"I WANT HER. AND I WILL HAVE HER . . ."

There was a hissing sound. Hamid struggled toward wakefulness, fear and puzzlement playing through his dreams. He looked across the floor at the pile of blankets that was the Blab's nest. "You okay, baby?"

No answer. Only the hissing, maybe louder now. For an instant his mind hung in a kind of mouse-and-snake paralysis. The sound was from the dataset; the picture-flat remained dark.

"Blab?" He had never seen her like this. Her eyes were open wide, rings of white showing around the irises. Her forelegs reached beyond the blankets. The talons were extended and had slashed deep into the plastic flooring.

He got up, started toward her. The hissing from the dataset formed a voice, and the voice spoke. "I want her. Human, I want her."

"How did you get access? You have no business disturbing us." Silly talk, but it broke the nightmare spell of this waking.

"My name is Tines." Hamid suddenly remembered the claw on the Ravna&Tines logo. "We have made generous offers. We have been patient. That is p⸍⸍ ⸍⸍⸍ ⸍ ⸍⸍ve her. If it means the death of all ⸍⸍⸍ ⸍⸍⸍ ⸍⸍⸍ But I *will* have her."

D1287910

Other Books by Vernor Vinge:

VERNOR VINGE
THREATS
...and Other Promises

BAEN BOOKS

THREATS AND OTHER PROMISES

This is a work of fiction. All the characters and events portrayed in this book are fictional, and any resemblance to real people or incidents is purely coincidental.

Copyright © 1988 by Vernor Vinge

All rights reserved, including the right to reproduce this book or portions thereof in any form.

A Baen Books Original

Acknowledgments:
"Apartness" copyright © 1965 by *New Worlds SF*.
"Conquest by Default" copyright © 1968 by Vernor Vinge. First published in *Analog Science Fiction/Science Fact*.
"The Whirligig of Time" copyright © 1974 by Random House, Inc. First published in *Stellar One*.
"Gemstone" copyright © 1983 by Vernor Vinge. First published in *Analog Science Fiction/Science Fact*.
"Just Peace" copyright © 1971 by Vernor Vinge and William Rupp. First published in *Analog Science Fiction/Science Fact*.
"Original Sin" copyright © 1972 by Vernor Vinge. First published in *Analog Science Fiction/Science Fact*.
"The Blabber" copyright © 1988 by Vernor Vinge.

Baen Publishing Enterprises
260 Fifth Avenue
New York, N.Y. 10001

First printing, November 1988

ISBN: 0-671-69790-0

Cover art by E. M. Gooch

Printed in the United States of America

Distributed by
SIMON & SCHUSTER
1230 Avenue of the Americas
New York, N.Y. 10020

*To Gene Wolfe, who saw this book
in the library at Port-Mimizon,
many years from now.*

Acknowledgments:

I would like to thank Mike Gannis, Jim Frenkel, and Joan D. Vinge for advice about the Blabber.

More generally, I am grateful to all my editors (including those who have rejected my stories) for their help over the years.

CONTENTS

The year 1965 is special to me: I first sold a science-fiction story. That story, "Apartness," is also first in this collection. In the next few years I sold a number of stories (including one written before "Apartness"). My ideal length was around twelve thousand words: longer than that, I had trouble coordinating characters and detail. Eventually I became comfortable with novel-length stories, which is certainly an important thing if you want to make decent money. Short stories appear, are read, and then are forgotten. At best they form a midden of confused, pleasant memories, the basis for conversations between fans trying to remember stories they saw long ago.

My stories have often been anthologized, scattered through many books, orphans moving from home to home. Most publishers are reluctant to do one-author collections. So I was very pleased when Baen Books decided to publish True Names and Other Dangers (1987) and the present collection. Between them, they cover most of my short fiction.

1

The True Names *collection concentrates on stories involving computers and my view of where technical progress is likely to take us. That view is both optimistic and apocalyptic. In the collection you're reading now, you'll find stories that have a little less to do with computers. Several deal with "classic" sf situations, situations which I have always loved—and which I find extraordinarily unlikely. Over the years, I have had a running battle with myself, trying to reconcile my view of science and progress with my desire to have stories about aliens and space adventure. With the last story in this collection, "The Blabber," I think I have a compromise that accommodates both.*

"Apartness" was a successful story, anthologized in a Wollheim and Carr best-of-the-year collection. Such success was a dream come true for this beginning writer. But I wonder if the story's success had much connection with the question that originally brought me to write it: Why are there no "eskimos" in Antarctica? Is it too remote from potential colonists, or is the place that much less hospitable than the arctic? I did some reading, concluded that both reasons had some virtue. There might be a few places on the continent that could support pretechnical human settlers, but those colonists would need real motivation. So the question was to find such motivation. Once asked, that question answered itself—and the story darned near wrote itself.

APARTNESS

". . . But he saw a light! *On the coast*. Can't you understand what that means?" Diego Ribera y Rodrigues leaned across the tiny wooden desk to emphasize his point. His adversary sat in the shadows and avoided the weak glow of the whale oil lamp hung from the cabin's ceiling. During the momentary pause in the argument, Diego could hear the wind keening through the masts and rigging above them. He was suddenly, painfully conscious of the regular rolling of the deck and slow oscillations of the swinging lamp. But he continued to glare at the man opposite him, and waited for an answer. Finally Capitán Manuel Delgado tilted his head out of the shadows. He smiled unpleasantly. His narrow face and sharp black moustache made him look like what he was: a master of power—political, military, and personal.

"It means," Delgado answered, "people. So what?"

"That's right. People. On the Palmer Peninsula. The Antarctic Continent is inhabited. Why, finding humans in Europe couldn't be any more fantastic—"

"*Mire*, Señor Profesor. I'm vaguely aware of the

3

importance of what you say." There was that smile again. "But the *Vigilancia*—"

Diego tried again. "We simply have to land and investigate the light. Just consider the scientific importance of it all—" The anthropologist had said the wrong thing.

Delgado's cynical indifference dropped away and his young, experienced face became fierce. "Scientific import! If those slimy Australian friends of yours wanted to, they could give us all the scientific knowledge ever known. Instead they have their sympathizers"—he jabbed a finger at Ribera—"run all about the South World doing 'research' that's been done ten times as well more than two centuries ago. The pigs don't even use the knowledge for their own gain." This last was the greatest condemnation Delgado could offer.

Ribera had difficulty restraining a bitter reply, but one mistake this evening was more than enough. He could understand though not approve Delgado's bitterness against a nation which had been wise (or lucky) enough not to burn its libraries during the riots following the North World War. *The Australians have the knowledge, all right,* thought Ribera, *but they also have the wisdom to know that some fundamental changes must be made in human society before this knowledge can be reintroduced, or else we'll wind up with a South World War and no more human race.* This was a point Delgado and many others refused to accept. "But really, Señor Capitán, we *are* doing original research. Ocean currents and populations change over the years. Our data are often quite different from those we know were gathered before. This light Juarez saw tonight is the strongest evidence of all that things are different." And for Diego Ribera, it was especially important.

As an anthropologist he had had nothing to do during the voyage except be seasick. A thousand times during the trip he had asked himself why he had been the one to organize the ecologists and oceanographers and get them on the ship; now he knew. If he could just convince this bigoted sailor . . .

Delgado appeared relaxed again. "And too, Señor Profesor, you must remember that you 'scientists' are really superfluous on this expedition. You were lucky to get aboard at all."

That was true. El Presidente Imperial was even more hostile to scientists of the Melbourne School than Delgado was. Ribera didn't like to think of all the boot-licking and chicanery that had been necessary to get his people on the expedition. The anthropologist's reply to the other's last comment started out respectfully, almost humbly. "Yes, I know you are doing something truly important here." He paused. *To hell with it,* he thought, suddenly sick of his own ingratiating manner. *This fool won't listen to logic or flattery.* Ribera's tone changed. "Yeah, I know you are doing something *truly* important here. Somewhere up in Buenos Aires the Chief Astrologer to el Presidente Imperial looked at his crystal ball or whatever and said to Alfredo IV in sepulchral tones: 'Señor Presidente, the stars have spoken. All the secrets of joy and wealth lie on the floating Isle of Coney. Send your men southward to find it.' And so you, the *Vigilancia NdP,* and half the mental cripples in Sudamérica are wandering around the coast of Antarctica looking for Coney Island." Ribera ran out of breath and satire at the same time. He knew his long-caged temper had just ruined all his plans and perhaps put his life in danger.

Delgado's face seemed frozen. His eyes flickered over Ribera's shoulder and looked at a mirror strategically placed in the space between the door frame and the top of the cabin's door. Then he looked back at the anthropologist. "If I weren't such a reasonable man you would be orca meat before morning." Then he smiled, a sincere friendly grin. "Besides, you're right. Those fools in Buenos Aires aren't fit to rule a pigsty, much less the Sudamérican Empire. Alfredo I was a man, a superman. Before the war-diseases had died out, he had united an entire continent under one fist, a continent that no one had been able to unite with jet planes and automatic weapons. But his heirs, especially the one that's in now, are superstitious tramps. . . . Frankly, that's why I can't land on the coast. The Imperial Astrologer, that fellow Jones y Urrutia, would claim when we returned to Buenos Aires that I had catered to you Australian sympathizers and el Presidente would believe him and I would probably end up with a one-way ticket to the Northern Hemisphere."

Ribera was silent for a second, trying to accept Delgado's sudden friendliness. Finally he ventured, "I would've thought you'd like the astrologers; you seem to dislike us scientists enough."

"You're using labels, Ribera. I feel nothing toward labels. It is success that wins my affection, and failure my hate. There may have been some time in the past when a group calling themselves astrologers could produce results. I don't know, and the matter doesn't interest me, *for I live in the present.* In our time the men working in the name of astrology are incapable of producing results, are conscious frauds. But don't be smug; your own people have produced damn few results. And if it should ever come that the astrologers are successful, I will take up their arts without hesitation and denounce you and your Scientific Method as superstition—for that is what it would be in the face of a more successful method."

The ultimate pragmatist, thought Ribera. *At least there is one form of persuasion that will work.* "I see what you mean, Señor Capitán. And as to success: there is one way that you could land with impunity. A lot can happen over the centuries." He continued half-slyly, "What was once a floating island might become grounded on the shore of the continent. If the astrologers could be convinced of the idea . . ." He let the sentence hang.

Delgado considered, but not for long. "Say! That is an idea. And I personally would like to find out what kind of creature would prefer this icebox over the rest of the South World.

"Very well. I'll try it. Now get out. I'm going to have to make this look like it's all the astrologers' idea, and you are likely to puncture the illusion if you're around when I talk to them."

Ribera lurched from his chair, caught off balance by the swaying of the deck and the abruptness of his dismissal. Without a doubt, Delgado was the most unusual Sudamérican officer Ribera had ever met.

"*Muchísimas gracias*, Señor Capitán." He turned and walked unsteadily out the door, past the storm light by the entrance, and into the wind-filled darkness of the short Antarctic night.

The astrologers did indeed like the idea. At two-thirty in the morning (just after sunrise) the *Vigilancia, Nave del Presidente*, changed course and tacked toward the area of coast where the light had been. Before the sun had been up six hours, the landing boats were over the side and heading for the coast.

In his eagerness, Diego Ribera y Rodrigues had scrambled aboard the first boat to be launched, not noticing that the Imperial Astrologers had used their favored status on the expedition to commandeer the lead craft. It was a clear day, but the wind made the water choppy and frigid salt water was splattered over the men in the boat. The tiny vessel rose and fell, rose and fell with a monotony that promised to make Ribera sick.

"Ah, so you are finally taking an interest in our Quest," a reedy voice interrupted his thoughts. Ribera turned to face the speaker, and recognized one Juan Jones y Urrutia, Subassistant to the Chief Astrologer to el Presidente Imperial. No doubt the vapid young mystic actually believed the tales of Coney Island, or else he would have managed to stay up in Buenos Aires with the rest of the hedonists in Alfredo's court. Beside the astrologer sat Capitán Delgado. The good captain must have done some tremendous persuading, for Jones seemed to regard the whole idea of visiting the coast as his own conception.

Ribera endeavored to smile. "Why yes, uh—"

Jones pressed on. "Tell me; would you have ever suspected life here, you who don't bother to consult the True Fundamentals?"

Ribera groaned. He noticed Delgado smiling at his discomfort. If the boat went through one more rise-fall, Ribera thought he'd scream; it did and he didn't.

"I guess we couldn't have guessed it, no." Ribera edged to the side of the boat, cursing himself for having been so eager to get on the first boat.

His eyes roamed the horizon—anything to get away from the vacuous, smug expression on Jones' face. The coast was gray, bleak, covered with large boulders. The breakers smashing into it seemed faintly yellow or red where they weren't white foam—probably coloring from the algae and diatoms in the water; the ecology boys would know.

"Smoke ahead!" The shout came thinly through the air from the second boat. Ribera squinted and examined the coast minutely. There! Barely recognizable as smoke, the wind-distorted haze rose from some point hidden by the low coastal hills. What if it turned out to be some sluggishly active volcano? That depressing thought had not occurred to him before. The geologists would have fun, but it would be a bust as far as he was concerned. . . . In any case, they would know which it was in a few minutes.

Capitán Delgado appraised the situation, then spoke several curt commands to the oarsmen. The crew's cadence shifted, and the boat turned ninety degrees to move parallel to the shore and breakers five hundred meters off. The trailing boats imitated the lead craft's maneuver.

Soon the coast bent sharply inward, revealing a long, narrow inlet. The night before, the *Vigilancia* must have been directly in line with the channel in order for Juarez to see the light. The three boats moved up the narrow channel. Soon the wind died. All that could be heard of it was a chill whistle as it tore at the hills which bordered the channel. The waves were much gentler now and the icy water no longer splashed into the boats, though the men's parkas were already caked with salt. Earlier the water had seemed faintly yellow; now it appeared orange and even red, especially farther up the inlet. The brilliant bacterial contamination contrasted sharply with the dull hills, hills that bore no trace of vegetation. In the place of plant life, uniformly gray boulders of all sizes covered the landscape. Nowhere was there snow; that would come with the winter, still five months in the future. But to Ribera this "summer" landscape was many times harsher than the bleakest winter scene in Sudamérica. Red water, gray hills. The only things that seemed even faintly normal were the brilliant blue sky, and the sun which cast long shadows into the drowned valley; a sun that seemed always at the point of setting even though it had barely risen.

Ribera's attention wandered up the channel. He forgot the sea sickness, the bloody water, the dead land. He could see *them;* not an ambiguous glow in the night, but people! He could see their huts, apparently made of stone and hides, and partly dug into the ground. He could see what appeared to be leather-hulled boats or kayaks along with a larger, white boat (now what could that be?), lying on the ground before the little village. He could see people! Not the expressions on their faces nor the exact manner of their clothing, but he could see them and that was enough for the instant. Here was something truly new; something the long dead scholars of Oxford, Cambridge, and UCLA had never learned, could never have learned. Here was something that mankind was seeing for the first and not the second or third or fourth time around!

What brought these people here? Ribera asked himself. From the few books on polar cultures that he had read at the University of Melbourne, he knew that generally populations are forced into the polar regions by competing peoples. What were the forces behind this migration? Who were these people?

The boats swept swiftly forward on the quiet water. Soon Ribera felt the hull of his craft scrape bottom. He and Delgado jumped into the red water and helped the oarsmen drag the boat onto the beach. Ribera waited impatiently for the two other boats, which carried the scientists, to arrive. In the meantime, he concentrated his attention on the natives, trying to understand every detail of their lives at once.

None of the aborigines moved; none ran; none attacked. They stood where they had been when he had first seen them. They did not scowl or wave weapons, but Ribera was distinctly aware that they were not friendly. No smiles, no welcome grimness. They seemed a proud people. The adults were tall, their faces so grimy, tanned, and withered that the anthropologist could only guess at their race. From the set of their lips, he knew that most of them lacked teeth. The natives' children peeped around the legs of their mothers, women who seemed old enough to be great grandmothers. If they had been Sudaméricans, he would have estimated their average age as sixty or seventy, but he knew that it couldn't be more than twenty or twenty-five.

From the pattern of fatty tissues in their faces, Ribera thought he could detect evidence of cold adaption; maybe they were Eskimos, though it would have been physically impossible for that race to migrate from one pole to the other while the North World War raged. Both their parkas and the kayaks appeared to be made of seal hide. But the parkas were ill-designed and much bulkier than the Eskimo outfits he had seen in pictures. And the harpoons they held were much less ingenious than the designs he remembered. If these people were of the supposedly extinct Eskimo race, they were an extraordinarily primitive branch of it. Besides, they were much too hairy to be full-blooded Indians or Eskimos.

With half his mind, he noticed the astrologers glance at the village and dismiss it. They were after the Isle of Coney, not some smelly aborigines. Ribera smiled bitterly; he wondered what Jones' reaction would be if the astrologer ever learned that Coney had been an amusement park. Many legends had grown up after the North World War and the one about Coney Island was one of the weirdest. Jones led his men up one of the nearer hills, evidently to

get a better view of the area. Capitán Delgado hastily dispatched twelve crewmen to accompany the
mystics. The good sailor obviously recognized what a
position he would be in if any of the astrologers were
lost.

Ribera's mind returned to the puzzle: Where were
these people from? How had they gotten here? Perhaps that was the best angle on the problem: people
don't just sprout from the ground. The pitiful kayaks—
they weren't true kayaks; they didn't enclose the
lower body of the user—could hardly transport a
person ten kilometers over open water. What about
that large white craft, further up the beach? It seemed
a much sturdier vessel than the hide and bone
"kayaks." He looked at it more closely—the white
craft might even be made of fiberglass, a pre-War
construction material. Maybe he should get a closer
look at it.

A shout attracted Ribera's attention; he turned.
The second landing craft, bearing the majority of the
scientists, had grounded on the rocky beach. He ran
down the beach to the men piling out of the boat,
and gave them the gist of his conclusions. Having
explained the situation, Ribera selected Enrique
Cardona and Ari Juarez, both ecologists, to accompany him in a parley with the natives. The three men
approached the largest group of natives, who watched
them stonily. The Sudaméricans stopped several paces
before the silent tribesmen. Ribera raised his hands
in a gesture of peace. "My friends, may we look at
your beautiful boat yonder? We will not harm it."
There was no response, though Ribera thought he
sensed a greater tenseness among the natives. He
tried again, making the request in Portuguese, then
in English. Cardona attempted the question in
Zulunder, as did Juarez in broken French. Still no

acknowledgement, but the harpoons seemed to quiver, and there was an all but imperceptible motion of hands toward bone knives.

"Well, to hell with them," Cardona snapped finally. "C'mon, Diego, let's have a look at it." The short-tempered ecologist turned and began walking toward the mysterious white boat. This time there was no mistaken hostility. The harpoons were raised and the knives drawn.

"Wait, Enrique," Ribera said urgently. Cardona stopped. Ribera was sure that if the ecologist had taken one more step he would have been spitted. "Wait," Diego Ribera y Rodrigues continued. "We have plenty of time. Besides, it would be madness to push the issue." He indicated the natives' weapons.

Cardona noticed the weapons. "All right. We'll humor them for now." He seemed to regard the harpoons as an embarrassment rather than a threat. The three men retreated from the confrontation. Ribera noticed that Delgado's men had their pistols half drawn. The expedition had narrowly avoided a blood-bath.

The scientists would have to content themselves with a peripheral inspection of the village. In one way this was more pleasant than direct examination, for the ground about the huts was littered with filth. In a century or so this area would have the beginnings of a soil. After ten minutes or so the adult males of the tribe resumed their work mending the kayaks. Apparently they were preparing for a seal hunting expedition; the area around the village had been hunted free of the seals and sea birds that populated most other parts of the coast.

If only we could communicate with them, thought Ribera. The aborigines themselves probably knew (at least by legend) what their origins were. As it was,

Ribera had to investigate by the most indirect means. In his mind he summed up the facts he knew: the natives were of an indeterminate race; they were hairy, and yet they seemed to have some of the physiological cold weather adaptions of the extinct Eskimos. The natives were primitive in every physical sense. Their equipment and techniques were far inferior to the ingenious inventions of the Eskimos. And the natives spoke no currently popular language. One other thing: the fire they kept alive at the center of the village was an impractical affair, and probably served a religious purpose only. Those were the facts; now, who the hell were these people? The problem was so puzzling that for the moment he forgot the dreamlike madness of the gray landscape and the "setting" noonday sun.

A half hour and more passed. The geologists were mildly ecstatic about the area, but for Ribera the situation was becoming increasingly exasperating. He didn't dare approach the villagers or the white boat, yet these were the things he most wanted to do. Perhaps this impatience made him especially sensitive, for he was the first of the scientists to hear the clatter of rolling stones and the sound of voices over the shrill wind.

He turned and saw Jones and company descending a nearby hill at all but breakneck speed. One misstep and the entire group would have descended the hill on their backs rather than their feet. The rolling stones cast loose by their rush preceded them into the valley. The astrologers reached the bottom of the hill, far outdistancing the sailors delegated to protect them, and continued running.

"Wonder what's trying to eat them?" Ribera asked Juarez half-seriously.

As he plunged past Delgado, Jones shouted,

"—think we may have found it, Capitán—something man-made rising from the sea." He pointed wildly toward the hill they had just descended.

The astrologers piled into a boat. Seeing that the mystics really intended to leave, Delgado dispatched fifteen men to help them with the craft, and an equal number to go along in another boat. In a couple of minutes, the two boats were well into the channel and rowing fast toward open water.

"What the hell was that about?" Ribera shouted to Capitán Delgado.

"You know as much as I, Señor Profesor. Let's take a look. If we go for a little walk"—he nodded to the hill—"we can probably get within sight of the 'discovery' before Jones and the rest reach it by boat. You men stay here." Delgado turned his attention to the remaining crewmen. "If these primitives try to confiscate our boat, demonstrate your firearms to them—on them.

"The same goes for you scientists. As many men as possible are going to have to stay here to see that we don't lose that boat; it's a long, wet walk back to the *Vigilancia*. Let's go, Ribera. You can take a couple of your people if you want."

Ribera and Juarez set out with Delgado and three ship's officers. The men moved slowly up the slope, which was made treacherous by its loose covering of boulders. As they reached the crest of the hill the wind beat into them, tearing at their parkas. The terrain was less hilly but in the far distance they could see the mountains that formed the backbone of the peninsula.

Delgado pointed. "If they saw something in the ocean, it must be in that direction. We saw the rest of the coast on our way in."

The six men started off in the indicated direction.

The wind was against them and their progress was slow. Fifteen minutes later they crossed the top of a gentle hill, and reached the coast. Here the water was a clean bluish-green and the breakers smashing over the rocky beach could almost have been mistaken for Pacific waters sweeping into some bleak shore in the Province of Chile. Ribera looked over the waves. Two stark, black objects broke the smooth, silver line of the horizon. Their uncompromising angularity showed them to be artificial.

Delgado drew a pair of binoculars from his parka. Ribera noted with surprise that the binoculars bore the mark of the finest optical instruments extant: U.S. Naval war surplus. On some markets, the object would have brought a price comparable to that of the entire ship *Vigilancia*. Capitán Delgado raised the binoculars to his eyes and inspected the black forms of the ocean. Thirty seconds passed. "*¡Madre del Presidente!*" he swore softly but with feeling. He handed the binocs to Ribera. "Take a look, Señor Profesor."

The anthropologist scanned the horizon, spotted the black shapes. Though winter sea ice had smashed their hulls and scuttled them in the shallow water, they were obviously ships—atomic or petroleum powered, pre-War ships. At the edge of his field of vision, he noticed two white objects bobbing in the water; they were the two landing boats from the *Vigilancia*. The boats disappeared every few seconds in the trough of a wave. They moved a little closer to the two half-sunken ships, then began to pull away. Ribera could imagine what had happened: Jones had seen that the hulks were no different from the relics of the Argentine navy sunk off Buenos Aires. The astrologer was probably fit to be tied.

Ribera inspected the wrecks minutely. One was

half capsized and hidden behind the other. His gaze roamed along the bow of the nearer vessel. There were letters on that bow, letters almost worn away by the action of ice and water upon the plastic hull of the ship.

"My God!" whispered Ribera. The letters spelled: S—*Hen*—k—V—*woe*—d. He didn't need to look at the other vessel to know that it had once been called *Nation*. Ribera dumbly handed the binoculars to Juarez.

The mystery was solved. He knew the pressures that had driven the natives here. "If the Zulunders ever hear about this . . ." Ribera's voice trailed off into silence.

"Yeah," Delgado replied. He understood what he had seen, and for the first time seemed somewhat subdued. "Well, let's get back. This land isn't fit for . . . it isn't fit."

The six men turned and started back. Though the ship's officers had had an opportunity to use the binoculars, they didn't seem to understand exactly what they had seen. And probably the astrologers didn't realize the significance of the discovery, either. That left three, Juarez, Ribera, and Delgado, who knew the secret of the natives' origin. If the news spread much further, disaster would result, Ribera was sure.

The wind was at their backs but it did not speed their progress. It took them almost a quarter-hour to reach the crest of the hill overlooking the village and the red water.

Below them, Ribera could see the adult male natives clustered in a tight group. Not ten feet away stood all the scientists, and the crewmen. Between the two groups was one of the Sudaméricans. Ribera squinted and saw that the man was Enrique Cardona. The ecologist was gesturing wildly, angrily.

"Oh, no!" Ribera sprinted down the hill, closely followed by Delgado and the rest. The anthropologist moved even faster then the astrologers had an hour before, and almost twice as fast as he would have thought humanly possible. The tiny avalanches started by his footfalls were slow compared to his speed. Even as he flew down the slope, Ribera felt himself detached, analytically examining the scene before him.

Cardona was shouting, as if to make the natives understand by sheer volume. Behind him the ecologists and biologists stood, impatient to inspect the village and the natives' boat. Before him stood a tall, withered native, who must have been all of forty years old. Even from a distance the native's bearing revealed intense, suppressed anger. The native's parka was the most impractical of all those Ribera had seen; he could have sworn that it was a crude, sealskin imitation of a double-breasted suit.

Almost screaming, Cardona cried, "God damn it, why can't we look at your boat?" Ribera put forth one last burst of speed, and shouted at Cardona to stop his provocation. It was too late. Just as the anthropologist arrived at the scene of the confrontation, the native in the strange parka drew himself to his full height, pointed to all the Sudaméricans, and screeched (as nearly as Ribera's Spanish-thinking mind could record), "—*in di nam niutrantsfals mos yulisterf*—"

The half-raised harpoons were thrown. Cardona went down instantly, transfixed by three of the weapons. Several other men were hit and felled. The natives drew their knives and ran forward, taking advantage of the confusion which the harpoons had created. A painfully loud *BAM* erupted beside Ribera's ear as Delgado fired his pistol, picking off the leader of the natives. The crewmen recovered from their shock, began firing at the aborigines. Ribera whipped his pistol from a pouch at his side and blasted into the swarm of primitives. Their single shot pistols emptied, the scientists and crew were reduced to knives. The next few seconds were total chaos. The knives rose and fell, gleaming more redly than the water in the cove. The anthropologist half stumbled over squirming bodies. The air was filled with hoarse shouts and sounds of straining men.

The groups were evenly matched and they were cutting each other to pieces. In some still calm part of his mind Ribera noticed the returning boats of the astrologers. He glimpsed the crewmen aiming their muskets, waiting for a clear shot at the primitives.

The turbulence of the fray whirled him about, out of the densest part of the fight. They had to disengage; another few minutes and there wouldn't be one in ten left standing on the beach. Ribera screamed this to Delgado. Miraculously the man heard him and agreed; retreat was the only sane thing to do. The Sudaméricans ran raggedly toward their boat, with the natives close behind. Sharp cracking sounds came from over the water. The crewmen in the other boats were taking advantage of the dispersion between pursuers and pursued. The Sudaméricans reached their boat and began pushing it into the water. Ribera and several others turned to face the natives. Musket fire had forced most of the primitives back, but a few still ran toward the shore, knives drawn. Ribera reached down and snatched a small stone from the ground. Using an almost forgotten skill of his "gentle" childhood, he cocked his arm and snapped the rock forward in a flat trajectory. It caught one of the natives dead between the eyes with a sharp *smack*. The man plunged forward, fell on his face, and lay still.

Ribera turned and ran into the shallow water after the boat. He was followed by the rest of the rearguard. Eager hands reached out from the boat to pull him aboard. A couple more feet and he would be safe.

The blow sent him spinning forward. As he fell, he saw with dumb horror the crimson harpoon which had emerged from his parka just below the right side pocket.

Why? Must we forever commit the same blunders over and over, and over again? Ribera didn't have time to wonder at this fleeting incongruous thought, before the redness closed about him.

A gentle breeze, carrying the happy sounds of distant parties, entered the large windows of the bungalow and caressed its interior. It was a cool night, late in summer. The first mild airs of fall made the darkness pleasant, inviting. The house was situated on the slight ridge which marked the old shore line of La Plata; the lawns and hedges outside fell gently away toward the general plain of the city. The faint though delicate light from the oil lamps of that city defined its rectangular array of streets, and showed its buildings uniformly one or two stories high. Further out, the city lights came to an abrupt end at the waterfront. But even beyond that there were the moving, yellow lights of boats and ships navigating La Plata. Off to the extreme left burned the bright fires surrounding the Naval Enclosure, where the government labored on some secret weapon, possibly a steam-powered warship.

It was a peaceful scene, and a happy evening; preparations were almost complete. His desk was littered with the encouraging replies to his proposals. It had been hard work but a lot of fun at the same time. And Buenos Aires had been the ideal base of operations. Alfredo IV was touring the western provinces. To be more precise, el Presidente Imperial and his court were visiting the pleasure spots in Santiago (as if Alfredo had not built up enough talent in Buenos Aires itself). The Imperial Guard and the Secret Police clustered close by the monarch (Alfredo was more afraid of a court coup than anything else), so Buenos Aires was more relaxed then it had been in many years.

Yes, two months of hard work. Many important people had to be informed, and confidentially. But the replies had been almost uniformly enthusiastic, and it appeared that the project wasn't known to those who would destroy its goal; though of course the simple fact that so many people had to know increased the chances of disclosure. But that was a risk that had to be taken.

And, thought Diego Ribera, *it's been two months since the Battle of Bloody Cove.* (The name of the inlet had arisen almost spontaneously.) He hoped that the tribe hadn't been scared away from that spot, or, infinitely worse, driven to the starvation point by the massacre. If that fool Enrique Cardona had only kept his mouth shut, both sides could have parted peacefully (if not amicably) and some good men would still be alive.

Ribera scratched his side thoughtfully. Another inch and he wouldn't have made it himself. If that harpoon had hit just a little further up. . . . Someone's quick thinking had added to his initial good luck. That someone had slashed the thick cord tied to the harpoon which had hit Ribera. If the separation had not been made, the cord would most likely have been pulled back and the harpoon's barb engaged. Even as miraculous was the fact that he had survived the impalement and the poor medical con-

ditions on board the *Vigilancia*. Physically, all the
damage that remained was a pair of neat, circular
scars. The whole affair was enough to give you religion, or, conversely, scare the hell out of you. . . .

And come next January he would be headed back,
along with the secret expedition which he had been
so energetically organizing. Nine months was a long
time to wait, but they definitely couldn't make the
trip this fall or winter, and they really did need time
to gather just the right equipment.

Diego was taken from these thoughts by several
dull thuds from the door. He got up and went to the
entrance of the bungalow. (This small house in the
plushiest section of the city was evidence of the
encouragement he had already received from some
very important people.) Ribera had no idea who the
visitor could be, but he had every expectation that
the news brought would be good. He reached the
door, and pulled it open.

"*Mkambwe Lunama!*"

The Zulunder stood framed in the doorway, his
black face all but invisible against the night sky. The
visitor was over two meters tall and weighed nearly
one hundred kilos; he was the picture of a superman.
But then, the Zulunder government made a special
point of using the super-race type in its dealings with
other nations. The procedure undoubtedly lost them
some fine talent, but in Sudamérica the myth held
strong that one Zulunder was worth three warriors of
any other nationality.

After his first outburst, Ribera stood for a moment in horrified confusion. He knew Lunama vaguely
as the Highman of Trueness—propaganda—at the
Zulunder embassy in Buenos Aires. The Highman
had made numerous attempts to ingratiate himself
with the academic community of la Universidad de

Buenos Aires. The efforts were probably aimed at recruiting sympathizers against that time when the disagreements between the Sudamérican Empire and the Reaches of Zulund erupted into open conflict.

Wildly hoping that the visit was merely an unlucky coincidence, Ribera recovered himself. He attempted a disarming smile, and said, "Come on in, Mkambwe. Haven't seen you in a long time."

The Zulunder smiled, his white teeth making a dazzling contrast with the rest of his face. He stepped lightly into the room. His robes were woven of brilliant red, blue and green fibers, in defiance of the more somber hues of Sudamérican business suits. On his hip rested a Mavimbelamake 20 mm. *revolver*. The Zulunders had their own peculiar ideas about diplomatic protocol.

Mkambwe moved lithely across the room and settled in a chair. Ribera hurried over and sat down by his desk, trying unobtrusively to hide the letters that lay on it from the Zulunder's view. If the visitor saw and understood even one of those letters, the game would be over.

Ribera tried to appear relaxed. "Sorry I can't offer you a drink, Mkambwe, but the house is as dry as a desert." If the anthropologist got up, the Zulunder would almost certainly see the correspondence. Diego continued jovially, desperately trying to dredge up reminiscences. ("Remember that time your boys whited their faces and went down to la Casa Rosada Nueva and raised hell with the—".)

Lunama grinned. "Frankly, old man, this visit is business." The Zulunder spoke with a dandyish, pseudo-Castilian accent, which he no doubt thought aristocratic.

"Oh," Ribera answered.

"I hear that you were on a little expedition to Palmer Peninsula this January."

"Yes," Ribera replied stonily. Perhaps there was still a chance; perhaps Lunama didn't know the whole truth. "And it was supposed to be a secret. If el Presidente Imperial found out that your government knew about it—"

"Come, come, Diego. That isn't the secret you are thinking of. I know that you found what happened to the *Hendrik Verwoerd* and the *Nation*."

"Oh," Ribera replied again. "How did you find out?" he asked dully.

"You talked to many people, Diego," he waved vaguely. "Surely you didn't think that every one of them would keep your secret. And surely you didn't think you could keep something this important from us." He looked beyond the anthropologist and his tone changed. "For three hundred years we lived under the heels of those white devils. Then came the Retribution in the North and—"

What a quaint term the Zulunders use for the North World War, thought Ribera. It had been a war in which every trick of destruction—nuclear, biological, and chemical—had been used. The mere residues from the immolation of China had obliterated Indonesia and India. Mexico and América Central had disappeared with the United States and Canada. And North Africa had gone with Europe. The gentlest wisps from that biological and nuclear hell had caressed the Southern Hemisphere and nearly poisoned it. A few more megatons and a few more disease strains and the war would have gone unnamed, for there would have been no one to chronicle it. This was the Retribution in the North which Lunama so easily referred to.

"—and the devils no longer had the protection of their friends there. Then came the Sixty-Day struggle for Freedom."

There were both black devils and white devils in those sixty days—and saints of all colors, brave men struggling desperately to avert genocide. But the years of slavery were too many and the saints lost, not for the first time.

"At the beginning of the Rising we fought machine guns and jet fighters with rifles and knives," Lunama continued, almost self-hypnotized. "We died by the tens of thousands. But as the days passed *their* numbers were reduced, too. By the fiftieth day *we* had the machine guns, and *they* had the knives and rifles. We boxed the last of them up at Kapa and Durb," (he used the Zulunder terms for Capetown and Durban) "and drove them into the sea."

Literally, added Ribera to himself. *The last remnants of White Africa were physically pushed from the wharves and sunny beaches into the ocean.* The Zulunders had succeeded in exterminating the Whites, and thought they succeeded in obliterating the Afrikaner culture from the continent. Of course they had been wrong. The Afrikaners had left a lasting mark, obvious to any unbiased observer; the very name Zulunder, which the present Africans cherished fanatically, was in part a corruption of English.

"By the sixtieth day, we could say that not a single White lived on the continent. As far as we know, only one small group evaded vengeance. Some of the highest ranking Afrikaner officials, maybe even the Prime Minister, commandeered two luxury vessels, the *SR Hendrik Verwoerd* and the *Nation.* They left many hours before the final freedom drive on Kapa."

Five thousand desperate men, women and children crammed into two luxury ships. The vessels had raced across the South Atlantic, seeking refuge in Argentina. But the government of Argentina was having troubles of its own. Two light Argentine patrol boats badly damaged the *Nation* before the Afrikaners were convinced that Sudamérica didn't offer shelter.

The two ships had turned south, possibly in an attempt to round Tierra del Fuego and reach Australia. That was the last anyone had heard of them for more than two hundred years—till the *Vigilancia*'s exploration of the Palmer Peninsula.

Ribera knew that an appeal to sympathy wouldn't dissuade the Zulunder from ordering the destruction of the pitiful colony. He tried a different tack. "What you say is so true, Mkambwe. But please, please don't destroy these descendants of your enemies. The tribe on the Palmer Peninsula is the only polar culture left on Earth." Even as Ribera said the words, he realized how weak the argument was; it could only appeal to an anthropologist like himself.

The Zulunder seemed surprised, and with a visible effort shelved the terrible history of his continent. "Destroy them? My dear fellow, whyever would we do that? I just came here to ask if we might send several observers from the Ministry of Trueness along on your expedition. To report the matter more fully, you know. I think that Alfredo can probably be convinced, if the question is put persuasively enough to him.

"Destroy them?" He repeated the question. "Don't be silly! They are *proof* of destruction. So they call their piece of ice and rock Nieutransvaal, do they?" He laughed. "And they even have a Prime Minister, a toothless old man who waves his harpoon at Sudaméricans." Apparently Lunama's informant had actually been on the spot. "And they are even more primitive than Eskimos. In short, they are savages living on seal blubber."

He no longer spoke with foppish joviality. His

eyes flashed with an old, old hate, a hate that was pushing Zulund to greatness, and which might eventually push the world into another hemispheric war (unless the Australian social scientists came through with some desperately needed answers). The breeze in the room no longer seemed cool, gentle. It was cold and the wind was coming from the emptiness of death piled upon megadeath through the centuries of human misery.

"It will be a pleasure for us to see them enjoy their superiority." Lunama leaned forward even more intensely. "They finally have the apartness their kind always wanted. *Let them rot in it—*"

For several years after that first sale, one editor rejected my every story with praise for how much he had liked "Apartness." I think he was referring to the parts of the story that have a moral for our times. I didn't have any bright ideas along those lines—but I did think that other stories might be possible in the same future.

I had enjoyed Chad Oliver's stories and I thought it would be fun to imagine what social science might look like coming out of an entirely different milieu. Modern anthropologists seem full of cultural relativism and self-conscious tolerance. Would it be possible to have a story in some wider context, with an anthropology based on alien motives? I wanted a culture that was technologically superior to ours, workable, and yet so painfully different that accepting it would be hard even for open-minded people with our outlook.

So what would be sufficiently alien? Ever since high school, I've been fascinated with the notion of anarchy. Every anarchical scheme has some set of

*assumptions for why the participants will cooperate.
(You can usually spot the assumption in the names:
anarcho-communism, anarcho-capitalism. . . .) There's
a fundamental problem all such plans must face: how
to prevent the formation of power groups large enough
to in fact be the government. In the next story,
"Conquest by Default," I attempted a frontal assault
on this question.*

*An aside: Many naive behaviors are seen in begin-
ning writers. One is the use of oddball spellings and
unpronounceable names. The names in this story
have haunted it from the beginning. I had just taken
a descriptive linguistics course, and I was enthusiastic: My aliens can close their noses—true nasal stops
and fricatives are possible! In the version John W.
Campbell bought back in 1967, I represented a voiceless nasal stop by the letter "p" with tilde and a
voiced nasal fricative by the letter "v" with tilde.
John told me he didn't think it would get past the
typesetters. He was right. In all its incarnations—till
now—the names have been misrepresented. And even
now, such oddball symbols can be hard to print. Our
kindly editor, Jim Baen, offered to accept photoready
copy from me—so that I could set the type exactly as
it should be. Alas, desktop publishing is still in my
future. So I have chosen to represent the voiceless
nasal stop as "%" and the voiced nasal fricative as
"#".*

CONQUEST BY DEFAULT

This all happened a long time ago, and almost twenty light-years from where we're standing now. You honor me here tonight as a humanitarian, as a man who has done something to bring a temporary light to the eternal darkness that is our universe. But you deceive yourselves. I made the situation just civilized enough so that its true brutality, shed of bloody drapery, can be seen.

I see you don't believe what I say. In this whole audience I suspect that only a Melmwn truly understands—and she better than I. Not one of you has ever been kicked in the teeth by these particular facts of life. Perhaps if I told you the story as it happened to me—I could make you *feel* the horror you hear me describe.

Two centuries ago, the %wrlyg Spice & Trading Company completed the first interstellar flight. They were thirty years ahead of their nearest competitors. They had a whole planet at their disposal, except for one minor complication . . .

* * *

The natives were restless.

My attention was unevenly divided between the beautiful girl who had just introduced herself, and the ancient city that shimmered in the hot air behind her.

Mary Dahlmann. That was a hard name to pronounce, but I had studied Australian for almost two years, and I was damned if I couldn't say a name. I clumsily worked my way through a response. "Yes, ah, Miss, ah, Dahlmann. I am Ron Melmwn, and I am the new Company anthropologist. But I thought the vice president for Aboriginal Affairs was going to meet me."

Ngagn Che# dug me in the ribs. "Say, you really can speak that gabble, can't you, Melmwn?" he whispered in Mikin. Che# was Vice President for Violence—an O.K. guy, but an incurable bigot.

Mary Dahlmann smiled uncertainly at this exchange. Then she answered my question. "Mr. Horlig will be right along. He asked me to meet you. My father is Chief Representative for Her Majesty's Government." I later learned that Her Majesty was two centuries dead. "Here, let me show you off the field." She grasped my wrist for a second—an instant. I guess I jerked back. Her hand fell away and her eagerness vanished. "This way," she said icily, pointing to a gate in the force fence surrounding the %wrlyg landing field. I wished very much I had not pulled away from her touch. Even though she was so blond and pale, she was a woman, and in a weird way, pretty. Besides, *she* had overcome whatever feelings she had against *us*.

There was an embarrassed silence, as the five of us cleared the landing craft and walked toward the gate.

The sun was bright—brighter than ours ever shines over Miki. It was also very dry. There were no clouds in the sky. Twenty or thirty people worked in the field. Most were Mikin, but here and there were clusters of Terrans. Several were standing around a device in the corner of the field where the fence made a joint to angle out toward the beach. The Terrans knelt by the device.

Orange fire flickered from the end of the machine, followed by a loud *guda-bam-bam-bam*. Even as my conscious mind concluded that we were under fire, I threw myself on the ground and flattened into the lowest profile possible. You've heard the bromide about combat making life more real. I don't know about that, but it's certainly true that when you are flat against the ground with your face in the dirt, the whole universe looks different. That red-tan sand was *hot*. Sharp little stones bit into my face. Two inches before my face a clump of sage had assumed the dimensions of a #ola tree.

I cocked my head microscopically to see how the others were doing. They were all down, too. Correction: that idiot Earthgirl was still standing. More than a second after the attack she was still working toward the idea that someone was trying to kill her. Only a dement or a Little Sister brought up in a convent could be so dense. I reached out, grabbed her slim ankle, and jerked. She came down hard. Once down, she didn't move.

Ngagn Che# and some accountant, whose name I didn't remember, were advancing toward the slug-thrower. That accountant had the fastest low-crawl I have ever seen. The Terrans frantically tried to lower the barrels of their gun—but it was really primitive and couldn't search more than five degrees. The little accountant zipped up to within twenty meters of the gun, reached into his weapons pouch, and tossed a grenade toward the Earthmen and their weapon. I dug my face into the dirt and waited for the explosion. There was only a muffled thud. It was a gas bomb—not frag. A green mist hung for an instant over the gun and the Terrans.

When I got to them, Che# was already complimenting the accountant on his throw.

"A private quarrel?" I asked Che#.

The security chief looked faintly surprised. "Why no. These fellows"—he pointed at the unconscious Terrans—"belong to some conspiracy to drive us off the planet. They're really a pitiful collection." He pointed to the weapon. It was composed of twenty barrels welded to three metal hoops. By turning a crank, the barrels could be rotated past a belt cartridge feeder. "That gun is hardly more accurate than a shrapnel bomb. This is nothing very dangerous, but I'm going to catch chaos for letting them get within the perimeter. And I can tell you, I am going to scorch those agents of mine that let these abos sneak in. Anyway, we got the pests alive. They'll be able to answer some questions." He nudged one of the bodies over with his boot. "Sometimes I think it would be best to exterminate the race. They don't occupy much territory but they sure are a nuisance.

"See," he picked up a card from the ground and handed it to me. It was lettered in neat Mikin: MERLYN SENDS YOU DEATH. "Merlyn is the name of the 'terrorist' organization—it's nonprofit. I think. Terrans are a queer lot."

Several Company armsmen showed up then and Che# proceeded to bawl them out in a very thorough way. It was interesting, but a little embarrassing, too. I turned and started toward the main gate. I still had to meet my new boss—Horlig, the Vice President for Abo Affairs.

Where was the Terran girl? In the fuss I had completely forgotten her. But now she was gone. I ran back to where we stood when the first shots were fired. I felt cold and a little sick as I looked at the ground where she had fallen. Maybe it had been a superficial wound. Maybe the medics had carried her off. But whatever the explanation, a pool of blood almost thirty centimeters wide lay on the sand. As I watched, it soaked into the sand and became a dark brown grease spot, barely visible against the reddish-tan soil. As far as appearances go, it could have been human blood.

Horlig was a Gloyn. I should have known from his name. As it was, I got quite a surprise when I met him. With his pale gray skin and hair, Herul Horlig could easily be mistaken for an Earthman. The Vice President for Aboriginal Affairs was either an Ostentatious Simplist or very proud of his neolithic grandparents. He wore wooden shin plates and a black breech-clout. His only weapon was a machine dartgun strapped to his wrist.

It quickly became clear that the man was unhappy with me as an addition to his staff. I could understand that. As a professional, my opinions might carry more weight with the Board of Directors and the President than his. Horlig did his best to hide his displeasure, though. He seemed a hard-headed, sincere fellow who could be ruthless, but nevertheless believed whatever he did was right. He unbent considerably during our meal at Supply Central. When I mentioned I wanted to interview some abos, he surprised me by suggesting we fly over to the native city that evening.

When we left Central, it was already dark. We walked to the parking lot, and got into Horlig's car. Three minutes later we were ghosting over the suburbs of Adelaide-west. Horlig cast a practiced eye upon the queer rectangular street pattern below, and brought us down on the lawn of a two-story wood house. I started to get out.

"Just a minute, Melmwn," said Horlig. He grabbed a pair of earphones and set the TV on pan. I didn't say anything as he scanned the quiet neighborhood for signs of hostile activity. I was interested: usually a Simplist will avoid using advanced defense techniques. Horlig explained as he set the car's computer on SENTRY and threw open the hatch:

"Our illustrious Board of Directors dictates that we employ 'all security precautions at our disposal.' Bunk. Even when these Earth creatures attack us, they are less violent than good-natured street brawlers back home. I don't think there have been more than thirty murders in this city since %wrlyg landed twenty years ago."

I jumped to the soft grass and looked around. Things really were quiet. Gas lamps lit the cobblestone street and dimly outlined the wood buildings up and down the lane. Weak yellow light emerged from windows. From down the street came faint laughter of some party. Our landing had gone unnoticed.

Demoneyes. I stepped back sharply. The twin yellow disks glittered maniacally, as the cat turned to face us, and the lamps' light came back from its eyes. The little animal turned slowly and walked disdainfully across the lawn. This was a bad omen indeed. I would have to watch the Signs very carefully tonight. Horlig was not disturbed at all. I don't think he knew I was brought up a witch-fearer. We started up the walk toward the nearest house.

"You know, Melmwn, this isn't just any old native we're visiting. He's an anthropologist, Earth style. Of course, he's just as insipid as the rest of the bunch, but our staff is forced to do quite a bit of liaison work with him."

An anthropologist! This was going to be interesting, both as an exchange of information and of research procedures.

"In addition, he's the primary representative chosen by the Australian *gowernmen'* . . . a *gowernmen'* is sort of a huge corporation, as far as I can tell."

"Uh-huh." As a matter of fact, I knew a lot more about the mysterious *government* concept than Horlig. My Scholarate thesis was a theoretical study of macro organizations. The paper was almost rejected because my instructors claimed it was an analysis of a patent impossibility. Then came word that three macro organizations existed on Earth.

We climbed the front porch steps. Horlig pounded on the door. "The fellow's name is Nalman."

I translated his poor pronunciation back to the probable Australian original: Dahlmann! Perhaps I could find out what happened to the Earthgirl.

There were shuffling steps from within. Whoever it was did not even bother to look us over through a spy hole. Earthmen were nothing if not trusting. We were confronted by a tall, middle-aged man with thin, silvery hair. His hand quavered slightly as he removed the pipe from his mouth. Either he was in an extremity of fear or he had terrible coordination.

But when he spoke, I knew there was no fear. "Mr. Horlig. Won't you come in?" The words and tone were mild, but in that mildness rested an immense confidence. In the past I had heard that tone only from Umpires. It implied that neither storm, nor struggle, nor crumbling physical prowess could upset the mind behind the voice. That's a lot to get out of six quiet words—but it was all there.

When we were settled in Scholar Dahlmann's den, Horlig made the introductions. Horlig understood Australian fairly well, but his accent was atrocious.

"As you must surely know, Scholar Dahlmann, the objective voyage time to our home planet, Epsilon Eridani II, is almost twelve years. Three days ago

the third %wrlyg Support Fleet arrived and assumed
a parking orbit around the Earth. At this instant,
they soar omnipotent over the lands of your people."
Dahlmann just smiled. "In any case, the first passen-
gers have been unfrozen and brought down to the
%wrlyg Ground Base. This is Scholar Ron Melmwn,
the anthropologist that the Company has brought in
with the Fleet."

From behind his thick glasses, Dahlmann inspected
me with new interest. "Well, I certainly am happy to
meet a Mikin anthropologist. Our meeting is something of a first I believe."

"I think so, too. Your institutions are ill-reported
to us on Miki. This is natural since %wrlyg is primar-
ily interested in the commercial and immigration
prospects of your Northern Hemisphere. I want to
correct the situation. During my stay I hope to use
you and the other Terrans for source material in my
study of your history and, uh, government. It's especially good luck that I meet a professional like
yourself."

Dahlmann seemed happy to discuss his people and
soon we were immersed in Terran history and cultures. Much of what he told me I knew from reports
received, but I let him tell the whole story.

It seems that two hundred years before, there was
a high technology culture in the Northern Hemisphere. The way Dahlmann spoke, it was very nearly
Mikin caliber—the North People even had some primitive form of space flight. Then there was a war. A
war is something like a fight, only much bigger,
bigger even than an antitrust action. They exploded
more than 12,500 megatons of bombs on their own
cities. In addition, germ cultures were released to
kill anybody who survived the fusion bombs. Without radiation screens and panphagic viruses, it was a
slaughter. Virtually all the mammals in the Northern

Hemisphere were destroyed, and according to Dahlmann, there was, for a while, the fear that the radiation poisons and disease strains would wipe out life
in the South World, too.

It is very difficult to imagine how anything like
that could get started in the first place—the cause of
"war" was one of the objects of my research. Of
course the gross explanation was that the Terrans
never developed the Umpire System or the Concept
of Chaos. Instead they used the gargantuan organizations called "governments." But the underlying question was why they chose this weird governmental
path at all. Were the Terrans essentially subhuman—or
is it just luck that we Mikins discovered the True
Way?

The war didn't discourage the Terrans from their
fundamental errors. Three governments rose from
the ashes of the war. The Australian, the Sudaméreican,
and the Zulunder. Even the smallest nation, Australia, had one thousand times as many people as the
%wrlyg Spice & Trading Company. And remember
that %wrlyg is already as big as a group can get
without being slapped with an antitrust ruling by the
Umpires.

I forgot my surroundings as Dahlmann went on to
explain the present power structure, the struggle of
the two stronger nations to secure colonies in portions of the Northern Hemisphere where the war
poisons had dissipated. This was a very dangerous
situation, according to the Terran anthropologist, since
there were many disease types dormant in the Northern Hemisphere. That could start hellish plagues in
the South World, for the Terrans were still more
than a century behind the technology they had
achieved before the blowup.

Through all this discussion, Horlig maintained an
almost contemptuous silence, not listening to what

we were saying so much as observing us as specimens. Finally he interrupted. "Well, I'm glad to see you both hit it off so well. It's getting too late for me though. I'll have to take your leave. No, you don't have to come back just yet, Melmwn. I'll send the car back here on auto after I get to Base."

"You don't have to bother with that, Horlig. Things look pretty tame around here. I can walk back."

"No," Horlig said definitely. "We have regulations. And there is always this Merlyn, you know."

The Merlyn bunglers didn't frighten me, but I remembered that cat's Demoneyes. Suddenly I was happy to fly back. After Horlig had left, we returned to the den and its dim gas mantle lamps. I could understand why Dahlmann's eyesight was so bad— you try reading at night without electric lights for a couple decades and you'll go blind, too. He rummaged around in his desk and drew out a pouch of "tobacco." He fumbled the ground leaves into the bowl of his pipe and tamped them down with a clumsy forefinger. I thought he was going to burn his face when he lit the mixture. Back home, anyone with coordination that poor would be dead in less than two days, unless he secluded himself in a pacific enclave. This Terran culture was truly alien. It was different along a dimension we had never imagined, except in a few mathematical theories of doubtful validity.

The Terran sat back and regarded me for a long moment. Behind those thick lenses his eyes loomed large and wise. Now I was the one who seemed helpless. Finally he pulled back the curtains and inspected the lawn and the place where the car had rested. "I believe, Scholar Melmwn, that you are a reasonable and intelligent individual. I hope that you are even more than that. Do you realize that you are attending the execution of a race?"

This took me completely by surprise. "What! What do you mean?"

He appeared to ignore my question. "I knew when you people first landed and we saw your machines: our culture is doomed. I had hoped that we could escape with our lives—though in our own history, few have been so lucky. I hoped that your social sciences would be as advanced as your physical. But I was wrong.

"Your vice president for Aboriginal Affairs arrived with the Second %wrlyg Fleet. Is genocide the %wrlyg policy or is it Horlig's private scheme?"

This was too much. "I find your questions insulting, Terran! The %wrlyg Company intends you no harm. Our interests are confined to reclaiming and colonizing areas of your planet that you admit are too hot for you to handle."

Now Dahlmann was on the defensive. "I apologize, Scholar Melmwn, for my discourtesy. I dived into the subject too hastily. I don't mean to offend you. Let me describe my fears and the reasons for them. I believe that Herul Horlig is not content with the cultural destruction of Earth. He would like to see all Terrans dead. Officially his job is to promote cooperation between our races and to eliminate possible frictions. In fact, he has played the opposite role. Since he arrived, his every act has increased our mutual antagonism. Take for instance, the 'courtesy call' he made to the Zulunder capital. He and that armed forces chief of yours, Noggin Chem—is that how you pronounce the name?"

"Ngagn Che#," I corrected.

"They breezed into Pret armed to the teeth—fifteen air tanks and a military air-space craft. The Zulunder government requested that Horlig return the spaceship to orbit before they initiated talks. In response, the Mikins destroyed half the city. At the time I hoped that it was just the act of some demented gunner, but Horlig staged practically the same performance at Buenos Aires, the capital of Sudamérica. And this time he had no pretext whatsoever, since the Américans bent over backwards trying to avoid a clash. Every chance he gets, the man tries to prove how vicious Mikins can be."

I made a note to check on these events when I returned to Base. Aloud I said: "Then you believe that Horlig is trying to provoke terrorist movements like this Merlyn thing, so he'll have an excuse to kill all Terrans?"

Dahlmann didn't answer immediately. He carefully pulled back the curtain again and looked into the yard. The aircar had not yet returned. I think he realized that the mikes aboard the car could easily record what we were saying. "That's not quite what I mean, Scholar Melmwn. I believe that Horlig *is* Merlyn."

I snorted disbelief.

"I know it sounds ridiculous—but everything fits. Just take the word 'Merlyn.' In Australian this refers to a magician who lived ages ago in England—that was one of the great pre-war nations in the Northern Hemisphere. At the same time it is a word that easily comes to the lips of a Mikin since it is entirely pronounceable within your phoneme system—it contains no front oral stops. With its magical connotations, it is designed to set fear in Mikins. The word Merlyn is a convenient handle for the fear and hatred that Mikins will come to associate with Terran activities. But note—we Terrans are a very unsuperstitious lot, especially the Australians and the Zulunders. And very few Terrans realize how superstitious many Mikins—the witch-fearers and the demon-mongers— are. The Merlyn concept is the invention of a Mikin mind."

Dahlmann rushed on to keep me from interrupting. "Consider also: When terrorist attacks are thwarted and the Terrans captured, they turn out to be ill-equipped rumdums—not the skilled agents of some world-wide plot. But whenever great damage is done—say the detonation of the Company ammo stores last year—no one is caught. In fact, it is almost impossible to imagine how the job could be pulled off without Mikin technology. At first I discounted this theory, because so many Mikins were killed in the ammo blast, but I have since learned that you people do not regard such violence as improper business procedure."

"It depends on who you are working for. There are plenty of Violent Nihilists on Miki, and occasionally they have their own companies. If %wrlyg is one such, he's been keeping the fact a secret."

"What it adds up to is that Horlig is creating an artificial threat which he believes will eventually justify genocide. One last element of proof. You came in on a Fleet landing craft this afternoon, did you not? Horlig was supposed to greet you. He invited me out to meet you on the field, as the Chief Representative of Her Majesty's Government in Australia. This is the first friendly gesture the man has made in three years. As it happened I couldn't go. I sent my daughter, Mary. But when you actually landed, Horlig got a sliver from his shin board, or something equally idiotic, and so couldn't go onto the field—where just five minutes later a group of 'Merlyn's Men' tried to shoot the lot of you."

Mary Dahlmann. I stuttered over the next question. "How . . . how is your daughter, Scholar Dahlmann?"

Dahlmann was nonplussed for a moment. "She's fine. Apparently someone pulled her out of the line of fire. A bloody nose was the sum total of her injuries."

For some reason I felt great relief at this news. I looked at my watch; it was thirty minutes to midnight, the witching hour. Tonight especially I wanted to get back to Base before Demonsloose. And I hadn't known that Merlyn was the name of a wizard. I stood up. "You've certainly given me something to think about, Dahlmann. Of course you know where my sympathies ultimately lie, but I'll be alert for signs of the plot you speak of, and I won't tell anyone what you've told me."

The Terran rose. "That's all I ask." He led me out of the den, and into the darkened mainroom. The wood floor creaked comfortingly beneath the thick carpet. Crystal goblets on wood shelving were outlined in faint glistening reflection from the den light. To the right a stairway led to the second floor. Was *she* up there sleeping, or out with some male? I wondered.

As we approached the door, something much more pertinent occurred to me. I touched Dahlmann's elbow; he stopped, ready to open the door. "A moment, Scholar Dahlmann. All the facts you present fit another theory; namely, that some Terran, expert in Mikin ways, yourself perhaps, has manufactured Merlyn and the rumor that members of the %wrlyg Company are responsible for the conspiracy."

I couldn't tell for sure, but I think he smiled. "Your counter-proposal does indeed fit the facts. However, I am aware of the power that you Mikins have at your disposal, and how futile resistance would be." He opened the door. I stepped out onto the porch. "Good night," he said.

"Good night." I stood there for several seconds, listening to his retreating footsteps, and puzzling over our last exchange.

I turned and was halfway across the porch when a

soft voice behind me asked, "And how did you like Daddy?" I jumped a good fifteen centimeters, spun around with my wrist gun extended. Mary Dahlmann sat on a wooden swing hung from the ceiling of the porch. She pushed the swing gently back and forth. I walked over and sat down beside her.

"He's an impressive and intelligent man," I answered.

"I want to thank you for pulling me down this afternoon." Her mind seemed to jump randomly from one topic to another.

"Uh, that's O.K. There really wasn't too much danger. The gun was so primitive that I imagine it's almost as unpleasant to be behind it as in front. I would've thought you'd be the first to recognize it as an attack. You must be familiar with Australian weapons."

"Are you kidding? The biggest gun I've ever seen was a 20mm rifle in a shooting exhibition."

"You mean you've never been under fire until today?" I saw that she hadn't. "I didn't mean to be insulting, Miss Dahlmann. I haven't really had much first-hand information about Terrans. That's one reason why I'm here."

She laughed. "If you're puzzled about us, then the feeling is mutual. Since my father became Chief Representative, he's been doing everything he can to interview Mikins and figure out the structure of your culture. I'll bet he spent half the night pumping you. As an anthropologist, you should be the best source he can find."

Apparently she wasn't aware of her father's true concerns.

"In the last three years we've managed to interview more than fifteen of you Mikins. It's crazy. You're all so different from one another. You claim you are all from the same continent, and yet each individual appears to have an entirely different cultural background. Some of you don't wear clothes at all, while others go around with every inch of their skin covered. Some, like Horlig, make a fetish of primitiveness. But we had one fellow here who had so many gadgets with him that he had to wear powered body armor. He was so heavy, he busted my father's favorite chair. We can't find any common denominator. Mikins believe in one god, or in many, or in none. At the same time, many of you are dreadfully superstitious. We've always wondered what aliens might be like, but we never guessed that— What's the matter?"

I pointed shakily at the creature in the street. She placed a reassuring hand on my arm. "Why, that's just a cat. Don't you have catlike creatures on Miki?"

"Certainly."

"Why the shock then? Are your cats poisonous or something?"

"Of course not. Many people keep them as pets. It's just that it's a bad sign to see one at night—an especially bad sign if it looks at you and its eyes glow." I was sorry when she withdrew her hand.

She looked at me closely. "I hope you won't be angry, Mr. Melmwn, but this is exactly what I mean. How can a race that travels between the stars believe in ill or good omens? Or have you developed magic as a science?"

"No, that's not it. Many Mikins don't believe in signs at all, and depending on whether you are a demon-monger or a witch-fearer, you recognize different signs. As for how I personally can believe in nonempirical, nonscientific signs—that's easy. There are many more causal relations in this universe than Mikin science will ever discover. I believe that witch-fearers have divined a few of these. And though I am quite a mild witch-fearer, I don't take any chances."

"But you are an anthropologist. I should think in

your studies you would see so many different attitudes and superstitions that you would disregard your own."

I watched carefully as the cat went round the corner of the house. Then I turned to look at Mary Dahlmann. "Is that how it is with Terran anthropologists? Perhaps then I should not translate my occupation as 'anthropology.' Before %wrlyg, I was employed by the Ana#og Pacific Enclave & Motor Corporation. A fine group. As anthropologist, my job was to screen the background attitudes of perspective employees. For instance, it just wouldn't do to have a Cannibal and a Militant Vegetarian work next to each other on the production line—they'd kill each other inside of three hours, and the corporation would lose money."

She pushed the swing back with an agitated kick. "But now we're back where we started. How can a single culture produce both cannibals and 'militant' vegetarians?"

I thought about it. Her question really seemed to go beyond cultures entirely—right to the core of reality. I had practiced my specialty within the Mikin framework—where such questions never came up. Maybe I should start with something basic.

"Our system is founded on the Concept of Chaos. The universe is basically a dark and unhappy place—a place where evil and injustice and randomness rule. The ironic thing is that the very act of organization creates the potential for even greater ruin. Social organizations have a natural tendency to become monopolistic and inflexible. When they finally break down, it is a catastrophic debacle. So, we must accept a great deal of disorder and violence in our lives if we are to avoid a complete blowup later.

"Every Mikin is free to *try* anything. Naturally, in order to survive, groups of people cooperate—and from this you get the tens of thousands of organizations, corporations, and convents that make our civilization. But no group may become monopolistic. This is why we have Umpires. I don't think you have anything comparable. Umpires see that excessively large organizations are never formed. They keep our society from becoming rigid and unresponsive to the natural world. Our system has lasted a very long time." *Much longer than yours*, I added to myself.

She frowned. "I don't understand. Umpires? Is this some sort of police force? How do they keep governments from forming? What's to keep the Umpires from becoming a government themselves?"

If I didn't watch out, I was going to learn more about Miki than I did about Earth. Mary's questions opened doors I never knew existed. My answer was almost as novel to me as it was to her. "I suppose it's because the Umpire tradition is very old with us. With one minor exception, all Mikins have had this tradition for almost four thousand years. The Umpires probably originated as a priest class serving a number of different nomad tribes. There never were many Umps. They go unarmed. They have bred for intelligence and flexibility. There's quite a bit of, uh, mystery—which we take for granted—surrounding them. I believe that they live under the influence of some rather strange drugs. You might say that they are brainwashed. In all history, there is no period in which they have sought power. Though they spend most of their lives in the abstract study of behavior science, their real task is to watch society for signs of bigness.

"There's one watching %wrlyg right now. If he decides that %wrlyg is too big—and that's a distinct possibility, since there are almost twelve thousand %wrlyg employees altogether—the Ump will issue an, uh, antitrust ruling, describing the situation and ordering certain changes. There is no appeal. Defiance of an antitrust ruling is the only deed that is recognized by all Mikins as a sin. When there is such defiance, all Mikins are bound to take antitrust action—that is, to destroy the criminal. Some antitrust actions have involved fusion bombs and armies—they're the closest thing we have to wars."

She didn't look convinced. "Frankly, I can't imagine how such a system could avoid becoming a dictatorship of 'Umpires'. "

"I feel the same incredulity about your civilization."

"How big are your 'organizations'?"

"It might be a single person. More than half the groups on Miki are just families or family groups. Anything goes unless it threatens stability—or becomes too large. The largest groups allowed are some of the innocuous religious types—the Little Brother Association, for instance. They preach approximately the principles I read of in your Christianity. But they don't proselytize, and so manage to avoid antitrust rulings. The largest 'hardware' organizations have about fifteen thousand employees."

"And how can a company support interstellar operations?"

"Yes, that's a very tricky point. %wrlyg had to cooperate with several hundred industrial groups to do it. They came mighty close to antitrust."

She sat silently, thinking all this over. Then she asked, "When can we expect an antitrust ruling against the Australian government?"

I laughed. "You don't have to worry about that. No offense, but antitrust can only apply to human groupings."

She didn't like that at all, but she didn't argue it either. Instead she came back with, "Then that means we also don't have Umpire protection if %wrlyg commits genocide upon us."

That was a nasty conclusion but it fitted the letter of custom. Killing millions of humans would warrant antitrust, but Terrans weren't human.

For an instant I thought she was laughing, low and bitter. Then her face seemed to collapse and I knew she was crying. This was an unpleasant turn of events. Awkwardly, I put my arm around her shoulders and tried to comfort her. She no longer seemed to me an abo, but simply a person in pain. "Please, Mary Dahlmann. My people aren't monsters. We only want to use places on your planet that are uninhabited, that are too dangerous for you. Our presence will actually make Earth safer. When we colonize the North World, we'll null the radiation poisons and kill the war viruses."

That didn't stop the tears, but she did move closer into my arms. Several seconds passed and she mumbled something like, "History repeats." We sat like that for almost half an hour.

It wasn't until I got back to Base that I remembered that I had been out between Demonsloose and Dawn without so much as a Hexagram.

I got my equipment installed the next day. I was assigned an office only fifty-four hundred meters from the central supply area. This was all right with me since the site was also quite near the outskirts of Adelaide-west. Though the office was made entirely of local materials, the style was old #*imw*#. The basement contained my sleeping and security quarters, and the first floor was my office and business machines. The surface construction was all hand-polished hardwood. The roof was tiled with rose marble and furnished with night chairs and a drink mixer. At the center of the roof was a recoilless rifle and a live map of the mine field around the building. It was all just like home—which is what I had specified when I had signed the contract back on Miki. I had expected some chiseling on the specifications once we got out in the boondocks, but %wrlyg's integrity was a pleasant surprise.

After I checked out the equipment, I called Horlig and got a copy of his mission log. I wanted to check on Dahlmann's charges. Horlig was suspiciously unhappy about parting with the information, but when I pointed out that I was without a job until I got background info, he agreed to squirt me a copy. The incidents were more or less as Dahlmann had described them. At Pret, though, the Zulunders attacked the air tanks with some jury-rigged anti-aircraft weapon—so the retaliation seemed justified. There was also one incident that Dahlmann hadn't mentioned. Just five days before, Che#—on Horlig's orders—burned the food supplies of the Sudamérican colony at Panamá, thus forcing the Terran explorers to return to the inhabited portions of their continent. I decided to keep a close watch on these developments. There could be something here quite as sinister as Dahlmann claimed.

Later that day, Horlig briefed me on my first assignment. He wanted me to record and index the Canberra Central Library. The job didn't appeal at all. It was designed to keep me out of his hair. I spent the next couple weeks getting equipment together. I found Robert Dahlmann especially helpful. He telegraphed his superiors in Canberra and they agreed to let us use Terran clerical help in the recording operation. (I imagine part of the reason was that they were eager to study our equipment.) I never actually flew to Canberra. Horlig had some deputy take the gear out and instruct the natives on how to use it. It turned out Canberra library was huge—almost as big as the Information Services library at home. Just supervising the indexing computers was a full-time job. It was a lot more interesting than I thought it would be. When the job was done I would have many times the source material I could have collected personally.

A strange thing: as the weeks went by, I saw more and more of Mary Dahlmann. Even at this point I was still telling myself that it was all field work for my study of Terran customs. One day we had a picnic in the badlands north of Adelaide. The next she took me on a tour of the business district of the city—it was amazing how so many people could live so close together day after day. Once we even went on a train ride all the way to Murray Bridge. Railroads are stinking, noisy and dirty, but they're fun— and they transport freight almost as cheaply as a floater does. Mary had that spark of intelligence and good humor that made it all the more interesting. Still I claimed it was all in the cause of objective research.

About six weeks after my landing I invited her to visit the %wrlyg Base. Though Central Supply is only four or five kilometers from Adelaide-west, I took her in by air, so she could see the whole Base at once. I think it was the first time she had ever flown.

The %wrlyg Primary Territory is a rectangular area fifteen by thirty kilometers. It was ceded by the Australian government to the Company in gratitude for our intercession in the Battle of Hawaii, seventeen years before. You might wonder why we didn't just put all our bases in the Northern Hemisphere, and ignore the Terrans entirely. The most important reason was that the First and Second Fleets hadn't had the equipment for a large-scale decontamination job. Also, every kilogram of cargo from Miki requires nearly 100,000 megatons of energy for the voyage to Earth: this is expensive by any reckoning. We needed all the labor and materials the locals could provide. Since the Terrans inhabited the Southern Hemisphere only, that's where our first base had to be.

By native standards %wrlyg paid extremely good wages. So good that almost thirty thousand Terrans were employed at the Ground Base. Many of these individuals lived in an area just off the Base, which Mary referred to as Clowntown. Its inhabitants were understandably enamored with the advantages of Mikin technology. Though their admiration was commendable, the results were a little ludicrous. Clowntowners tried to imitate the various aspects of Mikin life. They dressed eccentrically—by Terran standards—and adopted a variety of social behaviors. But their city was just as crowded as regular Australian urban areas. And though they had more scraps of our technology than many places in Australia, their city was filthy. Anarchy just isn't practical in such close quarters. They had absorbed the superficial aspects of our society without ever getting down to the critical matters of Umpires and antitrust. Mary had refused to go with me into Clowntown. Her reason was that police protection ceased to exist in that area. I don't think that was her real reason.

Below us, the blue sea and white breakers met the orange and gray-green bluffs of the shore. The great Central Desert extended right up to the ocean. It was difficult to believe that this land had once supported grass and trees. Scattered randomly across the sand and sage were the individual office and workshops of Company employees. Each of these had its own unique appearance. Some were oases set in the desert. Others were squat gray forts. Some even looked like Terran houses. And, of course, a good number were entirely hidden from sight, the property of Obscurantist employees who kept their location secret even from %wrlyg. Taken as a whole, the Base looked like a comfortable Metropolitan area on the A1 W1 peninsula. But, if the Company had originally based in the Northern Hemisphere, none of the amenities would have been possible. We would have had to live in prefab domes.

I swung the car in a wide arc and headed for the central area. Here was the robot factory that provided us with things like air tanks and drink mixers— things that native labor couldn't construct. Now we could see the general landing area, and the airy columns of Supply Central. Nearby was housing for groups that believed in living together: the sex club, the Little Brothers. A low annex jutted off from the Little Brothers building—the creche for children born of Non-Affective parents. They even had some half-breed Terran-Human children there. The biologists had been amazed to find that the two species could interbreed—some claimed that this proved the existence of a prehistoric interstellar empire.

I parked the car and we took the lift to the open eating area at the top of Supply Central. The utilitarian cafeteria served the Extroverts on the Company staff. The position afforded an excellent view of the sailing boats and surfers as well as three or four office houses out in the sea.

We were barely seated when two Terran waiter-servants came over to take our order. One of them favored Mary with a long, cold look, but they took my order courteously enough.

Mary watched them go, then remarked, "They hate my guts, do you know that?"

"Huh? Why should they hate you?"

"I'm, uh, 'consorting' with the Greenies. That's you. I knew one of those two in college. A real nice guy. He wanted to study low-energy nuclear reactions: prewar scientists never studied that area thoroughly. His life ended when he discovered that you people know more than he'll ever discover, unless he starts over from the beginning on your terms. Now he's practically a slave, waiting on tables."

"A slave he's not, girl. %wrlyg just isn't that type of organization. That fellow is a trusted and well cared for servant—an employee, if you will. He can pack up and leave any time. With the wages we pay, we have Terrans begging for jobs."

"That's exactly what I mean," Mary said opaquely. Then she turned the question around. "Don't you feel any hostility from your friends, for running around with an 'Earthie' girl?"

I laughed. "In the first place, I'm not running around. I'm using you in my studies. In the second place, I don't know any of these people well enough yet to have friends. Even the people I came out with were all in deep freeze, remember.

"Some Mikins actually support fraternization with the natives—the Little Brothers for instance. Every chance they get, they tell us to go out and make love—or is that verb just plain 'love'?—to the natives. I think there are some Company people who are definitely hostile toward you people—Horlig and Che#, for example. But I didn't ask their permission, and, if they want to stop me, they'll have to contend with this," I tapped the dart gun on my wrist.

"Oh?" I think she was going to say something more when the servants came out and placed the food on our table. It was good, and we didn't say anything for several minutes. When we were done we sat and watched the surfers. A couple on a powered board were racing a dolphin across the bay. Their olive skins glistened pleasantly against the blue water.

Finally she spoke. "I've always been puzzled by that Horlig. He's odd even for a Mikin—no offense.

He seems to regard Terrans as foolish and ignorant cowards. Yet as a person, he looks a lot more like a Terran than a Mikin."

"Actually, he's a different subspecies from the rest of us. It's like the difference between you and Zulunders. His bone structure is a little different and his skin is pale gray instead of olive green. His ancestors lived on a different continent than mine. They never developed beyond a neolithic culture there. About four hundred years ago, my race colonized his continent. We already had firearms then. Horlig's people just shriveled away. Whenever they fought us, we killed them; and whenever they didn't, we set them away in preserves. The last preserve Gloyn, died about fifty years ago, I think. The rest interbred with the mainstream. Horlig is the nearest thing to a full-blooded Gloyn I've seen. Maybe that's why he affects primitiveness."

Mary said, "If he weren't out to get us Terrans, I think I could feel sorry for him."

I couldn't understand that comment. Horlig's race may have been mistreated in the past, but he was a lot better off than his ancestors ever were.

Three tables away, another couple was engaged in an intense conversation. Gradually it assumed the proportions of an argument. The man snapped an insult and the woman returned it with interest. Without warning, a knife appeared in her hand, flashed at the other's chest. But the man jumped backward, knocking over his chair. Mary gasped, as the man brought his knife in a grazing slash across the woman's middle. Red instantly appeared on green. They danced around the tables, feinting and slashing.

"Ron, do something! He's going to kill her."

They were fighting in a meal area, which is against Company regs, but on the other hand, neither was using power weapons. "I'm not going to do anything, Mary. This is a lovers' quarrel."

Mary's jaw dropped. "A lovers' quarrel? What—"

"Yeah," I said, "they both want the same woman." Mary looked sick. As soon as the fight began, a Little Brother at the other end of the roof got up and sprinted toward the combatants. Now he stood to one side, pleading with them to respect the holiness of life, and to settle their differences peacefully. But the two weren't much for religion. The man hissed at the Little Brother to get lost before he got spitted. The woman took advantage of her opponent's momentary inattention to pink his arm. Just then a Company officer arrived on the roof and informed the two just how big a fine they would be subject to if they continued to fight in a restricted area. That stopped them. They backed away from each other, cursing. The Little Brother followed them to the lift as he tried to work out some sort of reconciliation.

Mary seemed upset. "You people lead sex lives that make free love look like monogamy."

"No, you're wrong, Mary. It's just that every person has a different outlook. It's as if all Earth's sex customs coexisted. Most people subscribe to some one type." I decided not to try explaining the sex club.

"Don't you have marriage?"

"That's just what I'm saying. A large proportion of us do. We even have a word analogous to your *missus—a*. For instance, Mrs. Smith is aSmith. I would say that nearly fifteen percent of all Mikins are monogamous in the sense you mean it. And a far greater percentage never engage in the activities you regard as perversions."

She shook her head. "Do you know—if your group had appeared without a superior technology, you would have been locked up in an insane asylum? I like you personally, but most Mikins are so awfully weird."

I was beginning to get irritated. "You're the one that's nuts. The %wrlyg employees here on Earth were deliberately chosen for their intelligence and compatibility. Even the mildly exotic types were left at home."

Mary's voice wavered slightly as she answered. "I . . . I guess I know that. You're all just so terribly different. And soon all the ways I know will be destroyed, and my people will all be dead or like you—more probably dead. No, don't deny it. More than once in our history we've had episodes like the colonization of Gloyn. Six hundred years ago, the Europeans took over North America from the stone-age Indians. One group of Indians—a tribe called the Cherokee—saw that they could never overcome the invaders. They reasoned that the only way to survive was to adopt European ways—no matter how offensive those ways appeared. The Cherokee built schools and towns; they even printed newspapers in their own language. But this did not satisfy the Europeans. They coveted the Cherokee lands. Eventually they evicted the Indians and forced-marched the tribe halfway across the continent into a desert preserve. For all their willingness to adapt, the Cherokee suffered the same fate that your Gloyn did.

"Ron, are you any different from the Europeans—or from your Mikin ancestors? Will my people be massacred? Will the rare survivor be just another Mikin with all your aw . . . all your alien customs? Isn't there any way you can save us from yourselves?" She reached out and grasped my hand. I could see she was fighting back tears.

There was no rationalizing it: I had fallen for her. I silently cursed my moralistic Little Brother upbringing. At that moment, if she had asked it, I would have run right down to the beach and started swimming for Antarctica. The feel of her hand against mine and the look in her eyes would have admitted to no other response. For a moment, I wondered if she was aware of the awful power she had. Then I said, "I'll do everything I can, Mary. I don't think you have to worry. We've advanced a long way since Gloyn. Only a few of us wish you harm. But I'll do anything to protect your people from massacre and exploitation. Is that enough of a commitment?"

She squeezed my hand. "Yes. It's a greater commitment than has been made in all the past."

"Fine," I said, standing up. I wanted to get off this painful subject as fast as possible. "Let me show you some of our equipment."

I took her over the Abo Affairs Office. The AAO wasn't a private residence-office, but it did bear Horlig's stamp. Even close up, it looked like a Gloyn rock-nest—a huge pile of boulders set in a marshy—and artificial—jungle. It was difficult, even for me, to spot the location of the recoilless rifles and machine guns. Inside, the neolithic motif was maintained. The computing equipment and TV screens were hidden behind woven curtains, and lighting came indirectly through chinks in the boulders. Horlig refused to employ Terrans, and his Mikin clerks and techs hadn't returned from lunch.

At the far end of the "room" a tiny waterfall gushed tinkling into a pool. Beyond the pool was Horlig's office, blocked from direct view by a rock partition. I noticed that the pool gave us an odd, ripply view into his office. That's the trouble with these "open" architectural forms: they have no real rooms, or privacy. In the water I could see the upside-down images of Horlig and Che#. I motioned Mary to be quiet, and knelt down to watch. Their voices were barely audible above the sound of falling water.

Che# was saying—in Mikin, of course: "You've been sensible enough in the past, Horlig. My suggestion is just a logical extension of previous policy. Once he's committed I'm sure that %wrlyg won't have any objections. The Terrans have provided us with almost all the materials we needed from them. Their usefulness is over. They're vermin. It's costing the Company two thousand man-hours a month to provide security against their attacks and general insolence." He waved a sheaf of papers at Horlig. "My plan is simple. Retreat from Ground Base for a couple weeks and send orbital radiation bombs over the three inhabited areas. Then drop some lethal viruses to knock off the survivors. I figure it would cost one hundred thousand man-hours total, but we'd be permanently rid of this nuisance. And our ground installations would be undamaged. All you have to do is camouflage some of our initial moves so that the Company officers on the Orbital Base don't catch—"

"Enough!" Horlig exploded. He grabbed Che# by the scruff of his cape and pulled him up from his chair. "You putrid bag of schemings. I'm reporting you to Orbit. And if you ever even *think* of that plan again, I personally will kill you—if %wrlyg doesn't do it first!" He shoved the Vice President for Violence to the floor. Che# got up, ready to draw and fire, but Horlig's wrist gun pointed directly at the other's middle. Che# spat on the floor and backed out of the room.

"What was that all about?" Mary whispered. I shook my head. This was one conversation I wasn't going to translate. Horlig's reaction amazed and pleased me. I almost liked the man after the way he had handled Che#. And unless the incident had been staged for my benefit, it shattered Robert Dahlmann's theory about Merlyn and Horlig. Could Che# be the one masquerading as a Terran rebel?

He had just used Terran sabotage as an excuse for genocide.

Or was Merlyn simply what it appeared to be: a terrorist group created and managed by deranged Terrans? Things were all mixed up.

Ngagn Che# stalked out of the passage that led to Horlig's office. He glared murderously at Mary and me as he swept past us toward the door hole.

I looked back into the pool, and saw the reflection of Horlig's face looking back out at me. Perhaps it was the ripple distortion from the waterfall, but he seemed just as furious with my eavesdropping as he had been with Che#. If it had been a direct confrontation, I would've expected a fight. Then Horlig remembered his privacy field and turned it on, blanking out my view.

My library project proceeded rapidly to a conclusion. Everything was taped, and I had 2e7 subjects cross-indexed. The computerized library became my most powerful research tool. Dahlmann hadn't been kidding when he said that the pre-war civilization was high class. If the North Americans and Asians had managed to avoid war, they probably would have sent an expedition to Miki while we were still developing the fission bomb. Wouldn't that have been a switch—the Terrans colonizing our lands!

In the two hundred years since the North World War, the Australians had spent a great deal of effort in developing social science. They hadn't given up their government mania, but they had modified the concept so that it was much less malevolent than in the past. Australia now supported almost eleven million people, at a fairly high standard of living. In fact, I think there was probably less suffering in Australia than there is in most parts of Miki. Too bad their way of life was doomed. The Terrans were people—

they were human. (And that simple conclusion was the answer to the whole problem, though I did not see it then.) In all my readings, I kept in mind the solution I was looking for: some way to save the Terrans from physical destruction, even if it was impossible to save their entire culture.

As the weeks passed, this problem came to overshadow my official tasks. I even looked up the history of the Cherokee and read about Elias Boudinot and Chief Sequoyah. The story was chillingly similar to the situation that was being played out now by the Mikins and the Terrans. The only way that the Terrans could hope for physical safety was to adopt Mikin institutions. But even then, wouldn't we eventually wipe them out the same way President Andrew Jackson did the Cherokee? Wouldn't we eventually covet all the lands of Earth?

While I tried to come up with a long-term solution, I also kept track of Che#'s activities. Some of his men were pretty straight guys, and I got to know one platoon leader well. Late one evening about ten weeks after my landing, my armsman friend tipped me off that Che# was planning a massacre the next day in Perth.

I went over to see Horlig that night. From his reaction to Che#'s genocide scheme, I figured he'd squash the massacre plan. The Gloyn was working late. I found him seated behind his stone desk in the center of the AAO rock-nest. He looked up warily as I entered. "What is it, Melmwn?"

"You've got to do something, Horlig. Che# is flying three platoons to Perth. I don't know exactly what type of mayhem he's planning, but—"

"Rockingham."

"Huh?"

"Che# is flying to Rockingham, not Perth." Horlig watched me carefully.

"You knew? What's he going to do—"

"I know because he's doing the job at my suggestion. I've identified the abos who blew up our ammo warehouse last year. Some of the ringleaders are Rockingham city officials. I'm going to make an example of them." He paused, then continued grimly, as if daring me to object. "By tomorrow at this time, every tenth inhabitant of Rockingham will be dead."

I didn't say anything for a second. I couldn't. When I finally got my mouth working again, I said with great originality, "You just can't do this, Horlig. We've had a lot more trouble from the Sudaméricans and the Zulunders than we've ever had from the Australians. Killing a bunch of Aussies will just prove to everyone that Mikins don't want peace. You'll be encouraging belligerence. If you really have proof that these Rockingham officials are Merlyn's Men, you should send Che# out to arrest just those men and bring them back here for some sort of Company trial. Your present action is entirely arbitrary."

Horlig sat back in his chair. There was a new frankness and a new harshness in his face. "Perhaps I just made it all up. I'll fabricate some proof too, when necessary."

I hadn't expected this admission. I answered, "%wrlyg's Second Son himself is coming down from Orbit tomorrow morning. Perhaps you thought he wouldn't know of your plans until they were executed. I don't know why you are doing this, but I can tell you that the Second Son is going to hear about it the minute he gets off the landing craft."

Horlig smiled pleasantly. "Get out."

I turned and started for the door. I admit it: I was going soft in the brain. My only excuse is that I had been associating with the natives too long. They generally say what they think because they have the protection of an impartial and all-powerful police force. This thought occurred to me an instant before I heard the characteristic sound of wrist gun smacking into palm. I dived madly for the floor as the first 0.07 mm dart hit the right boulder of the door hole. The next thing I knew I was lying in the cubbyhole formed by two or three large boulders knocked loose by the blast. My left arm was numb; a rock splinter had cut through it to the bone.

In the next couple seconds, Horlig fired about twenty darts wildly. The lights went out. Rocks weighing many tons flew about. The rock nest had been designed for stability, but this demolition upset the balance and the whole pile was shifting into a new configuration. It was a miracle I wasn't crushed. Horlig screamed. The shooting stopped. Was he dead? The man was nuts to fire more than a single dart indoors. He must have wanted me pretty bad.

As the horrendous echoes faded away, I could hear Horlig swearing. The pile was unrecognizable now. I could see the sky directly between gaps in the rocks. Moonlight came down in silvery shafts through suspended rock dust. Half-human shapes seemed to lurk in the rubble. I realized now that the nest was much bigger than I had thought. To my left an avalanche of boulders had collapsed into some subterranean space. The surface portion of the nest was only a fraction of the total volume. Right now Horlig could be right on the other side of a nearby rock or one hundred meters away—the pile shift had been that violent.

"You still kicking, Melmwn, old man?" Horlig's voice came clearly. The sound was from my right, but not too close. Perhaps if I moved quietly enough I could sneak out of the pile to my air car. Or I could play dead and wait for morning when Horlig's employees came out. But some of those might be partners in Horlig's scheme—whatever it was. I decided to try the first plan. I crawled over a nearby boulder, made a detour around an expanse of moonlit rock. My progress was definitely audible—there was too much loose stuff. Behind me, I could hear Horlig following. I stopped. This was no good. Even if I managed to make it out, I would then be visible from the pile, and Horlig could shoot me down. I would have to get rid of my opponent before I could escape. Besides, if he got away safely, Horlig could have Che#'s sentries bar me from the landing field the next day. I stopped and lay quietly in the darkness. My arm really hurt now, and I could feel from the wetness on the ground that I had left a trail of blood.

"Come, Melmwn, speak up. I know you're still alive." I smiled. If Horlig thought I was going to give my position away by talking, he was even crazier than I thought. Every time he spoke, I got a better idea of his position.

"I'll trade information for the sound of your voice, Melmwn." Maybe he was not quite so nuts after all. He knew my greatest failing: curiosity. If Horlig should die this night, I might never know what his motives were. And I was just as well armed as he. If I could keep him talking I stood to gain just as much as he.

"All right, Horlig. I'll trade." I had said more than I wanted to. The shorter my responses the better. I listened for the sound of movement. But all I heard was Horlig's voice.

"You see, Melmwn, I am Merlyn." I heard a slithering sound as he moved to a new position. He was revealing everything to keep me talking. Now it was my turn to say something.

"Say on, O Horlig."

"I should have killed you before. When you overheard my conversation with Che#. I thought you might have guessed the truth."

I had received a lot of surprises so far, and this was another. Horlig's treatment of Che#'s genocide scheme had seemed proof that Horlig couldn't be Merlyn. "But why, Horlig? What do you gain? What do you want?"

My opponent laughed. "I'm an altruist, Melmwn. And I'm a Gloyn; maybe the last full-blooded Gloyn. The Terrans are not going to be taken over by you the way you took over my people. The Terrans are people; they are human—and they must be treated as such."

I guess the idea must have been floating around in my mind for weeks. The Terrans were human, and should be treated as such. Horlig's statement triggered the whole solution in my mind. I saw the essential error of the Cherokee and of all my previous plans to save the Terrans. Horlig's motive was a complete surprise, but I could understand it. In a way he seemed to be after the same thing as I—though his methods couldn't possibly work. Maybe we wouldn't have to shoot it out.

"Listen Horlig. There's a way I can get what you want without bloodshed. The Terrans can be saved." I outlined my plan. I talked for almost two minutes.

As I finished, a dart smashed into a boulder thirty meters from my position. Then Horlig spoke. "I will not accept your plan. It is just what I'm fighting against." He seemed to be talking to himself, repeating a cycle that played endlessly, fanatically in his own brain. "Your plan would make the Terrans carbon-copy Mikins. Their culture would be destroyed as thoroughly as mine was. It is far better to die fighting you monsters than to lie down and let you take over. That's why I became Merlyn. I give the rebellious Terran elements a backbone, secret information, supplies. In my capacity as a Mikin official, I provoke incidents to convince the spineless ones of the physical threat to their existence. The Australians are the most cowardly of the lot. Apparently their government will accept any indignity. That's why I must be especially brutal at Rockingham tomorrow."

"Your plan's insane," I blurted without thinking. "%wrlyg could destroy every living thing on Earth without descending from orbit."

"Then that is better than the cultural assassination you intend! We will die fighting." I think he was crying. "I grew up on the last preserve. I heard the last stories. The stories of the lands and the hunting my people once had, before you came and killed us, drove us away, talked us out of everything of value. If we had stood and fought then, I at least would never have been born into the nightmare that is your world." There was silence for a second.

I crept slowly toward the sound of his voice. I tucked my left arm in my shirt to keep it from dragging on the ground. I guessed that Horlig was wounded too, from the slithery sound he made when he moved.

The man was so involved in his own world that he kept on talking. It's strange, but now that I had discovered a way to save the Terrans, I felt doubly desperate to get out of the rock-nest alive. "And don't, Melmwn, be so sure that we will lose to you this time. I intend to provoke no immediate insurrection. I am gathering my forces. A second robot factory was brought in with the Third Fleet. %wrlyg's Second Son is coming down with it tomorrow. With Che#'s forces on the West Coast it will be an easy matter for Merlyn's Men to hijack the factory and its floater. I already have a hidden place, in the midst of all the appropriate ore fields, to set it up. Over the years, that factory will provide us with all the weapons and vehicles we need. And someday, someday we will rise and kill all the Mikins."

Horlig sounded delirious now. He was confusing Gloyn and Terran. But that robofactory scheme was not the invention of a delirious mind—only an insane one. I continued across the boulders—under and around them. The moon was directly overhead and its light illuminated isolated patches of rock. I knew I was quite near him now. I stopped and inspected the area ahead of me. Just five meters away a slender beam of moonlight came down through a chink in the rock overhead.

"Tomorrow, yes, tomorrow will be Merlyn's greatest coup."

As Horlig spoke I thought I detected a faint agitation in the rock dust hung in that moonbeam. Of course it might be a thermal effect from a broken utility line, but it could also be Horlig's breath stirring the tiny particles.

I scrambled over the last boulder to get a clear shot that would not start an avalanche. My guess was right. Horlig sprang to his feet, and for an instant was outlined by the moonlight. His eyes were wide and staring. He was a Gloyn warrior in shin boards and breech-clout, standing in the middle of his wrecked home and determined to protect his way of life from the alien monsters. He was only four hundred years too late. He fired an instant before I did. Horlig missed. I did not. The last Gloyn disappeared in an incandescent flash.

I was in bad shape by the time I got out to my car and called a medic. The next couple hours seem like someone else's memories. I woke the Ump at 0230. He wasn't disturbed by the hour; Umpires can take anything in stride. I gave him the whole story and my solution. I don't think I was very eloquent, so either the plan was sharp or the Ump was especially good. He accepted the whole plan, even the ruling against %wrlyg. To be frank, I think it was a solution that he would have come to on his own, given time—but he had come down from the Orbital Base the week before, and had just begun his study of the natives. He told me he'd reach an official decision later in the day and tell me about it.

I flew back to my office, set all the protection devices on auto, and blacked out. I didn't wake until fifteen hours later, when Ghuri Kym—the Ump—called and asked me to come with him to Adelaide.

Just twenty-four hours after my encounter with Horlig, we were standing in Robert Dahlmann's den. I made the introductions. "Umpire Kym can read Australian but he hasn't had any practice with speaking, so he's asked me to interpret. Scholar Dahlmann, you were right about Herul Horlig—but for the wrong reasons." I explained Horlig's true motives. I could see Dahlmann was surprised. "And Che#'s punitive expedition to the West Coast has been called off, so you don't have to worry about Rockingham." I paused, then plunged into the more important topic. "I think I've come up with a way to save your species from extinction. Ghuri Kym agrees."

Kym laid the document on Dahlmann's desk and spoke the ritual words. "What's this?" asked Dahlmann, pointing at the Mikin printing.

"The English is on the other side. As the representative of the Australian government, you have just been served with an antitrust ruling. Among other things, it directs your people to split into no fewer than one hundred thousand autonomous organizations. Ngagn Che# is delivering similar documents to the Sudamérican and Zulunder governments. You have one year to effect the change. You may be interested to know that %wrlyg has also been served and must split into at least four competitive groups."

%wrlyg had been served with the antitrust ruling that morning. My employers were very unhappy with my plan. Kym told me that the Second Son had threatened to have me shot if I ever showed up on Company property again. I was going to have to lay low for a while, but I knew that %wrlyg needed all the men they could get. Ultimately, I would be forgiven. I wasn't worried: the risk-taking was worth while if it saved the Terrans from exploitation.

I had expected an enthusiastic endorsement from Dahlmann, but he took the plan glumly. Kym and I spent the next hour explaining the details of the ruling to him. I felt distinctly deflated when we left. From the Terran's reaction you'd think I had ordered the execution of his race.

Mary was sitting on the porch swing. As we left the house, I asked Kym to return to the Base without me. If her father hadn't been appreciative, I thought that at least Mary would be. She was, after all, the one who had given me the problem. In a way I had done it all for her.

I sat down on the swing beside her.

"Your arm! What happened?" She passed her hand gently over the plastic web dressing. I told her about Horlig. It was just like the end of a melodrama. There was admiration in her eyes, and her arms were around me—boy gets girl, et cetera.

"And," I continued, "I found a way to save all of you from the fate of the Cherokee."

"That's wonderful, Ron. I knew you would." She kissed me.

"The fatal flaw in the Cherokee's plan was that they segregated themselves from the white community, while they occupied lands that the whites wanted. If they had been citizens of the United States of America, it would not have been legal to confiscate their lands and kill them. Of course we Mikins don't even have a word for 'citizen,' but Umpire law extends to all humans. I got the Umpire to declare that Terrans are a human species. I know it sounds obvious, but it just never occurred to us before.

"Genocide is now specifically barred, because it would be monopolistic. An antitrust ruling has already been served on Australia and the other Earth governments."

Mary's enthusiasm seemed to evaporate somewhat. "Then our governments will be abolished?"

"Why, yes, Mary."

"And in a few decades, we will be the same as you with all your . . . perversions and violence and death?"

"Don't say it that way, Mary. You'll have Mikin cultures, with some Terran enclaves. Nothing could have stopped this. But at least you won't be killed. I've saved—"

For an instant I thought I'd been shot in the face. My mind did three lazy loops, before I realized that Mary had just delivered a round-house slap. "You green-faced thing," she hissed. "You've saved us nothing. Look at this street. Look! It's quiet. No one's killing anyone. Most people are tolerably happy. This suburb is not old, but its way of life is—almost five hundred years old. We've tried very hard in that time to make it better, and we've succeeded in many ways. Now, just as we're on the verge of discovering how all people can live in peace, you monsters breeze in. You'll rip up our cities. 'They are too big' you say. You'll destroy our police forces. 'Monopolistic enterprise' you call them. And in a few years we'll have a planet-wide Clowntown. We'll have to treat each other as animals in order to survive on these oh-so-generous terms you offer us!" She paused, out of breath, but not out of anger.

And for the first time I saw the real fear she had

tried to express from the first. She was afraid of dying—of her race dying; everybody had those fears. But what was just as important to her was her home, her family, her friends. The shopping center, the games, the theaters, the whole concept of courtesy. My people weren't going to kill her body, that was true, but we were destroying all the things that give meaning to life. I hadn't found a solution—I'd just invented murder without bloodshed. Somehow I had to make it right.

I tried to reach my arm around her. "I love you, Mary." The words came out garbled, incomprehensible. "I love you, Mary," more clearly this time.

I don't think she even heard. She pushed away hysterically. "Horlig was the one who was right. Not you. It is better to fight and die than—" she didn't finish. She hit frantically and inexpertly at my face and chest. She'd never had any training, but those were hard, determined blows and they were doing damage. I knew I couldn't stop her, short of injuring her. I stood up under that rain of blows and made for the steps. She followed, fighting, crying.

I stumbled off the steps. She stayed on the porch, crying in a low gurgle. I limped past the street lamp and into the darkness.

So there you have it: anarchy stabilized by antitrust laws! I certainly wouldn't suggest that in our real world, where antitrust laws are chiefly used to maintain monopolies of power. With my alien invaders, the "laws" were more a matter of religious custom. Still, I suspect that the scheme's success must be the most alien thing about my aliens.

I didn't pursue the future history that spans "Apartness" and "Conquest by Default"; yet post-War Earth has been the background of many of my stories. This is not because I am deeply pessimistic, but because a post-War environment slows down technical progress enough that there is time to ponder it. Barring a worldwide catastrophe, I believe that technology will achieve our wildest dreams, and soon. When we raise our own intelligence and that of our creations, we are no longer in a world of human-sized characters. At that point we have fallen into a technological "black hole," a technological singularity. There is very little anyone from our era can say about events in that singularity (though I edge around it in

Marooned in Realtime *and* True Names and Other Dangers—*both from Baen Books*).

Fifty years, a century after the Great War, the horror may be gone but there might be a feeling of sadness for the lost "golden age," for the mistakes that were made. I think that theme is clear in "Apartness" and "Conquest by Default." These stories have little editorializing about the cause of the Great War or the nature of the aggressors; such issues are irrelevant to my protagonists, even if I have strong feelings about policies that exist in our present.

I did write one story, though, where villainy in our era was of direct importance to the action in the story. A story of grand revenge demands grand villainy.

Back around 1970, I noticed a comment in Aviation Week that the planned Sprint anti-ballistic missile could go from launch to 60,000 feet in four seconds. Scale that up just a little bit and there are fairly likely, fairly obvious consequences. The idea went onto a 3-by-5 card and into the little wooden box where I kept inspirations deferred. Eventually, it became "The Whirligig of Time." It was published in 1974, long before SDI. Nevertheless, I think it points up a rarely mentioned aspect of strategic offense/defense.

THE WHIRLIGIG OF TIME

The defense station high in the Laguna Mountains had been on alert since dawn. The clear fall day had passed without event, and now the dark was closing in over the pine-covered hills. A cool, dry wind blew among the trees, nudged at the deep layers of pine needles and slid around the defense station's armored cupolas. Overhead, between the dark silhouettes of the pines, the stars were out, brighter and more numerous than they could ever seem in a city's sky.

To the west, limning the dark Pacific, a narrow band of greenish yellow was all that was left of day, and the city was a fine dusting of light spread inward from the ocean. From the Laguna Mountains, eighty kilometers inland, the city seemed a surrealistic carpet of tiny glowing gems—the most precious of the treasures this station had been constructed to protect.

This was the last moment of comfortable tranquility that this land would know for many, many centuries.

The life in the forest—the birds asleep in the trees, the squirrels in their holes—heard and felt nothing; but deep within the station men looked out into space with microwave eyes, saw the tiny specks rising beyond the polar horizon, plotted their trajectories and predicted that hell would burn in heaven and on earth this night.

On the surface, concrete and steel cowlings whirred open to reveal the lasers and ABMs now tracking the enemies falling out of space. The birds fluttered nervously about their trees now, disturbed by the noises below, and a faint red light shone up from the holes in the ground. Yet from the next ridgeline over, the night would still have seemed silent, and the starlit pine forest undisturbed.

Halfway up in the northern sky, three new stars lit, so bright that a blue-white day shone on the forest, still silent. Their glare faded swiftly through orange to red and guttered out, leaving a play of pale green and gold to spread through the sky. Those pastel colors were the only visible sign of the immense fog of charged particles the explosions had set between ground radars and the missiles that were yet to come. The men in the station held their fire. The explosions had not completely blinded them— they still had a proxy view of part of the battle space from a synchronous satellite—but the distance to their targets was far too great.

In the skies to the north and east more miniature stars were visible—mostly defensive fires. The unnatural aurora spread from horizon to horizon, yet in the west the lights of the city glowed as placidly, as beautifully as before the end began.

Now the defenders' radars could pick up the enemy warheads falling out of the ionospheric fog that had concealed them. But not one of the incoming missiles was targeted on the city to the west—all

were falling in toward the defense station and the
ICBM bases in the desert to the east. The defenders
noticed this but had no time to puzzle over it. Their
own destruction was seconds away unless they acted.
The station's main laser fired, and the pines and the
hills flashed red by its reflected light. The ten-
centimeter beam was a hundred-kilometer-tall thread
of fire, disappearing only at the top of the sensible
atmosphere where there was no more air to be ion-
ized. Its sound, the sound of whole tons of air being
turned into plasma, was a bone-shattering crack that
echoed off the distant hills to sweep back and forth
across the land.

Now there was nothing left asleep in the forest.

And when the beam itself was gone, there—high
in the sky—hung a pale blue thread, with a nob of
faintly glowing yellow and gold at one end. The first
target, at least, had been destroyed; the beam was so
energetic it created its own miniature aurora as it
passed through the ionosphere, and the knob at the
end of it marked a vaporized target.

Then the other lasers began firing, and the sky was
crisscrossed by strange red lightning. The ABMs
streaking from the hillside contributed their own
peculiar roar to this local armageddon. The tiny rockets were like flecks of molten metal spewed up on
rays of fire and smoke. Their success or failure was
determined in the scant five seconds of their powered flight—five seconds in which they climbed more
than thirty kilometers into the sky. The spaces above
the hills were filled with bright new stars, and the
more frequent—yet less impressive—glows that
marked successful laser interceptions.

For seventy-five seconds the battle in the spaces
over the defense station continued. During that time
the men could do little but sit and watch their
machines—the defense demanded microsecond re-

flexes, and only the machines could provide that. In those seventy-five million microseconds, the station destroyed dozens of enemy missiles. Only ten of the attacking bombs got through; bright blue flashes on the eastern horizon marked the end of the ICBM bases there. Yet even those ten might have been intercepted, if only the station had not held back its reserve, waiting for the attack that must sooner or later come upon the great city to the west.

Seventy-five seconds—and the city they waited to protect still lay glowing beneath the yellow-green sky.

And then, from the middle of the gleaming carpet that was the city, one more new star was born. In an astronomical sense, it was a very small star; but to itself and to what lay nearby, it was an expanding, gaseous hell of fission-fusion products, neutrons and x-rays.

In seconds the city ceased to be, and the defenders in the mountains realized why all the enemy missiles had been targeted on military installations, realized what must be happening to the larger cities all across the land, realized how much easier it had been for the enemy to smuggle his bombs into the nation's cities than to drop them in along ballistic trajectories.

From where the yacht floated, a million kilometers above the ecliptic and six million behind the Earth in its orbit, the home planet was a marbled bluish ball, nearly as bright as a full moon yet only a quarter the size. The moon itself, a couple of degrees further out from the sun, shone twice as bright as Venus. The rest of heaven seemed infinitely far away, misty sweeps of stars at the bottom of an endless well.

By the blue-white sunlight, the yacht was a three-hundred-meter silver crescent, devoid of fins and aerials and ports. In fact, the only visible marking was the Imperial escutcheon—a scarlet wreath and a five-pointed star—just short of the nose.

But from within, a large part of that hull was not opaque. Arching over the main deck it was as clear, as transparent, as the air of a desert night; and the lords and ladies attending the Prince's birthday party could see the Earth-Moon system hanging just above the artificial horizon created by the intersection of deck and hull. The scene was lost on most of them. Only a few ever bothered to look up into the strange sky. They were the fifteenth generation of an aristocracy that regarded the entire universe as its just due. They would have been just as bored—or just as amused—at Luna or back on the Avstralijan Riviera on Earth.

In all the two-million-ton bulk of the yacht, perhaps only four or five people were really aware of the surrounding emptiness:

Vanja Biladze floated near the center of the yacht's tiny control cabin—he liked to keep it at zero gee—steadying himself with one hand draped negligently around a wall strap. His three-man crew sat belted down to control saddles before the computer inputs and the holoscreens. Biladze gestured at the gray-white cone that tumbled slowly across the central screen. "Do you have any idea what it is, Boblanson?" he asked the fifth man in the control cabin.

The little man called Boblanson had just entered the cabin from the kennels below decks, and he still looked a bit green about the gills. His rickets-bent hands held tightly to the wall straps as his balding head bobbed about in an attempt to focus on the screen. The three crewmen seemed as intrigued by this twisted dwarf as by what the long-range scope was throwing on their screen. The men were new to the Imperial yacht, and Biladze guessed they had never before seen a non-Citizen in person. Outside of the Preserves, about the only place one could be found was in the Emperor's menageries.

Boblanson's nearsighted eyes squinted for a long moment at the screen. The ship's computer had superimposed a reticle on the image, indicating the cone was about a meter wide and perhaps three meters long. Ranging figures printed below the reticle showed the object was more than two hundred kilometers away. Even at that range the synthetic aperture scope resolved a lot of detail. The cone was not a smooth, uniform gray but was scored with hundreds of fine lines drawn parallel to its axis. There were no aerials or solar panels protruding from the cone. Every fifteen seconds the base of the object rotated into view, a dark uninformative hole.

The little man licked his lips nervously. If it had been possible to grovel in zero gee, Biladze was sure that Boblanson would have done so. "It is marvelous, Your Eminence. An artifact, to be sure."

One of the crewmen rolled his eyes. "We know that, you idiot. The question is, would the Prince be interested in it? We were told you are his expert on pre-Imperial spacecraft."

Boblanson bobbed his head emphatically, and the rest of his body bobbed in sympathy. "Yes, Eminence. I was born in the Prince's Kalifornija Preserve. For all these centuries, my tribes have passed from father to son the lore of the Great Enemy. Many times the Prince has sent me to explore the glowing ruins within the Preserves. I have learned all I can of the past."

The crewman opened his mouth—no doubt to give his acid opinion of illiterate savages who pose as archeologists—but Biladze broke in before the other could speak. The crewman was new to the Court, but not so new that he could get away with insulting the Prince's judgment. Biladze knew that every word spoken in the control cabin was monitored by Safety Committee agents hidden elsewhere in the ship, and every maneuver the crew undertook was analyzed by the Safety Committee's computers. Citizens of the Empire were used to surveillance, but few realized just how pervasive any eavesdropping could be until they entered the Imperial Service. "Let me rephrase Kolja's question," said Biladze. "As you know, we're tracking back along Earth's orbit. Eventually—in another fifteen hours, if we hadn't stopped for this thing—we will be far enough back to encounter objects in trojan orbits. Now there is some reason to believe that at least a few of the probes launched into Earthlike orbits eventually wound up near Earth's trojan points—"

"Yes, Eminence, I suggested the idea," said Boblanson. *So there is spirit in you after all*, thought Biladze with surprise; perhaps the little man knew that the Prince's pets sometimes counted for more than an Imperial Citizen. And the fellow's education obviously went beyond the folk tales his tribe passed from generation to generation. The idea of looking for artifacts near the trojan points was clever, though Biladze guessed that careful analysis would show it to be impractical for at least two different reasons. But the Prince rarely bothered with careful analysis.

"In any case," continued Vanja Biladze, "we've found something, but it's nowhere near our destination. Perhaps the Prince will not be interested. After all, the chief reason for this excursion is to celebrate his birthday. We are not sure if the Emperor and the Prince and all the gentle people attending will really be too happy if we interrupt them with this matter. But we know that you have the special confidence of the Prince when it comes to his collection of pre-Imperial space probes. We hoped—"

We hoped you'd take us off the hook, fellow, thought Biladze. His predecessor at this job had been executed by the teen-age prince. His crime: interrupting the boy at dinner. For the thousandth time, Biladze wished he were back in the old-time Navy—where research had been disguised as maneuvers—or even back on Earth in some Gruzijan lab. The closer a Citizen came to the centers of power, the more of a madhouse the universe became.

"I understand, Eminence," said Boblanson, sounding as if he really did. He glanced once more at the screen, then back at Biladze. "And I assure you that the Prince would hate to pass this up. His collection is immense, you know. Of course it contains all the moon landers ever launched. They are rather easy to find, given your Navy's maps. He even has a couple of Martian probes—one Republican and one launched by the Great Enemy. And the surviving near-Earth satellites are generally quite easy to find, too. But the solar and outer planet probes—those are extremely difficult to recover, since they are no longer associated with any celestial body but roam through an immense volume of space. He has only two solar probes in his entire collection, and both were launched by the Republic. I've never seen anything like this," he motioned jerkily at the tumbling white cone on the screen. "Even if it were launched by your ancestors in the days of the Republic, it would still be a find. But if it belonged to the Great Enemy, it would be one of the Prince's favorite acquisitions, without doubt." Boblanson lowered his voice. "And frankly, I think it's conceivable that this spacecraft was not launched by either the Republic or the Great Enemy."

"What!" The exclamation came simultaneously from four throats.

The little man still seemed nervous and half-nauseated, but for the first time Biladze saw an almost hypnotic quality about him. The fellow was diseased, half-crippled. After all, he had been raised in a poisoned and desolate land, and since coming to the Imperial Service he had apparently been used to explore the radioactive ruins of the Great Enemy's cities. Yet with all that physical abuse, the mind within was still powerful, persuasive. Biladze wondered whether the Emperor realized that his son's pet was five times the man the Prince was.

"Yes, it would be fantastic," said Boblanson. "Mankind has found no evidence of life—much less intelligent life—anywhere else in the universe. But I know . . . I know the Navy once listened for signals from interstellar space. The possibility is still alive. And this object is so strange. For example, there is no communication equipment sticking through its hull. I know that you of the Empire don't use exterior aerials—but in the time of the Republic, all spacecraft did. And, too, there are no solar panels, though perhaps the craft had an isotopic power source. But the pattern of rays along its hull is the strangest thing of all. Those grooves are what you might expect on a meteorite or space probe—after it had come down through a planetary atmosphere. But there is simply no explanation for finding such an ablated hull out in interplanetary space."

That certainly decides the question, thought Biladze. Everything the non-Citizen had said was on tape somewhere, and if it ever came out that Vanja Biladze had passed up an opportunity to obtain an extraterrestrial artifact for the Prince's collection, there would be need for a new pilot on the Imperial yacht. "Kolja, get on the printer, and tell the Lord Chamberlain what Boblanson has discovered here." Perhaps that phrasing would protect him and the crew if the whirling gray cone did not interest the Prince.

Kolja began typing the message on the intraship

printer. Theoretically, a Citizen could talk directly to the Lord Chamberlain, since that officer was a bridge of sorts between the Imperial Court and its servants. In fact, however, the protocol for speaking with any member of the aristocracy was so complex that it was safest to deal with such men in writing. And occasionally, the written record could be used to cover your behind later on—if the nobleman you dealt with was in a rational mood. Biladze carefully read the message as it appeared on the readout above the printer, then signaled Kolja to send it. The word ACKNOWLEDGED flashed on the screen. Now the message was stored in the Chamberlain's commbox on the main deck. When its priority number came up, the message would appear on the screen there, and if the Lord Chamberlain were not too busy supervising the entertainment, there might be a reply.

Vanja Biladze tried to relax. Even without Boblanson's harangue he would have given an arm and a leg to close with the object. But he was far too experienced, far too cautious, to let such feelings show. Biladze had spent three decades in the Navy—whole years at a time in deep space so far from Earth-Luna and the pervasive influence of the Safety Committee that the home world might as well not have existed. Then the Emperor began his crackdown on the Navy, drawing them back into near-Earth space, subjecting them to the scrutiny accorded his other Citizens and outlawing what research they had been able to get away with before. And with the new space drive, no point in the solar system was more than hours from Earth, so such close supervision was practical. For many officers, the change had been a fatal one. They had grown up in space, away from the Empire, and they had forgotten—or else never learned—how to mask their feelings and behave with appropriate humility. But Biladze remembered well. He had been

born at Suhumi in Gruzija, a favorite resort of the
nobility. For all the perfection of Suhumi's blind-
ingly white beaches and palm dotted parks, death
had been waiting every moment for the disrespectful
Citizen. And when he had moved east to Tiflis, to
the technical schools, life was no less precarious. For
in Tiflis there were occasional cases of systematically
disloyal thoughts, thoughts which upset the Safety
Committee far more than accidental disrespect.

If that had been the sum of his experience on
Earth, Biladze, like his comrades, might have forgotten how to live with the Safety Committee. But in
Tiflis, in the spring of his last year at the Hydrome-
chanical Institute, he met Klaša. Brilliant, beautiful
Klaša. She was majoring in heroic architecture, one
of the few engineering research fields the Emperors
had ever tolerated on Earth. (After all, statues like
the one astride Gibraltar would have been impossible without the techniques discovered by Klaša's
predecessors.) So while his fellow officers managed
to stay in space for whole decades at a time, Vanja
Biladze had returned to Tiflis, to Klaša, again and
again.

And he never forgot how to survive within the
Imperial system.

Abruptly, Biladze's attention returned to the white-
walled control room. Boblanson was eyeing him with
a calculating stare, as if making some careful judgment. For a long moment, Biladze returned the
gaze. He had seen only four or five non-Citizens in
the flesh, though he had been piloting the Imperial
yacht for more than a year. The creatures were always stunted, most often mindless—simple freaks
kept for the amusement of noblemen with access to
the vast Amerikan Preserves. This Boblanson was
the only clever one Biladze had ever seen. Still, he
found it hard to believe that the frail man's ancestors

had been the Great Enemy, had struggled with the Republic for control of Earth. Very little was known about those times, and Biladze had never been encouraged to study the era, but he did know that the Enemy had been intelligent and resourceful, that it had never been totally defeated until it finally launched a sneak attack upon the Republic. The enraged Republic beat back the attack, then razed the Enemy's cities, burned its forests and left its entire continent a radioactive wasteland. Even after five centuries, the only people living in that ruin were the pitiful non-Citizens, the final victims of their own ancestors' treachery.

And the victorious Republic had gone on to become the world Empire.

That was the story, anyway. Biladze could doubt or disbelieve parts of it, but he knew that Boblanson was the ultimate descendant of a people who had opposed the establishment of the Empire. Vanja briefly wondered what version of history had been passed down the years to Boblanson.

Still no answer on the printer readout. Apparently the Lord Chamberlain was too busy to be bothered.

He said to Boblanson, "You are from the Kalifornija Preserve?"

The other bobbed his head. "Yes, Eminence."

"Of course I've never been there, but I've seen most of the Preserves from low orbit. Kalifornija is the most terrible wasteland of them all, isn't it?" Biladze was breaking one of the first principles of survival within the Empire: he was displaying curiosity. That had always been his most dangerous failing, though he rationalized things by telling himself that he knew how to ask safe questions. There was nothing really secret about the non-Citizens—they were simply a small minority living in areas too desolate to be settled. The Emperor was fond of parading the poor creatures on the holo, as if to say to his Citizens: "See what becomes of my opponents." Certainly it would do no harm to talk to this fellow, as long as he sounded appropriately impressed by the Enemy's great defeat and yet greater treachery.

Boblanson gave another of his frenetic nods. "Yes, Eminence. I regret that some of my people's greatest and most infamous fortresses were in the southern part of Kalifornija. It is even more to my regret that my particular tribe is descended from the subhumans who directed the attack on the Republic. Many nights around our campfires—when we could find enough wood to make a fire—the Oldest Ones would tell us the legends. I see now that they were talking of reaction-drive missiles and pumped lasers. Those are primitive weapons by the Empire's present standards, but they were probably the best that either side possessed in those days. I can only thank your ancestors' courage that the Republic and justice prevailed.

"But I still feel the shame, and my dress is a penance for my ancestry—it is a replica of the uniform worn by the damned creatures who inspired the Final Conflict." He pulled fretfully at the blue material, and for the first time Biladze really noticed the other's clothing. It wasn't that Boblanson's dress was inconspicuous. As a mater of fact, the blue uniform—with its twin silver bars on each shoulder—was ludicrous. In the zero gee of the control cabin, the pants were continually floating up, revealing Boblanson's bent, thin legs. Before, Biladze had thought it was just another of the crazy costumes the Imperial family decreed for the creatures in the menagerie, but now he saw that the sadism went deeper. It must have amused the Prince greatly to take this scarecrow and dress him as one of the Enemy, then have him grovel and scuttle about. The Imperial family never forgot its opponents, no matter how far removed they were in time or space.

Then he looked back into the little man's eyes and realized with a chill that he had seen only half the picture. No doubt the Prince had ordered Boblanson to wear the uniform, but in fact the non-Citizen was the one who was amused—if there was any room for humor behind those pale blue eyes. It was even possible, Biladze guessed, that the man had maneuvered the Prince into ordering that he be dressed in this way. So now Boblanson, descendant of the Great Enemy, wore that people's full uniform at the Court of the Emperor. Biladze shivered within himself, and for the first time put some real credit in the myths about the Enemy's subtlety, their ability to deceive and to betray. This man still remembered whatever had happened in those ancient times—and with greater feeling than any member of the Imperial family.

The word ACKNOWLEDGED vanished from the screen over the printer and was replaced by the Lord Chamberlain's jowly face. The crew bowed their heads briefly, tried to appear self-composed. The Chamberlain was unusually content to communicate by printer, so apparently their message—when it finally got his attention—was of interest.

"Pilot Biladze, your deviation from the flight plan is excused, as is your use of the Prince's pet." He spoke ponderously, the wattles swaying beneath his chin. Biladze hoped that old Rostov's implied criticism was *pro forma*. The Lord Chamberlain couldn't afford to be as fickle as most nobles, but he was a hard man, willing to execute his patrons' smallest whim. "You will send the creature Boblanson up here. You will maintain your present position relative to the unidentified object. I am keeping this circuit open so that you will respond directly to the

Emperor's wishes." He stepped out of pickup range, ending the conversation as abruptly as if he had been talking to a computer. At least Biladze and his crew had been spared the trouble of framing a properly respectful response.

Biladze punched HATCH OPEN, and Boblanson's keepers entered the cabin. "He's supposed to go to the main deck," Biladze said. Boblanson glanced briefly at the main screen, at the enigma that was still slowly turning there, then let his keepers bind him with an ornamental leg chain and take him into the hallway beyond. The hatch slid shut behind the trio, and the crew turned back to the holographic image above the printer.

The camera sending that picture hadn't moved, but Rostov's obese hulk was no longer blocking the view and there was a lot to see. The yacht had been given to the Prince by the Emperor on the boy's tenth birthday. As with any Imperial gift, the thing was huge. The main deck—with its crystal ceiling-wall open to all heaven—could hold nearly two thousand people. At least that many were up there now, for this party—the whole twenty hour outing—celebrating the Prince's eighteenth birthday.

Many of the lords and ladies wore scarlet, though some had costumes of translucent and transparent pastels. The lights on the main deck had been dimmed, and the star clouds, crowned by Earth-Luna, hung bright above the revelers—an incongruous backdrop to the festivities. That these people should be the ones to rule those worlds . . .

Scattered through the crowd, he caught patches of gray and brown—the uniforms of the traybearers, doing work any sensible culture would reserve to machines. The servants scuttled about, forever alert to their betters' wishes, forever abjectly respectful. That respect must have been mainly for the

benefit of Safety Committee observers, since most
of the partygoers were so high on thorn-apple or
even more exotic drugs that they wouldn't have
known it if someone spit in their eye. The pro-
ceedings were about three-quarters of the way to
being a full-blown orgy. Biladze shrugged to himself.
It was nothing new—this orgy would simply be bigger than usual.

Then the tiny figures of Boblanson and his keepers
came in from the right side of the holoscreen. The
two Citizens walked carefully, their shoulders down,
their eyes on the floor. Boblanson seemed to carry
himself much the same, but after a moment Bilazde
noticed that the little man shot glances out to the
right and left, watching everything that went on. It
was amazing. No Citizen could have gotten away
with such brazen arrogance. But Boblanson was not a
Citizen. He was an animal, a favored pet. You kill an
animal if it displeases you, but you don't put the same
social constraints on it that you would upon a human.
No doubt even the Safety Committee passed over
the fellow with only the most cursory inspection.

As the figures walked off to the left, Biladze leaned
to the right to follow them in the holo and saw the
Emperor and his son. Paša III was seated on his
mobile throne, his costume a cascade of scarlet and
jewels. Paša's face was narrow, ascetic, harsh. In
another time such a man might have created an
empire rather than inherited one. As it was, Paša
had consolidated the autocracy, taking control of all
state functions—even and especially research—and
turning them to the crackpot search for reincarnators.

On only one issue could Paša be considered soft:
his son was just eighteen today, yet the boy had
already consumed the resources and the pleasures of
a thousand adolescences. Saša X, dressed in skintight
red breeches and diamond-encrusted belt, stood next

to his father's throne. The brunette leaning against
him had a figure that was incredibly smooth and full,
yet the Prince's hand slid along her body as negligently as if he were stroking a baluster.

The keepers prostrated themselves before the throne
and were recognized by the Emperor. Biladze bit
back a curse. The damn microphone wasn't picking
up their conversation! How would he know what
Paša or his son wanted if he couldn't hear what was
going on? All he was getting were music and laughter
—plus a couple of indecent conversations close by
the mike. This was the type of bungle that made the
position of Chief Yacht Pilot a short-lived one, no
matter how careful a man was.

One of his crew fiddled with the screen controls,
but nothing could really be done at this end. They
would see and hear only what the Lord Chamberlain
was kind enough to let them see and hear. Biladze
leaned toward the screen and tried to pick out from
the general party noises the conversation passing
between Boblanson and the Prince.

The two keepers were still prostrate at Paša's feet.
They had not been given permission to rise. Boblanson
remained standing, though his posture was cringing
and timid. Servants insinuated themselves through
the larger crowd to distribute drinks and candies to
the Imperial party.

The Emperor and his son seemed totally unaware
of this bustle of cringing figures about them. It was
strange to see two men set so far above the common
herd. And it all brought back a very old memory. It
had been the summer of his last year at Tiflis, when
he had found both Klaša and the freedom of the
Navy. Many times during that summer, he and Klaša
had flown into the Kavkaz to spend the afternoon
alone in the alpine meadows. There they could speak
their own minds, however timidly, without fear of

being overheard. (Or so they thought. In later years, Biladze realized how terribly mistaken they had been. It was blind luck they were not discovered.) On those secret picnics, Klaša told him things that were never intended to go beyond her classes. The architecture students were taught the old forms and the meaning of the inscriptions to be found upon them. So Klaša was one of the few people in all the Empire with any knowledge of history and archaic languages, however indirect and fragmentary. It was dangerous knowledge, yet in many ways fascinating: In the days of the Republic, Klaša asserted, the word "Emperor" had meant something like "Primary Secretary," that is, an elected official—just as on some isolated Navy posts, the men elect a secretary to handle unit funds. It was an amazing evolution—to go from elected equal to near godling. Biladze often wondered what other meanings and truths had been twisted by time and by the kind of men he was watching on the holoscreen.

"—Father. I think it could be exactly what my creature says." The audio came loud and abrupt as the picture turned to center on the Prince and his father. Apparently Rostov had realized his mistake. The Chamberlain had almost as much to lose as Biladze if the Emperor's wishes were not instantly gratified.

Biladze breathed a sigh of relief as he picked up the thread of the conversation. Saša's high-pitched voice was animated: "Didn't I tell you this would be a worthwhile outing, Father? Here we've already run across something entirely new, perhaps from beyond the Solar System. It will be the greatest find in my collection. Oh, Father, we must pick it up." His voice rose fractionally.

Paša grimaced, and said something about Saša's "worthless hobbies." Then he gave in—as he almost always did—to the wishes of his son. "Oh very well, pick the damned thing up. I only hope it's half as interesting as your creature here," he waved a gem-filthy arm at Boblanson, "says it is."

The non-Citizen shivered within his blue uniform, and his voice became a supplicating whine. "Oh, dear Great Majesty, this trembling animal promises you with all his heart that the artifact is perfectly fit to all the greatness of your Empire."

Even before Boblanson got the tongue-twisting promise out of his mouth, Biladze had turned from the holo and was talking to his men. "Okay. Close with the object." As one of the crew tapped the control board, Biladze turned to Kolja and continued, "We'll pick it up with the third-bay waldoes. Once we get it inside, I want to check the thing over. I remember reading somewhere that the Ancients used reaction jets for attitude control and thrust—they never did catch on to inertial drive. There just might be some propellant left in the object's tanks after all these years. I don't want that thing blowing up in anybody's face."

"Right," said Kolja, turning to his own board.

Biladze kept an ear on the talk coming from the main deck—just in case somebody up there changed his mind. But the conversation had retreated from the specifics of this discovery to a general discussion of the boy's satellite collection. Boblanson's blue figure was still standing before the throne, and every now and then the little man interjected something in support of Saša's descriptions.

Vanja pushed himself off the wall to inspect the approach program his crewman had written. The yacht was equipped with the new drive and could easily attain objective accelerations of a thousand gravities. But their target was only a couple hundred kilometers away and a more delicate approach was in order: Biladze pressed the PROGRAM INITIATE, and the ship's display showed that they were moving toward the artifact at a leisurely two gravities. It should take nearly two hundred seconds to arrive, but that was probably within Saša's span of attention.

One hundred twenty seconds to contact. For the first time since he had called Boblanson into the control cabin ten minutes earlier, Biladze had a moment to ponder the object for himself. The cone was an artifact; it was much too regular to be anything else. Yet he doubted that it was of extraterrestrial origin, no matter what Boblanson thought. Its orbit had the same period and eccentricity as Earth's, and right now it wasn't much over seven million kilometers from Earth-Luna. Orbits like that just aren't stable over long periods of time. Eventually such an object must be captured by Earth-Luna or be perturbed into an eccentric orbit. The cone couldn't be much older than man's exploration of space. Biladze wondered briefly how much could be learned by tracing the orbit back through some kind of dynamical analysis. Probably not much.

Right now the only difference between its orbit and Earth's was the inclination: about three degrees. That might mean it had been launched from Earth at barely more than escape velocity, along a departure asymptote pointing due north. Now what conceivable use could there be for such a trajectory?

Ninety seconds to contact. The image of the slowly tumbling cone was much sharper now. Besides the faint scoring along its hull, he could see that the dull white surface was glazed. It really did look as if it had passed through a planet's atmosphere. He had seen such effects only once or twice before, since with any inertial drive it was a simple matter to decelerate before entering an atmosphere. But Biladze could imagine that the Ancients, having to depend on rockets for propulsion, might have used aerodynamic braking to save fuel. Perhaps this was a returning space probe that had entered Earth's atmosphere at too shallow an angle and skipped back into space, lost forever to the Ancients' primitive technology. But that still didn't explain its narrow, pointed shape. A good aerodynamic brake would be a blunt body. This thing looked as if it had been designed expressly to minimize drag.

Sixty seconds to contact. He could see now that the black hole at its base was actually the pinched nozzle of a reaction jet—added proof that this was an Earth-launched probe from before the Final Conflict. Biladze glanced at the holoscreen above the printer. The Emperor and his son seemed really taken with what they were seeing on the screen set before the throne. Behind them stood Boblanson, his poor nearsighted eyes squinting at the screen. The man seemed even stranger than before. His jaws were clenched and a periodic tic cut across his face. Biladze looked back at the main screen; the little man knew more than he had revealed about that mysterious cone. If he had not been beneath their notice, the Safety Committee would have long since noticed this, too.

Thirty seconds. What was Boblanson's secret? Biladze tried to connect the centuries-deep hatred he had seen in Boblanson with what they knew about the tumbling white cone: It had been launched around the time of the Final Conflict on a trajectory that might have pointed northwards. But the object hadn't been intended as a space probe since it had evidently acquired most of its speed while still within Earth's atmosphere. No sensible vehicle would move so fast within the atmosphere . . .

. . . *unless it was a weapon.*

The thought brought a sudden numbness to the

pit of Biladze's stomach. The Final Conflict had been fought with rocket bombs fired back and forth over the North Pole. One possible defense against such weapons would be high acceleration antimissile missiles. If one such missed its target, it might very well escape Earth-Luna—to orbit the sun, forever armed, forever waiting.

Then why hadn't his instruments detected a null bomb within it? The question almost made him reject his whole theory, until he remembered that quite powerful explosions could be produced with nuclear fission and fusion. Only physicists knew such quaint facts, since null bombs were much easier to construct once you had the trick of them. But had the Ancients known that trick?

Biladze casually folded his arms, kept his position by hooking one foot through a wall strap. Somewhere inside himself a voice was screaming: *Abort the approach, abort the approach!* Yet if he were right and if the bomb in that cone were still operable, then the Emperor and the three highest tiers of the nobility would be wiped from the face of the universe.

It was an opportunity no man or group of men had had since the Final Conflict.

But it's not worth dying for! screamed the tiny, frightened voice.

Biladze looked into the holoscreen at the hedonistic drones whose only talent lay in managing the security apparatus that had suppressed men and men's ideas for so long. With the Emperor and the top people in the Safety Committee gone, political power would fall to the technicians—ordinary Citizens from Tiflis, Luna City, Eastguard. Biladze had no illusions: ordinary people have their own share of villains. There would be strife, perhaps even civil war.

But in the end, men would be free to go to the stars, from where no earthly tyranny could ever recall them.

Behind the Emperor and the nobles, Boblanson cringed no more. A look of triumph and hatred had come into his face, and Biladze remembered that he had said this would be a gift fit for the Empire.

And so your people will be revenged after all these centuries, thought Biladze. As vengeance it was certainly appropriate, but that had nothing to do with why he, Vanja Biladze, floated motionless in the control cabin and made no effort to slow their approach on the tumbling cone. He was scared as hell. Mere vengeance was not worth this price. Perhaps the future would be.

They were within a couple thousand meters of the object now. It filled the screen, as if it whirled just beyond the yacht's hull. Biladze's instruments registered some mild radioactivity in the object's direction.

Good-bye, Klaša.

Six million kilometers from Earth, a new star was born. In an astronomical sense, it was a very small star, but to itself and what lay nearby it was an expanding plasmatic hell of fission-fusion products, neutrons and gamma rays.

"The Whirligig of Time" wasn't hard to sell (Judy-Lynn del Rey bought it for Stellar One), but it did pick up an interesting rejection along the way: One editor bounced the story, saying that it was too patriotic. Hmm. Too polemical, I could understand, or too trite . . . but too patriotic? I felt much as I would if someone had told me that my stories were too unpatriotic (though I suppose unpatriots are more likely to be on the receiving end of unpleasant midnight visits from the police).

One last earthly story before this collection departs the solar system: It is a cliche that writers put their own experiences and their own pain into their stories (a cliche that is not always true, fortunately). (George R. R. Martin treated this notion in his beautiful story "Portraits of His Children." I am convinced that story won a Nebula but not a Hugo because the authors—who are the Nebula voters—felt special kinship with the protagonist of the story.) In my case, an unhappy vacation as a child—and a happy vacation many years later in New Zealand—

came together with a random idea from the ol' idea box. The result is a story that turns and turns, surely the most unbalanced thing I have ever written. Stan Schmidt rejected it, then wrote me three months later, asking to see it again. I'm very glad he bought it. Even if "Gemstone" never quite decides what it wants to be, it means something to me:

GEMSTONE

The summer of 1957 should have been Sanda's most wonderful vacation. She had known about her parents' plans since March, and all through the La Jolla springtime, all through the tedious spring semester of her seventh grade, she had that summer to dream about.

Nothing ever seemed so fair at first, and turned out so vile:

Sanda sat on the bedroom balcony of her grandmother's house and looked out into the gloom and the rain. The pine trees along the street were great dark shadows, swaying and talking in the dusk. A hundred yards away, toward downtown Eureka, the light of a single street lamp found its way through pines to make tiny glittering reflections off the slick street. As every night these last four weeks, the wind seemed stronger when the daylight departed. She hunched down in her oversized jacket and let the driven mist wash at the tears that trickled down her face. Tonight had been the end, just the end. Daddy and Mom would be here in six days, and two or

three days after that the three of them would drive
back home. Six days. Sanda unclenched her jaws and
tried to relax her face. How could she last? She
would have to see Grandma at least for meals, at
least to help around the house. And every time she
saw Grandma she would feel the shame and know
that she had ruined things.

And it isn't all my fault! Grandmother had her
secrets, her smugness, her ignorance—flaws Sanda
had never imagined during those short visits of years
passed.

In the hallway beyond the bedroom, the Gemstone was at it again. Sanda felt a wave of cold wash
over her. For a moment the dark around her and the
balcony beneath her knees were not merely chill and
wet, but glacially frozen, the center of a lifeless and
friendless waste. It was funny that now that she *knew*
the house was haunted and *knew* precisely the thing
that caused these moods, it was not nearly as frightening
as before. In fact, it was scarcely more than an incon-
venience compared to the *people* problems she had.

It had not always been this way. Sanda thought
back to the beginning of the summer, trying to imagine blue skies and warm sun. Those first few days
had been like the other times she remembered in
Eureka. Grandmother's house sat near the end of its
street, surrounded by pines. The only other trees
were a pair of small palms right before the front
steps. (These needed constant attention. Grandma
liked to say that she kept them here just so her
visitors from San Diego would never feel homesick.)
The house had two storeys, with turrets and dormers
coming out of the attic. Against the blue, cloudless
sky it looked like a fairy-tale castle. The Victorian
gingerbread had been carefully maintained through
the years, and in its present incarnation gleamed
green and gold.

Her parents had left for San Francisco after a one-day stay. The summer conference at USF was starting that week, and they weren't yet sure they had an apartment. Sanda's first night alone with Grandma had been everything she imagined. Even though the evening beyond the porch was turning chill, the living room still held its warmth. Grandma set her old electric heater in the middle of the carpeted floor so that it shone on the sofa side of the room. Then she walked around the book-lined walls pretending to search for the thing she so liked to show her grandchild.

"Not here, not here. Oh my, I hardly ever look at it nowadays. I forget where . . ." Sanda tagged along, noticing titles where her earlier, younger self had been impressed only by color and size. Grandma had a complete collection of *National Geographics*. Where most families put such magazines in boxes and forget them, Grandmother had every issue there, as though they were some grand encyclopedia. And for Sanda, they were. On her last visit she had spent many an afternoon looking through the pictures. It was the only item she remembered for sure from this library. Now she saw dozens of books on polar exploration, meteorology, biology. Grandfather Beauchamp had been a great man, and Grandmother kept the library and its books, plaques, and certificates in honor of his memory.

"Ah, here it is!" She pulled the huge notebook down from its central position. She led Sanda back to the sofa. "Too big to sit in my lap, now, aren't you?" They grinned at each other and she opened the book across their laps, then put her arm across Sanda's shoulders.

The book was precisely organized. Every newspaper clipping, photo, article, was framed and had a short legend. Some of the pictures existed nowhere else in the world. Others could be found in articles in magazines like the *National Geographic* from the '20s and '30s. Rex Beauchamp had been on the "Terra Nova" expedition in 1910. If it hadn't been for a knee injury he would actually have been on Scott's tragic journey to the South Pole. Sanda sucked in her breath and asked the same question she had asked once before, "And so if his knee had been okay, why, he would have died with the others—and would never have met you, and you would never have had Dad, and—"

Grandma slapped the notebook. "No. I know Rex. He would have made the difference. If they had just waited for him to get well, they could have made it back to the coast."

It was an answer she had heard before, but one she wanted to hear again. Sanda sat back and waited for the rest of the story. After World War I, the Beauchamps had emigrated from Great Britain, and Grandfather participated in several American expeditions. There were dozens of pictures of him on shipboard and in the brave little camps the explorers had established along the Antarctic coast. Rex Beauchamp had been very handsome and boyish even in middle age, and it made Sanda proud to see him in those pictures—though he was rarely the center of attention. He always seemed to be in the background, or in the third row of the group portraits. Grandma said he was a doer and not a talker. He never had a college degree and so had to serve in technician and support jobs. But they depended on him nevertheless.

Not all the pictures were of ice and snow. Many of the expeditions had worked out of Christchurch, New Zealand. On one occasion, Grandmother had gone along that far. It had been a wonderful vacation for her. She had pictures of the city and its wide, circu-

lar harbor, and others of her visiting the North Island and Maori country with Grandfather.

Sanda raised her eyes from the picture collection
as her grandmother spoke. There were things in this
room that illustrated her story more spectacularly
than any photographs. The area around the sofa was
brightly lit by one of the beautiful stained-glass lamps
that Grandma had in every room. But at the limits of
its light, the room glowed in mysterious blue and red
and yellow from the higher panes in the glass. Dark
polished wood edged the carpet and the moldings of
every doorway. Beyond the electric heater she could
see the Maori statues the Beauchamps had brought
back from their stay at Rotorua. In normal light those
figures carved in wooden relief seemed faintly comi-
cal, their pointed tongues stuck out like weapons,
their hands held claw-like. But in the colored dimness the mother-of-pearl in their eyes shone almost
knowingly, and the extended tongues were no childish aggression. Sanda wriggled with a moment of
delicious fright. The Maori were all civilized now,
Grandmother said, but they had been more hideously ferocious than any savages on Earth.

"Do you still have the *meri*, Grandma?"

"Yes indeed." She reached into the embroidered
sewing stand that sat next to her end of the sofa and
withdrew a graceful, eight-inch piece of stone. One
end fit the hand, while the other spread out in a
smooth, blunt-edged oval. It was beautiful, and no
one but someone like Grandma—or a Maori—could
know its true purpose. "This is what they fought
with, not like American Indians with spears and ar-
rows." She handed it to Sanda, who ran her fingers
over the smoothness. "It's so short you have to come
right up to your enemy and *whack!* right across the
forehead." Sanda tried to imagine but couldn't.
Grandma had so many beautiful things. Sanda had

once overheard her mother complain to Daddy that these were thefts from an ancient heritage. Sanda couldn't see why; she was sure that Grandpa had paid for these things. And if he hadn't brought them back to Eureka, so many fewer people could have admired them.

Grandma talked on, well past Sanda's La Jolla bedtime. The girl found herself half hypnotized by the multicolored shadows of the lamp and the pale red from the heater. That heater sat on newspapers.

Sanda felt herself come wide awake. "That heater, Grandma. Isn't it dangerous?"

The woman stopped in mid-reminiscence. "What? No, I've had it for years. And I'm careful not to set it on the carpet where it might stain."

"But those newspapers. They're brown, almost burned."

Grandma looked at the heater. "My, you're a big girl now, to worry about such things. I don't know . . . Anyway, we can turn it off now. You should be going to bed, don't you think?"

Sanda was to sleep in the same room her father had used when he was little. It was on the second floor. As they walked down the hall to the bedroom, Grandma stopped by the heavy terrarium she kept there. Dad and Mother hadn't known quite what to make of it: the glass box was something new. Grandma had placed it so the wide skylight gave it sun through most of the day. Now moonlight washed over the glass and the stones. Pale reflections came off some of the smaller rocks. Grandma switched on the hall light and turned everything mundane. The terrarium was empty of life. There was nothing there but rocks of odd sizes mixed with river-washed gravel. It was like the box Sanda kept her pet lizards in. But there were not even lizards in this one. The only concessions to life were little plastic flowers, "planted" here and there in the landscape.

Grandma smiled wanly. "I think your Dad believes I'm crazy to put something like this here."

Sanda looked at the strange display for a moment and then suggested, "Maybe if you used real flowers?"

The old woman shook her head. "I like artificial ones. You don't have to water them. They never fade or die. They are always beautiful." She paused and Sanda remained diplomatically silent. "Anyway, it's the rocks that are the important thing here. I showed you pictures of those valleys your grandfather helped discover: the ones that don't have any snow in them, even though they're hundreds of miles inside Antarctica. These rocks are from one of those valleys. They must have been sitting there for thousands of years with nothing but the wind to upset them. Rex kept his collection in boxes down in the basement, but I think they are so much nicer up here. This is a little like what they had before."

Sanda looked into the cabinet with new interest. Some of the stones were strange. A couple looked like the meteorites she had seen in the Natural History Museum back home. And there was another, about the size of her head, that had a vaguely regular pattern in the gray and black minerals that were its substance.

Minutes later, Sanda was tucked into her father's old bed, the lights were out, and Grandmother was descending the stairs. Moonlight spread silver on the window sills, and the pines beyond were soft, pale, bright. Sanda sighed and smiled. So far, things were just as she dreamed and just as she remembered.

The last she wondered as she drifted off to sleep was why Grandmother put flowers in the terrarium if she really wanted to imitate the bleak antarctic valleys.

*   *   *

That first day was really the last when everything went totally well. And looking back on it, Sanda could see symptoms of many of the things that were later to make the summer so unpleasant.

Physically everything was just as she remembered. The stair railings were a rich, deeply polished wood that she hardly ever saw in La Jolla. Everywhere was carpeting, even on the stairs. The basement was cool and damp and filled with all the mysterious things that Grandfather had worked with. But there were so many things that Grandma did and believed that were *wrong*. Some—like the flowers—were differences of opinion that Sanda could keep her mouth shut about. Others—like Grandma's use of the old electric heater—were really dangerous. When she spoke about those, Grandmother didn't seem to believe or understand her. The older woman would smile and tell her what a big girl she was getting to be, but it was clear she was a little hurt by the suggestions, no matter how diplomatically put. Finally Sanda had taken a plastic mat off the back porch and slipped it under the heater in place of the newspapers. But Grandma noticed, and furthermore pointed out that the dirty mat had stained the beautiful carpet—just the thing the nice clean newspapers had been there to prevent. Sanda had been crushed: she'd been harmful when she wanted to be helpful. Grandmother was very good about it; in the end— after she cleaned the carpet—she suggested putting the mat between the newspapers and the heater. So the incident ended happily, after all.

But this sort of thing seemed to happen all the time: Sanda trying to do something different, some hurt being caused to property or Grandma, and then sincere apology and reconciliation. Sanda began to feel a little haggard, and to watch the calendar for a different reason than before. Just being with Grandma had been one of the big attractions of this summer. Both she and Grandma were *trying,* but it wasn't working. Sometimes Sanda thought that—no matter how often Grandma said Sanda was a young grown-up now—she still thought Sanda was five years old. She had seriously wanted Sanda to take afternoon naps. Only when the girl assured her that her parents no longer required naps did she relent. And Grandma never told her to do anything. She always asked Sanda "wouldn't you like to" do whatever she wanted. It was awfully hard to smile and say "oh yes, that would be fun" when in fact it was a chore she would rather pass up. At home it was so much easier: Sanda did as she was told, and did not have to claim to love it.

A week later the fair weather broke. It rained. And rained. And rained. And when it wasn't raining it was cloudy; not cloudy as in La Jolla, but a dripping, misty cloudiness that just promised more rain. Grandma said it was often this way; Sanda had just been lucky on the previous visits.

And it was about this time she began to be afraid of the upstairs. Grandmother slept downstairs, though she stayed up very late at night, reading or sewing. She would be easy to call if anything . . . bad happened. That did not help. At first it was like an ordinary fear of darkness. Some nights a person is just more fidgety than others. And after the weather turned bad it was easy to feel scared, lying in bed with the wind and the rattle of rain against the windows. But this was different. The feeling increased from night to night. It wasn't quite a feeling that something was sneaking up on her. More it was a sense of utter desolation and despair. Sometimes it seemed as if the room, the whole house, were gone and she was in just the antarctic wilderness that Grandfather had explored. She had no direct visions of this—just the feeling of cold and lifelessness extending forever. *Grandfather's ghost?*

Late one night Sanda had to go to the bathroom, which was down on the first floor next to Grandmother's bedroom. It was almost painful to move—so afraid was she of making a sound, of provoking whatever caused the mood that filled her room. When she passed the terrarium in the hallway, the feeling of cold grew stronger and her legs tensed for a sprint down the stairs. Instead she forced herself to stand still, then to walk slowly around the glass cage. Something in there was causing it. The terror was insidious, growing as she stood there—almost as if what caused this now knew it had a "listener." Sanda slept at the foot of the stairs that night.

After that, when night came and Grandmother had tucked her in, Sanda would creep out of bed, unwrap her sleeping bag, and quietly carry it onto the balcony that opened off her room. The extra distance and the extra wall reduced the psychic cold to a tolerable level. Many nights it was rainy, and it was always chill and a bit windy, but she had bought a really good sleeping bag for the Scouts, and she had always liked to camp out. Nevertheless, it wore her down to sleep like that night after night, and made it harder to be diplomatic and cheerful during the days.

In the daytime there was far less feeling of dread upstairs. Sanda didn't know whether this was because the second floor was basically a sunny, cheerful place or whether the ghost "slept" during the day. Whenever she walked past the terrarium she looked carefully into it. After a while, she thought she had the effect narrowed down to one particular rock—the skull-sized one with the strangely regular patterns of gray and black. As the days passed, the position of some of the rocks changed. There had been five plastic flowers in the terrarium when Sanda first saw it; now there were three.

There was one other mystery—which under other circumstances would have been very sinister, but which seemed scarcely more than an intriguing puzzle now. Several times, usually on stormy nights, a car parked in the grass just off the other side of the street, about forty yards north of the house. That was all; Sanda had noticed it only by accident. It looked like a '54 Ford. Once a match flared within the cab, and she saw two occupants. She smiled smugly, wistfully to herself; she could imagine what they were up to. But she was wrong. One night, when the rain had stopped yet clouds kept out the stars, the driver got out and walked across the street toward the house. He moved silently, quickly. Sanda had to lean out from the balcony to see him crouch in the bushes next to the wall where the electric power meter was mounted. He spent only half a minute there. She saw a tiny point of light moving over the power meter and the utility cables that came down from the telephone pole at the street. Then the phantom meter reader stood and ran back across the street, quietly relatching the door of his Ford. The car sat for several more minutes—as if they were watching the house for some sign of alarm—and then drove away.

She should have told Grandma. But then, if she were being as open as a good girl should be with a grandmother, she would have also confessed her fear of the upstairs and the terrarium. Those fears were shameful, though. Even if *real*, they were the type of childish thing that could only make her situation with Grandma worse. Grandmother was a clever person. Sanda knew that if she told her about the mysterious car, the older woman would either dismiss the story—or question her in sufficient detail to discover that Sanda was sleeping on the balcony.

So she dithered—and in the end told someone else.

Finding that someone else had been a surprise; she hadn't really known she was looking. Whenever the weather dried a little, Sanda tried to get outdoors. The city library was about three miles away, an easy ride on her father's old bicycle. Of course Grandmother had been uneasy about Sanda carrying library books in the saddle baskets of the bike. There was always the risk of splashing water or a sudden rainstorm. It was just another of the polite little conflicts they had. One or the other of them could always see some objection to a given activity. In the end—as usual—they compromised, with Sanda taking grocery bags and a little waxed paper for the books.

Today wasn't wet, though. The big blocks of cloud left plenty of space for the blue. To the northwest, the plume from the paper mill was purest white across the sky. The sun was warm, and the gusty breeze dry. It was the sort of day she once thought was every day in Eureka.

Sanda took a detour, biking back along the street away from town. The asphalt ended about thirty yards past Grandmother's lot. There were supposed to be more houses up here, but Grandma didn't think much of them. She passed one. It looked like a trailer used as a permanent home. A couple old cars, one looking very dead, were in front. The trees came in close to the road here, blocking out the sun. It felt a little like those great forests they'd driven through to get to Eureka. Even after a half day of sun, there was still a slow dripping from the needles. Everything was so green it might as well be dipped in paint. Once she had liked that.

She went a lot farther south than she had before.

The road stopped at a dead end. A one-storey, red-shingled house was the last thing on the street. It was a real house, but it reminded Sanda of the trailer. It was such a different thing from Grandmother's house. There were a lot of small houses in La Jolla, but the weather back home was so dry and mild that buildings didn't seem to wear out. Here Sanda had the feeling that the damp, the cold, and the mildew were forever warring on the houses. This place had been losing the fight for some time.

She circled around the end of the road—and almost ran into a second bicyclist.

Sanda stopped abruptly and awkwardly. (The center bar on the bike was a little high for her.) "Where did you come from?" she asked a bit angrily.

The boy was taller than Sanda, and looked very strong. He must be at least fifteen years old. But his face was soft, almost stupid-looking. He waved at the red-shingled house. "We live here. Who are you?"

"Sanda Beauchamp."

"Oh, yeah. You're the girl staying with the old English lady."

"She is not an old lady. She's my grandmother."

He was silent for a moment, the baby-face expressionless. "I'm Larry O'Malley. Your grandmother is okay. Last summer I did her lawn."

Sanda untangled herself from the bicycle and they walked their bikes back the way she had come. "She has regular gardeners now."

"I know. She's very rich. Even more than last year."

Grandma wasn't rich. It was on the tip of her tongue to contradict him, but his second statement made her pause, puzzled. *Even more than last year?*

They had walked all the way back to Grandmother's before Sanda knew it. Larry wasn't really sullen. She wasn't sure yet if he was smart or stupid; she knew he wasn't as old as he looked. His father was a real lumberjack, which was neat. Most of Sanda's parents' friends were geologists and things like that.

They parked their bikes at the steps, and Sanda took him in to see Grandmother. As she had expected, the elder Beauchamp was not thrilled with Sanda's plans for the afternoon.

She looked uncertainly at the boy. "But, Larry, isn't that a long ride?"

Sanda was not about to let Larry blow it. "Oh no, Grandma, it's not much farther than the library. Besides, I haven't been to a movie in so long," which was true, though Grandmother's television did a great job of dragging in old movies from the only available station.

"What's the film? It's such a nice day to waste inside a theater."

"Oh, they're playing movies from the early fifties." That sounded safe. Grandma had complained more than once about the immorality of today's shows. Besides, if she heard the title, she would be sure to refuse.

Grandmother seemed almost distraught. Then she agreed, and walked out to the screened porch with them. "Come back before four."

"We will. We will." And they were off. She didn't know if it was the weather, or meeting Larry, or the prospect of the movie, but suddenly she felt wonderful.

The Thing from Outer Space. That's what it said on the marquee. She felt a little guilty deceiving Grandma about the title. It wasn't really the sort of show her parents would want her to see. But just seeing a movie was going to be fun. It was like home. This theater reminded her a lot of the Cove in La Jolla. After they got their tickets they drifted down to the movie posters.

And Sanda began to feel a chill that was not in the air and that was not the vicarious thrill of watching a scary show. This *Thing* was supposed to be from outer space, yet the posters showed arctic wastes. . . .

She found herself walking more slowly, for the first time letting the boy do most of the talking. Then they were inside, and the movie had begun.

It was a terrible thing, almost as if God had created a personal warning, a personal explanation for Sanda Rachel Beauchamp. *The Thing* was what had been after her all these weeks. Oh, a lot of the details were different. The movie took place in the arctic; the alien monster—the Thing—was crudely man-shaped. Sanda sat, her face slack, all but hypnotized by these innocently filmed revelations. About halfway through the movie, Larry nudged her and asked if she were okay. Sanda just nodded.

The Thing had been stranded. In the polar wastes the temperature and lack of predators allowed it to survive a very long time. The dry antarctic valleys Grandpa discovered might be even better; Things from long, long ago would be right at the surface, not hidden beneath hundreds of feet of ice. The creature would be like a time bomb waiting to be discovered. When exposed to light and warmth—as Grandma had done by putting it in the sunny terrarium—it would come to life. The movie Thing looked for blood. Sanda's Thing seemed after something more subtle, more terrible.

Sanda was scarcely aware when the movie ended, so perfectly did its story merge with the greater terror she now felt. It was still middle afternoon, but the berglike clouds had melded together, thick and deep and dark. The wind was picking up, driving through her sweater and carrying occasional drops of wet. They recovered their bikes, Sanda dazed, Larry O'Malley silently observant.

It was uphill most of the way back, but now the wind was behind them. The forests beyond the town were blackish green, sometimes turned gray by passing mist. The scene didn't register with her. All she could think of was the cold and the ice and the thing waiting for her up ahead.

Larry reached out to grab her handlebars as the bike angled toward the ditch. "Really. What's the matter?"

And Sanda told him. About the strangely mottled antarctic rock and the terrarium. About its movement and the desolation it broadcast.

The boy didn't say anything when she finished. They worked laboriously up a hill past neat houses, some of them Victorian, none as beautiful as Grandmother's. As usual, traffic was light—nonexistent by the standards of home. They rode side by side with the entire road to themselves. Finally they reached the top and started down a gentle slope. Still Larry hadn't said anything. Sanda's haze of terror was broken by sudden anger. She pedaled just ahead of him and waved her hand in his face. "*Hey!* I was talking to you. Don't you believe me?"

Larry blinked, his wide face expressionless. He didn't seem to take offense. He spoke, but didn't directly answer her question. "I think your Grandma is a smart person. And I always thought she had some strange things in that house. She put the rock up there; she must know something about it. You should ask her straight out. Or do you think *she* wants to hurt you, too?"

Sanda lagged back even with Larry and felt a little bit ashamed. She should have brought this up with Grandma weeks ago. She knew why she had not. After all the little conflicts and misunderstandings, she had been afraid that a fearful story like this would have weakened her position even further, would have reinforced Grandma's view of her as a child. Saying these things out loud seemed to make them smaller. But having said them, she could also see that there was something *real* here, something to fear, or at least to be concerned about. She looked at Larry and smiled with some respect. Perhaps he wasn't very imaginative—after all, nothing seemed to disturb him—but being with him was like suddenly finding the ground in the surf, or waking up from a bad dream.

Blocks of mist chased back and forth around them, but they were still dry when they got home. They stood for a moment on the grassy shoulder of the road.

"If you want to go to the sand dunes tomorrow, we should start early. It's a long ride from here." She couldn't tell if he had already forgotten her story, or if he was trying to reassure her.

"I'll have to ask Grandmother," *about that and certain other things.* "I'll see you tomorrow, anyway."

Larry pedaled off toward his house, and Sanda walked the bike around to the tool shed. Grandma came out to the back porch, and worried over the damp on Sanda's sweater. She seemed nervous, and relieved to see Sanda back.

"My, you've been gone so long. I've got some sandwiches made up in the kitchen." As they walked into the house, Grandma asked her about the movie and about Larry. "You know, Sanda, I think the O'Malley boy is nice enough. But I'm not sure your Mum and Dad would want you spending so much time with him. Your interests are so different, don't you think?"

Sanda was not really listening. She took the other's hand. It was a child-like gesture that stopped the older woman short. "Grandma, there's something I've *got* to talk to you about. Please."

"Of course, Sanda."

They sat down, and the girl told her of the terror that soaked the upstairs every night so strongly that she must sleep on the balcony.

Grandma smiled tentatively and patted Sanda's hand. "I'll wager it's those Maori statues. They would scare anyone, especially in the dark. I shouldn't have told you all those stories about them. They're just wood and—"

"It's not them, Grandmother." Sanda tried to keep the frustration out of her voice. She looked out of the kitchen, down the hall into the living room. She could see one of the statues there, sticking its tongue at her. It was lovely, and frightening in a fun sort of way, but that was all. "It's the terrarium, and especially one rock there. When I'm near it, I can feel the cold get stronger."

"Oh, dear." Grandmother looked down at her hands and avoided Sanda's eyes. For a moment she seemed to be talking only to herself. "You must be very sensitive."

Sanda's eyes widened. Even after all this time, she hadn't really expected anyone to believe. And now she saw that Grandma had known something about this all along.

"Oh, Sanda, I'm so sorry. If I thought you could sense it, I would never have put you up there." She reached out to touch Sanda, and smiled. "There really is nothing to fear. That's my, uh, Gemstone." She stumbled on the name, looked faintly worried. "It has always been a little secret of your grandfather's and mine. If I tell you about it, will you keep the secret, too?"

The girl nodded.

"Let's go up there, and I'll show you. You're right that the stone can make you feel things. . . ."

* * *

As Grandma had told her before, Rex Beauchamp had found the Gemstone on one of the first expeditions into the dry valleys. He probably should have turned his discovery over to the expedition's collection. But in those early days there was a more casual attitude about individual finds, and besides, Grandfather was continually shunted aside from the credit he deserved. He was simply the fellow who fixed all the little things that went wrong. After retirement he hoped to set up his own small lab here, to look into this and several other mysteries he had come across over the years.

Grandfather had kept the Gemstone in a special locker down in the lab/basement. He hoped to imitate its original environment. At first Grandpa thought the rock was some special crystal that stored and reflected back the emotions of those around it. When he held it in his hand, he could feel the winds and desolation of the antarctic. If he touched it an hour later, he felt vague reflections of his mood *at the time of the previous encounter*.

When he cut it with a lapidary saw, the mental shriek of pain showed both of them the Gemstone was not psychic mineral, but a living thing.

"We never told anyone what we had discovered. Not even your father. Rex kept it in the basement, and as cold as possible. He was so afraid that it would die." They had reached the second floor and were walking down the short hallway toward the terrarium. The skylight was pale gray, and rain was beginning to splatter off it. The cold and loneliness were not quite as sharp as after dark, but it took an effort for Sanda to approach the rock.

"I looked at it differently. It seemed to me that if the Gemstone could survive all those centuries of no food, no water—well then, maybe it was tough. Maybe even it would like light and warmth. After your grandfather died, I took the stone and put it in this nice aquarium box up here where there is light. I know it is alive; I think it likes it up here."

Sanda looked down at the black and grey whorls that marked its rough exterior. The shape was not symmetrical, but it was regular. Even without the chill beating against her mind she should have known it was alive. "What . . . what does it eat?"

"Um." Grandma paused for just a second. "Some of the rocks. Even those flowers. I have to replace them now and again. But it's mindless. It's never done much more than what Rex originally noticed. It's just that now—up here in the light—it does them a bit more often." She saw the pain on Sanda's face. "You can feel the stone even that far away?" she asked wonderingly.

Grandma reached down and touched the top of the Gemstone with the palm of her hand. She winced. "Ah, it is projecting that old cold-and-desolate pattern. I can see why that bothers you. But it's not intended to be hurtful. I think it's just the creature's memory of the cold. Now just wait. It takes a minute or so for it to change. In some ways it's more like a plant than an animal."

The psychic chill faded. What remained was not threatening, but—with her present sensitivity—was unsettling. Grandma motioned her closer. "Here. Now you put your hand on it, and you'll see what I mean."

Sanda advanced slowly, her eyes on her grandmother's face. Above them, the rain droned against the skylight. *What if it's all a lie?* thought Sanda. Could the creature take people over and make them go after others?

But now that the mental pressure was gone, it seemed just a little bit unbelievable. She touched the Gemstone first with her fingertips and then with the flat of her hand. Grandmother's hand was still on the rock, though not quite touching hers. Nothing happened. It was cold as any rock might be in this room. The surface was rough, though regular. The seconds passed and slowly she felt it: It was Grandma! Her smile, a wave of affection—and behind that, disappointment and an emptiness more muted than the stone usually broadcast. Still, there was a warmth where before there had been only cold.

"Oh, Grandmother!" The older woman put her arm across Sanda's shoulders, and for the first time in weeks, the girl thought there might be a lasting reconciliation. Sanda's hand strayed from the Gemstone and brushed through the pebbles that were its bed. They were ordinary. The Gemstone was the only strange thing in the terrarium. Wait. She picked up a smallish pebble and held it in the light, scarcely noticing the sudden tension in Grandma's arm. The tiny rock might have been glassy except for the milky haze on its surface. It felt almost greasy. "This isn't a real rock, is it, Grandma?"

"No. It's plastic. Like the flowers. I just think it's pretty."

"Oh." She dropped it back into the terrarium. Another time, she might have been more curious. For now, everything was swamped by her relief in discovering that what had terrorized her for so long was not a threat but something very wonderful. "Thank you. I was so afraid." She laughed a little ruefully. "I really made a fool of myself this afternoon, telling Larry I thought the Gemstone was some kind of monster."

Grandmother's arm slipped away from her shoulder. "Sanda, you mustn't—" she began sharply. "Really, Sanda, you mustn't be going out with the O'Malley boy. He's simply too old for you."

Sanda's reply was casually argumentative; she was

still immersed in a rosy feeling of relief. "Oh, Gran. He's going into ninth grade this fall. He's just big for his age."

"No. I'm sure your mother and dad would be very upset with me if I let you be off alone with him."

The sharpness of her tone finally came through to Sanda. Grandma had on her determined look. And suddenly the girl felt just as determined. There was no valid reason for her not to see Larry O'Malley. Grandma had hinted around at this before: she thought her neighbors up the road were lower class, both in background and present accomplishment. If there was one thing really wrong with Grandmother it was that she looked down on some people. Sanda even suspected that she was racially prejudiced. For instance, she called Negroes "colored people."

The double injustice of Grandma's demand was too much. Sanda thrust out her quivering jaw. "Grandmother, I'll go out with him if I want. You just don't want me to see him because he's poor . . . because he's Irish."

"*Sanda!*" The older woman seemed to shrink in upon herself. Her voice was choked, hard to understand. "I had so looked forward to this summer with you. B-but you're not the nice little girl you once were." She stepped around Sanda and hurried down the stairs.

Sanda looked after her, open-mouthed. Then she felt tears turning into sobs, and rushed into her bedroom.

She sat on the bedroom balcony and looked out into the gloom and the rain. The pine trees along the street were great dark shadows, swaying and talking in the dusk. From a hundred yards away, the light of a single street lamp found its way through the pines to make tiny glittering reflections off the slick street.

She hunched down in her oversized jacket and let the driven mist wash at the tears that trickled down her face. Daddy and Mom would be here in six days. Six days. Sanda unclenched her jaws and tried to relax her face. How could she last?

She had sat here for hours, going around and around with these questions, never quite getting the pain rationalized, never quite finding a course of action that would not be still more painful. She wondered what Grandma was doing now. There had been no call to supper, or to help with supper. But there had been no sounds of cooking either. She was probably in her room, going through the same thing Sanda was. Grandma's last words . . . they almost described her own grief all these weeks.

Grandmother had looked so small, so frail. Sanda was almost as tall as she, but rarely thought about it. It must have been hard for Grandma to have a guest she thought of as a child, a guest to whom she must always show the most cheerful face, a guest with whom every disagreement was a tiny failure.

And even this vacation had not been all bad. There had been the evenings when the weather was nice and they had stayed out on the screened porch to play caroms or Scrabble. Those had been just as good as before—better in some ways, now that she could understand Grandma's little jokes and appreciate her impish grin when she made some clever countermove.

The girl sighed. She had been through these thoughts several times in the last hours. Each time she returned to them, they seemed to gain strength over the recriminations. She knew that in the end she would go downstairs, and try to make up. And maybe . . . maybe this time it could really work. This break had gone so deep and hurt so much that maybe they could start out in a new way.

She stood up and breathed the clean, cold, wet air. The keening of the Gemstone in the back of her mind was a prod now. There was more than cold in the Gemstone's call; there was a loneliness she knew came in part from those around it.

As Sanda turned to enter the bedroom, a flash of headlights made her look back. A car was driving slowly by. . . . It looked like a '54 Ford. She stayed very still until it was out of sight, then dropped to her knees so that just her head was above the balcony. If this were like the other visitations . . .

Sure enough, a couple minutes passed and the Ford was back—this time without its lights. It stopped on the other side of the road. The rain was heavy, and the wind came in gusts now. Sanda wasn't sure, but it looked like *two* people got out of the car. Yes. There were two. They ran toward the house, one for the power meter, the other heading out of sight to her left.

This was more than the mysterious intruders had ever done before. And somehow there was a purposefulness in it tonight. As if this were no rehearsal. Sanda leaned out from the balcony. Her curiosity was fast giving way to fear. Not the psychic, moody fear the Gemstone broadcast, but a sharp, call-to-action type of fear. *What is that guy doing?* The dark figure maneuvered a small light, and something else. There was a snapping noise that came faintly to her over the rain.

And then she knew. It wasn't just the power cable that came down to that side of the house; the phone line did, too.

Sanda whirled and dived back into her bedroom, shedding the jacket as she ran. She sprinted by the terrarium, barely conscious of the mood emerging from the Gemstone.

Grandmother stood at the bottom of the stairs,

looking as if she were about to come up. She appeared tired, but there was a wan smile on her face. "Sanda, dear, I—"

"Grandma! Somebody's trying to break in. *Somebody's trying to break in!*" Sanda came down the stairs in two crashing leaps. There was a shadow on the porch where no shadow should have been. Sanda slammed the bolt to just as the doorknob began to turn. Behind her, Grandmother stared in shocked silence. Sanda spun and ran toward the kitchen. Once they had the intruders locked out, what could she and Gran do without a phone?

She nearly ran into him in the kitchen. Sanda sucked in a breath so hard she squeaked. He was big and hooded. He also had a knife. Strange to see such a man in the middle of the glistening white kitchen— the homey, comforting, *safe* kitchen.

From the living room came the sound of splintering wood and Grandmother screamed. Running footsteps. Something metal being kicked over. Grandmother screamed again. "Shut your mouth, lady. I said, *shut it.*" The voice—though not the tone—was vaguely familiar. "Now where is that prissy little wimp?"

"I got her in here," called the man in the kitchen. He caught Sanda's upper arm in a grip as painful as any physical punishment she had ever received and marched her into the living room.

Grandma looked okay, just scared and very small next to the fellow holding her. Even with the hooded mask, Sanda thought she recognized him. It was the clerk from the little grocery store they shopped at. Behind them, the electric heater lay face down, its cherry coils buried in the carpet.

The clerk shook Grandma at every syllable he spoke. "All right, lady. There's just one thing we want. Show us where they are and we'll go." This was the sense of what he said, though not the precise words. Many of those words were ones Sanda knew but had previously heard only from the rougher girls in gym class, where there was much smirking and giggling over their meaning. Here, said in deadly anger, those words were themselves an assault.

"I've a couple rings—"

"Lady, you're rich and we know how you got it."

Grandma's voice was quaking. "No, just my husband's investments." That was true: Sanda had overheard Grandma telling Sanda's surprised father the size of Rex Beauchamp's estate.

The clerk slapped her. "Liar. Two or three times a year you bring a diamond into Arcata Gems. A rough diamond. Your husband was the big-time explorer." There was sarcasm in the words. "Somewhere he musta found quite a pile of 'em. Either that or you got a diamond machine in your basement." He laughed at his joke, and suddenly the girl saw through several mysteries. *Not in the basement—upstairs.*

"We know you got 'em. We want 'em. We want 'em. We want 'em. We—" As he spoke, he slapped her rhythmically across the face. Someone was screaming; it was Sanda. She barely knew what she did then. From the corner of her eye she saw Grandma's *meri* lying on the sewing table. She swept it up with her free hand and pivoted swiftly around her captor, swinging the flattened stone club into the clerk's chest just below the ribs.

The man went down, dragging Grandmother to her knees. He sat on the floor for several seconds, his mouth opening and closing soundlessly. Finally he could take great, gasping breaths. "I'll. Kill. Her." He came to his feet, one hand still on Grandma's shoulder, the other weaving a knife back and forth in front of Sanda.

The other fellow grabbed the *meri* from Sanda's

hand and pulled the girl back from the clerk. "No. Remember."

The clerk pressed his knife hand gently against his chest, and winced. "Yeah." He pushed Grandmother down onto the sofa and approached Sanda.

"Lady, I'm gonna cut on your kid till you start talking." He barely touched the knife to Sanda's forearm. It was so sharp that a thin line of red oozed, yet the girl scarcely felt it.

Grandma came off the sofa. "Stop! Don't touch her!"

He looked around at her. "Why?"

"I-I'll show you where the diamonds are."

The clerk was genuinely disappointed. "Yeah?"

"You won't hurt us afterwards?"

The one holding Sanda touched his mask. "All we want are the diamonds, lady."

Pause. "Very well. They're in the kitchen."

Seconds later, Mrs. Beauchamp showed them where. She opened the cabinet where she kept flour and sugar and withdrew a half-empty bag of rock salt. The clerk grabbed it from her, then swept the salt and pepper and sugar bowl off the kitchen table. He carefully upended the bag of rock salt and spread it so that no piece sat on another. "Do you see anything?" he said.

The other man spent several minutes examining the table. "One," he said, and moved a tiny stone to the edge of Grandmother's china rack. It looked glassy except for a milky haze on its surface. "Two." He looked some more.

No one spoke. The only sounds were the clerk's harsh breathing and the steady throbbing of rain against the windows. The night beyond the windows was black. The nearest neighbors were hidden beyond trees.

"That's all. Just the two."

The clerk's obscenities would have been screamed if his chest had been up to it. In a way, his quiet intensity was more frightening. "You sold ten of these the last three years. You claim you're down to *two* ?"

Grandma nodded, her chin beginning to quiver.

"Do you believe her?"

"I don't know. But maybe it doesn't matter. We've got all night, and I want to cut on that girl. Either way, I'll get what's due me." He motioned with his knife. "C'mere you."

"Just as well. I think they recognize you." The vise on Sanda's upper arm tightened and she found herself pushed toward the point of the knife.

"Smell something burning?" her captor said abruptly.

The clerk's eyes widened, and he stepped out of the kitchen to look down the hall. "Jesus, yes! The carpet and some newspapers. It's that heater."

"Unplug the heater. Roll the carpet over it. This place burns, we got nothing to search!"

"I'm trying." There were awkward shuffling sounds. "Need help."

The man holding Sanda looked at the two women. She saw his hand tighten on his knife. "I know where the rest of them are," Grandma suddenly said.

He grabbed her, too, and hustled them to the basement door. Sanda was shoved roughly through. She crashed backwards against the rack of brooms and fell down the steps, into the darkness. A second later Grandma's frail body fell on top of hers. The door slammed, and they heard the key turn in the lock.

The two of them lay dazed for a second. Next to her face, Sanda could smell the moldy damp of the stairs. Part of a mop seemed to be strung across her neck. "Are you okay, Grandmother?"

Her answer was immediate. "Yes. Are you?"

"Yes."

Grandma gave an almost girlish laugh. "You make rather a good pillow to land on, dear." She got up carefully and switched on the stairs light. There was that impish smile on her face. "I think they may have outsmarted themselves."

She led Sanda further down the steps and switched on another light. The girl looked around the small basement, made even smaller by the old sample crates and Grandma's laundry area. There was no way out of here, no windows set at ground level. What was Grandmother thinking of?

The older woman turned and slammed shut the interior hatch that Grandfather had mounted in the stairwell. Sanda began to see what she had in mind: The top of the stairs could be locked from the kitchen side, but this heavy door was now locked from their side!

Grandmother walked across the floor toward a stack of cases that sat under the living room. "Rex wanted this to be his laboratory. He was going to refrigerate— actually try to imitate polar conditions. That turned out to be much too expensive, but the heavy doors he installed can be useful. . . . Help me with these crates, please, Sanda."

They were heavy, but Grandma didn't care if they went crashing to the floor. In minutes Sanda saw that they were uncovering another stairway, one that must open into the living room. "If they can put the fire out as easily as they should, then we'll simply wait them out. Even a small fire can be seen from the street and I'll wager the Fire Department will be here straight away. But if the fire wins free and the whole house goes . . ." There were new tears streaking her face. She swayed slightly on her feet, and Sanda realized that the older woman had been limping.

Sanda put her arm about her grandmother's waist. "Are you sure you're okay?"

Grandma looked at her and smiled. Her face was a little bit puffy, swelling from the blows to it. "Yes, dear." She bowed her head and touched her front teeth. "But my dentist will be overjoyed by all this, I fear."

Grandmother turned back to the door and wiped at a quartz port set in the metal. "I still don't know why Rex wanted this stair up to the living room. P'raps he just felt obligated to use both the surplus hatches he bought."

Sanda looked through the tiny window. It was a viewpoint on the living room she had never imagined. They were looking through the decorative drapes that covered the wall behind the sofa.

The robbers had pulled off their masks and were madly dragging furniture—including the sofa—away from the blaze. They had rolled the carpet over the fire, but it was still spreading, leaking out toward the TV and the Maori statues on the far wall.

The floor itself was starting to burn.

The men in the living room saw this, too. The clerk shouted something that came only faintly through the insulated walls. Then they ran out of view. The fire spread up the legs of the TV and onto a Maori statue. For a moment, the figure blazed in a halo of light. Flames played from the twisted hands, from the thrusting tongue.

The lights in the basement went out, but the red glow through the quartz window still lit Grandma's face. "They couldn't save it. They couldn't save it." Her voice was barely audible.

Heavy banging at the other hatch, the one to the kitchen. Sanda knew that was no rescue, but murder denied. The banging ceased almost immediately; these two witnesses would live to tell their story.

She looked back through the quartz. The fire was spreading along the far wall. Their side of the living room was untouched. Even the drapes seemed undamaged.

"I've got to go out there, Sanda."

"No! . . . I-I'm sorry, Gran. If they couldn't save it, we can't."

"Not the house, Sanda. I'm going to save the Gemstone." There was the strain of physical exertion in her voice, but the girl couldn't see what she was doing. Only Grandma's face was lit by the rose and yellow light. She was not pushing on the door; Sanda could see that much.

"You can't risk your life for diamonds, Grandma. Dad and Mom have money. You can stay—"

The older woman grunted as though pushing at something. "You don't understand. The diamonds have been wonderful. I could never have lived so free with just the money Rex left me. Poor Rex. The Gemstone was his greatest find. He knew that. But he kept it in a freezer down here, and never saw the miracle it really is.

"Sanda, the Gemstone is not just a thing that eats plastic flowers and passes diamonds. It is not just a thing that sends out feelings of cold and emptiness— those are simply its memories of Antarctica.

"Next to you and your dad—and your mum—I value the Gemstone more than anything. When I put my hand on it, it glows back at me—you felt that, too. It is friendly, though it scarce seems to know me. But when I touch it long enough, I feel Rex there, I feel the times he must have touched the stone . . . and almost I feel that he is touching me."

She grunted; Sanda heard something spinning on oiled bearings. There was a popping noise from the hatch and Sanda guessed it could be pushed open now.

"The fire is along the outer wall. I have room to get to the stairs. I can pick up the Gemstone and get

out down the back stairs—on the other side of the
house from the fire. You'll be safe staying here. Rex
was very thorough. The basement is an insulated
hull, even over the ceiling. The house could burn
right down and you'd not be harmed."

"No, I'm going with you."

Grandmother took a breath. There was the look on
her face of someone who must do something very
difficult. "Sanda. *If you ever loved me*, you will obey
me now; stay here."

Sanda's arms hung numb at her sides. If you *ever*
loved me . . . It was many years before she could live
with her inaction of the next few seconds.

Grandma pushed the door back. The drapes parted
and there was a wave of heat, like standing near a
bonfire. The air was full of popping and cracking, but
the drapes that swung into the opening were not yet
singed. Gran pulled the cloth away and pushed the
door shut. Through the quartz window Sanda saw
her moving quickly toward the stairs. She started up
them—was almost out of sight— when she looked
down, puzzlement on her face.

Sanda saw the fire burning out of the wall beneath
her an instant before the stairs collapsed and Grandmother disappeared. The house groaned and died
above her.

"Grand*ma!*" Sanda crashed against the metal door,
but it would not open now; ceiling timbers had fallen
across it. The scene beyond the quartz was no longer
recognizably a home. The fire must have burned
behind the walls and up under the stairwell. Now
much of the second floor had collapsed onto the first.
Everything she could see was a glowing jumble. The
heat on her face was like looking through a kiln
window. Nothing out there could live.

And still the heat increased. The fallen center of
the upstairs left a natural flue through the skylight.

For a few moments the heat and rushing winds lived in equilibrium, and the flames steadied to uniform brilliance. Brief stillness in hell.

She would have felt it sooner if she had been waiting for it, or if its mood hadn't been so different from all that went on about her: a chime of happiness, clear and warm. The feeling of sudden freedom and escape from cold.

Then she saw it: Its surface was no longer black and gray. It glowed like the ends of the burning timbers but with overtones of violet that seemed to penetrate its body. And now that it moved, she could see the complete regularity of its shape. The Gemstone was a cross between a four-legged starfish and a very small pillow. It moved nimbly, gracefully through the red jumble beyond the quartz window, and Sanda could feel its exuberance.

Grandfather had been wrong. Grandmother had been wrong. The cold and desolation it had broadcast were not memories of antarctic centuries, but a wordless cry against what *still* was cold and dark to it. How could she have missed it before? Daddy's dog, Tyrann, did the same thing: locked out on a misty winter night he keened and keened his misery for hours.

Gemstone had been alone and cold much, much longer.

And now—like a dog—it frisked through the brightness, eager and curious. It stopped and Sanda felt its puzzlement. It pushed down into the chaos that had been the stairs. The puzzlement deepened, shaded into hurt. Gemstone climbed back out of the rubble.

It had no head, no eyes, but what she saw in its mind now was clear; it felt her and was trying to find where she was hiding. When it "saw" her it was like a searchlight suddenly fixing on a target; all its attention was on her.

Gemstone scuttled down from its perch and swiftly crossed the ruins. It climbed the wood that jammed shut the door and—from inches away—seemed to peer at her. It scampered back and forth along the timber, trying to find some way in to her. Its mood was a mix of abject friendliness, enthusiasm, and curiosity that shifted almost as fast as the glowing colors of its body. Before tonight it had taken minutes to change from one mood to another; before, it had been frozen to near unconsciousness. All those centuries before, it had been barely alive.

Sanda saw that it was scarcely more intelligent than she imagined dogs to be. It wanted to touch her and didn't realize the death that would bring. Gemstone climbed back to the little window and touched a paw to the quartz. The quartz grew cloudy, began to star. Sanda felt fear, and Gemstone immediately pulled back.

It didn't touch the quartz again, but rubbed back and forth across the surface of the door. Then it settled against the door and let Sanda "pet" it with her mind. This was a little like touching it had been before. But now the memories and emotions were deeper and changed quickly at her wish:

There was Grandmother, alive again. She felt Grandma's hand resting on her (its) back. Wistful sometimes, happy sometimes, lonely often. Before that there was another, a man. Grandpa. Bluff, inquisitive, stubborn. Before that . . . Colder than cold, not really conscious, Gemstone sensed light all around the horizon and then dark. Light and darkness. Light and darkness. Antarctic summer and antarctic winter. In its deadened state, the seasons were a flickering that went on for time the little mind in the starfish body could not comprehend.

And before that . . .

Wonderful warmth, even nicer than now. Being cuddled flesh against flesh. Being valued. There were many friends, personalities strange to Sanda but not unknowable. They all lived in a house that moved, that visited many places—some warm and pleasant, some not. It remembered the coldest. In its curiosity, Gemstone wandered away from the house, got so very cold that when the friends came out to search, they could not find. Gemstone was lost.

And so the long time of light-and-dark, light-and-dark had begun.

The pure, even hell of the fire lasted only a few minutes. Gemstone whimpered in her mind as the walls began to fall, and the wind-driven cycle of flame faltered. The hottest places were in the center of what had been the living room, but Gemstone remained propped against Sanda's door, either for her company or in hopes she could bring back the warm.

Rain was winning against fire. Steam and haze obscured the glowing ruins. There might have been sirens.

She felt Gemstone chill and slowly daze. Its tone was now the nearly mindless dirge of all the weeks before. Sanda slid to the floor. And cried.

"Gemstone" takes place in 1957. I've wondered what became of Sanda and her wonderful pet. I suppose there is some room for sequels. One idea that sticks in my mind: Sanda ends up an artist, living in Arizona. She specializes in pottery. She is admired for the brushwork she does while the glaze is still hot. She has the most marvelous collection of kilns, all connected by narrow tunnels to a large one that is always fired. . . .

Only twice have I collaborated on fiction. Ordinarily, it's a good way to work just as hard as ever—but only get paid half as much. (Keith Laumer summed up the problems in the title of his essay for the SFWA Bulletin: "How to Collaborate without Getting Your Head Shaved.") There were these two times, though. Once was with my then-wife, Joan D. Vinge. We wrote "The Peddler's Apprentice," an oft-reprinted story (most recently in True Names and Other Dangers from Baen Books). In that story, I wrote the first part, got bogged down, and Joan *finished it. The circumstances of the other collaboration were quite different: My friend Bill Rupp and I simply wanted to write an adventure story. We plotted the thing together, using various ideas we had been collecting. For instance, we both admired Poul Anderson's approach to conflict adventures, the way he acknowledges the right that adheres in some wise to almost any cause. Bill wrote the first draft, and I revised it. John W. Campbell bought it for Analog. (Sadly, this was the last sale I ever made to John. He died just a few months later.)*

JUST PEACE

In its orbit about Jupiter, an artificial star flickered briefly, its essence oscillating between matter and energy. The complex disturbance generated by those pulsations spread out from the Solar System—in violation of several classical theories of simultaneity—at many times the speed of light.

Nineteen light-years away, a receiver on the second planet of the star delta Pavonis picked the signal out from the universal static of ultrawave radiation and . . .

Chente felt a slight, though abrupt, lurch as gravity fell to New Canadian normal. That was the only sign that the transmission had been accomplished. The cage's lights didn't even flicker.

("We can't know, of course, the exact conditions which faced your predecessor. His report is eighteen months overdue, however, so that we must expect the worst.")

Chente took a deep breath and stood, feeling for the moment exaltation: three times before he had sat in the transmission cage, and each time he had been disappointed.

(". . . believe you are ready, Chente. What can I say to a man about to travel nineteen light-years in an instant? For that matter, what will I say to the man who remains behind?")

The exit was behind his chair. Chente hit the control plate, and the hatch slid silently into the wall. Beyond was the control cubby of a ramscoop starship. Chente scrambled through the opening and stood in the small space behind the control saddle. The displays were all computer driven, and rather quaint. Neat lettering above one of the consoles read: INTERNATIONAL BUSINESS MACHINES OF CANADA—the original Canada back on Earth. Chente had spent hundreds of hours working out in a mock-up of this famous control room, but the real thing was subtly different. Here the air felt completely dead, sterile. The mock-up on Earth had been occupied by occasional technicians, whereas no one but Chente's predecessor had been in this room for more than a century. And it had been more than three centuries since the robot craft had sailed out of the Solar System.

A monument to empires passed, Chente thought as he slipped onto the saddle.

"Who goes there?" a voice asked in English.

Chente looked at the computer's video pickup. He had had plenty of practice with a similar think-box on Earth: the mech was barely sentient, but the best mankind could produce in the old days. Chente's superiors had theorized that after three hundred twenty years such a brain would be more than a little irrational. The human responded carefully, "Vicente Quintero y Jualeiro, agent of the Canadian Hegemony." He placed his ID before the pickup. Of course it was a fake—the Canadian Hegemony had ceased to exist one hundred years earlier. But the computer probably wouldn't accept any more recent authority.

"I have already received Vicente Quintero y Jualeiro."

It really is senile, thought Chente. "That is so. But another copy of Quintero remains on Earth, and was used for this latest transmission."

A long pause. "Very well, sir, I am at your disposal. I so rarely receive visitors, I—You require a situation report, of course." The vocoder's pleasant baritone assumed a sing-song tone, as if repeating some long-considered excuse. "After my successful landing on delta Pavonis II, I sent Earth a favorable report on the planet— Sir, most pertinent criteria *were* favorable. I see now my mistake . . . but it would have taken a new program to avoid making it. Shortly thereafter I received an initial transmission of fifteen hundred colonists together with enough ova and sperm to breed a colony. By 2220, the New Canada colony had a population of 8,250,000.

"Then . . . then the great planetary disturbance occurred."

Chente held up his hand. "Please. The Hegemony received your reports through 2240. We've reestablished contact to find out what's happened since then."

"Yes, sir. But I must report all the truth first. I wish no one to say that I have failed. I warned of the core collapse several weeks before it occurred. Yet still, most of the colony was destroyed. The disruption was so great, in fact, that the very continental outlines were changed.

"Sir, I have done my best to help the survivors, but their descendants have regressed terribly, have even formed warring nation-states. These groups covet every fragment of surviving technology. They stole my communication bombs so that I could no longer report to Earth. They have even attacked my own person, and attempted to cannibalize me. Fortunately my defenses are—" The computer broke off, and remained silent.

"What's the matter?"

"A small party is now climbing the hill I stand upon."

"Do they look hostile?"

"They are always hostile toward me, but this group is not armed. I suspect they saw the coronal discharge that accompanied your arrival. They probably drove here from Freetown."

"A city?" said Chente.

"Yes, a city-state which has remained neutral in the current warfare. It's built over the ruins of Firstlanding, the settlement I helped to found. Would you like to see our visitors?"

Chente leaned forward. "Of course!"

A large screen lit up to show a grass-covered slope. Coming up the hill toward the ship were twelve men and a woman. Beyond them, beyond the hill, the ocean stretched away unbroken to the horizon.

"¡Madre de Dios!" Chente gasped. On the old maps this hilltop was 3,500 kilometers inland. The continental outlines certainly had been changed by the catastrophe.

"Say again, sir?" said the computer.

"Never mind." Chente ignored the view and concentrated on the people who would soon be questioning him.

They made an interesting study in contrasts. To the left, a man and woman walked almost in lock step, though they remained discreetly apart. The man was dressed in simple black trousers and a short coat. His hat was stiff and wide-brimmed. The woman wore a long black dress that revealed nothing of her from below the neck. Her reddish hair was drawn back and tied with a black ribbon, and her grim face showed no sign of makeup. The two short men in the center wore jumpsuits, apparently modeled after the original colonists' dress. To the right, eight nearly naked men bent beneath an elaborate litter carrying a young male. As the group stopped, the litter was lowered, and he stepped jauntily to earth. The fellow's upper body was heavily oiled. He wore skintight breeches with an enormous codpiece. The grimly dressed couple on the left looked straight ahead, trying to avoid the sight of their companion on the far right.

"You see the cultural fragmentation that has occurred here on New Canada," the computer remarked.

"How far are they now?"

"Twenty meters."

"I may as well meet them. Off load the equipment that came through with me."

"Yes, sir." A hatch slid open and he entered the air lock beyond. Seconds later he was standing ankle-deep in turquoise grass, beneath a pale, pale blue sky. A slow breeze pushed with remarkable force against his jumpsuit: sea level air pressure on New Canada was almost twice Earth's. He was about to greet his visitors when the somber woman spoke, her voice tense with surprise.

"Chente!"

Chente bowed. "You have the advantage of me, ma'am. I take it you know my predecessor."

"The past tense would be more appropriate, Freeman Quintero. Your twin was murdered more than a year ago," the fellow in the skin-tight pants said, and smiled at the woman. Chente saw that in spite of his athletic build and flamboyant dress, the man was in his forties. The woman, on the other hand, seemed much younger than she had at a distance. Now she kept silent, but her companion said, "It was one of *your* ships he died on, you slave-holding animal." The shirtless dandy just shrugged.

"Please, gentlemen." The fat man in the center spoke up. "Recall that the condition of your presence here requires a certain mutual cordiality"—glares flickered back and forth between Shirtless and the puritans—"or at least courtesy. Mr. Quintero, I am Bretaign Flaggon, mayor of Freetown and governor of Wundlich Island. Welcome.

"The lady is Citizeness Martha Blount, ambassadress to Wundlich from the Commonwealth of New Providence, and," he rushed on as if trying to make both the introductions at once, "this gentleman is Bossman Pier Balquirth, Ambassador to Wundlich from the Ontarian Confederacy."

The woman seemed to have recovered from her initial surprise. Now she spoke with solemn formality. "New Providence regards you as our honored guest and citizen. Our nation awaits your—"

"Not so fast, Mistress Blount," Bossman Pier interrupted. "You aren't the only people brimming over with hospitality. I believe Freeman Quintero would be much more comfortable in a society which does not condemn dancing and music as a crime against nature."

"*Please!*" Flaggon repeated, "let's not have propaganda spoil the arrival of a visitor from the Mother World. As mayor, I wish to offer you any assistance you require, Mr. Quintero. I, uh . . . *Ah!* I will hold a banquet in your honor tonight. Of course, we will invite guests from both New Providence and Ontario." He sighed unhappily, recognizing the inevitable. "You can settle things then."

A faint hissing announced the opening of the freight

port in the ship's hull. A lift slid down the ancient metal surface with Chente's "luggage."

"Mr. Quintero y Jualeiro," the computer's vocoder boomed from a hidden speaker, "have you further orders at this time?"

"No. I will keep in touch."

"Beyond this hill I cannot protect you, sir."

"I'll survive."

"Yes, sir," doubtfully.

"Damned machine," Bossman Pier said softly. His perpetual grin had vanished. "It should be helping us. Instead it shoots at anyone trying to make entrance. We had to leave most of our boys at the base of the hill or we couldn't have got this close. Can I help you with that equipment?"

Chente stepped between Balquirth's servants and the freight lift.

"No thanks. I can carry it myself."

The Ontarian smiled knowingly. "Perhaps you will survive, after all."

As they walked down the hillside, Vicente kept silent. *So I died here*, he thought. Well, that was no great surprise. But that he had been killed by the very colonists he had been sent to help made his mission seem doubly difficult. What had happened on New Canada these last one hundred thirty years?

The lush grass on the hilltop thrived everywhere. He was no botanist, but it looked like some terrestrial type brought by the first colonists. Other vegetation was less familiar. Large ferns and broad-leafed plants stood in scattered clumps. The trees looked like giant flowers: their trunks rose straight and tall, with purple foliage sprouting from the top. Except for the grass, the land had a strong Jurassic aspect. Chente half expected a large reptile to pop out of the bushes.

They had reached the base of the hill when his

expectation materialized. A meter-wide *something* flew low over their heads, then circled above a nearby ridge.

"A gretch," Bretaign Flaggon said. "They're really quite common around here. That poor little fellow must have lost his mother."

The "poor little fellow" looked like a cross between a reptile and a buzzard. Chente grimaced. A nice place for a lifelong vacation. He'd never cared for paleontology.

At the base of the hill they stopped by a large three-wheeled vehicle and a group of armed men with bicycles. The powered tricycle was driven from a bench above and behind the passenger compartment. A brass tank and a piston cylinder sat below the driver's seat.

"Steamer?" Vicente asked, as he climbed into the cab.

"Quite right," Balquirth said. He swung up onto his slave-powered litter and looked down at Quintero. "If you're wise, you'll use something time-tested." He patted the satin pillows.

Flaggon and his driver climbed onto the upper bench, while Martha Blount and her aide got in with Chente. The armed bicyclists started down the road, and the auto got off with a jerk and a jump. The deep cushions could not disguise the absence of an adequate suspension, and acrid black smoke drifted from the fire box into the passenger compartment. Behind them, Bossman Pier's bearers were having no trouble keeping pace.

Minutes later the auto was puffing down a long slope that gave an overview of Freetown. The city was built around a crescent-shaped bay protected on the north by a huge granitic outcropping. Except for that headland, the bay was open to the sea.

"Have many storms?" he said to Martha.

"Dreadful ones," the woman answered, unsmiling. "But the tsunamis are worse—that's why the ships you see are anchored so far out. They come in to port only for loading."

The city rested on a sequence of terraces that climbed steeply up from the water's edge. Each terrace was split down the middle by a narrow, copper-paved street, while steps and coppered ramps provided communication between one level and the next.

Chente noticed that on the first three tiers the buildings were mostly warehouses and sheds. Nearly all these structures were made of wood and had a brand-new look. But above the third tier, the buildings were of massive stone construction, eroded and weather beaten. The most peculiar thing about the stone buildings was their long, narrow shape, their sharp, pointed ends. The prows of those stone arcs pointed uniformly out to sea.

Martha Blount followed his gaze. "The Freetowners use those wooden buildings for temporary storage of sea freight. They can count on everything in the first three terraces being leveled every two years or so. Beyond the third level, the tsunamis attenuate and the water breaks over the bows of the buildings."

The auto turned onto the fourth tier's main street, and slowed even further to get through the swarm of Freetowners moving to and from the stone-encased bazaars.

Chente shook his head in wonder. "You people certainly have managed to adapt."

"Adapt!" The New Providencian ambassador turned toward him, for the first time showing an emotion: rage. "We were nearly wiped out in the Cataclysm. That computer-driven monster up there on the hill gave us a real prize. With an advanced technology a colony on this planet could get along, but with that technology lost the place is a Hell. Adapt? Look—" She pointed out of the cab. They were passing near the edge of the terrace now, by blocks of gray rubble, stumpy walls. "Life on New Canada is a constant struggle simply to maintain ourselves. And all the while we're weighed down by those sybarites." She waved her hand back toward Bossman Pier's litter, some fifteen meters away. "They drain our resources. They fight us at every turn . . ." Her voice trailed off and she sat looking at Chente. For a moment some new emotion flickered across her face, but then she became impassive. Chente suddenly realized the reason for her silence: it was the second time around for Martha. No doubt she had sat in this same vehicle eighteen months earlier, and had had the same conversation with his predecessor.

Martha's hand moved toward him, then retreated. She said softly, "You really are Chente . . . alive again." Her tone became businesslike. "Be more careful, this time, will you please? Your knowledge, your equipment . . . many people would kill to get them." She was silent the rest of the way into town.

At sunset the heavy layers of dust in New Canada's atmosphere transformed the pale-blue sky into orange, red, and greenish brown. From where Chente sat within the Freetown banquet hall, the sky light shone through narrow, horizontal slits cut high up in the west wall to play gentle pastels of orange and green down upon the waiters and chattering guests. It was a most colorful tribute to volcanism.

The sky light faded slowly toward gray as the last unpleasant course of the meal was served. Above them, electric lamps mounted on large silver wheels were lit. Clusters of rubies and emeralds hung like clouds of colored stars around the glowing filaments. Occasionally the earth trembled faintly, causing the wheels to sway as if a slight breeze had touched them.

The meal over, Bretaign Flaggon rose to deliver "a few words of welcome to our star-crossed [sic] visitor." Chente couldn't decide whether the phrase was a pun or a malaprop. The speech droned on and eventually the Earthman succeeded in ignoring it.

The hall's wide floor was covered from wall to wall with what could only be gold. The soft yellow metal behaved like some slow sea beneath the weight of the banquet tables and constant passage of human feet: tiny ripples barely a centimeter high stood frozen in its surface. New Canada had everything the Spanish Conquistadores had ever dreamed of. But this virtue was symtomatic of a serious vice. Heavy metals were plentiful near the planet's surface simply because New Canada's interior was much more poorly differentiated than Earth's. The starship's computer had reported this fact to its makers on first landing here, but had failed to notice that the process of core formation was ongoing. The cataclysm that hit the colony one hundred fifty years earlier was evidence of this continuing process. The abundance of metallic salts on the surface meant that less than one percent of New Canada's land area could be used for farming. And those same salts made the sea life uniformly poisonous. In contrast to the opulent banquet hall, the food served had been scarcely more than a spicy gruel.

". . . Mr. Quintero." Applause sounded as Flaggon finished talking. The mayor motioned for Chente to rise and speak. The Earthman stood and bowed briefly. The applause was equally enthusiastic from the three groups seated at the horseshoe banquet table. On his right sat the Ontarian delegation, consisting of Bossman Pier, three associates, and a crowd of scantily dressed odalisques—all ensconced on piles of wide, deep pillows. Chente had been placed at the middle of the horseshoe with the Freetowners, while Martha Blount and her people sat along the left leg of the horseshoe. All through the meal, while the Ontarians caroused and the Freetowners chattered, the New Providencians had kept silent.

Finally the applause died, and people waited. From above them the tiny lights burned fiercely, but the stark shadows they cast held abysmal gloom. Chente saw a certain measure of fear in their attentive silence. No doubt many of them had sat right here less than two years before, and watched a man identical to the one they saw now. Intellectually they might accept the idea of duplicative transport, but historians had assured Chente that without a lifetime of experience no one could really accept such a thing. To his audience Chente was a man come back from the dead. Perhaps he could take advantage of this fear.

"I will be brief, as most of you will have heard this speech before." There was an uneasy movement and various exchanges of glances. Bossman Pier seemed the only one left with a smile on his face. "Your planet is undergoing a core collapse. A century ago a core tremor sank half a continent and virtually destroyed your civilization. Recently Earth has been able to reestablish communications with the starship on the hill behind Freetown. The link we have established is a tenuous one and you can't expect material aid. But Earth does have knowledge it can place at your disposal. Ultimately the core collapse will proceed to completion, and about ten million 'Cataclysms' worth of energy will be released. If this happens all at once, no life above the microbe level will be left on the planet. But, if it happens uniformly over a million-year period, you would never even be aware of the change. From the frequency of earthquakes, you know that the latter possibility has already been ruled out. My mission is to discover where between these two extremes the truth lies. For it is entirely possible that a future Cataclysm will be powerful enough to wreck your civilization as it is now, yet mild enough so that with adequate forewarning and preparation you can survive."

Flaggon bobbed his head. "We understand, sir. And, as we did with your predecessor, we will cooperate to the limit of our resources."

Chente decided to pounce on the double meaning in Flaggon's inept phrasing. "Yes, I've heard about the splendid help you gave my predecessor. He is dead, I've been told." He waved down Flaggon's stammered clarification. "Ladies and gentlemen, someone among you killed me. That was an act that threatened all of New Canada. If I am killed again, there may be no more replacements, and you will face the core collapse in ignorance." Chente wondered briefly if he hadn't just invited his assassination with that last threat, but it was too late to retract it.

The distressed Flaggon again pledged his help. Both Balquirth and Martha Blount chorused similar promises.

"Very well, I'll need transportation for an initial survey. From my discussion with the ship's computer before this banquet, I've decided that the best place to start is the islands that were formerly the peaks of the Heavenraker Mountains."

Martha Blount came to her feet. "Citizen Quintero, one of our Navy's finest dirigibles is tied down here at Freetown. We could be ready to go in twenty-two hours, and it won't take more than another day to reach the Heavenraker Islands." On the other side of the horseshoe, Balquirth cleared his throat noisily and stood up. Martha Blount rushed on. "Don't . . . don't make the same mistake the first Quintero did. He accepted Ontarian hospitality rather than ours, only to die on an Ontarian ship."

Chente looked at the Bossman.

"Her story is true, but misleading," Balquirth said easily. He had the air of someone telling a lie that he expected no one to believe—or else a self-evident truth that needed no earnest protestations to support itself. "The first Quintero had the good judgment to use Ontarian transportation. But his death occurred when the ship we assigned him was attacked by the forces of some other state." He looked across the table at Martha Blount.

The Earthman didn't respond directly. "Mayor Flaggon, what's the weather like along the Heavenraker chain this time of year?"

The mayor looked to an aide, who said, "In late spring? Well, there are no hurricanes likely. Matter of fact, the Heavenrakers rarely get any bad storms. But the underground 'weather' is something else again. Freetown alone loses three or four ships a year out there—smashed by tsunamis as they sail close to shore."

"In that case I'd prefer to go by aircraft."

Balquirth shrugged amiably. "Then I must leave you to the clutches of Mistress Blount. I don't have a single flier in port, and Mayor Flaggon doesn't have a single flier in his state."

"Your concern is appreciated in any case, Bossman. Citizen Blount, I'd like to discuss my plans in more detail with your people."

"Tomorrow?" She seemed close to a triumphant smile.

"Fine." Vicente began to sit down, then straightened. "One more thing. According to the starship's computer, all nine communications bombs are missing from their storage racks up on the hill."

In order to generate ultrawave distortions matter must needs be annihilated. Chente referred to the specially constructed nuclear bombs whose detonation could be modulated to carry information at superlight speeds. Such devices lacked the "bandwidth" to transmit the pattern of a human being—Earth's government used the tiny star that orbited where Callisto had once been for that job. Nevertheless, each of the communication bombs could be set to generate the equivalent of ten megatons of TNT, so they could do considerable damage if they were not hoisted into space prior to use.

The silence lengthened. Finally Chente said coldly, "I see. Your nation-states are playing strategic deterrence. That's a dangerous game, you recall. It cost Earth more than three hundred million lives a few centuries back. Your colony is in enough trouble without it."

His listeners nodded their agreement, but Chente saw—with a sick feeling—that his words were no more than platitudes to them.

The New Providencian airship *Diligence* flew south for a day and a half before it reached the first of the Heavenrakers. Chente saw a small village and a few farms in a sheltered bay near the coast, but the rest of the island was naked black rock. This was the first stop on a tour that would take them over 2,700 kilometers to the East Fragge, the Greenland-sized island that had once been the eastern end of the largest New Canadian continent. Chente had chosen this course since he wanted a baseline of observations along the planet's equator, and the Heavenrakers were the most convenient landmasses stretching along such a path. The survey went quickly, thanks to the help of the islanders, though they seemed happy only when the *Diligence* and its guns were preparing to depart.

Three days later the dirigible hung in the clear blue sky over the west coast of the Fragge. All around them thunder sounded. For hundreds of kilometers along the coast they could see tiny rivulets of cherry-colored molten rock dribbling off into the surf, converting the water into a low-lying fog beneath them. Looking inland at the extent of the frozen lava, Chente could see that the land-forming process had added thousands of square kilometers to the area.

Quintero turned to his companion at the railing. Martha Blount hadn't really changed in these last four days, but she had been revealed in a new aspect. For one thing, she had traded her full-length dress for a gray jumpsuit that covered her but hinted at a lot more than the dress had. From their discussions on the journey out he had found her to have a quick and lively mind that belied her outward reserve and convinced him that she had earned her high position. At times he found her interest in his equipment and plans somewhat too intense, and her political views too rigid, but he knew better than to expect anything else under the circumstances. And the more he knew of her, the more certain he was that her presence here was not motivated strictly by political interest: there had been something between Martha and the first Chente.

He gestured at the red and black landscape shimmering in the superheated air below them. "Are you sure you still want to come down with my landing party?"

She nodded. "I certainly do. It's not as dangerous as it looks. We'll be going many kilometers inland before we set down. I'm—doing a little reconnaissance here myself. I've never been in this part of the world."

*   *   *

Further conversation became impossible as the nuclear jets lit up to angle the *Diligence* down toward the black ridges that thrust up between the rivulets of fire. The jets were just one of many anachronisms in the New Providencian military machine. Apparently they had been salvaged from one of the colony's original helicopters. With them, the dirigible could make nearly fifty kilometers per hour in level flight.

The *Diligence* flew inland until the ground below was solid and cold. The airship descended rapidly, then leveled off just before its nose skid rasped across the jagged volcanic slag. Heavy grapnels were thrown out and the ship was drawn to Earth.

Vicente called to Ship's Captain Oswald, "Who'll be in charge of my ground party?"

"Flight corporal Nord," the officer said, pointing to a tall, muscular man, who together with three others was dragging explosives and equipment out of the *Diligence*'s cramped hold. "We'll stay on the ground just long enough to drop you off, Citizen Quintero. We're at the mercy of every breeze down here. We'll come back for you in twenty-two hours, unless you signal us earlier." He glanced at Martha. "Citizen Blount, I suggest you forego this landing. The country is pretty rough."

Martha looked back at him, and seemed faintly annoyed. "No, I insist."

Oswald frowned, but did not press the matter. "Very well. See you in a day or so."

Nord and two of the riflemen were the first to hit ground. Martha followed them. Then came Vicente, loaded down with his own special equipment. Two more riflemen with the explosives brought up the rear.

The landing site was a flat area at the top of a

narrow ridge. The seven of them clambered down the hillside as the huge aircraft's engines throttled up. By the time they reached the bottom of the ravine that followed the ridge, the *Diligence* was already floating five hundred meters over their heads.

"Let's follow this gorge inland a bit," said Quintero. "From what I could see before we landed, it should widen out to where we can do some blasting without risking an avalanche."

"Anything you say," Nord replied indifferently. Chente watched the man silently as the other moved on ahead. One way or another, this would not be a routine exploration.

The New Providencians spent most of the afternoon setting off explosives in the slag. Their firecrackers were bulky and heavy, and the work went slowly. The bombs didn't amount to more than half a ton of TNT, a microscopically small charge to obtain any information about conditions within the planet. Fortunately Chente's instruments didn't measure mechanical vibrations as such, but considerably more subtle effects. Even so he had to rely on coincidence counters and considerable statistical analysis to derive a picture of what went on hundreds of kilometers below.

Toward evening the sky became overcast and it began to drizzle. Chente called off their work. In fact, his survey was now complete, and his grim conclusions were beyond doubt. A stiff breeze kept anyone from suggesting that they call down the *Diligence*. Even with perfect visibility, Oswald probably couldn't have brought the airship in against that wind.

By the time they set up camp in a deep hollow— almost a cave—beneath the cliff face, they were all thoroughly soaked. Nord put two of his men on watch at the entrance to the hollow, and the rest of the party took to their sleeping bags.

As the hours passed, the rain fell more heavily, and from the west the steady hissing of the lava masked nearly all other sounds. Abruptly, the cylinder that rested in Chente's hand vibrated against his palm: someone was tampering with his equipment. Chente raised his head and looked about the cavelet. The darkness was complete. He couldn't even see the sleeping bag he lay in. But now the years of training paid off: Chente relaxed, suppressed all background noise and listened for nearby sounds. There! At least one person was standing in his immediate vicinity. The fellow's breathing was shallow, excited. Farther away, toward the equipment cache, he could now hear even fainter sounds.

Quintero slipped quietly out of the sleeping bag which he had prudently left unbuttoned and moved toward the cavelet entrance, lifting and lowering his feet precisely to avoid the irregularities he remembered in the rocky ground. He probably would have got clear anyway, as the distant hissing and the sound of rain covered whatever sounds he made. He didn't dare pick up any equipment, however; he was forced to settle on what he'd kept with him.

Twenty meters out into the rain, he turned and lay down behind a small, sharp hummock of lava. He drew his tiny pistol. Several minutes passed. These were the most cautious assassins he had ever seen. As if to rebut the thought, two of the guards' hand torches lit. Their yellow beams shone down upon his and Martha's sleeping bags. The two other guards held their rifles trained on the bags, ready to fusillade.

Before the riflemen could utter more than gasps of astonishment, Chente shouted, "Out here!" All but one of the men turned toward his voice. Chente raised his pistol and shot the one who still had his rifle pointed at the sleeping bags. There was no report or flash, but his target virtually exploded.

The hand torches were doused as everyone scrambled for cover. "Martha!" he shouted. "Get out. Run off to the side!"

He couldn't tell whether she had, but he kept up a steady covering fire, sending stone chips flying in all directions off the cavelet's entrance.

Then someone stuck one of the torches on a pole and hoisted it up. The others moved briefly into the open to fire all at once down upon his exposed position. But the Earthman got off one last shot—into the explosives.

The concussion smashed the ground up into his face, and he never heard the cliffside fall across the cavelet, entombing his enemies.

Someone was shaking him, and he felt a nose and a forehead nestled against the back of his neck. "Chente, please don't die again, please," came Martha's voice.

Chente stirred and looked into the wet darkness. His ears were buzzing, and the left side of his head was one vast ache.

"You all right?" he asked Martha.

"Yes," she said. Her hands tightened momentarily against him, but her voice was much calmer. Now that he was conscious she retreated again into a shell of relative formality. "The others must be dead though. The whole overhang came down on them. I followed the edge of the landfall trying to find you. You were not more than a couple of meters beyond it."

"You knew about this plan beforehand?" Chente's soft question was almost a statement.

"Yes—I mean, *no*. There were rumors that our Special Weapons Group killed the first Chente in an unsuccessful attempt to take his communications bomb. I believed those rumors. We used one of our bombs in the Nuclear Exchange of Year 317. The Special Weapons people have devised new uses, new delivery systems for our two remaining bombs, but what they really need are more nukes. In the last few months, I've had reports that the Weapons people are more eager than ever to get another bomb, that they have some special need for it. When you arrived, I was sure that between the Ontarians and our Weapons Group someone would try to kill you."

Chente shook his head, trying to end the buzzing pain. The motion only made him want to be sick. Finally he said, "Their assassination attempt seems incredibly clumsy. Why didn't they just do away with me once we were airborne?"

Now the Providencian ambassador seemed completely in control of herself. She said quietly, "That was partly my doing. I knew the Weapons people were waiting for another agent to be sent from Earth. When you came through, I made sure you were assigned to an airship crewed by regular Navy men. I was sure it was safe. For years Oswald has been part of the Navy faction opposed to the Special Weapons Group. But somehow they must have got through to him, and at least a few of his crewmen. Their murder attempt was clumsy, but it was a lot more than I had expected, under the circumstances."

Chente sat up and propped his head against his hands. This morass of New Providencian intrigue was not completely unexpected, but it was ludicrous. Even if the conspirators could dig his bomb out of the avalanche, it could not be fused without a voice-code spoken by Chente himself. He saw now his mistake in not revealing that fact upon landing. He had thought that all his dire warnings about the colonists' common peril would be enough to get co-operation. The situation was all the more ludicrous since he had seen how real the danger of core collapse was.

"Martha, do you know what I discovered during my survey?"

"No." She sounded faintly puzzled by this sudden change in topic.

"In one hundred fifty years or so there will be another core tremor, about as serious as the one you call the Cataclysm. You people simply don't have time to fight among yourselves. Your only option is to cooperate, to develop a technology advanced enough to ensure your survival."

"I see . . . Then the Special Weapons Group are fools as well as murderers. We should be working together to win the Ontarian war, so we can put all our resources into preparing for the next Cataclysm."

Chente wondered briefly if he were hallucinating. He tried again to explain. "I mean the war itself must be ended; not through victory, but simply through an end of hostilities. You need the Ontarians as much as they need you."

She shook her head stubbornly. "Chente, you don't realize what a ruthless, hedonistic crew the Ontarian rulers are. Until they're eliminated, New Providence will go on bleeding, so that no steps can be taken to protect us from the next Cataclysm."

Chente sighed, realizing that further argument would get him nowhere: he knew his own planet's history too well. He changed the subject. "Are there any settlements on the Fragge?"

"No cities, but there is at least one village about five hundred kilometers southeast of here. It's in the single pocket of arable land that's been discovered on the Fragge."

"That doesn't sound too bad. If we start out before dawn, we may be able to avoid Oswald's—"

"Chente, between here and wherever that village is, there's not a single plant or animal we can eat without poisoning ourselves."

"You'd rather take your chance with Oswald?"

"Certainly. It's obvious that not everyone aboard the *Diligence* was in on this."

"Martha, I think we can make it through to that village." He felt too dizzy to explain how. "Will you come along?"

Even in the darkness, he thought he felt a certain amount of amusement in her answer. "Very well . . . I could hardly return to the *Diligence* alone, anyway. It would give away the fact that you're out here somewhere." Her hand brushed briefly across his shoulder.

They started inland at the morning's first light, following along the bottom of one of the innumerable tiny ravines cut through the black rock. A temporary but good-sized stream ran down the middle so that they had to walk along the steep, rough ground near the side of the ravine. The buzzing was gone from Chente's head, but some of the dizziness remained. He was beginning to think that his inner ear had been "tumbled" by the explosion, giving him a permanent, though mild, case of motion sickness.

Martha appeared to be in much better condition. Quintero noticed that since she had made up her mind to come along, she seemed to be doing her best to ignore the fact that they were without food, or a reliable means of navigation.

Toward noon they drank rain water from a shallow puddle in the rocks. Twice during the afternoon Chente thought he heard the engines of the *Diligence*, nearly masked by the volcanic thunder to the west. By late afternoon, he estimated they were twenty kilometers inland—excellent progress, considering the ground they were crossing. The ravine became steadily shallower, until finally they left the lava fields and crossed into a much older country-side. The cloud cover swept away and the westering sun shone down from an orange-red sky upon the savannah-like plain ahead of them. That plain was not covered by grass, but by low, multiple-rooted plants that rose like thick green spiders from the ground.

Chente glanced at the sun, and then at the girl who trudged doggedly on beside him. Her initial reserves of energy were gone now and her face was set in lines of fatigue. "Rest break," he said, as they entered the greenery. They dropped down onto plants which, despite their disquieting appearance, felt soft and resilient—something like iceplant back on Earth. The abrupt movement made the world spin giddily around Chente's head. He waited grimly until the wave of dizziness passed, then pulled an oblong case from a pocket and began fiddling. Finally Martha spoke, her tired voice devoid of sarcasm, "Some Earthside magic? You're going to materialize some food?"

"Something like that." A small screen flashed to life on the wide side of the oblong. He sharpened the image, but it was still no more than abstract art to the uninitiated: a mixed jumble of blue and green and brown. He didn't look up as he said, "Martha, did you know that the starship left several satellites in orbit before it landed on New Canada?"

She leaned closer to him, looked down at the screen. "Yes. If you know where to look you can often see them at night."

"They were put up for your colony's use, and though you no longer have receiving equipment, they are still in working order."

"And this thing—"

". . . Is reading from a synchronous satellite some 40,000 kilometers up. This picture shows most of the Fragge."

Martha's fatigue was forgotten. "We never dreamed the satellites could still work. I feel like God looking down on things this way. Now we can find that village easily."

"Yes—" Using the controls at the side of the display he began to follow the Fragge's coastline at medium resolution.

Martha spoke up again. "I think we're seeing the north coast now. At least, the part that isn't under cloud looks like the last map I saw. The village is to the southeast of us, so you're not going to find much of anything—"

Chente frowned, looked more closely at the screen, then increased the magnification. It was as if the camera had been dropped straight toward the ground. The tiny bay at the center of the screen swelled to fill the entire display. Now they were looking down through late afternoon haze at a large natural harbor. Chente identified thirty or forty piers and a number of ships. All along the waterfront buildings cast long, incriminating shadows. He pushed a button and five tiny red lights glowed over the image of one of those buildings.

Martha was silent for a long moment. She looked more closely at the picture, and finally she said, "Those ships, they're Ontarian. They have an entire naval base hidden away there. The scum! I can imagine what they're planning: to build up a large secret reserve, and then tempt us into a major battle. Why, Chente, this changes our entire naval situation. It—" Suddenly she seemed to realize that she was not sitting in some intelligence briefing, but was instead stranded thousands of kilometers from the people who could use this discovery.

Chente made no comment, but returned the magnification to its previous level. He followed the coastline all the way around to the south and eventually found two other settlements, both small villages.

"Now let's try to find some food," he said. "If I'm oriented properly, I've got the picture centered on our location." He stepped up the magnification. On the enlarged scale they could see individual hillocks and identify the small stream they had crossed half a kilometer back. Toward the top of the picture, a collection of spikelike shadows stretched several millimeters. He magnified the image still further.

"Animals," Chente said. "They look better than two meters long."

"Then they're buzzards."

"Buzzards?"

"Yes, herbivores. The next largest thing we know about on the Fragge is a predator not much more than a meter long."

Chente grinned at her. "I think I've materialized that food for you."

She looked dubious. "Only if I can acquire a taste for copper salts in my meat."

"Perhaps we can do something about that." He looked at the scale key that flickered near the bottom of the picture. "That herd isn't more than five thousand meters away. I hadn't expected luck this good. How long till sunset? Two hours?"

Martha glanced at the sun, which hung some thirty degrees off the stony ridges behind them. "More like ninety minutes."

"We'll have buzzard soup yet. Come on."

The pace he set was a slow one, but in their present state it was about the best they could do. The spidery vegetation caught at their feet and the ground was not nearly as level as it looked. An hour and three quarters passed. Behind them the sun had set, and only the reddish sky-glow lighted their way. Chente touched Martha's elbow, motioned her to bend low. If they spooked the herd now, they would have a hungry night. They crawled over a broad hill crest, then lay down to scan the plain beyond. They had not been too cautious: the herd was some five hundred meters down the slope, near a waterhole. Chente almost laughed; buzzards, indeed! They certainly hadn't been named by the first-generation colonists. In this light the creatures might almost have been mistaken for tall men stooped over low against the ground. Their thin wings were clasped behind their backs as they walked slowly about.

Chente chose a medium-sized animal that was browsing away from the main group. He silently took his pistol from his coverall and aimed. The beast screamed once, then ran fifteen meters, right into the waterhole, where it collapsed. The others didn't need two warnings. The herd stampeded off to Chente's right. The creatures didn't run or fly—they bounded, in long, wing-assisted leaps. The motion reminded Chente of the impalas he had seen in the San Joaquin valley. In fact, their ecological niche was probably similar. *In which case*, he thought, *we'd better watch out for whatever passes for lions around here*.

The humans picked themselves up, and walked slowly down toward the abandoned waterhole. Vicente waded cautiously into the shallow, acrid-smelling water. The top of the buzzard's head was blown off. It was probably dead, but he didn't take any chances with it. By the time he got the hundred-kilo carcass out of the pool the short twilight was nearly ended. Martha took over the butchering—though she remarked that buzzards didn't have much in common with the farm animals she was used to. Apparently she had not spent her whole life administrating. He watched her work in the gathering darkness, glad for her help and gladder for her presence.

When the beast was cut into small enough pieces, Chente took a short cylinder from his coveralls and fed some of the meat into it. There was a soft buzzing sound, and then he pressed a cup into Martha's hand. "Buzzard soup. Minus the heavy metal salts."

He could just make out her silhouette as she slowly raised the cup to her lips and drank. She gagged several times but got it all down. When Chente had his first taste he understood her reaction. The sludge didn't *taste* edible.

"This will keep us alive?" Martha asked hoarsely.

"For a number of weeks, anyway. Over a longer time we'd need dietary supplements." He continued feeding the buzzard to the processor, and bagging the resulting slop.

"Why hasn't Earth given us the secret of this device, Vicente? Only one percent of New Providence has soil free from metallic poisons, and Ontario is only three or four times better off. With your processor we could conquer this planet."

He shook his head. "I doubt it. The machine is a good deal more complicated than it looks. On Earth, the technology to build one has existed for less than thirty years. It's not enough to remove the heavy metals from the meat. The result would still be poisonous—or at least nonnutritious. This thing actually reassembles the protein molecules it rips apart. For the technique to be of any use to you, we'd have to ship a factory whole. You just—"

Chente heard a faint hiss above and behind him. Martha screamed. As he whirled and drew his pistol he was bowled over by something that had glided in on them in virtual silence. Chente and the birdlike carnivore spun over in the spider-weed, the thing's beak searching for his face and throat but finding Chente's upthrust forearm instead. The claws and beak were like knives thrust into his chest and arm. He fired his pistol and the explosion sent the attacker into pieces all over him.

Chente rolled to a sitting position and played fire around the unseen landscape in case there were others waiting. But all he heard was vegetation and earth exploding as the water within them was brought violently to a boil.

The whole thing hadn't lasted more than ten seconds. Now the night was silent again. Chente had the impression that his attacker had been built more like a leopard than a bird. New Canada's dense atmosphere and low gravity made some peculiar things possible.

"Are you all right, Chente?"

The question made him aware of the slick flow of blood down his forearm, of the gashes across his ribs. He swore softly. "No bones broken, but I got slashed up. Are these creatures venomous?"

"No." He heard her move close.

"Good. The first-aid equipment I've got should be enough to keep me going, then. Let's get our stuff away from this waterhole or we'll be entertaining visitors all night long." He got stiffly to his feet.

They collected the bags of processed meat and then walked three hundred meters or so from the waterhole, where they settled down in the soft spiderweed. Chente took a pain killer, and for a while everything seemed hazy and pleasant. The night was mild, even warm. The humidity had dropped steadily during the afternoon, so that the ground felt dry. A heavy breeze pushed around them, but there were no identifiable animal sounds: New Canada had yet to invent insects, or their equivalent. The sky seemed clear, but the stars were not so numerous as in an earthly sky. Chente guessed that the upper-atmosphere haze cut out everything dimmer than magnitude three or four. He looked for Sol near the head of the Great Bear but he wasn't even sure he had spotted that constellation. More than anything else, this sky made him feel far from home.

He lay back, going over in his mind what he had discovered since his arrival. When his predecessor had failed to report, they had tried to prepare him more thoroughly for his return to New Canada. But none of the historians, none of the psychologists had guessed what an extreme social system had developed here. It must have begun as an attempt by the shattered colony to reform society after the Cataclysm, forging a fragile unity from zealous allegiance. But now it bled the warring nations dry, while blinding the people to the possibility of peace, and what was worse, to the absolute necessity of working together. By rights he should now be a hero among the New Canadians. By rights they should be taking the technical advice he could give to increase what small chances there might be to survive the next core tremor. Instead, he was marooned on this forlorn continent, and the only person who had any real desire to help him was just as much an hysterical nationalist as everyone else.

But his mission still remained, even if he couldn't get the locals to cooperate in saving themselves. In spite of its terrible problems, New Canada was a more viable colony than most. After four centuries of space flight, Earth knew how rare are habitable planets. Man's colonies were few. If those failed, there would be no hope for mankind ever to expand itself beyond the Solar System, and eventually the entire race would die of its own stagnation.

Somehow, he had to end this internecine fighting, or at least eliminate the possibility of nuclear war.

Somehow he had to force the colonists to fight for survival. At the moment he could see only one possibility. It was a long shot and deception was its essence. How much deception, and of whom, he tried not to consider.

"Martha?"

"Yes?" She huddled tentatively against him, all reserve finally gone.

"We're going to make for that Ontarian base rather than the village south of here."

She stiffened. "What? No! In spite of what some of my people tried to do to you, the Ontarians are still worse. Why—"

"Two reasons. First, that naval base is only two hundred fifty kilometers away, not five hundred. Second, I mean to stop this warfare between your two states. There must be peace."

"A just peace? One where we won't have our mines expropriated by the Ontarians? One where we get our fair share of the farmland? One where feudalism is outlawed?"

Chente sighed. "Yes." *Something like that.*

"Then I'll do anything to help you. But how can going to the Ontarians bring peace?"

"You remember those red blips on my display? Those were signals from the transponders that are on each of the communications bombs. If I've been keeping count properly, this means that the Ontarians have all their nuclear weapons stored at this base. If I tell them of New Providence's treachery, and offer my services, I may eventually get a crack at those bombs."

"It might work. Certainly, the world isn't safe as long as those fanatics have the bomb, so perhaps it's worth the risk."

Quintero didn't answer. He gave one quick glance around, saw no "leopards" in the pale starlight. Then he drew Martha into his arms and kissed her, and wondered how many times he had kissed her before.

Two hundred and fifty kilometers in five days would have been no burden for Chente if he had started fresh and uninjured. As it was, however, his dizziness and wounds slowed him down to the point where Martha could move as fast as he. Fortunately it didn't rain again and the nights remained warm. Waterholes were easily detected from orbit, and when they ran out of food after three days they had no trouble getting more meat—this time without having to fight for it.

But by the morning of the fifth day, they were both near the limit of their resources. Through the haze of pain-killer drugs and motion-sickness pills, the landscape gradually became unreal to Chente. He knew that soon he would stop walking, and no effort of will would get him moving again.

Beside him, Martha occasionally staggered. She walked flat-footedly now, no longer trying to favor her blisters. He could imagine the state of her feet after five days of steady walking.

Ahead stretched a long hill, its crest some five thousand meters away. Chente stopped and studied his display. "Just over that hill and we're home—"

Martha nodded, tried to smile. The news seemed to give them new strength and they reached the crest in less than ninety minutes. Below them lay the harbor they had discovered five days earlier on Chente's display. It was separated from the sea by overlapping headlands some ten kilometers further north. South of the green and brown buildings were the unpoisoned farmlands which apparently supported the base.

They looked down on the base only briefly, then silently started toward it. The possibility that they

might be shot out of hand had occurred to them, but
now they were too tired to worry much about it.

They were picked up by a patrol before they reached
the tilled fields. The soldiers didn't shoot, but it was
obvious that the visitors were unwelcome. Chente
was relieved of his hardware and he and Martha
were hustled into an olive-drab car that performed
much more efficiently than the huffer Mayor Flaggon
drove. Apparently the Ontarians could make fairly
good machinery, when ostentation didn't require otherwise. Their captors made no attempt to prevent
them from looking about as they drove through the
base toward the water's edge, and Chente forced his
tired mind to take in all he could. They tooled over
the brick-paved road past row after row of warehouses—a testament to Ontarian perseverance. To
bring so much equipment and material must have
taken many carefully planned voyages. And to avoid
Providencian detection, the supply convoys would
have had to be small and inconspicuous.

They turned parallel to the long stone quay and
drove between huge earthen reservoirs—presumably
filled with vegetable oils—and piles of kindling. Further along the quay they passed several cruisers and
a battleship. New Canadian ships were noticeably
smaller than their counterparts in the old-time na-
vies of Earth. A battleship here might run eight
thousand tons and mount six 25-centimeter guns. A
fleet of airships sat on the mudflats across the bay.
No wonder Balquirth had had no fliers to spare on
Wundlich.

Finally they stopped before a long three-story building that looked a good deal more permanent than the
wooden warehouses. The driver unlocked the door
to the passenger compartment and said, "Out." Two
soldiers covered them with what looked like four-

barreled shotguns as they followed the driver up the
steps to the building's wide doorway.

The inside of the building was quite a contrast to
the camouflaged exterior: deep-blue carpets covered
the floor while paintings and tapestries were hung
from the polished silver walls. Filament lamps glittered along the windowless hallway. They were led
stumbling up two flights to a massive wooden door.
One of the guards tapped lightly, and a muffled,
though familiar, voice from beyond the door said,
"Enter."

They did so and found Pier Balquirth surrounded
by aides and a pair of curvaceous secretaries. "Freeman Quintero! I should have guessed it was you.
And the lovely, though girdle-bound, Miss Blount.
Indeed, no longer girdle-bound—?" He raised his
eyebrows. "Sit down, please. I have the feeling you
may fall down if you don't. I apologize that I don't
give you a chance to rest before talking, but a decent
regard for Machiavelli demands that I ask some questions while your defenses are down. Whatever happened to Captain Oswald and his gallant crew?"

Chente brought the Ontarian up to date. As he
spoke, Balquirth removed a cigar from his desk and
lit up. He drew in several puffs and exhaled green
smoke. Finally he waved his hand in amusement.
"That's pretty sloppy work for the Special Weapons
Group, but I suppose they were trying to make your
death seem an accident. I hope this opens your eyes,
Freeman. Though the Special Weapons Group is the
most ruthless bureaucracy within the tight little to-
talitarian state that calls itself New Providence, the
other Groups aren't much better. New Providence
may be slightly ahead of the Ontarian Confederation
technologically, but they use their advantage simply

to make life unbearable for their 'Citizens', and to spread misery to other folks as well."

Martha glared dully at Balquirth but kept silent. Chente recalled Balquirth's casual, almost reckless attitude back in Freetown. He came close to smiling. A dandy and a fool are not necessarily the same thing. "You know, I think you drove me into the arms of New Providence just to create this situation."

Balquirth looked faintly embarrassed. "That's close to the truth. I stuck my neck way out to get your predecessor on one of my vessels. The first Quintero completed his survey, and told me his discoveries —I'm sure you've made these same discoveries by now—but he wouldn't believe that a loose confederation like Ontario could handle the preparations for this core tremor. He kept insisting that both New Providence and Ontario must somehow unite and work together. These are nice sentiments, but he just didn't realize how intolerant and uncompromising Miss Blount's friends can be. When the New Providencians killed him, my government—and myself in particular—were the goats.

"This time I thought I'd let you go with the Providencians. They'd try to kill you and steal your gadgets, but I knew that without your active cooperation they wouldn't get much use out of them. And I knew you were too stubborn to let them cajole you over to their side. If you were killed, then they would look bad. If by some quirk they didn't manage to kill you, I was pretty sure that you would realize what an unpleasant bunch they are.

"I am truly pleased that you survived, however. Can we depend on your help, or are you even more stubborn than I had guessed?"

Chente didn't answer immediately. "Are you in charge here?"

Pier chuckled. "As those things go in the Ontarian

Confederacy—yes. We've got men and material from four major bossdoms here, and their chiefs are at each other's throat half the time. But the base was my idea, and the Bossmanic Council in Toronto has appointed me temporarily superior to the three other bossmen involved."

The answer gave Chente a moment to think. In his way, the Ontarian was just as likable and just as much the capable fanatic as Martha. The only difference was that by accident of birth, one was supporting a loose feudal confederation and the other a more industrialized, more centralized regime. And both were so in love with their systems that they put national survival before the survival of the entire colony. Finally he said, "Your plan has convinced me—hell, it practically killed me. If you'll bring in the things they confiscated, I may be able to show you something you can use." Beside him, Martha's expression became steadily darker, though she still maintained her silence.

The bossman turned to one of his secretaries: "Darlene, go out and have Gruzinsky bring in any equipment he's holding. The rest of you leave, too—except Maclen, Trudeau, and our guests," he gestured at Chente and Martha. Chente glanced at his companion, wondered why Balquirth had permitted her to remain. Then he realized that the Ontarian had guessed his involvement with Martha, and was gauging his truthfulness by the exhausted woman's reactions.

A soldier brought in the various items taken from Chente and Martha, and placed them on the low table that sat before Balquirth's empillowed throne. The bossman picked up Chente's weapon. It looked vaguely like a large-caliber pistol, except that the bore was filled with a glassy substance.

"This does what I think it does?" Bossman Pier asked.

"Yes. It's an energy weapon—but the radiation is in the submillimeter range, so there isn't much ionization along the beam path, and your target can't see where your fire is coming from. But you'll find this more interesting." He pulled the satellite display toward himself and pushed the green button on its side. The tiny screen lit up to show a section of coast and ocean. Balquirth was silent for several seconds. "Very pretty," he said finally, but the banter was gone from his voice. "I never guessed the satellites were still working."

"The colonial planners built them to last. They didn't expect you would be able to go up and repair them."

"Hm-m-m. Too bad they didn't build our ground receivers the same way. What's that?" Balquirth interrupted himself to point at a tiny white "vee" set in the open ocean between two wide cumulous cloud banks.

"A ship of some kind. Let's have a closer look." Chente stepped up the magnification. The craft was clearly visible, its white wake streaming out far behind it.

"Why, that's the *Ram!*" one of the Ontarian officers exclaimed. "This is incredible! That ship left thirty-three hours ago. She must be hundreds of kilometers out, and yet we can see her as if we were flying over in an airship. When was this picture taken?"

"Less than a second ago. The coverage is live."

"What area can be observed with this gadget?"

"Everything except the poles, though high resolution pictures are available only up to latitude 45 degrees."

"Hm-m-m, we could reconnoiter the entire Inner Ocean." Pier touched one of the knobs. Now that

Chente had activated the device it responded to the Ontarian's direction. The *Ram*'s image dwindled, slid to one side, and they looked down on an expanse of cloud-stippled ocean. Chente started. Almost off the left side of the screen was a cluster of wake "vees". Balquirth increased the magnification until the formation filled the screen.

"Those aren't ours," one of the officers said finally.

"Clearly," said Balquirth. "It's equally clear that this is a New Providencian fleet, Colonel Maclen. And their wakes point our way."

"Looks like four Jacob class battleships, half a dozen cruisers, and twenty destroyers," said the second, older officer. "But what are those ships in the trailing squadron?" His eyes narrowed. "They're troop transports!"

"Now, I wonder what an invasion force would be doing in this innocent part of the world," said Pier.

The older officer didn't smile at the flippancy. "From their wake angles I estimate they're making thirty kilometers an hour, Bossman. If I read the key on the screen right, that means we have less than forty-four hours."

Chente glanced across at Martha, saw her eyes staring back at him. Now he knew why the Special Weapons people had wanted another bomb. Pier noticed their exchange of looks.

"Any idea why this invasion should coincide with your arrival, Freeman Quintero?"

"Yes. My guess is that certain Providencian groups discovered your base here some months ago, but deferred attack until they could get still another nuclear bomb—namely the one I brought—for their stockpile."

The bossman nodded, then seemed to put the matter aside. "Admiral Trudeau, I intend to meet them at sea. We have neither the shore batteries nor the garrison to take them on at the harbor entrance."

The officer nodded, looking unhappy. "But even with this much warning," he nodded at the screen, "they've still caught us with our pants down. I only have three cruisers, two battleships, and a handful of escort craft in port. We can't stop four Jacob class battlewagons and a half dozen cruisers with that, Bossman."

"We have the bombs, sir," Colonel Maclen broke in.

"You Army sorts are all alike, Colonel," Admiral Trudeau snapped. "The only time you ever used a bomb, it was smuggled into New Providencian territory and exploded on the ground. On the open sea we need at least twenty kilometers clearance between our fleet and the target. It's mighty hard to sneak a dirigible, or a torpedo boat, across a gap that wide."

Maclen had no answer to the criticism. Chente suddenly saw an opportunity to get at the Ontarian bombs and perhaps to destroy the Providencian nuclear capability in the bargain. He said, "But those comm bombs were mounted on drive units powerful enough to boost them out of the atmosphere. Why don't you alter the drive program and let them deliver themselves?" The three Ontarians looked at him open-mouthed. Beside him he heard Martha gasp.

Balquirth said, "You can make such alterations?"

Chente nodded. "As long as we know the target's position, I'll have no problem."

Martha gave an inarticulate cry of rage as she lunged across the table, picked up the recon display and flung it to the floor. Maclen and Trudeau grabbed her, forced her away from the table. Balquirth retrieved the display. The picture on the screen still glowed crisp and true. He shook his head sadly at Martha. "That's it, then. Trudeau, sound general alarm. I want some kind of fleet ready to sail in twenty-two hours."

The Navy man left without a word. Balquirth turned back to the Earthman. "You're wondering why I don't keep the fleet here, and lob the bomb out to sea when the enemy comes in range?"

Chente considered wearily. "That would be the prudent thing to do—if you trusted me."

"Right. Unfortunately, I don't trust you that far. I'll let you decide which bomb you want, and let you supervise the launch, but I'd rather not risk this base on the possibility of a change in your heart. We may not have many ships here yet, but the physical plant we've developed makes this one of the best naval bases in our confederation—whether it remains secret or not."

Chente nodded. Martha murmured something; Balquirth turned to her and bowed almost graciously. "You may come along, too, if you wish, Miss Blount."

The *Fearsome*, Admiral Trudeau's flagship, displaced seventy-three hundred tons and could run at better than forty kilometers per hour. She was doing at least that now. Chente stood on the bridge and looked out over the foredeck. After being treated by Ontarian medics, he had slept most of the preceding day. He felt almost normal now, except for a stiffness in his arm and side, and occasional attacks of vertigo.

He had studied naval types of the Twentieth Century quite thoroughly back home, and in many ways the *Fearsome* was a familiar craft. But there were differences. The Ontarian construction had a faintly crude, misshapen appearance. Standardized production techniques were only beginning to appear in the Confederacy. And without petroleum resources or coal, the nations of New Canada were forced to use vegetable oils or wood to fire their boilers—the greasy black smoke that spouted from the *Fearsome*'s stacks was enough to cause a queasy stomach even if his inner ear and the rolling sea were not. The ship had a huge crew. Apparently its auxiliary devices were not connected to the central power plant. Even the big deck guns needed work squads to turn and angle them. In a sense the *Fearsome* was a cross between a Roman galley and a 1910 battleship.

So far Chente's jury-rigged plans had gone much more smoothly than he had dared to hope. At Balquirth's direction, Colonel Maclen had shown him the maximum security storage bunker where Ontario's five nuclear weapons were located. Only one was needed for this mission, but the Earthman had been allowed to check the missiles' drive units in making his selection. Apparently, neither Maclen or Balquirth realized that a simple adjustment of the drive unit could render the bomb itself permanently unusable. It had taken Chente only a moment to so adjust four of the five weapons.

Now the hastily formed Ontarian fleet was under full steam, with the bomb launch less than an hour away. In addition to the *Fearsome*, the fleet contained the battleship *Covenant* and two large cruisers —essentially as protection for that one bomb. When they were within missile range of the Providencians the Ontarian fleet would turn away, and Balquirth and Chente would take the bomb aboard the motorized boat which now sat near the *Fearsome*'s stern. Not until then would Chente be allowed to touch the bomb's trigger.

Chente looked down at Martha, who sat beside him on the bridge, gazing fixedly out at the ocean. Her wrists had been manacled, but when the sea got choppy, Admiral Trudeau had removed the cuffs so that she could more easily keep her balance. She had not spoken a single word for the last three hours, had seemed almost like a disinterested spectator. Chente touched her shoulder, but she continued to ignore him.

The starboard hatch opened and Balquirth, dressed now in utility coveralls and a slicker, stepped onto the bridge. He spoke briefly with Trudeau, then approached the Earthman. "We've got problems, Freeman. This storm has kicked up a bit faster than the weather people predicted. We can't spot our fleet on the display, and the New Providencian force will be under cloud cover in another fifteen minutes."

Chente shrugged, and the gesture brought a sharp pain to his side. "No matter. That satellite we're reading from was also intended for navigation. It's got radar powerful enough to scan the ocean. We'll be able to keep track of the other fleet almost as easily as if there were no storm at all."

"Ah, good. Let's go below and take a look at the display, then. You said we could launch the missile from twenty-five kilometers out?"

"That's the effective range. Actually the bomb's drive unit could push it much farther, but it wasn't designed as a weapon, so it would be terrifically inaccurate at greater ranges."

Chente and Balquirth left the bridge and went carefully down the steep ladderway to the charthouse. The sky was completely overcast now, and a gathering squall obscured the horizon. He could barely make out the forms of the escort craft, far off to the side. The hard cold wind that sleeted across the *Fearsome* presaged the storm's arrival.

The charthouse was hidden from the direct blast of the wind by several armored buttresses and a gun turret. Five armed seamen stood at the entrance; once they recognized Balquirth, there was no trouble getting inside. The charthouse itself was well insulated from the outside, as the instruments it housed required better care than men did. Balquirth had had all of Chente's equipment stowed here, along with the communications bomb, a two-meter-long cylinder of black plastic that rested in a case of native velvet near the cabin's interior bulkhead.

Maclen sat beside some bulky and primitive wireless equipment. The young colonel held a repeating slug gun at the ready position. He was the room's only occupant. Apparently Pier trusted only his top aides with this Pandora's box of Earthly artifacts.

"All secure, sir," Maclen said. "I let the navigator take some charts but no one else has been by."

"Very good, Colonel," said Balquirth. "All right, Freeman, it's all yours."

Chente approached the brass chart table and the satellite receiver. He fiddled briefly with the controls, and the screen turned gray. A tiny point of light moved slowly from left to right across the top of the screen, then returned to the left margin and started across again. "That's the scanning trace from the satellite. It's illuminating a square kilometer as it moves across the ocean. The satellite's maser isn't powerful enough to light up a larger area, so the picture must be built up from a sequence of scans." The tiny blip of light shifted down about a millimeter with each scan, but still nothing showed in its track. Finally, two golden blips appeared, and in the scan below that, another blip.

"The Providencians," Balquirth said, almost to himself.

Chente nodded. "At this resolution, it's difficult to see individual ships, but you get the idea of their formation."

"What's that red blip?" Bossman Pier pointed to the newest apparition.

"That must be a transponder on one of the Providencian bombs. All the communications bombs transmit a uhf signal in response to microwave from the satellite. I suppose that originally the gimmick was used to find dud bombs that fell back to the surface without detonating."

"So they really thought they were going to wipe us out," said Pier. "This is even better than I had hoped."

The scanning dot moved relentlessly across the screen, shifting down with each pass to reveal more and more of the Providencian fleet. Finally they could see the echelon structure of the enemy forces. For ten more scans, no new blips appeared. Then a single red blip showed up far south of the enemy fleet. Chente caught his breath.

Balquirth looked across the table at him. "How far is that bomb from us?" he said quietly.

Chente held up his hand, and watched the scanning dot continue across the screen. He remembered Martha's remarks about the Providencians having special delivery systems. Then the scanning dot showed the leading elements of the Ontarian fleet—just six lines below the red dot. "Less than ten kilometers, Bossman."

Balquirth didn't reply. He looked at the display's key, then rattled off some instructions into a speaking tube. General quarters sounded. Seconds later Chente heard the *Fearsome*'s big deck guns fire.

Finally Balquirth spoke to Chente. His voice was calm, almost as if their peril were someone else's. "How do you suppose they detected our fleet?"

"There are a number of ways. Martha said the Providencians were experimenting with a lot of gadgets of their own design. In fact they may not have detected us. That bomb is probably aboard a small, unmanned boat. They may just keep it thirty or forty kilometers ahead of their fleet. Then if it hears the sounds of propellers nearby it detonates."

"Ah, yes. Research and development—isn't it wonderful."

They stood waiting in silence. Ten kilometers away, a barrage of heavy artillery was arcing down on the cause of that innocuous red blip. Any second now they would discover just how cleverly the New Providencians had designed their delivery system.

From outside the windowless charthouse came screams. No other sounds, just screams. Chente smelled fire, noticed the insulation around the closed hatch was beginning to smoke. He and Balquirth hit the deck, and Maclen was not far behind. The bomb's searing flash had crossed the ten kilometers separating them at the speed of light, but they would have to wait almost seven seconds for the water-borne shock wave to arrive.

Chente heard a monstrously loud ripping sound, felt the deck smash into his chest and head. He was not conscious when the air-borne shock wave did its job, peeling back the charthouse bulkhead and part of the deck above them.

Chente woke with rain in his face, and the muffled sound of exploding ammunition and burning fuel all around. Behind all these sounds, and nearly as insistent, was a steady roar—the last direct evidence of the nuclear explosion.

The Earthman rolled over, cursing as he felt the stitches the Ontarian doctors had put in his side come apart. His head rang, his nose was bleeding, and his ears felt stuffed with cotton. But as he shook the rain out of his eyes he saw that the others in the charthouse had not fared so well. On the other side of the cabin, Maclen's body was sprawled, headless. Nearer, Balquirth lay unmoving, a pool of blood spreading from his mouth.

For a few moments Chente sat looking stupidly at

the scene, wondering why he was alive. Then he began to think. His plans to destroy the Providencian bombs were ruined now that the Ontarian fleet had been destroyed. Or were they? Suddenly he realized that this turn of events might give him hope of completing his mission and still escaping both groups. Chente struggled to his feet, and noticed the deck was listing—or was it only his sense of balance gone awry again? He recovered the recon display and his pistol, then picked the communications bomb from its case. The bomb didn't mass more than fifteen kilograms, but it was an awkward burden.

Outside the charthouse the mutilated guards' bodies lay amid twisted metal. The ship's paint was scorched and curling even in the rain. The after part of the ship was swallowed by flame, and the few people he saw alive were too busy to notice him.

Martha. The thought brought him up short, and he reconsidered the possibilities. Then he turned and started toward the bridge. He could see the gaping holes where the glass had been blown out of the bridge's ports. Anybody standing by those ports would be dead now.

Then he saw her, crawling along the gangway above. The deck listed a full ten degrees as he pulled himself up a ladderway to reach her. "Let's get off this thing!" he shouted over the explosions and the fire. He caught her arm and helped her to her feet.

"What—?" She shook her head. A trickle of blood ran from one ear down her neck. Her face was smeared with grime and blood.

He could barely hear her voice, and realized the explosion must have deafened them all. He held onto her and shouted again into her good ear. For a moment she relaxed against him, then pulled back, and he saw her lips mouth: "Not with . . . traitor!"

"But I was never going to use that bomb on your

people. It was just a trick to get at the Ontarian bombs." It was the biggest lie he'd told her yet, but he knew she wanted to believe it.

He pointed toward the *Fearsome*'s stern, and shouted, "To the launch!" She nodded and they staggered across the tilting, twisted deck, toward the flames and the sound of explosions. Everyone they met was going in the opposite direction, and seemed in no mood to stop and talk.

Now there was only one narrow path free of flames, and the heat from either side was so intense it blistered their skin even as they ran through it. Then they were beyond the flames, on the relatively undamaged stern. Chente saw that the motor launch had been torn loose from its after mooring cable, and now its stern hung down, splashing crazily in the water. Several bodies lay unmoving on the scorched deck, but no one else was visible. They crawled down to where the bow of the launch stuck up over the railing. Chente had almost concluded they were alone on the stern, when Balquirth stepped from behind the wreckage next to the launch's moorings.

The Ontarian swayed drunkenly, one hand grasping the jagged and twisted metal for support. His other hand held a slug gun. The lower part of his face was covered with blood. Chente staggered toward him, and shouted, "Thought you were dead. We're going ahead with your plan."

Through the blood, Pier almost seemed to smile. He gestured at Martha. "No . . . Quintero," his voice came faintly over the sounds of rain and fire, ". . . think you've turned your coat . . ."

He raised the pistol, but Chente was close to him now. The Earthman lunged, knocking the gun aside with his bomb, and drove his fist hard into Pier's stomach. The other crumpled. Chente staggered back, clinging to the rail for support. It struck him that the fight must have looked like a contest between drunks.

He turned to Martha, and waved at the launch. "We'll have to jump for it, before that other cable breaks."

She nodded, her face pale with cold and fear. They were cut off from the rest of the ship by the spreading fire, and even as he spoke the *Fearsome* tilted another five or ten degrees. He climbed over the rail and jumped. The drop was only three meters, but his target was moving and he was holding the bomb. He hit hard on his bad side and rolled down the launch's steeply sloping deck.

Gasping for breath he dragged himself back up the deck and waved to Martha above him. She stood motionless, her fists tightly clenched about the railing. For a moment, Chente thought she would balk, but she slipped over the railing and jumped, her arms outstretched. He managed to break her fall and they both went sprawling. They crawled clumsily down the bobbing deck toward the craft's cockpit. Martha struggled through the tiny hatch, and Chente pushed the bomb after her. Then he turned and fired at the remaining mooring cable.

The launch knifed into the water and for a moment submerged completely, but somehow Chente managed to keep from being washed away. The boat bobbed back to the surface, and he scrambled into the cockpit.

From his talks with Balquirth, Quintero knew the boat had a steam-electric power plant—it was ordinarily used for espionage work. Looking over the control panel, Chente decided that this was the most advanced Ontarian mechanism he had encountered—just the kind of luck they needed. He depressed the largest switch on the board and felt a faint humming beneath his feet. He eased the throttle forward. As the launch pulled slowly away from the foundering *Fearsome*, he thought he heard the whine and snick of small arms fire caroming off the boat's hull; apparently Balquirth was not easily put out of action. But now it was too late to stop their escape. The *Fearsome* was soon lost to sight amid the deep swells and pounding rain. The last Chente saw and heard of the Ontarian fleet was a pale orange glow through the storm, followed by a sound that might have been thunder. Then they were alone with the storm.

The storm was bad enough in itself. The tiny cabin spun like a compass needle, and several times Chente was afraid the boat would capsize. Somehow Martha managed to tie down the equipment and dig a couple of life jackets out of a storage cubby.

Chente fastened the recon screen to the control board, and inspected the radar display. On high resolution he could distinguish every vessel in the area. Even his motor launch showed—or at least the transponder on his communications bomb did. They would have no trouble navigating through this storm, if they didn't sink. He briefly thanked heaven that the comm bombs were about as clean as anything that energetic can be: nearly all the destruction was radiated as soft X rays. At least they didn't have to worry that the rain was drenching them in radioactive poisons.

"Now what?" Martha shouted finally. She had wedged herself in the corner, trying to keep her balance.

Chente hesitated. He had three choices. He could flee the scene immediately; he could use his bomb to destroy the Providencians and their remaining bomb—just as he and Balquirth had planned; or he could indulge in more treachery. The first option would leave the Providencians with a bomb, and an enormous advantage in the world. The second option would be difficult to execute; at this point Martha might be stronger than he was. He might have to kill her. Besides, if he exploded his bomb, he would have no way to make his report to Earth.

That left treachery. "We're going to try to get picked up by one of the ships in the Providencian fleet."

Twenty minutes passed. At the top of the screen the launch's blip moved closer and closer to the red dot that represented the last Providencian bomb. He kept the screen angled so that Martha didn't have a clear view of it.

They should be able to see the ship before much longer. He leaned his head close to Martha and said, "Do you know any signals that would keep them from shooting us out of hand?" He pointed at the electric arc lamp mounted in the windscreen.

Her voice came back faintly over the wind. "I know some diplomatic codes. We update them every fifteen days—they just might respect them."

"We'll have to chance it." Chente helped her light the arc lamp. But there was nothing to see except storm. Chente guided the launch so that its image on the screen approached the other. As they swung over the top of a swell, they saw a long gray shadow not more than two hundred meters ahead. It appeared to be an auxiliary craft, probably a converted cargo ship.

Chente reached across the panel and tapped new instructions into the display. Now the machine was reading the transponder's position from its internal direction finders. Beside him at the control panel, Martha awkwardly closed and opened the signaler's shutter. For nearly thirty seconds there was no reply. Chente held his breath. He expected that this particular ship would be manned by Special Weap-

ons people, who might well be trigger-happy and
extremely suspicious. On the other hand, depending
on what they expected of the Ontarians, the weapons
people might be cocksure and careless.

Finally a light high on one of the ship's masts
blinked irregularly. "They acknowledge. They want
us to move in closer."

Chente worked the electric boat closer and closer
to the ship. Martha continued sending. They were
about fifty meters out now, and they could make out
the details of the other vessel. Quintero looked closely
at his display, then scanned the ship's foredeck. He
noticed a shrouded boat lashed down near the bow.
Its position agreed with the location of the blip on
his display. This was better than he had hoped. That
was the twin of the robot boat that had nearly destroyed the Ontarian fleet.

He took one hand from the wheel, drew his pistol
and fired a single low-power bolt. The thick windscreen shattered, throwing slivers of glass all around.
He stepped the pistol's power to full and aimed at
the other vessel's bow.

"No!" Martha screamed as she rammed him against
the bulkhead. She was tall and strong and she fought
desperately. They careened wildly about the cabin
for several seconds before Chente got a solid, close-
fisted blow to her solar plexus. She collapsed without
a sound, and the Earthman whirled back to face the
deadlier enemy.

The ship's main guns were turned toward him, but
he was below them now. He sprayed fire all along
the vessel, concentrating on the smaller deck guns
and the shrouded boat. Clouds of steam quickly obscured the glowing craters his pistol gouged in the
ship's hull, and then the fuel supply aboard the robot
boat exploded in a ball of orange-red flame hot enough
to melt the controls of the bomb within.

There was the sparkle of automatic fire from up in the ship's masts, and the cockpit seemed to shred around him. He fired upward blindly.

Chente grabbed the wheel and turned about. The seconds passed but there was no more Providencian gunfire. The sounds of the burning ship quickly faded behind them and they were alone.

They drove steadily west for three hours. The seas fell. Just as the sun set, the cloud cover in the far west moved aside so that the sun shone red and gold through the narrow band between horizon and cloud.

His reconnaissance screen showed no sign of pursuit. More importantly, there was only one transponder blip glowing on Chente's display—his own.

The tiny launch was slowing, and finally Chente decided to try to fire its boiler. He eased the throttle back to null, and the boat sat bobbing almost gently in the sea the sun turned gold.

"Martha?" No response. "I had to do it."

"Had to?" Her tone showed despair and unbelieving indignation. She looked briefly up at him through her rain-plastered hair. "How many Providencians did you kill today?"

Chente didn't answer. The rationalizations that men use for killing other men stuck in his throat, at least for the moment. Finally he said, "I told you, I told the Ontarians: Unless you work together you will all be wiped out. But it didn't do any good just to say it. Now, Ontario and New Providence have a mutual enemy: me. I have the only nuclear weapon left, and I have means to deliver it. Soon I will control territory, too. Your nations will spend their energies to develop the technology to defeat me, and in the end you may be good enough to meet your real peril."

But Martha had resumed her study of the deck, and made no reply.

Chente sighed, and began to pull back the deck plates that should cover the boiler.

The sun set and the first stars of twilight shone through the gap between the clouds and the horizon. Nineteen light-years away, his likeness must still be awaiting his report. In a few weeks, Chente would make that report, using the Ontarian communications bomb. But the people of the New Canada would never know it, for that bomb was the lever he would use to take over some small Ontarian fiefdom. Already he must begin casting the net of schemes and the machinations that would stretch one hundred years into this miserable planet's future. It was small consolation to hope that his likeness would live to see other worlds.

There are a lot of things I like about "Just Peace." As a collaboration it went very smoothly. Bill and I had lots of small things in our idea boxes that found a nice home here: the Canadian background, the danger of colonizing a planet whose core was about to undergo a phase change.

Chente's background on Earth was vague. This was deliberate. I assume Earth had already gone through the technological singularity I mentioned before. We see about as much of Earth as we could understand. One major aspect of Earth's technology leaks into this story: the duplicative transport used to bring Chente to New Canada. Not much is made of it here, but I find the idea immensely intriguing. If we could make exact copies of someone (not just clones, but exact down to quantum limits) what would this do to our concept of ego? The idea has been in sf for many years (at least back to Algis Budrys' Rogue Moon and Poul Anderson's We Have Fed Our Sea). I think there is plenty of mileage left in the gimmick. This is just one (and one of the simplest) of the problems that I see looming in our future. Our most basic beliefs—the concept of self itself—are in for rough times.

Alien contact stories have always been a favorite of mine. I grew up with John Campbell's notion that the humans were short-lived, bright, and terribly aggressive compared to the wiser intellects of galactic civilization. Why not turn that around? Why not have a race even more short-lived, intelligent, and aggressive than humans? John's older/wiser races often tried to keep the human "superrace" confined to Earth. What would we do if confronted by aggressive primitives with the potential to run circles around us?

I hadn't seen any stories with this theme, but knowing science-fiction I guessed that such had already been written. I needed something more. Many human personalities are piled deep with interacting layers of shame and loneliness and hatred. My race would have even more inner turmoil. How to do it? A short lifespan would certainly intensify such problems, but I wanted something that would give individuals real reason to feel guilt. I remembered the extraordinary life cycle of the hugl (a non-sentient pest) in Silverberg and Garrett's Shrouded Planet. Maybe I could jazz that up, and apply it to an intelligent race. Thus was born:

ORIGINAL SIN

First twilight glowed diffusely from the fog. On the landscaped terraces that fell away from the hilltop, long rows of tiny crosses slowly materialized. Low trees dripped almost silently upon the sodden grass.

The officer in charge was young. This was his first assignment. And it was an assignment more important than most. He shifted his weight from one foot to the other. There must be something to do with his time—something to check, something to worry over; the machine guns. Yes. He could check those again. He moved rapidly up the narrow, concrete walk to where his gun crews manned their weapons. But the magazine feeds were all set, the muzzle chokes screwed down. Everything was just as proper as the last time he had checked, ten minutes earlier. The crews watched him silently, but resumed their whispered conversations as he walked away.

Nothing to do. Nothing to do. The officer stopped for a moment and stood trembling in the cool dampness. Christ, he was hungry.

Behind the troops, and even farther from the field

of crosses, the morning twilight defined the silhouettes of the doctors and priests attendant. Their voices couldn't carry through the soggy air, but he could see their movements were jerky, aimless. They had time on their hands, and that is always the greatest burden.

The officer tapped his heavy boot on the concrete walk in a rapid tattoo of frustration. It was so quiet here.

The mists hid the city that spread across the lowlands. If he listened carefully he could hear auto traffic below. Occasionally, a ship in the river would sound its whistle, or a string of railway freight cars would faintly crash and rattle as it moved along the wharves. Except for these links with the everyday world, he might as well be at the end of time here on the hilltop with its grasses, its trees. Even the air seemed different here—it didn't burn into his eyes, and there was only a hint of creosote and kerosene in its smell.

It was brighter now. The ground became green, the fog a cherry brown. With a sigh of anguished relief, the officer glanced at his watch. It was time to inspect the cross-covered hillside. He nearly ran out onto the grass.

Low hedges curved back and forth between the white crosses to form an intricate topiary maze. He must check that pattern one last time. It was a dangerous job, but hardly a difficult one. There were less than a thousand critical points and he had memorized the scheme the evening before. Every so often he broke stride to cock a deadfall, or arm a claymore mine. Many of the crosses rose from freshly turned earth, and he gave these an especially wide berth. The air was even cleaner here above the grass than it had been back by the machine-guns, and the deep wet sod sucked at his feet. He gulped back saliva and tried to concentrate on his job. So hungry. Why must he be tempted so?

Time seemed to move faster, and the ground brightened steadily beneath his running feet. Twenty minutes passed. He was almost done. The ground was visible for nearly fifty meters through the brownish mists. The city sounds were louder, more numerous. He must hurry. The officer ran along the last row of crosses, back toward friendly lines—the cool sooty concrete, the machine-guns, the trappings of civilization. Then his boots were clicking on the walkway, and he paused for three seconds to catch his breath.

He looked at the cemetery. All was still peaceful. The preliminaries were completed. He turned to run to his gun crews.

Five more minutes. Five more minutes, and the sun would rise behind the fog bank to the east. Its light would seep down through the mists, and warm the grass on the hillside. Five more minutes and children would be born.

What a glorious dump! They had me hidden in one of the better parts of town, on a slight rise about three kilometers east of the brackish river that split the downtown area in two. I stood at the tiny window of my "lab" and looked out across the city. The westering sun was a smudged reddish disk shining through the multiple layers of crap that city traffic pumped into the air. I could actually see bits of ash sift down from the high spaces above.

It was the rush hour. The seven-lane freeways that netted the city were a study in still life, with idling cars backed up thousands of meters at the interchanges. I could imagine the shark-faced drivers shaking their clawed fists at each other, frothing murderous threats. Even here on the rise, it was so hot and humid that the soot stuck to my sweating skin. Down in the city basin it must have been infernal.

Further across town was a cluster of skyscrapers, seventy and eighty stories high. Every fifteen seconds a five-prop airplane would cruise in from the east, make a one-eighty just above the rooftops, and attempt a landing at the airport between the skyscrapers and the river.

And beyond the river, misty in the depths of the smog, was the high ridgeline that blocked the ocean from view. The grayish-green expanse of the metropolitan cemetery ran across the whole northern end of the ridge.

Sounds like something out of a historical novel, doesn't it? I mean, I hadn't seen an aircraft in nearly seventy years. And as for cemeteries . . . This side of the millennium, such things just didn't exist—or so I had thought. But it was all here on Shima, and less than ten parsecs from mother Earth. It's not surprising if you don't recognize the name. Earthgov lists the planet's star as $+56°2966$. You can tell the Empire is trying to hide something when the only designation they have for a nearby K-star is a centuries-old catalog number. If you're old enough, though, you remember the name. Two centuries back, "Shima" was a household word. Not counting Earth, Shima was the second planet where man discovered intelligent life.

A lot has happened in two hundred years: the Not-Wars, the secession of the Free Human Worlds from Earthgov. Somewhere along the line, Earth casually rammed Shima under the rug. Why? Well, if nothing else, Earthgov is cautious (read: chicken). When humans first landed (remember spaceships?) on Shima, the native culture was paleolithic. Two centuries later, their technology resembled Earth's in the late Twentieth Century. Of course, that was no great shakes, but remember it took us thousands of years to get from stone ax to steam engine. It's really hard to imagine how the Shimans did it.

You can bet Earthgov didn't give 'em any help. Earth has always been scared witless by competition, while at the same time they don't have the stomach for genocide. So they pretend competition doesn't exist. The Free Worlds aren't like that. Over the last one hundred and fifty years, dozens of companies have tried to land entrepreneurs on the planet. The Earth Police managed to rub out every one of them.

Except for me (so far). But then, the people who hired me had had a lucky break. Earthgov occasionally imports Shimans to work as troubleshooters. (The Empire would import a lot more—Shimans are incredibly quick at solving problems that don't require background work—except that Earthpol can't risk letting the aliens return with what they learn.) Somehow one such contacted the spy system that Samuelson Enterprises maintains throughout the Empire. Samuelson got in touch with me.

Together, S.E. and the Shimans bribed an Earthman to look the other way when I made my appearance on Shima. Yes, some Earthcops do have a price—in this case it was the annual gross product of an entire continent. But the bribe was worth it. I stood to gain one hundred times as much, and Samuelson Enterprises had—in a sense—been offered one of the biggest prizes of all time by the Shimans. But that, as they say, is another story. Right now I had to come across with what the Shimans wanted, or we'd all have empty pockets—or worse.

You see, the Shimans wanted immortality. S.E. had impaled many a hick world on that particular gaff, but never like this. The creatures were really desperate: no Shiman had ever lived longer than twenty-five Earth months.

I leaned out to look at the patterns of soot on the window sill, trying at the same time to ignore the laboratory behind me. It was filled with equipment the Shimans thought I might need: microtomes, ultracentrifuges, electron microscopes—a real antique shop. The screwy thing was that I did need some of those gadgets. For instance, if I had used my *'mam'ri* at the prime integers, Earthpol would be there before I could count to three. I'd been on Shima four weeks, and considering the working conditions, I thought progress had been pretty good. But the Shimans were getting suspicious and very, very impatient. Samuelson had negotiated with them through third parties on Earth, and so hadn't been able to teach me the Shiman language. Sometime *you* try explaining biological chemistry with sign language and grunts. And these damn fidget brains seemed to think that a project was overdue if it hadn't been finished last week. I mean, the ol' Protestant Ethic stood like a naked invitation to hedonism next to what these underweight kangaroos practiced.

Three days earlier, they had posted armed guards inside my lab. As I stood glooming at the windowsill I could hear my three pals shuffling endlessly about the room, stopping every so often to poke into the equipment. Nothing short of physical violence could make them stay in one spot.

Sometimes I would look up from my bench to see one of them staring back at me. His gaze was not unfriendly—I've often looked at a steak just that way. When he saw me looking back, the Shiman would abruptly turn away, unsuccessfully trying to swallow slaver back from the multiple rows of inward curving teeth that covered his mouth. (Actually the creatures were omnivorous. In fact, they'd killed off virtually all animal life on the planet, and most of their vast population subsisted on cereal crops grown—in insufficient quantities—on well-defended collective farms.)

I could feel them staring at me right now. I had half a mind to turn around and show them a thing or three—Earthpol and its detection devices be damned.

This line of thought was interrupted as a sports car breezed up from the sentry gate three hundred meters away. I was housed in some sort of biological science complex. The place looked like a run-down Carnegie Library (if you remember what a library is), and was surrounded by hectares of blackened concrete. Beyond this were tank traps and a three-meter high barricade. Till now the only vehicles I had seen inside the compound were tracked military jobs.

The blue and orange sports car burned rubber as the driver skidded to a stop against the curb beneath my window. The driver bounded out of his seat, and double-timed up the walk. Typical. Shimans never slow down.

The passenger door opened, and a second figure appeared. Normal Shiman dress consists of a heavy jacket and a kilt which conceals their broad haunches and part of their huge feet. But this second fellow was wrapped from head to foot in black, a costume I had seen only once or twice before—some kind of penance outfit. And when he moved it wasn't with short rapid hops, but with longer slower strides, almost as if . . .

I turned back to my equipment. At most I had only seconds, not really enough time to set the devious traps I had prepared. The two were inside the building now. I could hear the rapid *thumpthumpthump* as the driver bounced up the stairs, and the softer sound of someone moving unseemly slow. But not slow enough. Through the door came the whistly buzz of Shiman talk. Perhaps those guards would do their job, and I would have a few extra seconds. No luck. The door opened. Driver and passenger stepped into my lab. With nearly Shiman haste, the veiled passenger whipped off the headpiece and dropped it to the floor. As expected, the face behind the veil was human. It was also female. The girl looked about the room expressionlessly. A sheen of sweat glistened on her skin. She brushed straight blond hair out of her face and turned to me.

"I wish to speak to Professor Doctor Hjalmar Kekkonen," she said. It was hard to believe that such a flat delivery could come from that sensuous mouth.

"That's one I'll grant," I said, wondering if she was going to read me my rights.

She didn't answer at once, and I could see the throb at her temple as she clenched her jaws. Her eyes, I noticed, were like her voice: pretty, but somehow dead and implacable. She pulled open her heavy black gown. Underneath she wore a frilly thing which wouldn't have been out of place in Tokyo—or with the Earth Police.

She stood at her full height and her gray eyes were level with mine. "It is hard for me to believe. Hjalmar Kekkonen holds the Chair of Biology at New London University. Hjalmar Kekkonen was the first commander of the Draeling Mercenary Division. Could anyone so brilliant act so stupidly?" Her flat sarcasm became honest anger. "I did my part, sir! Your appearance on Shima was undetected. But since you arrived you've been so 'noisy' that nothing could disguise your presence from my superiors in Earthpol."

Ah, so this was the cop Samuelson had bought. I should have guessed. She seemed typical of the egotistical squirts Earthpol uses. "Listen, Miss Whoever-you-are, I was thoroughly briefed. I've worn native textiles, I've eaten the stuff they call food here, I've even washed in gunk that makes me *smell* like a local. Look at this place—I don't have a single scrap of comfort."

"Well then, what is that?" She pointed at the coruscating pile of my 'mam'ri.

"You know damn well what it is. I told you I've been briefed. I've only used it on a Hammel base. Without that much analysis, the job would take years."

"Professor Kekkonen, you have been briefed by fools. We in the Earth Police can detect such activity easily—even from the other side of Shima." She began refastening the black robe. "Come with us now." You can always spot Earthgov types; the imperative is their favorite mode.

I sat down, propped my heels on the edge of the lab bench. "Why?" I asked mildly. Earthgov people irritate easy, too. Her face turned even paler as I spoke.

"It may be that Miss Tsumo hasn't made things clear, sir." I did a double take. It was the cop's native driver speaking English. The gook's accent was perfect, though he spoke half again as fast as a human would. It was as if some malevolent Disney had put the voice of Donald Duck in the mouth of a shark.

"Professor, you are here working for a group of the greatest Shiman governments. Twenty minutes ago, Miss Tsumo's managers made discovery of this fact. At any minute the Earth Police will order our governments to give you up. Our people all want to help you, but they have knowledge of the power of Earth. They will attempt to do what they are ordered. For the next five minutes, I have authority to take you from here—but— after that it will probably be too late."

The gook made a hell of a lot more sense than the Tsumo character. The sooner we holed up someplace new, the better. I swung my feet off the bench and grabbed the heavy black robe Tsumo held out to me. She kept silent, her face expressionless. I've met Earthcops before. In their own way, some of them are imaginative—even likeable. But this creature had all the personality of a five-day-old corpse.

The native driver turned to my guards and began whistling. They called in some ranking officer who inspected a sheaf of papers the driver had with him. I had just finished with the robe and veil combination when the commanding officer waved us all toward the door. We piled down the stairs and through the exit. Outside, there was no activity beyond the usual sentries that patrolled the perimeter.

As the driver entered the blue and orange car, I crawled onto the narrow bench behind the front seat. The car sank under my weight. I mass nearly one hundred kilos and that's a lot more than the average Shiman. The driver turned the ignition, and the kerosene-eating engine turned over a couple of times, died. Tsumo got into the front seat and shut the door.

Still no alarms.

I wiped the sweat from my forehead and looked out the grimy window. Shima's sun had set behind the smog bank but here and there across the city lingered small patches of gold where the sun's rays fell directly on the ground. Something was moving through the sky from the south. A native aircraft? But Shiman fliers all had wings. The cigar-shaped flier moved rapidly toward the city. Its surface was studded with turrets—vaguely reminiscent of the gun blisters on a Mitchell bomber. God, this place brought back memories. The vehicle crossed a patch of sunlit ground. Its shadow was at least two thousand meters long.

I tapped Tsumo on the shoulder and pointed at

the object that now hovered over the estuary beyond the city.

She glanced briefly into the sky, then turned to the native. "Sirbat," she said. "Hurry. Earthpol is already here." Sirbat—if that was the native's name—twisted the starter again and again. Finally the engine kicked over and stayed lit. Somehow all those whirling pieces of metal meshed and we were rolling toward the main gate. Sirbat leaned forward and punched a button on the dash. It was the car radio. The voice from the speaker was more resonant, more deliberate than is usual with Shimans.

Sirbat said, "The voice says, 'See the power of Earth over your city.'" The speaker paused as if to give everyone time to look up and see the airborne scrap heap over the estuary. Tsumo twisted about to face me. "That's the Earthpol 'flagship'. We tried to imagine what the Shimans would view as the warcraft of an advanced technology, and that's what we came up with. In a way, it's impressive."

I grunted. "Only a demented two-year-old could be impressed." Sirbat hissed, his lips curling back from his fangs. He had no chance to speak though, because we were rapidly coming up on the main gate. Sirbat slammed on the brakes. I was leaning against the front dash when we finally screeched to a stop beside the armored vehicle which guarded the gateway's steel doors.

Sirbat waved his papers out the window, and screamed impatiently. The turret man on the tank had aimed his machine gun at us, but I noticed he was looking back over his shoulder at the Earthpol flagship. The gunner's lips were peeled back in anger—or fear. Perhaps the floating mountain *was* somehow awesome to the Shiman psyche. I tried briefly to remember how I had felt about aircraft, back before the turn of the millennium.

Tsumo unobtrusively turned off the car radio, as a guard came over and snatched the clearance papers from Sirbat. The two natives began arguing over the authorization. From the tank, I could hear another radio. It wasn't the voice from the flagship. This sounded agitated and entirely Shiman. Apparently Earthpol was broadcasting on selected civilian frequencies. Score one against their side. If we could just get past this checkpoint before Earthpol made its ultimatum.

The guard waved to the tank pilot, who disappeared inside his vehicle. Ahead of us electric motors whined and the massive steel door swung back. Our sports car was already blasting forward as Sirbat reached out of the window and plucked his authorization from the guard's claws.

The city's streets were narrow, crowded, but Sirbat zipped our car from lane to lane like we were the only car around. Worst of all, Sirbat was the most conservative driver in that madhouse. I haven't moved so fast since the last time I was on skis. The buildings to right and left were a dirty gray blur. Ahead of us, though, things stood still long enough to get some sort of perspective. We were heading downtown—toward the river. Over the roofs of the tenements, and through a maze of wires and antennas, I could still see the bulk of the Earthpol flagship.

I grabbed wildly for support as the car screeched diagonally through an intersection. Seconds later we crashed around another corner and I could see all the way to the edge of the estuary.

Sirbat summarized the Earthpol announcement coming from the car radio. "He says he's Admiral Ohara—"

"—that would be Sergeant Oharasan," said Tsumo.

"—and he orders Berelesk to turn over the person-eater and doer of crimes, Hjalmar Kekkonen. If not, destruction will come from the sky."

Several seconds passed. Then the entire sky flashed red. Straight ahead that color was eye-searingly bright as a threadlike ray of red-whiteness flickered from flagship to bay. A shockwave-driven cloud of steam exploded where the beam touched water. Sirbat applied the brakes and we ran up over the curb, finally came to a stop against a utility pole. The shock wave was visible as it whipped up the canyon of the street. It smashed over our car, shattering the front windshield.

Even before the car shuddered to a stop, Sirbat was out. And Tsumo wasn't far behind. The Shiman quickly ripped the identification tags from the rear windshield and replaced them with—counterfeits?

In those seconds the city was quiet, Earthpol's gentle persuasion still echoing through the minds of its inhabitants. Tsumo looked up and down the street. "I hope you see now why we had to run. By now the city and national armies are probably on the hunt for us. Once cowed, the Shimans are dedicated in their servility."

I pulled the black veil of my robe more tightly down over my head and swore. "So? What now? This place can't be more than four kilometers from the lab. We're still dead ducks."

Tsumo frowned. "Dead—ducks?" she said. "What dialect do you speak?"

"English, damn it!" Youngsters are always complaining about my language.

Sirbat hustled around the rear of the sports car to the sidewalk. "Go quick," he said and grasped my wrist with bone-crushing force. "I hear police coming." As we ran toward a narrow alley, I glanced up the street. The place was right out of the dark ages. I'd like to take some of these young romantics and stuff them into a real, old-fashioned slum like that one. The buildings were better than three stories high, and crushed up against each other. Windows and tiny balconies competed in endless complication for open air. Fresh-laundered rags hung from lines stretched between the buildings—to become filthy in the sooty air. The stench of garbage was the only detail the scene seemed to lack.

The moment of stunned shock passed. Some Shimans ran wildly around while others sat and gnawed at the curbing. This was panic, and it made their previous behavior look tame. The buildings were emptying, and the screams of the trampled went right through the walls. If we had been just ten meters farther away from that alley, we'd never have made it.

We huddled near the end of the hot cramped alley amid the crumbling remains of a couple of skeletons, and listened to the cries from beyond. Now I could hear the police sirens, too—at least that's what I assumed the bass *boohoohoo* to be. I turned my head and saw that it was just centimeters from the saurian immensity of Sirbat's fangs.

The Shiman spoke. "You may be all right. At one time I had good knowledge of this part of the city. There is a place we may use long enough for you to make good on your agreement with Shima." I opened my mouth to tell this nightmare he was an idiot if he thought I could make progress with nothing more than paper and pencil. But he was already running back the way we had come. I glanced at Tsumo. She sat motionless against the rotting wall of the alley. Her face wasn't visible behind the thick veil, but I could imagine the flat, hostile glare in her gray eyes. The look that sank a thousand ships.

I drew the sticker from my sleeve and tested its edge. There was no telling who would come back for us. I wouldn't have put anything past our toothy friend—and Earthpol was as bad.

What a screwed-up mess. Why had I ever let Samuelson persuade me to leave New London? A guy could get killed here.

Sunrise. The disk blazed pale orange through the fog, and momentarily the world seemed clean, bright.

Silence. For those few seconds the muted sounds of the city died. The sun's warmth pressed upon the ground, penetrated the moist turf, and brought a call of life—and death—to those below.

The Shimans stood tense, and the silence stretched on: Ten seconds. Twenty. Thirty. Then:

A faint wail. The sound was joined by another, and another, till a hundred voices, all faint but together loud, climbed through the register and echoed off nearby hills.

The dying had discovered their mouths.

Near the middle of the green field, one cross among the thousands wavered and fell.

It was the first.

The fog blurred the exact form of the grayish creatures that spilled from the newly opened graves. As grave after grave burst open, the wailing screams died and a new sound grew—the low, buzzing hum of tiny jaws opening and closing, grinding and tearing. The writhing gray mass spread toward the edge of the field, and the ground it passed over was left brown, bare. A million mouths. They ate anything green, anything soft—each other. The horde reached the hedgework. There it split into a hundred feelers that searched back and forth through the intricate twisting of the maze. Where the hedge wall was narrow or low, the mouths began to eat their way through.

A command was given, and all along the crest of

*the hill the machine scatterguns whirred, spraying a
dozen streams of birdshot down on those points where
the horde was breaking out. The poisoned shot killed
instantly, by the thousands. And tens of thousands
were attracted by the newly dead into the field of
fire.*

*Only the creatures which avoided the simplest
branches of the maze escaped death by nerve poison.
And most of those survivors ran blindly into dead
ends, where claymore mines blasted their bodies apart.*

*Only the smartest, fastest thousand of the original
million reached the upper end of the maze. These
had grown fat since they climbed from their fathers'
graves, yet they still moved forward faster than a
man can walk. Not a blade of grass survived their
passage.*

I'll say one thing about my stay on Shima: it cured
me once and for all of any nostalgia I had felt for
pre-millennium Earth. Shima had the whole bag: the
slums, the smog, the overpopulation, the starvation—
and now this. I looked down from our hiding place at
the congregation standing below. The Shimans sang
from hymnals, and their quacking was at once alien
and familiar.

On the dais near the front of the room was a
podium—an altar, I should say. The candelabra on
the altar cast its weak light on the immense wooden
cross that stood behind it.

It took me all the way back to Chicago, circa
1940—when a similar scene had been weekly ritual.
Funny, that was one bit of nostalgia I had never
wished to part with. But after seeing those shark-
faced killers mouthing the same chants, I knew the
past would never seen the same. The hymn ended
but the congregation remained standing. Outside I
could hear the night traffic—and the occasional rum-

ble of military vehicles. The city was not calm. A million tons of hostile metal still sat in their sky.

Then the "minister" walked rapidly to the altar. The crowd moaned softly. He was dressed all in black, and I swear he had a clerical collar hung around the upper portion of his neckless body.

Tsumo shifted her weight, her thigh resting momentarily against mine. Our friend Sirbat had hidden us in this cramped space above the hall. He was supposedly negotiating with the reverends for better accommodations. The Earthpol girl peered through the smoked glass which shielded us from the congregations's view, and whispered, "Christianity is popular on Shima. A couple of Catholic Evangels introduced the cult here nearly two centuries ago. I suppose any religion with a Paul would have sufficed, but the Shimans never invented one of their own."

Below us, the parishioners settled back in their pews as the minister began some sort of speech—and that sounded kind of familiar, too. I glanced back at Tsumo's shadowed face. Her long blond hair glinted pale across her shoulders.

"Kekkonen," she continued, "do you know why Earthgov has quarantined Shima?"

An odd question. "Uh, they've made the usual 'cultural shock' noises but it's obvious they're just scared of the competition these gooks could provide, given a halfway decent technology. I'm not worried. Earthgov has never put enough store by human ingenuity and guts."

"Your problem, Professor Doctor, is that you can think of competition only on an economic level: a strange failing for one who considers himself so rough and tough. Look down there. Do you see those two at the end of the pew fight to hold the collection tray?"

The Shimans tugged the plate back and forth,

snarling. Finally, the larger of the two raked his claws across the other's face, opening deep red cuts. Shorty squealed and released the plate. The victor ponderously drew a fat wallet from his blouse and dropped several silver slugs into the tray, then passed it down the row, away from his adversary. Those near the struggle gave it their undivided attention, while from the front of the hall the minister droned on.

"Are you familiar with the Shiman life cycle, Professor." It was a statement.

"Certainly." And a most economical system it was. From birth the creatures lived to eat—anything and everything. Growing from a baby smaller than your fist, in less than two years the average Shiman massed sixty kilograms. Twenty-one months after birth a thousand embryos would begin to develop in his combined womb/ovary—no sex was necessary for this to happen, though occasionally the Shimans did exchange genetic material through conjugation. For the next three months the embryos developed in something like the normal mammalian fashion, drawing nourishment from the parent's circulatory system. When the fetuses were almost at term the womb filled most of the adult's torso, absorbed most of the adult's food intake. Finally—and I still didn't understand the timing mechanism, since it seemed to depend on external factors—the thousand baby Shimans ate their way out of the parent, and began their own careers.

"Then you know that parricide and genocide are a way of life with these monsters. Earthgov is not the stupid giant you imagine, Professor. The challenge Shima presents us transcends economics. The Shimans are very much like locusts, yet their average intelligence is far greater than ours. In another century they will be our technological equal. You entrepre-

neurs will lose more than profits dealing with them—
you'll be exterminated. The Shimans have only one
natural disadvantage and that is their short life span.
In twenty-four months, even *they* can't learn enough
to coordinate their genius." Her whisper became
soft, taut. "If you succeed, Professor, we will have
lost the small chance we have for survival."

Miss Iceberg was blowing her cool. "Hell, Tsumo,
I thought you were on our side. You're taking our
money, anyway. If you're really so in love with
Earthgov policy, why don't you blow the whistle on
me?"

The Earthpol agent was silent for nearly a minute.
At first I thought she was watching the services
below, but then I noticed her eyes were closed.
"Kekkonen, I had a husband once. He was an
Evangel—a fool. Missionaries were allowed on Shima
up to fifty years ago. That was probably the biggest
mistake that Earthgov has ever made: Before the
Christians came, the Shimans had never been able to
cooperate with one another even to the extent of
developing a language. The only thing they did together was to eat. Since they were faster and deadlier than anything else they would often come near
to wiping out all life on a continent; at which point,
they'd start eating each other and their own population would drop to near zero and stay there for
decades. But then the Christians came and filled
them with notions of sin and self-denial, and now the
Shimans cooperate with each other enough so they
can use their brains for something besides outsmart-
ing their next meal.

"Anyway, Roger was one of the last missionaries.
He really believed his own myths. I don't know if his
philosophies conflicted with Shiman dogma, or if

the monsters were just hungry one day: but my husband never came back."

I almost whistled. "O.K., so you don't like Shimans —but hating them won't bring your husband back. That would take the skills of a million techs and the resources of . . ." My voice petered out as I remembered that that was about the size bribe Samuelson had offered her. "Hm-m-m, I guess I'm getting the picture. You want things both ways: to have your husband back, and to have a little vengeance, too."

"Not vengeance, Professor Doctor. You are just rationalizing your own goals. Remember the things you have seen on Shima: The cannibalism. The viciousness. The constant state of war between the different races of the species. And above all the superhuman intelligence these monsters possess.

"You think it ridiculous for me to accept money on a project I want to fail. But never in a thousand years will I have another chance to make such a fortune— and you know a thousand years is too long. It would be so terribly simple for you to fail. I'm not asking you to give up the rewards promised you. Just make an error that won't be apparent until after the rejuvenation treatments are started and you have been paid."

If nothing else, Tsumo had the gall of ten. She was obviously an idealist: that is, someone who can twist his every vice into self-righteous morality. "You're nearly as ignorant as you are impudent. S.E. won't buy a pig in a poke. I don't get a cent till my process has boosted the Shiman life span past one century." That's the hell of immortality—you can't tell until the day after forever whether you really have the goods. "This is one cat you'll have to skin yourself."

Tsumo shook her head. "I intend to get that bribe, Kekkonen. The human race is second with me. But," she looked up and her voice hardened, "I've studied these creatures. If their life span is increased beyond ten years, there won't be any Samuelson Enterprises to pay you a century from now." Ah, so self-righteous.

The discussion was interrupted as a crack of light appeared in the darkness above us. Sirbat's burred voice came faintly. "We have moved the Bible classes from this part of the building. Come out." The light above silhouetted some curves I hadn't noticed before as Tsumo crawled through the tiny trap. I followed her, groaning. I never did learn what they used that cramped box for. Maybe the reverends spied on their congregations. You could never tell about those cannibals in the back pews.

We followed Sirbat down a low, narrow corridor into a windowless room. Another Shiman stood by a table in the center of the room. He looked skinny compared to our guide.

Sirbat shut the door, and motioned us to chairs by the table. I sat, but it was hardly worth the effort. The seat was so narrow I couldn't relax my legs. Shimans are bottom heavy. They don't really sit—they just lean.

Sirbat made the introductions. "This is Brother Gorst of the Order of Saint Roger. He keeps the rules at this church, by the authority of the Committee in Senkenorn. Gorst's father was probably my teacher in second school." Brother Gorst nodded shyly and the harsh light glinted starkly off his fangs. Our interpreter continued, "For this minute we are safe—from Shiman police and army forces. The Earth Police spaceship is still hanging over the water, but only Miss Tsumo can do anything about that. Gorst will help us, but we may not use these rooms for more than three days. They are needed for church purposes later this eightday. There is another time limit, too. You will not have my help after tomorrow morning. Naturally, Gorst has no knowledge of any Earth languages, so—"

I interrupted, "The devil you say! There's no such thing as half a success in this racket, Sirbat. What's the matter with you?"

The Shiman leaned across the table, his claws raking scratches in its plastic surface. "That is not your business, Worm!" he hissed into my face. Sirbat stared at me for several seconds, his jaws working spasmodically. Finally, he returned to his chair. "You will please take account of this. Things would not be so serious now if you had only given care to the Earthpol danger. If I were you I would be happy that Shima is still willing to take what you have to offer. At this time our governments take Earthpol's orders, but it is safe to say they hope by Christ's name that you are out of danger. Their attempts to get you will not be strong. The greatest danger still comes from *your* people."

The blond Earthpol agent took the cue. "We have at least forty-eight hours before Ohara locates us." She reached into a pocket. "Fortunately I am not so poorly equipped as Professor Kekkonen. This is police issue."

The pile she placed on the table had no definite form—yet was almost alive. A thousand shifting colors shone from within it. Except for its size, her 'mam'ri seemed unremarkable. Tsumo plunged her hand into it, and the device searched slowly across the table. Brother Gorst squeaked his terror, and bolted for the exit. Sirbat spoke rapidly to him, but the skinny Shiman continued to tremble. Sirbat turned to us. "The fact is, it's harder for me to talk with Gorst than with you. His special word knowledge has to do with right and wrong, while my special knowledge is of language. The number of words we have in common is small."

I guess two years isn't much time to learn to talk, read, write and acquire a technical education.

Finally Sirbat coaxed Gorst back to the table. Tsumo continued her spiel. "Don't be alarmed. I'm only checking to see that—" and she lapsed into Japanese. Old English just isn't up to describing modern technology. "That is, I'm making sure that our . . . shield against detection is still working. It is, but even so it doesn't protect us from pre-millennium techniques. So stay away from windows and open places. Also, my *o-mamori* can't completely protect us against—" She looked at me, puzzled. "How can I explain *fun*, Professor?"

"Hm-m-m. Sirbat, Earthpol has a weapon which could be effective against us even if we stay hidden."

"A gas?" the Shiman asked.

"No, it's quite insubstantial. Just imagine that . . . hell, that's no good. About the best I can say is that it amounts to a massive dose of bad luck. If the breaks run consistently against us, I'd guess *fun* might be involved."

Sirbat was incredulous, but he relayed my clumsy description on to Gorst, who seemed to accept the idea immediately.

Finally Sirbat spoke in English. "What an interesting thing. With this 'fa-oon' you no longer need to be responsible for your shortcomings. We used to have things like that, but now we poor Shimans are weighted down by reason and science."

Sarcasm yet! "Don't accuse *us* of superstition, Sirbat. You people are clever but you have a long way to catch up. In the last two centuries, mankind has achieved every material goal that someone at your level could even *state* in a logical way. And we've gone on from there. The methods—even the methodology—of Tsumo's struggle with Earthpol would be unimaginable to you, but I assure you that if she weren't protecting us, we would have been captured hours ago." I touched the police-issue *'mam'ri*. In addition to being our only defense against Earthpol, it was also my only hope for finishing my biological analysis of the Shimans. Apparently, the Earthpol agent really meant to keep her part of the bargain with Samuelson *et al*. Perhaps she thought I would foul things up *for* her. Fat chance.

"Before things blew up, I was pretty close to success. Only one real problem was left. Death for a Shiman isn't the sort of metabolic collapse we see in most other races. In a way you die backwards. If I'm gonna crack this thing, I've got to observe death firsthand."

Sirbat was silent for a long moment. It was the first time I'd seen a Shiman in a reflective mood. Finally he said, "As you have knowledge, Professor, we Shimans come to birth in great groups. The fact is that those who first saw life seven hundred and nine days before now will give up living tomorrow." He turned and spoke to Brother Gorst. The other bobbed his head and buzzed a response. Sirbat translated, "There is a death place only three kilometers from here. It is necessary for people of Gorst's Order to be on hand at the time of the group deaths. Brother Gorst says that he is willing to take you there. But it will not be possible for you to get nearer than fifty or sixty meters to the place of the deaths."

"That'll be fine," I said. "Fifteen minutes is all I need."

"Then this is a very happy chance, Professor. If it was not for the group death tomorrow, you would have to take nine more days here." As he spoke, a caterwauling rose from below us. Moments later someone was pounding at our door. Gorst scuttled over and opened it a crack. There was a hysterical consultation, then the reverend slammed the door and screamed at our interpreter.

"Christ help us!" said Sirbat. "There has been a smash out at the second school two kilometers from here. A large group of young is coming this way."

Gorst came back to his chair, then bounded up and paced around the room. From the way he chewed his lip, I guessed he was unhappy about the situation. Sirbat continued, "We have to make the decision of running or not running from the young persons."

"Are there any other hideouts you could dig up in this area?" I asked.

"No. Gorst is the only living person I have knowledge of in this place."

"Hm-m-m. Then I guess we'll just have to stay put."

Sirbat came to his feet. "You have little knowledge of Shiman conditions, Professor, or you wouldn't make that decision quite so easily. It is too bad. You are probably right. Our chances are near zero, one way or the other, but . . ." He snarled something at the other Shiman. Brother Gorst replied shortly. Sirbat said, "My friend is in agreement with you. We'll be safest at the top of the building." Gorst was already out the door. Tsumo scooped her 'mam'ri off the table, and we followed. A spiral stairway climbed twenty meters to end on a flat roof no more than ten meters square. A cross towered over the open space.

It was well past midnight. Below and around us were the sounds of running feet and automobile engines being lit. The cars screeched away from their parking slots, and headed west. One by one the lights in nearby buildings went out. The traffic got steadily noisier. Then after five or ten minutes, it subsided and the neighborhood was still.

The church spire reached several stories above the

nearby buildings, and from there we could see
Berelesk spread many kilometers, a mosaic of rough
gray rectangles. Shima's single moon had risen and
its light fell silver on the city. Near the horizon
bomb flashes shone through the thinning smog, and
I could hear the faint *thudadub* of artillery. Berelesk
wasn't on good terms with its neighbors.

Tsumo pulled at my arm. I turned. Vast, blue, the
glowing Earthpol ship hung above the bay. I jerked
my outfit's dark veil down across my face. It wouldn't
matter how good Tsumo's equipment was if her superiors actually eye-balled us.

Gorst hustled over to the low parapet, and leaned
out to look straight down. At the same time, Sirbat
studied the empty streets and quiet tenements. Finally I whispered, "So where's the action, Sirbat?"

The Shiman glanced at the Earthpol ship, then
sidled over to us. "Don't you see why things are so
quiet, Professor? More than three thousand children
are free in this part of Berelesk. And they are coming
our way. Everyone with any brain has run away from
here. Children will eat everything they see, and it
would be death to fight them: they run together and
they are very bright. In the end, they will be so full
that the authorities can take care of them one by
one. We are probably the only living older persons
within three kilometers—and that makes us the biggest pieces of food around."

Tsumo stood behind me, close to the cross. She
ignored us both as she played with her *'mam'ri*.
From the parapet Brother Gorst shrilled softly. "Gorst
is hearing them come," Sirbat translated. I turned to
look east. There were faint sounds of traffic and
artillery, but nothing else.

Several blocks away something bright lit the sides
of facing buildings. There was a muffled, concussive

thud. Sirbat and Gorst hissed in pain. The fire burned
briefly, then gutted out: the slums of Berelesk were
mostly stone—nonflammable, and much more important, inedible. Smoke rose into the sky, blocked
the moonlight and laid twisting shadows on the city.

Far away, something laughed, and someone screamed.
Voices growled and squabbled. Whatever they were,
they seemed to be having a good time. Four blocks
up the pike, a street lamp winked out, and there was
the sound of breaking glass. In the moonlight the
juveniles were fast-moving gray shadows that flitted
from doorway to doorway. The little bastards were
smart. They never exposed themselves unnecessarily
and they systematically smashed every street lamp
they passed. I didn't see anyone run across the street
until their skirmish line was nearly even with our
church. Behind those front lines more were coming.
[How big was the grade school, anyway?] Their luna-
tic screaming was all around us now. Tsumo looked
up from her work, for the first time acknowledging
our trivial problems. "Sirbat, aren't we safe from
them here? We're so far above the street."

The Shiman made a rude noise, but it was a soft
rude noise. "They will smell us even up here, and
don't doubt they will come this high. We're the best
food left. I wouldn't be surprised if the greater part
of the young people are there in the church right
now eating the wood seats and giving thought to our
downfall."

Feet pattered around below us, and I heard a low,
bubbly chuckle. I leaned over the parapet and looked
down on the church's main roof. A chorus of eager
shouts greeted my appearance, and something whistled up past my face. I ducked back, but I had
already seen more than enough. There was a mob of
them dancing on the deck below us. They were so
close I could see the white of their fangs and the

drool foaming down their chins. Except that they were near naked, the juveniles looked pretty much like adult Shimans.

Was there any real difference?

Tsumo might have a point after all—but that point would be entirely academic unless we could get out of this fix in one piece.

Gorst stood a meter behind the parapet with a quarterstaff in his claws. The first head that popped up would get a massive surprise. Sirbat paced back and forth, either panicking or thoughtful, I couldn't tell which. How long did we have before the juveniles came up the wall of the steeple? It was maddening: Properly used, Tsumo's *o-mamori* could easily defeat this attack, but at the same time such use would certainly put Earthpol onto our location. I looked around our tiny roof. There was unidentifiable equipment in the shadows beneath the parapet. Memories of a life two centuries past were coming back, and so were some ideas. The largest object, an ellipsoidal tank, sat near the base of the cross. A slender hose led from a valve on the tank. Half crouching, I ran across to the tank and felt its surface. The tank was cool, and the valve was covered with frost.

"Sirbat," I shouted over the competition from below, "What's this gadget?" The Shiman stopped his agonized pacing and glared at me briefly, then shouted at Gorst.

"That's a vessel of liquid natural gas," he translated the reply. "They use it to heat the church, and to . . . cook."

I looked at Sirbat and he looked back at me. I think he had the idea the instant he knew what the tank was. He came over to the tank and looked at the valve. I turned to follow the hose that stretched along the floor to a hole in the parapet.

"Kekkonen!" Tsumo's voice was tense. "If you attract Earthpol's notice, that disguise won't hold up." Over my shoulder I could see the glowing hulk of the gunboat. "Forget it, girl. If I can't do something with this tank, we'll all be dead in five minutes." Probably less: the juveniles were much louder now. We'd have to hope that if anyone was aboard the ship, they didn't believe in old-fashioned detection methods—like photoscanning computers.

The hose was slack and flexible. Four meters from the tank it entered a small valve set in the parapet. I began cutting at it with my knife. Behind me Sirbat said, "This looks good. The vessel is nearly full and its pressure is high." There were tearing sounds. "And it will get higher now."

That hose was tougher than it looked. It took nearly a minute, but finally I hacked through the thing. As I stood up, a head full of teeth appeared over the parapet next to me. I straight-armed the juvenile. It fell backwards, taking part of my sleeve in its claws. We were down to seconds now. I looked down at the hose in my hands and discovered the big flaw in our plan. How were we going to get this thing lit? Then I glanced at Sirbat. The Shiman was frantically jamming his coat under the tank. He stepped back and pointed something at the tank. A spark fell upon the coat, and soon yellow flames slid up the underside of the container. Even as those flames spread, he turned and ran to where I stood. But then he slowed, stopped, looked down at the object in his hand. For a long moment he just stood there.

"What's the matter? The lighter dead?"

". . . No." Sirbat answered slowly. He squeezed the small metal tube and a drop of fire spurted from the end. I swore and grabbed the lighter from Sirbat's hands. I leaned over the parapet and looked down. At least thirty juveniles were coming up the wall at us. Behind me Tsumo screamed. This was followed by a meaty thud. I looked up to see the Earthpol agent swing a long broom down on the head of a second monster. I guess she had finally found something more worrisome than her superiors in the sky to the west. Gorst was busy, too. He swept back and forth along the parapet with his quarterstaff. I saw him connect at least three times. The juveniles fell screeching to the roof below. Maybe that would occupy their brothers' appetites a few more moments.

I pushed our interpreter toward the gas tank. "Turn that damn valve, Sirbat." The Shiman returned to the tank. Now the flames licked up around the curving sides, keeping the valve out of reach. He ran to the other side of the cross, picked up some kind of rod and stuck it in the valve handle.

"Turn it, turn it," I shouted. Sirbat hesitated, then gave the lever a pull. No effect. He twisted the valve again. The hose bucked in my hand, as clear liquid spewed through it and arced out into space. That hose got *cold:* I could feel my hand going numb even as I stood there. I squeezed the lighter. A tiny particle of fire spurted out, missed the stream of gas. On my next try the burning droplet did touch the stream. Nothing happened.

I wrapped the hose in the corner of my jacket but it was still colder than a harlot's smile. This was probably my last chance to ignite the damn thing. Our gas pressure would fail soon enough, even if the juveniles didn't get me first.

The liquid gas left the hose as a coherent stream, but about five meters along its arc, the fluid began to mix with the air. Hah! I shook the lighter again and aimed it further out. The burning speck dropped through the aerated part of the stream. . . . The mist didn't burn—it exploded. I almost lost my footing as a roaring ball of blue-white flame materialized in the air five meters from the end of the hose. If that fireball had been any bigger we'd have been blown right off the roof. I pointed the hose down over the parapet. The roar of the flame masked their screams, but as I swept the fire along the wall below, I could see the juveniles fall away. The concussion alone must have been lethal. As I dragged the hose along the parapet, I could feel my face blister and my hands go numb. How long did I have before we ran out of gas, or even worse, before Sirbat's little fire exploded the tank? The ball of blue flame swept across the fourth wall, till no one was left there, till the wall was cracked and blackened. The roof and street below were littered with bodies.

Then Tsumo was dragging at my arm. I turned to see five or six gray forms leap from the trapdoor in the middle of our roof. I didn't have much choice: I turned the hose inward. Hunks of masonry flew past us as the exploding gas demolished the intruders along with the trapdoor, the center of the roof, and part of the cross. The floor buckled and I fell to one knee. That hose was some tiger's tail. If I dropped it, the top of the building would probably get blown off. Finally I managed to twist it around so the steam pointed outward again.

The explosion ended almost as suddenly as it had begun. All that was left was a ringing that roared in my ears. I was abruptly aware of the sweat dripping down the side of my nose, and the taste of dust and blood in my mouth. I dropped the hose and looked down at my numb hands. Was it the moonlight, or were they really bone white?

Over by the gas tank, Sirbat was busy putting out the fire he had set. He looked O.K. except that his

clothes were shredded. Tsumo stood by the parapet.
Her veil and one sleeve had been ripped away.
Brother Gorst lay face down beside the large hole
our makeshift flamethrower had put in the roof. If
anything was left alive in that hole, it was downright
unkillable.

The ringing faded from my ears, and I could hear
low-pitched sirens in the far distance. But I couldn't
hear a single juvenile, and the smell of barbecue
floated up from the street.

Sirbat nudged Gorst with his foot. The other's
clawed hand lashed out, barely missing our interpreter. The reverend sat up and groaned. Sirbat
glanced at us. "You all right?" he asked.

I grunted something affirmative, and Tsumo nodded. An ugly bruise covered her jaw and cheek, and
four deep scratches ran down her arm. She followed
my glance. "Never mind, I'll live." She pulled the
'mam'ri from her pocket. "You'll be pleased to know
that this has survived. What do we do now?"

It was Sirbat who answered. "Same as before.
We'll stay here this night. Tomorrow you'll be able
to see the group death you're so interested in." He
moved cautiously to the edge of the hole. The moon
was overhead now, and the damage was clearly visible. The room directly below us was gutted, and its
floor was partly burned through. The room below
that looked pretty bad, too. "First, we have to get
some way to go down through this hole."

Brother Gorst rolled onto his feet and looked briefly
at the destruction below. Then he ran to a small
locker near the edge of the roof. He pulled out a coil
of rope and threw it to Sirbat, who tied one end
about the cross. Our interpreter moved slowly, almost clumsily. I looked closely at him, but in the
moonlight he seemed uninjured. Sirbat pulled at the

rope, making sure it was fast. Then he tossed the other end into the hole. "If past experience is a guide," he said, "we won't have any more trouble this night. The young persons fight very hard, but they are bright and when they have knowledge that their chances are zero, they go away. Also, they fear flames more than any other thing." He turned and slowly lowered himself hand over hand into the darkness. The rest of us followed.

My hands weren't numb anymore. The rope felt like a brand on them. I slipped and fell the last meter to the floor. I stood up to see the two Shimans and Tsumo standing nearby. The Earthpol agent was fiddling with the *o-mamori*, trying to reestablish our cover.

What was left of the roof above us blocked the Earthpol ship from view. Through the jagged hole, the full moon spread an irregular patch of gray light on the wreckage around us. The floor had buckled and cracked under the explosion. Several large fragments from a marble table top rested near my feet. As my eyes became accustomed to the darkness, I could also see what was left of the juveniles who had used this route to surprise us on the roof. The room was a combination abattoir and ruin.

Gorst moved quickly to the west wall, dug into the rubble. His rummaging uncovered a ladder well: we wouldn't have to use that rope again. Brother Gorst bent over and crawled down into the hole he had uncovered. All this time Sirbat just stood looking at the floor. Gorst called to him, and he walked slowly over to the ladder.

I was right above Tsumo as we climbed down. Her progress was clumsy, slow. It was a good thing the rungs were set only fifteen centimeters apart. A single beam of moonlight found its way over my shoulder and onto those below me.

If I hadn't been looking in just the right spot, I could have missed what happened then. A screaming fury hurtled out of the darkness. Gorst, who was already on the floor below us, whirled at the sound, his claws extended. Then just before the juvenile struck, he lowered his arms, stood defenseless. Gorst paid for his stupidity as the juvenile slammed into him, knocking him flat. He was dead even before he touched ground: his throat was ripped out. Now the juvenile headed for us on the ladder.

A reflex three centuries old took over, and my knife was out of my sleeve and in my hand. I threw just before the creature reached Sirbat. One thing I knew was Shiman anatomy. Still, it was mostly luck that the knife struck the only unarmored section of its notochord. My fingers were just too ripped up for accurate throwing. The juvenile dived face first into the base of the ladder and lay still. For a long moment the rest of us were frozen, too. If more were coming, we didn't have a chance. But the seconds passed and no other creatures appeared. The three of us scrambled down to the floor. As I retrieved my knife, I noticed that the corpse's flesh was practically parboiled. The juvenile must have been too shook up by the explosion to run off with the rest of the pack.

Sirbat walked past Gorst's body without looking down at it. "Come on," he said. You'd think I had just threatened his life rather than saved it.

This was the first level where the main stairs were still intact. We followed Sirbat down them, into the darkness. I couldn't see a thing, and the stairs were littered with crap that had fallen in from the disaster area above us. Either Sirbat was a fool or he had some special reason to think we were safe. Finally, we reached a level where the electric lights were still working. Sirbat left the stairway, and we walked down a long, deserted corridor. He stopped at a half-open door, sniffed around, then stepped through the doorway and flicked on a light. "I have no doubt you'll be safe here for this night."

I looked inside. A bas relief forest had been cut in the walls and then painted green. Three wide cots were set near the middle of the room—on the only carpet I ever saw on Shima. And what did they use the place for? You got me.

But whatever its purpose, the room looked secure. A grated window was set in one wall—nothing was going to surprise us from that direction. And the door was heavy plastic with an inside lock.

Tsumo stepped into the room. "You're not staying with us?" she asked Sirbat.

"No. That would not be safe." He was already walking from the room. "Just keep memory, that you have to be up two hours before sunrise in order to get to the death place on time. Have your . . . machines ready."

The arrogant bastard! What was "safe" for us was not safe enough for him. I followed the Shiman into the hall, debating whether to shake some answers out of him. But there were two good arguments against such action: 1) he might end up shaking me, and 2) unless we wanted to turn ourselves over to Earthpol, we didn't have any choice but to play things his way. So I stepped back into the room and slammed the door. The lock fell to with a satisfying thunk.

Tsumo sat down heavily on one of the cots and pulled the *'mam'ri* from its pouch. She played awkwardly with it for several seconds. In the bright blue light, her bruise was a delicate mauve. Finally she looked up. "We're still undetected. But what happened tonight is almost certainly *fun*. There hasn't been a smashout from that particular school in nearly three years. If we stay here much longer, our . . . 'bad luck' is going to kill us."

I grunted. Tsumo was at her cheery best. "In that case, I'll need a good night's sleep. I don't want to have to do that job twice." I hit the light and settled down on the nearest bunk. Faint bands of gray light crossed the ceiling from the tiny window. The shadowed forest on the wall almost seemed real now.

Tomorrow was going to be tricky. I would be using unfamiliar equipment—Tsumo's *mam'ri*—out-of-doors and at a relatively great distance from the dying. Even an orgy of death would be hard to analyze under those conditions. And all the time, we'd have Earthpol breathing down our necks. Several details needed thorough thinking out, but every time I tried to concentrate on them, I'd remember those juveniles scrambling up the church steeple at us. Over the last couple of centuries I'd had contact with three nonhuman races. The best competition I'd come across were the Draelings—carnivores with creative intelligence about 0.8 the human norm. I had never seen a group whose combined viciousness and cunning approached man's. Until now: the Shimans *started* life by committing a murder. The well-picked skeletons in the alley showed the murders didn't stop with birth. The average human would have to practice hard to be as evil as a Shiman is by inclination.

Tsumo's voice came softly from across the room. She must have been reading my mind. "And they're smart, too. See how much Sirbat has picked up in less than two years. He could go on learning at that rate for another century—if only he could live that long. The average is as inventive as our best. Fifty years ago there wasn't a single steam engine on

Shima. And you can be sure we in Earthgov didn't help them invent one."

In the pale light I saw her stand and cross to my bunk. Her weight settled beside me. My frostbitten hand moved automatically across her back.

"Money is no good if you are dead—and we'll all die unless you fail tomorrow." A soft hand slipped across my neck and I felt her face in front of mine.

She tried awfully hard to convince me. Toward the end, there in the darkness, I almost felt sorry for little Miss Machiavelli. She kept calling me Roger.

Someone was shaking me. I woke to find Tsumo's face hovering hazily in the air above me. I squinted against the hellishly bright light, and muttered, "Whassamatter?"

"Sirbat says it's time to go to the cemetery."

"Oh." I swung my feet to the floor, and raised myself off the bunk. My hands felt like hunks of flayed meat. I don't know how I was able to sleep with them. I steadied myself against the bed and looked around. The window was a patch of unrelieved darkness in the wall. We still had a way to go before morning. Tsumo was dressed except for hood and veil, and she was pushing my costume at me.

I took the disguise. "Where the devil is Sirbat, anyway?" Then I saw him over by the door. On the floor. The Shiman was curled up in a tight ball. His bloodshot eyes roved aimlessly about, finally focused on me.

My jaw must have been resting on my chest. Sirbat croaked, "So, Professor, you have been getting knowledge of Shiman life all this time, but you did not ever take note of my condition. If it wasn't for the special substances I've been taking I would have been like this days ago." He stopped, coughed reddish foam.

O.K., I had been an idiot. The signs had all been there: Sirbat's relative plumpness, his awkward slowness the last few hours, his comments about not being with us after the morning. My only excuse is the fact that death by old age had become a very theoretical thing to me. Sure, I studied it, but I hadn't been confronted with the physical reality for more than a century.

But one oversight was enough: I could already see a mess of consequences ahead. I slipped the black dress over my head and put on the veil. "Tsumo, take Sirbat's legs. We'll have to carry him downstairs." I grabbed Sirbat's shoulders and we lifted together. The Shiman must have massed close to seventy-five kilos—about fifteen over the average adult's weight. If he had been on drugs to curb the burrowing instinct, he might die before we got him to the cemetery—and that would be fatal all the way around. Now we had a new reason for getting to that cemetery on time.

We hadn't gone down very many steps before Tsumo began straining under the load. She leaned to one side, favoring her left hand. Me, both hands felt like they were ready to fall off, so I didn't have such trouble. Sirbat hung between us, clutching tightly at his middle. His head lolled. His jaws opened with tiny whimpering sounds, and reddish drool dripped down his head onto the steps. It was obviously way past burrowing time for him.

Sirbat gasped out one word at a breath. "Left turn, first story."

Two more flights and we were on the ground. We turned left and staggered out the side door into a parking lot. No one was around this early in the morning. A sea fog had moved in and perfect halos hung around the only two street lamps left alight. It was so foggy we couldn't even see the other side of the lot. For the first time since I'd been on Shima, the air was tolerably clean.

"The red one," said Sirbat. Tsumo and I half dragged the Shiman over to a large red car with official markings. We laid Sirbat on the asphalt and tried the doors. Locked.

"Gorst's opener, in here." His clawed hand jerked upward. I retrieved the keys from his blouse, and opened the door. Somehow we managed to bundle Sirbat into the back seat.

I looked at Tsumo. "You know how to operate this contraption?"

Her eyes widened in dismay. Apparently she had never considered this flaw in our plans. "No, of course not. Do you?"

"Once upon a time, my dear," I said, urging her into the passenger seat, "once upon a time." I settled behind the wheel and slammed the door. These were the first mechanical controls I had seen in a long time, but they were grotesquely familiar. The steering wheel was less than thirty centimeters across (I soon found it was only half a turn from lock to lock). A clutch and shift assembly were mounted next to the wheel. With the help of Sirbat's advice I started the engine and backed out of the parking stall.

The car's triple headlights sent silver spears into the fog. It was difficult to see more than thirty meters into the murk. The only Shiman around was a half-eaten corpse on the sidewalk by the entrance to the parking lot. I eased the car into the street, and Sirbat directed me to the first turn.

This was almost worth the price of admission! It had been a long time since I'd driven any vehicle. The street we were on went straight to the river. I'll bet we were making a hundred kilometers per hour before three blocks were passed.

"Go, go you—" the rest was unintelligible. Sirbat

paused, then managed to say, "We'll be stopped for sure if you keep driving like a sleepwalker." The buildings on either side of the narrow street zipped by too fast to count. Ahead nothing was visible but the brilliant backglow from our headlights. How could a Shiman survive even two years if he drove faster than this? I swerved as something—a truck, I think—whipped out of a side street.

I turned up the throttle. The engine tried to twist off its moorings and the view to the side became a gray blur.

Three or four minutes passed—or maybe it wasn't that long. I couldn't tell. Suddenly Sirbat was screaming, "Left turn . . . two hundred meters more." I slammed on the brakes. Thank God they'd taught him English instead of modern Japanese—which doesn't really have quantitative terms for distance. We probably would have driven right through the intersection before Sirbat would come up with a circumlocution that would tell me how far to go and where to turn. The car skidded wildly across the intersection. Either the street was wet or the Shimans made their brake linings out of old rags. We ended up with our two front wheels over the curb. I backed the car off the sidewalk and made the turn.

Now the going got tough. We had to turn every few blocks and there were some kind of traffic signals I couldn't figure out. That tiny steering wheel was hell to turn. The skin on my hands felt like it was being ripped off. All the time Sirbat was telling me to go faster, faster. I tried. If he died there in the car it would be like getting trapped in a school of piranha.

The fog got thicker, but less uniform. Occasionally we broke into a clear spot where I could see nearly a block. We blasted up a sharply arched bridge, felt a brief moment of near-weightlessness at the top, and then were down on the other side. In the river that was now behind us, a boat whistled.

From the back set, Sirbat's mumbling became coherent English: "Earthman, do you have knowledge . . . how lucky you are?"

"What?" I asked. Was he getting delirious?

Ahead of me the road narrowed, got twisty. We were moving up the ridge that separated the city from the ocean. Soon we were above the murk. In the starlight the fog spread across the lands below, a placid cottony sea that drowned everything but the rocky island we were climbing. Earthpol's gunboat skulked north of us.

Finally Sirbat replied, "Being good is no trouble at all for you. You're . . . born that way. We have to work so . . . hard at it . . . like Gorst. And in the end . . . I'm still as bad . . . as hungry as I ever was. So hungry." His speech died in a liquid gurgle. I risked a look behind me. The Shiman was chewing feebly at the upholstery.

We were out of the city proper now. Far up, near the crest of the ridge, I could see the multiple fences that bounded the cemetery. Even by starlight I could see that the ground around us was barren, deeply eroded.

I pulled down my veil and turned the throttle to full. We covered the last five hundred meters to the open gates in a single burst of speed. The guards waved us through—after all, their job was to keep things from getting *out*—and I cruised into the parking area. There were lots of people around, but fortunately the street lights were dimmed. I parked at the side of the lot nearest the graveyard. We hustled Sirbat out of the car and onto the pavement. The nearest Shimans were twenty meters from us, but when they saw what we were doing they moved even further away, whispered anxiously to each other. We had a live bomb on our hands, and they wanted no part of it.

Sirbat lay on the pavement and stared into the sky. Every few seconds his face convulsed. He seemed to be whispering to himself. Delirious. Finally he said in English, "Tell him . . . I forgive him." The Shiman rolled onto his feet. He paused, quivering, then sprinted off into the darkness. His footsteps faded, and all we could hear were faint scratching sounds and the conversation of Shimans around us in the parking lot.

For a moment we stood silently in the chill, moist air. Then I whispered to Tsumo, "How long?"

"It's about two hours before dawn. I am sure Earthpol will penetrate my evasion patterns in less than three hours. If you stay until the swarming, you'll probably be caught."

I turned and looked across the rising fog bank. There were thirty billion people on this planet, I had been told. Without the crude form of birth control practiced at thousands of cemeteries like this one, there could be many more. And every one of the creatures was intelligent, murderous. If I finished my analysis, then they'd have practical immortality along with everything else, and we'd be facing them in our own space in a very short time . . . which was exactly what Samuelson wanted. In fact, it was the price he had demanded of the Shimans—that their civilization expand into space, so mankind would at last have a worthy competitor. And what if the Shiman brain was as far superior as timid souls like Tsumo claimed? *Well then, we will have to do some imitating, some catching up.* I could almost hear Samuelson's reedy voice speaking the words. Myself, I wasn't as sure: ever since we were kids back in Chicago, Samuelson had been kinda kinky about street-fighting, and about learning from the toughs he fought—me for instance.

"Give me that," I said, taking the *'mam'ri* from Tsumo's hand, and turning it to make my preliminary scan across the cemetery. Whether Samuelson and I were right or wrong, the next century was going to be damned interesting.

The sun's disk stood well clear of the horizon. The mazes and deadfalls and machine guns had taken their toll. Of the original million infants, less than a thousand had survived. They would be weeded no further.

Near the front of the pack, one of the smartest and strongest ran joyfully toward the scent of food ahead—where the first schoolmasters had set their cages. The child lashed happily at those around it, but they were wise and kept their distance. For the moment its hunger was not completely devastating and the sunlight warmed its back. It was wonderful to be alive and free and . . . innocent.

For many years, "Original Sin" was my favorite of all my stories. I thought I had said some important things about basic "human" issues. I liked the tantalizing glimpses of post-Singularity civilization ("remember spaceships?"). I deliberately wrote it without reference to any real technologies beyond 1940—the idea being that 1940 jargon should probably be as accurate as 1970 jargon in explaining the far future. The word-hacker in me was also intrigued by the Basic English vocabulary the aliens used. (It turned out to be surprisingly difficult to write in that vocabulary. Once I saw the Gettysburg address redone in Basic English; it seemed about as eloquent as the original. I didn't realize till writing this story what a feat that was.)

Nevertheless, I had more trouble selling "Original Sin" than almost anything I've written. The early versions were just too cryptic. It bounced and bounced and bounced. But usually the editors liked parts of it, and often they told me what they didn't like. Between the kind advice of Harlan Ellison and Ben Bova, I eventually wrote something that could sell.

*   *   *

I strongly believe that the most realistic hard-science extrapolations of progress lead us to the unknowable in just a few more decades. This is fine, but it makes things difficult for me as a writer of fiction! In my novel Marooned in Realtime *I had a brush with the singularity. After I finished that book, I felt a bit marooned myself. The closer my stories came to the singularity, the shorter the time scales and the less opportunity for the kind of adventure stories that I grew up with. Any future history following these events would be a short run over a cliff, into the abyss . . . with no human-equivalent aliens, no intelligible interstellar civilizations.*

If I wanted to build a future-history series, it seemed that I was stuck with honest extrapolation and a very quick end to human history—or a series that was overtly science-fictional, but secretly a fantasy since it would be based on the absence of the scientific progress that I see coming. I was stuck; the dilemma lasted about two years.

But now I think I have a solution, one that will be faithful to my ideas about progress but which will still allow me to write fiction with human-sized characters and interstellar adventure. In fact, it will let me look at the singularity from many different perspectives. (There are many different ways the singularity could happen, though our world will only see one.)

The solution? Basically I turned my extrapolations sideways, as you will see: The last story in this collection is a test flight into this new future. I hope you like it (since I'd like to do several novels here).

THE BLABBER

Some dreams take a long time in dying. Some get a last-minute reprieve . . . and that can be even worse.

It was just over two klicks from the Elvis revival to the center of campus. Hamid Thompson took the long way, across the Barkers' stubbly fields and through the Old Subdivision. Certainly the Blabber preferred that route. She raced this way and that across Ham's path, rooting at roach holes and covertly watching the birds that swooped close on her seductive calls. As usual, her stalking was more for fun than food. When a bird came within striking distance, the Blab's head would flick up, touching the bird with her nose, blasting it with a peal of human laughter. The Blab hadn't taken this way in some time; all the birds in her regular haunts had wised up, and were no fun anymore.

When they reached the rock bluffs behind the subdivision, there weren't any more roach holes, and the birds had become cautious. Now the Blab walked companionably beside him, humming in her own way: scraps of Elvis overlaid with months-old news commentary. She went a minute or two in silence . . . listening? Contrary to what her detractors might say, she could be both awake and silent for hours at a time—but even then Hamid felt an occasional buzzing in his head, or a flash of pain. The Blab's tympana could emit across a two-hundred-kilohertz band, which meant that most of her mimicry was lost on human ears.

They were at the crest of the bluff. "Sit down, Blab. I want to catch my breath." *And look at the view. . . . And decide what in heaven's name I should do with you and with me.*

The bluffs were the highest natural viewpoints in New Michigan province. The flatlands that spread around them were pocked with ponds, laced with creeks and rivers, the best farmland on the continent. From orbit, the original colonists could find no better. Water landings would have been easier, but they wanted the best odds on long-term survival. Thirty klicks away, half hidden by gray mist, Hamid could see the glassy streaks that marked the landing zone. The history books said it took three years to bring down the people and all the salvage from the greatship. Even now the glass was faintly radioactive, one cause for the migration across the isthmus to Westland.

Except for the forest around those landing strips, and the old university town just below the bluff, most everything in this direction was farmland, unending squares of brown and black and gray. The year was well into autumn and the last of the Earth trees had given up their colored leaves. The wind blowing across the plains was chill, leaving a crispness in his nose that promised snow someday soon. Hallowe'en was next week. Hallowe'en indeed. *I wonder if in Man's thirty thousand years, there has*

*ever been a celebration of that holiday like we'll be
seeing next week.* Hamid resisted the impulse to look
back at Marquette. Ordinarily it was one of his favorite places: the planetary capital, population four hundred thousand, a real city. As a child, visiting
Marquette had been like a trip to some far star
system. But now reality had come, and the stars
were so *close.* . . . Without turning, he knew the
position of every one of the Tourist barges. They
floated like colored balloons above the city, yet none
massed less than a thousand tonnes. And those were
their *shuttles.* After the Elvis revival, Hallowe'en
was the last big event on the Marquette leg of the
Tour. Then they would be off to Westland, for more
semi-fraudulent peeks at Americana.

Hamid crunched back in the dry moss that cush-
ioned the rock. "Well, Blabber, what should I do?
Should I sell you? We could both make it Out There
if I did."

The Blabber's ears perked up. "Talk? Converse?
Disgust?" She settled her forty-kilo bulk next to him,
and nuzzled her head against his chest. The purring
from her foretympanum sounded like some transcen-
dental cat. The sound was pink noise, buzzing through
his chest and shaking the rock they sat on. There
were few things she enjoyed more than a good talk
with a peer. Hamid stroked her black and white pelt.
"I said, should I sell you?"

The purring stopped, and for a moment the Blab
seemed to give the matter thoughtful consideration.
Her head turned this way and that, bobbing—a good
imitation of a certain prof at the University. She
rolled her big dark eyes at him, "Don't rush me!
I'm thinking. I'm thinking." She licked daintily at
the sleek fur at the base of her throat. And for all
Hamid knew, she really was thinking about what to
say. Sometimes she really seemed to try to under-

stand . . . and sometimes she almost made sense. Finally she shut her mouth and began talking.

"Should I sell you? Should I sell you?" The intonation was still Hamid's but she wasn't imitating his voice. When they talked like this, she typically sounded like an adult human female (and a very attractive one, Hamid thought). It hadn't always been that way. When she had been a pup and he a little boy, she'd sounded to him like another little boy. The strategy was clear: she understood the type of voice he most likely wanted to hear. Animal cunning? "Well," she continued, "*I* know what I think. Buy, don't sell. And always get the best price you can."

She often came across like that: oracular. But he had known the Blab all his life. The longer her comment, the less she understood it. In this case . . . Ham remembered his finance class. That was before he got his present apartment, and the Blab had hidden under his desk part of the semester. (It had been an exciting semester for all concerned.) "Buy, don't sell." That was a quote, wasn't it, from some nineteenth-century tycoon?

She blabbered on, each sentence having less correlation with the question. After a moment, Hamid grabbed the beast around the neck, laughing and crying at the same time. They wrestled briefly across the rocky slope, Hamid fighting at less than full strength, and the Blab carefully keeping her talons retracted. Abruptly he was on his back and the Blab was standing on his chest. She held his nose between the tips of her long jaws. "Say Uncle! Say Uncle!" she shouted.

The Blabber's teeth stopped a couple of centimeters short of the end of her snout, but the grip was powerful; Hamid surrendered immediately. The Blab jumped off him, chuckling triumph, then grabbed his sleeve to help him up. He stood up, rubbing his nose gingerly. "Okay, monster, let's get going." He waved downhill, toward Ann Arbor Town.

"Ha, ha! For sure. Let's get going!" The Blab danced down the rocks faster than he could hope to go. Yet every few seconds the creature paused an instant, checking that he was still following. Hamid shook his head, and started down. Damned if he was going to break a leg just to keep up with her. Whatever her homeworld, he guessed that winter around Marquette was the time of year most homelike for the Blab. Take her coloring: stark black and white, mixed in wide curves and swirls. He'd seen that pattern in pictures of ice-pack seals. When there was snow on the ground, she was practically invisible.

She was fifty meters ahead of him now. From this distance, the Blab could almost pass for a dog, some kind of greyhound maybe. But the paws were too large, and the neck too long. The head looked more like a seal's than a dog's. Of course, she could bark like a dog. But then, she could also sound like a thunderstorm, and make something like human conversation—all at the same time. There was only one of her kind in all Middle America. This last week, he'd come to learn that her kind were almost as rare Out There. A Tourist wanted to buy her . . . and Tourists could pay with coin what Hamid Thompson had sought for more than half his twenty years.

Hamid desperately needed some good advice. It had been five years since he'd asked his father for help; he'd be damned if he did so now. That left the University, and Lazy Larry. . . .

By Middle-American standards, Ann Arbor Town was *ancient*. There were older places: out by the landing zone, parts of Old Marquette still stood. School field trips to those ruins were brief—the pre-

fab quonsets were mildly radioactive. And of course
there were individual buildings in the present-day
capital that went back almost to the beginning. But
much of the University in Ann Arbor dated from just
after those first permanent structures: the University
had been a going concern for 190 years.

Something was up today, and it had nothing to do
with Hamid's problems. As they walked into town, a
couple of police helicopters swept in from Marquette,
began circling the school. On the ground, some of
Ham's favorite back ways were blocked off by University safety patrols. No doubt it was Tourist business. He might have to come in through the Main
Gate, past the Math Building. *Yuck*. Even after ten
years he loathed that place: his years as a supposed
prodigy; his parents forcing him into math classes he
just wasn't bright enough to handle; the tears and
anger at home, till he finally convinced them that he
was not the boy they thought.

They walked around the Quad, Hamid oblivious to
the graceful buttresses, the ivy that meshed stone
walls into the flute trees along the street. That was
all familiar . . . what was new was all the Federal cop
cars. Clusters of students stood watching the cops,
but there was no riot in the air. They just seemed
curious. Besides, the Feds had never interfered on
campus before.

"Keep quiet, okay?" Hamid muttered.

"Sure, sure." The Blab scrunched her neck back,
went into her doggie act. At one time they had been
notorious on campus, but he had dropped out that
summer, and people had other things on their minds
today. They walked through the main gate without
comment from students or cops.

The biggest surprise came when they reached Larry's slummy digs at Morale Hall. Morale wasn't old
enough to be historic; it was old enough to be in

decay. It had been an abortive experiment in brick construction. The clay had cracked and rotted, leaving gaps for vines and pests. By now it was more a reddish mound of rubble than a habitable structure. This was where the University Administration stuck tenured faculty in greatest disfavor: the Quad's Forgotten Quarter . . . but not today. Today the cop cars were piled two deep in the parking areas, and there were shotgun-toting guards at the entrance!

Hamid walked up the steps. He had a sick feeling that Lazy Larry might be the hardest prof in the world to see today. On the other hand, working with the Tourists meant Hamid saw some of these security people every day.

"Your business, sir?" Unfortunately, the guard was no one he recognized.

"I need to see my advisor . . . Professor Fujiyama." Larry had never been his advisor, but Hamid was looking for advice.

"Um." The cop flicked on his throat mike. Hamid couldn't hear much, but there was something about "that black and white off-planet creature." Over the last twenty years, you'd have to have been living in a cave never to see anything about the Blabber.

A minute passed, and an older officer stepped through the doorway. "Sorry, son, Mr. Fujiyama isn't seeing any students this week. Federal business."

Somewhere a funeral dirge began playing. Hamid tapped the Blab's forepaw with his foot; the music stopped abruptly. "Ma'am, it's not school business." Inspiration struck: why not tell something like the truth? "It's about the Tourists and my Blabber."

The senior cop sighed. "That's what I was afraid you'd say. Okay, come along." As they entered the dark hallway, the Blabber was chuckling triumph. Someday the Blab would play her games with the wrong people and get the crap beat out of her, but apparently today was not that day.

They walked down two flights of stairs. The lighting got even worse, half-dead fluorescents built into the acoustic tiling. In places the wooden stairs sagged elastically under their feet. There were no queues of students squatting before any of the doors, but the cops hadn't cleared out the faculty: Hamid heard loud snoring from one of the offices. The Forgotten Quarter—Morale Hall in particular—was a strange place. The one thing the faculty here had in common was that each had been an unbearable pain in the neck to someone. That meant that both the most incompetent and the most brilliant were jammed into these tiny offices.

Larry's office was in the sub-basement, at the end of a long hall. Two more cops flanked the doorway, but otherwise it was as Hamid remembered it. There was a brass nameplate: PROFESSOR L. LAWRENCE FUJIYAMA, DEPARTMENT OF TRANSHUMAN STUDIES. Next to the nameplate, a sign boasted implausible office hours. In the center of the door was the picture of a piglet and the legend: "If a student appears to need help, then appear to give him some."

The police officer stood aside as they reached the door; Hamid was going to have to get in under his own power. Ham gave the door a couple of quick knocks. There was the sound of footsteps, and the door opened a crack. "What's the secret password?" came Larry's voice.

"Professor Fujiyama, I need to talk to—"

"That's not it!" The door was slammed loudly in Hamid's face.

The senior cop put her hand on Hamid's shoulder. "Sorry, son. He's done that to bigger guns than you."

He shrugged off her hand. Sirens sounded from

the black and white creature at his feet. Ham shouted over the racket, "Wait! It's me, Hamid Thompson! From your Transhume 201."

The door came open again. Larry stepped out, glanced at the cops, then looked at the Blabber. "Well, why didn't you say so? Come on in." As Hamid and the Blab scuttled past him, Larry smiled innocently at the Federal officer. "Don't worry, Susie, this is official business."

Fujiyama's office was long and narrow, scarcely an aisle between deep equipment racks. Larry's students (those who dared these depths) doubted the man could have survived on Old Earth before electronic datastorage. There must be tonnes of junk squirreled away on those shelves. The gadgets stuck out this way and that into the aisle. The place was a museum—perhaps literally; one of Larry's specialties was archeology. Most of the machines were dead, but here and there something clicked, something glowed. Some of the gadgets were Rube Goldberg jokes, some were early colonial prototypes . . . and a few were from Out There. Steam and water pipes covered much of the ceiling. The place reminded Hamid of the inside of a submarine.

At the back was Larry's desk. The junk on the table was balanced precariously high: a display flat, a beautiful piece of night-black statuary. In Transhume 201, Larry had described his theory of artifact management: Last-In-First-Out, and every year buy a clean bed sheet, date it, and lay it over the previous layer of junk on your desk. Another of Lazy Larry's jokes, most had thought. But there really *was* a bed sheet peeking out from under the mess.

Shadows climbed sharp and deep from the lamp on Larry's desk. The cabinets around him seemed to lean inwards. The open space between them was covered with posters. Those posters were one small reason Larry was down here: ideas to offend every sensible faction of society. A pile of . . . something . . . lay on the visitor's chair. Larry slopped it onto the floor and motioned Hamid to sit.

"Sure, I remember you from Transhume. But why mention that? You own the Blabber. You're Huss Thompson's kid." He settled back in his chair.

I'm not Huss Thompson's kid! Aloud, "Sorry, that was all I could think to say. This is about my Blabber, though. I need some advice."

"Ah!" Fujiyama gave his famous polliwog smile, somehow innocent and predatory at the same time. "You came to the right place. I'm full of it. But I heard you had quit school, gone to work at the Tourist Bureau."

Hamid shrugged, tried not to seem defensive. "Yeah. But I was already a senior, and I know more American Thought and Lit than most graduates . . . and the Tourist caravan will only be here another half year. After that, how long till the next? We're showing them everything I could imagine they'd want to see. In fact, we're showing them more than there really *is* to see. It could be a hundred years before anyone comes down here again."

"Possibly, possibly."

"Anyway, I've learned a lot. I've met almost half the Tourists. But . . ." There were ten million people living on Middle America. At least a million had a romantic yearning to get Out There. At least ten thousand would give everything they owned to leave the Slow Zone, to live in a civilization that spanned thousands of worlds. For the last ten years, Middle America had known of the Caravan's coming. Hamid had spent most of those years—half his life, all the time since he got out of math—preparing himself with the skills that could buy him a ticket Out.

Thousands of others had worked just as hard. During the last decade, every department of American Thought and Literature on the planet had been jammed to the bursting point. And more had been going on behind the scenes. The government and some large corporations had had secret programs that weren't revealed till just before the Caravan arrived. Dozens of people had bet on the long shots, things that no one else thought the Outsiders might want. Some of those were fools: the world-class athletes, the chess masters. They could never be more than eighth rate in the vast populations of the Beyond. No, to get a ride you needed something that was odd . . . Out There. Besides the Old Earth angle, there weren't many possibilities—though that could be approached in surprising ways: there was Gilli Weinberg, a bright but not brilliant ATL student. When the Caravan reached orbit, she bypassed the Bureau, announced herself to the Tourists as a genuine American cheerleader and premier courtesan. It was a ploy pursued less frankly and less successfully by others of both sexes. In Gilli's case, it had won her a ticket Out. The big laugh was that her sponsor was one of the few non-humans in the Caravan, a Lothlrimarre slug who couldn't survive a second in an oxygen atmosphere.

"I'd say I'm on good terms with three of the Outsiders. But there are least five Tour Guides that can put on a better show. And you know the Tourists managed to revive four more corpsicles from the original Middle America crew. Those guys are sure to get tickets Out, if they want 'em." Men and women who had been adults on Old Earth, two thousand light years away and twenty thousand years ago. It was likely that Middle America had no more valuable export this time around. "If they'd just come a few years later, after I graduated . . . maybe made a name for myself."

Larry broke into the self-pitying silence. "You never thought of using the Blabber as your ticket Out?"

"Off and on." Hamid glanced down at the dark bulk that curled around his feet. The Blab was *awfully* quiet.

Larry noticed the look. "Don't worry. She's fooling with some ultrasound imagers I have back there." He gestured at the racks behind Hamid, where a violet glow played hopscotch between unseen gadgets.

The boy smiled. "We may have trouble getting her out of here." He had several ultrasonic squawkers around the apartment, but the Blab rarely got to play with high-resolution equipment. "Yeah, right at the beginning, I tried to interest them in the Blab. Said I was her trainer. They lost interest as soon as they saw she couldn't be native to Old Earth. . . . These guys are *freaks*, Professor! You could rain transhuman treasure on 'em, and they'd call it spit! But give 'em Elvis Presley singing Bruce Springsteen and they build you a spaceport on Selene!"

Larry just smiled, the way he did when some student was heading for academic catastrophe. Hamid quieted. "Yeah, I know. There are good reasons for some of the strangeness." Middle America had nothing that would interest anybody rational from Out There. They were stuck nine light years inside the Slow Zone: commerce was hideously slow and expensive. Middle American technology was obsolete and—considering their location—it could never amount to anything competitive. Hamid's unlucky world had only one thing going for it. It was a direct colony of Old Earth, and one of the first. Their greatship's tragic flight had lasted twenty thousand years, long enough for the Earth to become a legend for much of humankind.

In the Beyond, there were millions of solar systems known to bear human-equivalent intelligences.

Most of these could be in more or less instantaneous communication with one another. In that vastness humanity was a speck—perhaps four thousand worlds. Even on those, interest in a first-generation colony within the Slow Zone was near zero. But with four thousand worlds, that was enough: here and there was a rich eccentric, an historical foundation, a religious movement—all strange enough to undertake a twenty-year mission into the Slowness. So Middle America should be glad for these rare mixed nuts. Over the last hundred years there had been occasional traders and a couple of tourist caravans. That commerce had raised the Middle American standard of living substantially. More important to many— including Hamid—it was almost their only peephole on the universe beyond the Zone. In the last century, two hundred Middle Americans had escaped to the Beyond. The early ones had been government workers, commissioned scientists. The Feds' investment had not paid off: of all those who left, only five had returned. Larry Fujiyama and Hussein Thompson were two of those five.

"Yeah, I guess I knew they'd be fanatics. But most of them aren't even much interested in accuracy. We make a big thing of representing twenty-first-century America. But we both know what that was like: heavy industry moving up to Earth orbit, five hundred million people still crammed into North America. At best, what we have here is like mid-twentieth-century America—or even earlier. I've worked very hard to get our past straight. But except for a few guys I really respect, anachronism doesn't seem to bother them. It's like just being here with us is the big thing."

Larry opened his mouth, seemed on the verge of providing some insight. Instead he smiled, shrugged.

(One of his many mottos was, "If you didn't figure it out yourself, you don't understand it.")

"So after all these months, where did you dig up the interest in the Blabber?"

"It was the slug, the guy running the Tour. He just mailed me that he had a party who wanted to buy. Normally, this guy haggles. He—wait, you know him pretty well, don't you? Well, he just made a flat offer. A payoff to the Feds, transport for me to Lothlrimarre," that was the nearest civilized system in the Beyond, "and some ftl privileges beyond that."

"And you kiss your pet goodbye?"

"Yeah. I made a case for them needing a handler: me. That's not just bluff, by the way. We've grown up together. I can't imagine the Blab accepting anyone without lots of help from me. But they're not interested. Now, the slug claims no harm is intended her, but . . . do you believe him?"

"Ah, the slug's slime is generally clean. I'm sure he doesn't know of any harm planned . . . and he's straight enough to do at least a little checking. Did he say who wanted to buy?"

"Somebody—something named Ravna&Tines." He passed Larry a flimsy showing the offer. Ravna&Tines had a logo: it looked like a stylized claw. "There's no Tourist registered with that name."

Larry nodded, copied the flimsy to his display flat. "I know. Well, let's see. . . ." He puttered around for a moment. The display was a lecture model, with imaging on both sides. Hamid could see the other was searching internal Federal databases. Larry's eyebrows rose. "Hm*hm!* Ravna&Tines arrived just last week. It's not part of the Caravan at all."

"A solitary trader . . ."

"Not only that. It's been hanging out past the Jovians—at the slug's request. The Federal space net got some pictures." There was a fuzzy image of something long and wasp-waisted, typical of the Outsiders' ramscoop technology. But there were strange fins—almost like the wings on a sailplane. Larry played some algorithmic game with the display and the image sharpened. "Yeah. Look at the aspect ratio on those fins. This guy is carrying high-performance ftl gear. No good down here of course, but hot stuff across an enormous range of environment . . ." He whistled a few bars of "Nightmare Waltz." "I think we're looking at a High Trader."

Someone from the Transhuman Spaces.

Almost every university on Middle America had a Department of Transhuman Studies. Since the return of the five, it had been a popular thing to do. Yet most people considered it a joke. Transhume was generally the bastard child of Religious Studies and an Astro or Computer Science department, the dumping ground for quacks and incompetents. Lazy Larry had founded the department at Ann Arbor—and spent much class time eloquently proclaiming its fraudulence. Imagine, trying to study what lay *beyond* the Beyond! Even the Tourists avoided the topic. Transhuman Space existed—perhaps it included most of the universe—but it was a tricky, risky, ambiguous thing. Larry said that its reality drove most of the economics of the Beyond . . . but that all the theories about it were rumors at tenuous second hand. One of his proudest claims was that he raised Transhuman Studies to the level of palm reading.

Yet now . . . apparently a trader had arrived that regularly penetrated the Transhuman Reaches. If the government hadn't sat on the news, it would have eclipsed the Caravan itself. And *this* was what wanted the Blab. Almost involuntarily, Hamid reached down to pet the creature. "Y-you don't think there could really be anybody transhuman on that ship?" An hour ago he had been agonizing about parting with the Blab; that might be nothing compared to what they really faced.

For a moment he thought Larry was going to shrug the question off. But the older man sighed. "If there's anything we've got right, it's that no transhuman can think at these depths. Even in the Beyond, they'd die or fragment or maybe cyst. I think this Ravna&Tines must be a human-equivalent intellect, but it could be a lot more dangerous than the average Outsider . . . the tricks it would know, the gadgets it would have." His voice drifted off; he stared at the forty-centimeter statue perched on his desk. It was lustrous green, apparently cut from a flawless block of jade. *Green? Wasn't it black a minute ago?*

Larry's gaze snapped up to Hamid. "Congratulations. Your problem is a lot more interesting than you thought. Why would any Outsider want the Blab, much less a High Trader?"

". . . Well, her kind must be rare. I haven't talked to any Tourist who recognized the race."

Lazy Larry just nodded. Space is deep. The Blab might be from somewhere else in the Slow Zone.

"When she was a pup, lots of people studied her. You saw the articles. She has a brain as big as a chimp's, but most of it's tied up in driving her tympana and processing what she hears. One guy said she's the ultimate in verbal orientation—all mouth and no mind."

"Ah! A student!"

Hamid ignored the Larryism. "Watch this." He patted the Blab's shoulder.

She was slow in responding; that ultrasound equipment must be fascinating. Finally she raised her head. "What's up?" The intonation was natural, the voice a young woman's.

"Some people think she's just a parrot. She can play things back better than a high-fidelity recorder. But she also picks up favorite phrases, and uses them in different voices—and almost appropriately. . . . Hey, Blab. What's that?" Hamid pointed at the electric heater that Larry had propped by his feet. The Blab stuck her head around the corner of the desk, saw the cherry glowing coils. This was not the sort of heater Hamid had in his apartment.

"What's that . . . that . . ." The Blab extended her head curiously toward the glow. She was a bit too eager; her nose bumped the heater's safety grid. "*Hot!*" She jumped back, her nose tucked into her neck fur, a foreleg extended toward the heater. "Hot! Hot!" She rolled onto her haunches, and licked tentatively at her nose. "Jeeze!" She gave Hamid a look that was both calculating and reproachful.

"Honest, Blab, I didn't think you would touch it. . . . She's going to get me for this. Her sense of humor extends only as far as ambushes, but it can be pretty intense."

"Yeah. I remember the Zoo Society's documentary on her." Fujiyama was grinning broadly. Hamid had always thought that Larry and the Blab had kindred humors. It even seemed that the animal's cackling became like the old man's after she attended a couple of his lectures.

Larry pulled the heater back and walked around the desk. He hunched down to the Blab's eye level. He was all solicitude now, and a good thing: he was looking into a mouth full of sharp teeth, and somebody was playing the "Timebomb Song." After a moment, the music stopped and she shut her mouth. "I can't believe there isn't human equivalence hiding here somewhere. Really. I've had freshmen who did worse at the start of the semester. How could you get this much verbalization without intelligence to benefit from it?" He reached out to rub her shoulders. "You got sore shoulders, Baby? Maybe little hands ready to burst out?"

The Blab cocked her head. "I like to soar."

Hamid had thought long about the Heinlein scenario; the science fiction of Old Earth was a solid part of the ATL curriculum. "If she is still a child, she'll be dead before she grows up. Her bone calcium and muscle strength have deteriorated about as much as you'd expect for a thirty-year-old human."

"Hm. Yeah. And we know she's about your age." Twenty. "I suppose she could be an ego frag. But most of those are brain-damaged transhumans, or obvious constructs." He went back behind his desk, began whistling tunelessly. Hamid twisted uneasily in his chair. He had come for advice. What he got was news that they were in totally over their heads. He shouldn't be surprised; Larry was like that. "What we need is a whole lot more information."

"Well, I suppose I could flat out demand the slug tell me more. But I don't know how I can force any of the Tourists to help me."

Larry waved breezily. "That's not what I meant. Sure, I'll ask the Lothlrimarre about it. But basically the Tourists are at the end of a nine-light-year trip to nowhere. Whatever libraries they have are like what you would take on a South Seas vacation—and out of date, to boot. . . . And of course the Federal government of Middle America doesn't know what's coming off to begin with. Heh, heh. Why else do they come to me when they're really desperate? . . . No, what we need is direct access to library resources Out There."

He said it casually, as though he were talking about getting an extra telephone, not solving Middle America's greatest problem. He smiled complacently at Hamid, but the boy refused to be drawn in. Fi-

nally, "Haven't you wondered why the campus—
Morale Hall, in particular—is crawling with cops?"

"Yeah." *Or I would have, if there weren't lots
else on my mind.*

"One of the more serious Tourists—Skandr Vrinimis-
rinithan—brought along a genuine transhuman artifact. He's been holding back on it for months, hoping
he could get what he wants other ways. The Feds—
I'll give 'em this—didn't budge. Finally he brought
out his secret weapon. It's in this room right now."

Ham's eyes were drawn to the stone carving (now
bluish green) that sat on Larry's desk. The old man
nodded. "It's an ansible."

"Surely they don't call it that!"

"No. But that's what it is."

"You mean, all these years, it's been a lie that ftl
won't work in the Zone?" *You mean I've wasted my
life trying to suck up to these Tourists?*

"Not really. Take a look at this thing. See the
colors change. I swear its size and mass do, too. This
is a real transhuman artifact: not an intellect, of
course, but not some human design manufactured in
Transhuman space. Skandr claims—and I believe
him—that no other Tourist has one."

A transhuman artifact. Hamid's fascination was
tinged with fear. This was something one heard of in
the theoretical abstract, in classes run by crackpots.

"Skandr claims this gadget is 'aligned' on the Lothlrimarre commercial outlet. From there we can talk to
any registered address in the Beyond."

"Instantaneously." Hamid's voice was very small.

"Near enough. It would take a while to reach the
universal event horizon; there are some subtle limitations if you're moving at relativistic speeds."

"And the Catch?"

Larry laughed. "Good man. Skandr admits to a
few. This thing won't work more than ten light years

into the Zone. I'll bet there aren't twenty worlds in the Galaxy that could benefit from it—but we are *definitely* on one. The trick sucks enormous energy. Skandr says that running this baby will dim our sun by half a percent. Not noticeable to the guy in the street, but it could have long-term bad effects." There was a short silence; Larry often did that after a cosmic understatement. "And from your standpoint, Hamid, there's one big drawback. The mean bandwidth of this thing is just under six bits per minute."

"Huh? Ten seconds to send a single bit?"

"Yup. Skandr left three protocols at the Lothlrimarre end: ASCII, a Hamming map to a subset of English, and an AI scheme that guesses what you'd say if you used more bits. The first is Skandr's idea of a joke, and I wouldn't trust the third more than wishful thinking. But with the Hamming map, you could send a short letter—say five hundred English words— in a day. It's full-duplex, so you might get a good part of your answer in that time. Neat, huh? Anyway, it beats waiting twenty years."

Hamid guessed it would be the biggest news since first contact, one hundred years ago. "So . . . uh, why did they bring it to you, Professor?"

Larry looked around his hole of an office, smiling wider and wider. "Heh, heh. It's true, our illustrious planetary president is one of the five; he's been Out There. But I'm the only one with real friends in the Beyond. You see, the Feds are very leery of this deal. What Skandr wants in return is most of our zygote bank. The Feds banned any private sale of human zygotes. It was a big moral thing: 'No unborn child sold into slavery or worse.' Now they're thinking of doing it themselves. They really *want* this ansible. But what if it's a fake, just linked up to some fancy database on Skandr's ship? Then they've lost some genetic flexibility, and maybe they've sold some kids into hell—and got nothing but a colorful trinket for their grief.

"So. Skandr's loaned them the thing for a week, and the Feds loaned it to me—with close to *carte blanche*. I can call up old friends, exchange filthy jokes, let the sun go dim doing it. After a week, I report on whether the gadget is really talking to the Outside."

Knowing you, "I bet you have your own agenda."

"Sure. Till you showed up the main item was to check out the foundation that sponsors Skandr, see if they're as clean as he says. Now . . . well, your case isn't as important morally, but it's very interesting. There should be time for both. I'll use Skandr's credit to do some netstalking, see if I can find *anyone* who's heard of blabbers, or this Ravna&Tines."

Hamid didn't have any really close friends. Sometimes he wondered if that was another penalty of his strange upbringing, or whether he was just naturally unlikable. He had come to Fujiyama for help all right, but all he'd been expecting was a round of prickly questions that eventually brought *him* to some insight. Now he seemed to be on the receiving end of a favor of world-shaking proportions. It made him suspicious and very grateful all at once. He gabbled some words of abject gratitude.

Larry shrugged. "It's no special problem for me. I'm curious, and this week I've got the *means* to satisfy my curiosity." He patted the ansible. "There's a real favor I can do, though: so far, Middle America has been cheated occasionally, but no Outsider has used force against us. That's one good thing about the Caravan system: it's to the Tourists' advantage to keep each other straight. Ravna&Tines may be different. If this is really a High Trader, it might just make a grab for what it wants. If I were you, I'd keep close to the Blabber. . . . And I'll see if the slug will move one of the Tourist barges over the campus. If you stay in this area, not much can happen without them knowing.

"Hey, see what a help I am? I did nothing for your original question, and now you have a whole, ah, shipload of new things to worry about. . . ."

He leaned back, and his voice turned serious. "But I don't have much to say about your original question, Hamid. If Ravna&Tines turn out to be decent, you'll still have to decide for yourself about giving up the Blab. I bet every critter that thinks it thinks—even the transhumans—worry about how to do right for themselves and the ones they love. I—uh, oh damn! Why don't you ask your pop, why don't you ask Hussein about these things? The guy has been heartbroken since you left."

Ham felt his face go red. Pop had never had much good to say about Fujiyama. Who'd have guessed the two would talk about him? If Hamid had known, he'd never have come here today. He felt like standing up, screaming at this old man to mind his own business. Instead, he shook his head and said softly, "It's kind of personal."

Larry looked at him, as if wondering whether to push the matter. One word, and Ham knew that all the pain would come pouring out. But after a moment, the old man sighed. He looked around the desk to where the Blab lay, eyeing the heater. "Hey, Blabber. You take good care of this kid."

The Blab returned his gaze. "Sure, sure," she said.

Hamid's apartment was on the south side of campus. It was large and cheap, which might seem surprising so near the oldest university around, and just a few kilometers south of the planetary capital. The back door opened on kilometers of forested wilderness. It would be a long time before there was any land development immediately south of here. The original landing zones were just twenty klicks away. In a bad storm there might be a little hot stuff blown north. It might be only fifty percent of natural background radiation, but with a whole world to colonize, why spread towns toward the first landings?

Hamid parked the commons bicycle in the rack out front, and walked quietly around the building. Lights were on upstairs. There were the usual motorbikes of other tenants. *Something* was standing in back, at the far end of the building. Ah. A Hallowe'en scarecrow.

He and the Blab walked back to his end. It was past twilight and neither moon was in the sky. The tips of his fingers were chilled to numbness. He stuck his hands in his pockets, and paused to look up. The starships of the Caravan were in synch orbit at this longitude. They formed a row of bright dots in the southern sky. Something dark, too regular to be a cloud hung almost straight overhead. That must be the protection Larry had promised.

"I'm hungry."

"Just a minute and we'll go in."

"Okay." The Blab leaned companionably against his leg, began humming. She looked fat now, but it was just her fur, all puffed out. These temperatures were probably the most comfortable for her. He stared across the star fields. *God, how many hours have I stood like this, wondering what all those stars mean?* The Big Square was about an hour from setting. The fifth brightest star in that constellation was Lothlrimarre's sun. At Lothlrimarre and beyond, faster than light travel was possible—even for twenty-first century Old Earth types. If Middle America were just ten more light years farther out from the galactic center, Hamid would have had all the Beyond as his world.

His gaze swept back across the sky. Most everything he could see there would be in the Slow Zone. It extended four thousand light years inward from here, if the Outsiders were to be believed. Billions of star systems, millions of civilizations—trapped. Most would never know about the outside.

Even the Outsiders had only vague information about the civilizations down here in the Slow Zone. Greatships, ramscoops, they all must be invented here again and again. Colonies spread, knowledge gained, most often lost in the long slow silence. What theories the Slow Zone civilizations must have for why nothing could move faster than light—even in the face of superluminal events seen at cosmic distances. What theories they must have to explain why human-equivalent intelligence was the highest ever found and ever created. Those ones deep inside, they might at times be the happiest of all, their theories assuring them they were at the top of creation. If Middle America were only a hundred light years farther down, Hamid would never know the truth. He would love this world, and the spreading of civilization upon it.

Hamid's eye followed the Milky Way to the eastern horizon. The glow wasn't really brighter there than above, but he knew his constellations. He was looking at the galactic center. He smiled wanly. In twentieth-century science fiction, those star clouds were imagined as the homes of "elder races," godlike intellects. . . . But the Tourists call those regions of the galaxy the Depths. The Unthinking Depths. Not only was ftl impossible there, but so was sentience. So they guessed. They couldn't know for sure. The fastest round-trip probe to the edge of the Depths took about ten thousand years. Such expeditions were rare, though some were well documented.

Hamid shivered, and looked back at the ground. Four cats sat silently just beyond the lawn, watching the Blab. "Not tonight, Blab," he said, and the two of them went indoors.

The place looked undisturbed: the usual mess. He fixed the Blab her dinner and heated some soup for himself.

"Yuck. This stuff tastes like *shit*!" The Blab rocked back on her haunches and made retching sounds. Few people have their own childhood obnoxiousness come back to haunt them so directly as Hamid Thompson did. He could remember using exactly those words at the dinner table. Mom should have stuffed a sock down his throat.

Hamid glanced at the chicken parts. "Best we can afford, Blab." He was running his savings down to zero to cover the year of the Tourists. Being a guide was such a plum that no one thought to pay for it.

"Yuck." But she started nibbling.

As Ham watched her eat, he realized that one of his problems was solved. If Ravna&Tines wouldn't take him as the Blab's "trainer," they could hike back to the Beyond by themselves. Furthermore, he'd want better evidence from the slug—via the ansible he could get assurances directly from Lothlrimarre— that Ravna&Tines could be held to promises. The conversation with Larry had brought home all the nightmare fears, the fears that drove some people to demand total rejection of the Caravan. Who knew what happened to those that left with Outsiders? Almost all Middle American knowledge of the Beyond came from less than thirty starships, less than a thousand strangers. Strange strangers. If it weren't for the five who came back, there would be zero corroboration. Of those five . . . well, Hussein Thompson was a mystery even to Hamid: seeming kind, inside a vicious mercenary. Lazy Larry was a mystery, too, a cheerful one who made it clear that you better think twice about what folks tell you. But one thing came clear from all of them: space is deep. There were millions of civilized worlds in the Beyond, thousands of star-spanning empires. In such vastness, there could be no single notion of law and order. Cooperation and enlightened self-interest were common, but . . . nightmares lurked.

So what if Ravna&Tines turned him down, or couldn't produce credible assurances? Hamid went into the bedroom and punched up the news, let the color and motion wash over him. Middle America was a beautiful world, still mostly empty. With the agrav plates and the room-temperature fusion electrics that the Caravan had brought, life would be more exciting here than ever before. . . . In twenty or thirty years there would likely be another caravan. If he and the Blab were still restless—well, there was plenty of time to prepare. Larry Fujiyama had been forty years old when he went Out.

Hamid sighed, happy with himself for the first time in days.

The phone rang just as he finished with the news. The name of the incoming caller danced in red letters across the news display: *Ravna*. No location or topic. Hamid swallowed hard. He bounced off the bed, turned the phone pickup to look at a chair in an uncluttered corner of the room, and sat down there. Then he accepted the call.

Ravna was human. And female. "Mr. Hamid Thompson, please."

"T-that's me." *Curse the stutter*.

For an instant there was no reaction. Then a quick smile crossed her face. It was not a friendly smile, more like a sneer at his nervousness. "I call to discuss the animal. The Blabber, you call it. You have heard our offer. I am prepared to improve upon it." As she spoke, the Blab walked into the room and across the phone's field of view. Her gaze did not waver. Strange. He could see that the VIDEO TRANSMIT light was on next to the screen. The Blab began to hum. A moment passed and *then* she reacted, a tiny start of surprise.

"What is your improvement?"

Again, a half-second pause. Ravna&Tines were a lot nearer than the Jovians tonight, though apparently still not at Middle America. "We possess devices that allow faster-than-light communication to a world in the . . . Beyond. Think on what this access means. With this, if you stay on Middle America, you will be the richest man on the planet. If you choose to accept passage Out, you will have the satisfaction of knowing you have moved your world a good step out of the darkness."

Hamid found himself thinking faster than he ever had outside of a Fujiyama oral exam. There were plenty of clues here. Ravna's English was more fluent than most Tourists', but her pronunciation was awful. Human but awful: her vowel stress was strange to the point of rendering her speech unintelligible, and she didn't voice things properly: "pleess" instead of "pleez," "chooss" instead of "chooz."

At the same time, he had to make sense of what she was saying and decide the correct response. Hamid thanked God he already knew about ansibles. "Miss Ravna, I agree. That is an improvement. Nevertheless, my original requirement stands. I must accompany my pet. Only I know her needs." He cocked his head. "You could do worse than have an expert on call."

As he spoke, her expression clouded. Rage? She

seemed hostile toward him *personally*. But when he finished, her face was filled with an approximation of a friendly smile. "Of course, we will arrange that also. We had not realized earlier how important this is to you."

Jeeze. Even I can lie better than that! This Ravna was used to getting her own way without face-to-face lies, or else she had real emotional problems. Either way: "And since you and I are scarcely equals, we also need to work something out with the Lothlrimarre that will put a credible bond on the agreement."

Her poorly constructed mask slipped. "That is absurd." She looked at something off camera. "The Lothlrimarre knows nothing of us. . . . I will try to satisfy you. But know this, Hamid Thompson: I am the congenial, uh, *humane* member of my team. Mr. Tines is very impatient. I try to restrain him, but if he becomes desperate enough . . . things could happen that would hurt us all. Do you understand me?"

First a lie, and now chainsaw subtlety. He fought back a smile. *Careful. You might be mistaking raw insanity for bluff and bluster.* "Yes, Miss Ravna, I do understand, and your offer is generous. But . . . I need to think about this. Can you give me a bit more time?" *Enough time to complain to the Tour Director.*

"Yes. One hundred hours should be feasible."

After she rang off, Hamid sat for a long time, staring sightlessly at the dataset. What *was* Ravna? Through twenty thousand years of colonization, on worlds far stranger than Middle America, the human form had drifted far. Cross-fertility existed between most of Earth's children, though they differed more from one another than had races on the home planet. Ravna looked more like an Earth human than most of the Tourists. Assuming she was of normal height, she could almost have passed as an American of Middle East descent: sturdy, dark-skinned, black-haired.

There were differences. Her eyes had epicanthic folds, and the irises were the most intense violet he had ever seen. Still, all that was trivial compared to her manner.

Why hadn't she been receiving Hamid's video? Was she blind? She didn't seem so otherwise; he remembered her looking at things around her. Perhaps she was some sort of personality simulator. That had been a standard item in American science fiction at the end of the twentieth century; the idea passed out of fashion when computer performance seemed to top out in the early twenty-first. But things like that should be possible in the Beyond, and certainly in Transhuman Space. They wouldn't work very well down here, of course. Maybe she was just a graphical front end for whatever Mr. Tines was.

Somehow, Hamid thought she was real. She certainly had a human effect on him. Sure, she had a good figure, obvious under soft white shirt and pants. And sure, Hamid had been girl-crazy the last five years. He was so horny most of the time, it felt good just to ogle femikins in downtown Marquette stores. But for all-out sexiness, Ravna wasn't *that* spectacular. She had nothing on Gilli Weinberg or Skandr Vrinimi's wife. Yet, if he had met her at school, he would have tried harder to gain her favor than he had Gilli's . . . and that was saying *a lot*.

Hamid sighed. That probably just showed that *he* was nuts.

"I wanna go out." The Blab rubbed her head against his arm. Hamid realized he was sweating even though the room was chill.

"God, not tonight, Blab." He guessed that there was a lot of bluff in Ravna&Tines. At the same time, it was clear they were the kind who might just *grab* if they could get away with it.

"I wanna go out!" Her voice came louder. The

Blab spent many nights outside, mainly in the forest. That made it easier to keep her quiet when she was indoors. For the Blab, it was a chance to play with her pets: the cats—and sometimes the dogs—in the neighborhood. There had been a war when he and the Blab first arrived here. Pecking orders had been abruptly revised, and two of the most ferocious dogs had just disappeared. What was left was very strange. The cats were fascinated by the Blab. They hung around the yard just for a glimpse of her. When she was here they didn't even fight among themselves. Nights like tonight were the best. In a couple of hours both Selene and Diana would rise, the silver moon and the gold. On nights like this, when gold and silver lay between deep shadows, Hamid had seen her pacing through the edge of the forest, followed by a dozen faithful retainers.

But, *"Not tonight, Blab!"* There followed a major argument, the Blabber blasting rock music and kiddie shows at high volume. The noise wasn't the loudest she could make. That would have been physically painful to Ham. No, this was more like a cheap music player set way high. Eventually it would bring complaints from all over the apartment building. Fortunately for Hamid, the nearest rooms were unoccupied just now.

After twenty minutes of din, Hamid twisted the fight into a "game of humans." Like many pets, the Blab thought of herself as a human being. But unlike a cat or a dog or even a parrot, she could do a passable job of imitating one. The trouble was, she couldn't always find people with the patience to play along.

They sat across from each other at the dinette table, the Blab's forelegs splayed awkwardly across its surface. Hamid would start with some question—it didn't matter the topic. The Blab would nod wisely, ponder a reply. With most abstractions, anything she had to say was nonsense, meaningful only to tea-leaf readers or wishful thinkers. Never mind that. In the game, Hamid would respond with a comment, or laugh if the Blab seemed to be in a joke-telling behavior. The pacing, the intonation—they were all perfect for real human dialog. If you didn't understand English, the game would have sounded like two friends having a good time.

"How about an imitation, Blab? Joe Ortega. President Ortega. Can you do that?"

"Heh, heh." That was Lazy Larry's cackle. "Don't rush me. I'm thinking. I'm thinking!" There were several types of imitation games. For instance, she could speak back Hamid's words instantly, but with the voice of some other human. Using that trick on a voice-only phone was probably her favorite game of all, since her audience really *believed* she was a person. What he was asking for now was almost as much fun, if the Blab would play up to it.

She rubbed her jaw with a talon. "Ah yes." She sat back pompously, almost slid onto the floor before she caught herself. "We must all work together in these exciting times." That was from a recent Ortega speech, a simple playback. But even when she got going, responding to Hamid's questions, ad-libbing things, she was still a perfect match for the President of Middle America. Hamid laughed and laughed. Ortega was one of the five who came back, not a very bright man but self-important and ambitious. It said something that even his small knowledge of the Outside was enough to propel him to the top of the world state. The five were very big fish in a very small pond—that was how Larry Fujiyama put it.

The Blab was an enormous show-off, and was quickly carried away by her own wit. She began waving her forelegs around, lost her balance and fell off the chair. "Oops!" She hopped back on the chair, looked at Hamid—and began laughing herself. The two were in stitches for almost half a minute. This had happened before; Hamid was sure the Blab could not appreciate humor above the level of pratfalls. Her laughter was imitation for the sake of congeniality, for the sake of being a person. "Oh, God!" She flopped onto the table, "choking" with mirth, her forelegs across the back of her neck as if to restrain herself.

The laughter died away to occasional snorts, and then a companionable silence. Hamid reached across to rub the bristly fur that covered the Blab's forehead tympanum. "You're a good kid, Blab."

The dark eyes opened, turned up at him. Something like a sigh escaped her, buzzing the fur under his palm. "Sure, sure," she said.

Hamid left the drapes partly pulled, and a window pane cranked open where the Blab could sit and look out. He lay in the darkened bedroom and watched her silhouette against the silver and gold moonlight. She had her nose pressed up to the screen. Her long neck was arched to give both her head and shoulder tympana a good line on the outside. Every so often her head would jerk a few millimeters, as if something very interesting had just happened outside.

The loudest sound in the night was faint roach racket, out by the forest. The Blab was being very quiet—in the range Hamid could hear—and he was grateful. She really was a good kid.

He sighed and pulled the covers up to his nose. It had been a long day, one where life's problems had come out ahead.

He'd be very careful the next few days; no trips away from Marquette and Ann Arbor, no leaving the Blab unattended. At least the slug's protection looked solid. *I better tell Larry about the second ansible, though.* If Ravna&Tines just went direct to the government with it . . . that might be the most dangerous move of all. For all their pious talk and restrictions on private sales, the Feds would sell their own grandmothers if they thought it would benefit the Planetary Interest. Thank God they already had an ansible—or almost had one.

Funny. After all these years and all the dreams, that it was the Blab the Outsiders were after . . .

Hamid was an adopted child. His parents had told him that as soon as he could understand the notion. And somewhere in those early years, he had guessed the truth . . . that his father had brought him in . . . from the Beyond. Somehow Huss Thompson had kept that fact secret from the public. Surely the government knew, and cooperated with him. In those early years—before they forced him into Math—it had been a happy secret for him; he thought he had all his parents' love. Knowing that he was really from Out There had merely given substance to what most well-loved kids believe anyway—that somehow they are divinely special. His secret dream had been that he was some Outsider version of an exiled prince. And when he grew up, when the next ships from the Beyond came down . . . he would be called to his destiny.

Starting college at age eight had just seemed part of that destiny. His parents had been so confident of him, even though his tests results were scarcely more than bright normal. . . . That year had been the destruction of innocence. He wasn't a genius, no matter how much his parents insisted. The fights, the tears, their insistence. In the end, Mom had left Hussein Thompson. Not till then did the man relent, let his child return to normal schools. Life at home was never the same. Mom's visits were brief, tense

. . . and rare. But it wasn't for another five years that Hamid learned to hate his father. The learning had been an accident, a conversation overheard. Hussein had been *hired* to raise Hamid as he had, to push him into school, to twist and ruin him. The old man had never denied the boy's accusations. His attempts to "explain" had been vague mumbling . . . worse than lies. . . . If Hamid was a prince, he must be a very hated one indeed.

The memories had worn deep grooves, ones he often slid down on his way to sleep. . . . But tonight there was something new, something ironic to the point of magic. All these years . . . it had been the Blab who was the lost princeling. . . !

There was a hissing sound. Hamid struggled toward wakefulness, fear and puzzlement playing through his dreams. He rolled to the edge of the bed and forced his eyes to see. Only stars shone through the window. The Blab. She wasn't sitting at the window screen anymore. She must be having one of her nightmares. They were rare, but spectacular. One winter's night Hamid had been wakened by the sounds of a full-scale thunderstorm. This was not so explosive, but . . .

He looked across the floor at the pile of blankets that was her nest. Yes. She was there, and facing his way.

"Blab? It's okay, baby."

No reply. Only the hissing, maybe louder now. *It wasn't coming from the Blab.* For an instant his fuzzy mind hung in a kind of mouse-and-snake paralysis. Then he flicked on the lights. No one here. The sound was from the dataset; the picture flat remained dark. *This is crazy.*

"Blab?" He had never seen her like this. Her eyes were open wide, rings of white showing around the

irises. Her forelegs reached beyond the blankets.
The talons were extended and had slashed deep into
the plastic flooring. A string of drool hung from her
muzzle.

He got up, started toward her. The hissing formed
a voice, and the voice spoke. "I want her. Human, I
want her. And I will have her." Her, the Blab.

"How did you get access? You have no business
disturbing us." Silly talk, but it broke the nightmare
spell of this waking.

"My name is Tines." Hamid suddenly remembered the claw on the Ravna&Tines logo. Tines.
Cute. "We have made generous offers. We have
been patient. That is past. I will have her. If it
means the death of all you m-meat animals, so be it.
But I *will* have her."

The hissing was almost gone now, but the voice
still sounded like something from a cheap synthesizer.
The syntax and accent were similar to Ravna's. They
were either the same person, or they had learned
English from the same source. Still, Ravna had seemed
angry. Tines sounded flat-out nuts. Except for the
single stutter over "meat," the tone and pacing were
implacable. And that voice gave away more than
anything yet about why the Outsider wanted his pet.
There was a *hunger* in its voice, a lust to feed or to
rape.

Hamid's rage climbed on top of his fear. "Why
don't you just go screw yourself, comic monster! We've
got *protection*, else you wouldn't come bluffing—"

"Bluffing! *Bluffiiyowru*—" the words turned into
choked gobbling sounds. Behind him, Hamid heard
the Blab scream. After a moment the noises faded. "I
do not bluff. Hussein Thompson has this hour learned
what I do with those who cross me. You and all your
people will also die unless you deliver her to me. I
see a ground car parked by your . . . house. Use it to

take her east fifty kilometers. Do this within one hour, or learn what Hussein Thompson learned—that *I do not bluff.*" And Mr. Tines was gone.

It has to be a bluff! If Tines has that power, why not wipe the Tourists from the sky and just grab the Blab? Yet they were so stupid about it. A few smooth lies a week ago, and they might have gotten everything without a murmur. It was as if they couldn't imagine being disobeyed—or were desperate beyond reason.

Hamid turned back to the Blab. As he reached to stroke her neck, she twisted, her needle-toothed jaws clicking shut on his pyjama sleeve. "Blab!"

She released his sleeve, and drew back into the pile of blankets. She was making whistling noises like the time she got hit by a pickup trike. Hamid's father had guessed those must be true blabber sounds, like human sobs or chattering of teeth. He went to his knees and made comforting noises. This time she let him stroke her neck. He saw that she had wet her bed. The Blab had been toilet-trained as long as he had. Bluff or not, this had thoroughly terrified her. Tines claimed he could kill everyone. Hamid remembered the ansible, a god-damned telephone that could dim the sun.

Bluff or madness?

He scrambled back to his dataset, and punched up the Tour Director's number. Pray the slug was accepting more than mail tonight. The ring pattern flashed twice, and then he was looking at a panorama of cloud tops and blue sky. It might have been an aerial view of Middle America, except that as you looked downward the clouds seemed to extend forever, more and more convoluted in the dimness. This was a picture clip from the ten-bar level over Lothlrimarre. No doubt the slug chose it to soothe human callers, and still be true to the nature of his home world—a subjovian thirty thousand kilometers across.

For five seconds they soared through the canyons of cloud. *Wake up, damn you!*

The picture cleared and he was looking at a human—Larry Fujiyama! Lazy Larry did not look surprised to see him. "You got the right number, kid. I'm up here with the slug. There have been developments."

Hamid gaped for an appropriate reply, and the other continued. "Ravna&Tines have been all over the slug since about midnight. Threats and promises, mostly threats since the Tines critter took their comm. . . . I'm sorry about your dad, Hamid. We should've thought to—"

"*What?*"

"Isn't that what you're calling about? . . . Oh. It's been on the news. Here—" The picture dissolved into a view from a news chopper flying over Eastern Michigan farmland. It took Hamid a second to recognize the hills. This was near the Thompson spread, two thousand klicks east of Marquette. It would be past sunup there. The camera panned over a familiar creek, the newsman bragging how On-Line News was ahead of the first rescue teams. They crested a range of hills and . . . where were the trees? Thousands of black lines lay below, trunks of blown-over trees, pointing inevitably inward, toward the center of the blast. The newsman babbled on about the meteor strike and how fortunate it was that ground zero was in a lake valley, how only one farm had been affected. Hamid swallowed. That farm . . . was Hussein Thompson's. The place they lived after Mom left. Ground zero itself was obscured by rising steam—all that was left of the lake. The reporter assured his audience that the crater consumed all the land where the farm buildings had been.

The news clip vanished. "It was no Middle American nuke, but it wasn't natural, either," said Larry. "A lighter from Ravna&Tines put down there two hours ago. Just before the blast, I got a real scared call from Huss, something about 'the tines' arriving. I'll show it to you if—"

"No!" Hamid gulped. "No," he said more quietly. How he had hated Hussein Thompson; how he had loved his father in the years before. Now he was gone, and Hamid would never get his feelings sorted out. "Tines just called me. He said he killed my—Hussein." Hamid played back the call. "Anyway, I need to talk to the slug. Can he protect me? Is Middle America really in for it if I refuse the Tines thing?"

For once Larry didn't give his "you figure it" shrug. "It's a mess," he said. "And sluggo's waffling. He's around here somewhere. Just a sec—" More peaceful cloud-soaring. Damn, damn, damn. Something bumped gently into the small of his back. The Blab. The black and white neck came around his side. The dark eyes looked up at him. "What's up?" she said quietly.

Hamid felt like laughing and crying. She was very subdued, but at least she recognized him now. "Are you okay, Baby?" he said. The Blabber curled up around him, her head stretched out on his knee.

On the dataset, the clouds parted and they were looking at both Larry Fujiyama and the slug. Of course, they were not in the same room; that would have been fatal to both. The Lothlrimarre barge was a giant pressure vessel. Inside, pressure and atmosphere were just comfy for the slug—about a thousand bars of ammonia and hydrogen. There was a terrarium for human visitors. The current view showed the slug in the foreground. Part of the wall behind him was transparent, a window into the terrarium.

Larry gave a little wave, and Hamid felt himself smiling. No question who was in a zoo.

"Ah, Mr. Thompson. I'm glad you called. We have a very serious problem." The slug's English was perfect, and though the voice was artificial, he sounded like a perfectly normal Middle American male. "Many problems would be solved if you could see your way clear to give—"

"No." Hamid's voice was flat. "N-not while I'm alive, anyway. This is no business deal. You've heard the threats, and you saw what they did to my father." The slug had been his ultimate employer these last six months, someone rarely spoken to, the object of awe. None of that mattered now. "You've always said the first responsibility of the Tour Director is to see that no party is abused by another. I'm asking you to live up to that."

"Um. Technically, I was referring to you Middle Americans and the Tourists in my caravan. I know I have the power to make good on my promises with them. . . . But we're just beginning to learn about Ravna&Tines. I'm not sure it's reasonable to stand up against them." He swiveled his thousand-kilo bulk toward the terrarium window. Hamid knew that under Lothlrimarre gravity the slug would have been squashed into the shape of a flatworm, with his manipulator fringe touching the ground. At one gee, he looked more like an overstuffed silk pillow, fringed with red tassels. "Larry has told me about Skandr's remarkable Slow Zone device. I've heard of such things. They are *very* difficult to obtain. A single one would have more than financed my caravan. . . . And to think that Skandr pleaded his foundation's poverty in begging passage. . . . Anyway, Larry has been using the 'ansible' to ask about what your blabber really is."

Larry nodded. "Been at it since you left, Hamid.

The machine's down in my office, buzzing away. Like Skandr says, it is aligned on the commercial outlet at Lothlrimarre. From there I have access to the Known Net. Heh, heh. Skandr left a *sizable* credit bond at Lothlrimarre. I hope he and Ortega aren't too upset by the phone bill I run up testing this gadget for them. I described the Blab, and put out a depth query. There are a million subnets, all over the Beyond, searching their databases for anything like the Blab. I—" His happy enthusiasm wavered, "Sluggo thinks we've dug up a reference to the blabber's race. . . ."

"Yes, and it's frightening, Mr. Thompson." It was no surprise that none of the Tourists had heard of a blabber. The only solid lead coming back to Larry had been from halfway around the galactic rim, a nook in the Beyond that had only one occasional link with the rest of the Known Net. That far race had no direct knowledge of the blabbers. But they heard rumors. From a thousand light years below them, deep within the Slow Zone, there came stories . . . of a race matching the Blab's appearance. The race was highly intelligent, and had quickly developed the relativistic transport that was the fastest thing inside the Zone. They colonized a vast sphere, held an empire of ten thousand worlds—all without ftl. And the tines—the name seemed to fit—had not held their empire through the power of brotherly love. Races had been exterminated, planets busted with relativistic kinetic energy bombs. The tines' technology had been about as advanced and deadly as could exist in the Zone. Most of their volume was a tomb now, their story whispered through centuries of slow flight toward the Outside.

"Wait, wait. Prof Fujiyama told me the ansible's bandwidth is a tenth of a bit per second. You've had less than twelve hours to work this question. How can you possibly know all this?"

Larry looked a little embarrassed—a first as far as Hamid could remember. "We've been using the AI protocol I told you about. There's massive interpolation going on at both ends of our link to Lothlrimarre."

"I'll bet!"

"Remember, Mr. Thompson, the data compression applies only to the first link in the chain. The Known Net lies in the Beyond. Bandwidth and data integrity are very high across most of its links."

The slug sounded very convinced. But Hamid had read a lot about the Known Net; the notion was almost as fascinating as ftl travel itself. There was no way a world could have a direct link with all others—partly because of range limitations, mainly because of the *number* of planets involved. Similarly, there was no way a single "phone company" (or even ten thousand phone companies!) could run the thing. Most likely, the information coming to them from around the galaxy had passed through five or ten intermediate hops. The intermediates—not to mention the race on the far rim—were likely nonhuman. Imagine asking a question in English of someone who also speaks Spanish, and that person asking the question in Spanish of someone who understands Spanish and passes the question on in German. This was a million times worse. Next to some of the creatures Out There, the slug could pass for human!

Hamid said as much. "F-furthermore, even if this *is* what the sender meant, it could still be a lie! Look at what local historians did to Richard the Third, or Mohamet Rose."

Lazy Larry smiled his polliwog smile, and Hamid realized they must have been arguing about this already. Larry put in, "There's also this, sluggo: the nature of the identification. The tines must have something like hands. See any on Hamid's Blabber?"

The slug's scarlet fringe rippled three quick cycles. Agitation? Dismissal? "The text is still coming in. But I have a theory. You know, Larry, I've always been a great student of sex. I may be a 'he' only by courtesy, but I think sex is fascinating. It's what makes the 'world go around' for so many races." Hamid suddenly understood Gilli Weinberg's success. "So. Grant me my expertise. My guess is the tines exhibit *extreme* sexual dimorphism. The males' forepaws probably are hands. No doubt it's the males who are the killers. The females—like the Blab—are by contrast friendly, mindless creatures."

The Blab's eyes rolled back to look at Hamid. "Sure, sure," she murmured. The accident of timing was wonderful, seeming to say *Who is this clown?*

The slug didn't notice. "This may even explain the viciousness of the male. Think back to the conversation Mr. Thompson had. These creatures seem to regard their own females as property to exploit. Rather the ultimate in sexism." Hamid shivered. That *did* ring a bell. He couldn't forget the *hunger* in the tines's voice.

"Is this the long way to tell me you're not going to protect us?"

The slug was silent for almost fifteen seconds. Its scarlet fringe waved up and down the whole time. Finally: "Almost, I'm afraid. My caravan customers haven't heard this analysis, just the threats and the news broadcasts. Nevertheless, they are tourists, not explorers. They demand that I refuse to let you aboard. Some demand that we leave your planet immediately. . . . How secure is this line, Larry?"

Fujiyama said, "Underground fiberoptics, and an encrypted laser link. Take a chance, sluggo."

"Very well. Mr. Thompson, here is what you can expect from me:

"I can stay over the city, and probably defend against direct kidnapping—unless I see a planetbuster coming. I doubt very much they have that set up, but if they do—well, I don't think even you would want to keep your dignity at the price of a relativistic asteroid strike.

"I can *not* come down to pick you up. That would be visible to all, a direct violation of my customers' wishes. On the other hand," there was another pause, and his scarlet fringe whipped about even faster than before, "if you should appear, uh, up here, I would take you aboard my barge. Even if this were noticed, it would be a *fait accompli*. I could hold off my customers, and likely our worst fate would be a premature and unprofitable departure from Middle America."

"T-that's very generous." *Unbelievably so.* The slug was thought to be an honest fellow—but a very hard trader. Even Hamid had to admit that the claim on the slug's honor was tenuous here, yet he was risking a twenty-year mission for it.

"Of course, *if* we reach that extreme, I'll want a few years of your time once we reach the Outside. My bet is that hard knowledge about your Blabber might make up for the loss of everything else."

A day ago, Hamid would have quibbled about contracts and assurances. Today, well, the alternative was Ravna&Tines. . . . With Larry as witness, they settled on two years' indenture and a pay scale.

Now all he and the Blab had to do was figure how to climb five thousand meters straight up. There was one obvious way.

It was Dave Larson's car, but Davey owed him. Hamid woke his neighbor, explained that the Blab

was sick and had to go into Marquette. Fifteen minutes later, Hamid and the Blab were driving through
Ann Arbor Town. It was a Saturday, and barely into
morning twilight; he had the road to himself. He'd
half expected the place to be swarming with cops and
military. If Ravna&Tines ever guessed how easy it
was to intimidate Joe Ortega . . . If the Feds knew
exactly what was going on, they'd turn the Blab over
to Tines in an instant. But apparently the government was simply confused, lying low, hoping it
wouldn't be noticed till the big boys upstairs settled
their arguments. The farm bombing wasn't in the
headline list anymore. The Feds were keeping things
quiet, thereby confining the mindless panic to the
highest circles of government.

The Blab rattled around the passenger side of the
car, alternately leaning on the dash and sniffing in
the bag of tricks that Hamid had brought. She was
still subdued, but riding in a private auto was a
novelty. Electronics gear was cheap, but consumer
mechanicals were still at a premium. And without a
large highway system, cars would never be the rage
they had been on Old Earth; most freight transport
was by rail. A lot of this could change because of the
Caravan. They brought one hundred thousand agrav
plates—enough to revolutionize transport. Middle
America would enter the Age of the Aircar—and for
the first time surpass the homeworld. So saith Joe
Ortega.

Past the University, there was a patch of open
country. Beyond the headlights Hamid caught glimpses
of open fields, a glint of frost. Hamid looked up
nervously every few seconds. Selene and Diane hung
pale in the west. Scattered clouds floated among the
Tourist barges, vague grayness in the first light of
morning. No intruders, but three of the barges were
gone, presumably moved to orbit. The Lothlrimarre

vessel floated just east of Marquette, over the warehouse quarter. It looked like the slug was keeping his part of the deal.

Hamid drove into downtown Marquette. Sky signs floated brightly amid the two-hundred-story towers, advertising dozens of products—some of which actually existed. Light from discos and shopping malls flooded the eight-lane streets. Of course the place was deserted; it was Saturday morning. Much of the business section was like this—a reconstruction of the original Marquette as it had been on Earth in the middle twenty-first century. That Marquette had sat on the edge of an enormous lake, called Superior. Through that century, as Superior became the splashdown point for heavy freight from space, Marquette had become one of the great port cities of Earth, the gateway to the solar system. The Tourists said it was legend, ur-mother to a thousand worlds.

Hamid turned off the broadway, down an underground ramp. The Marquette of today was for show, perhaps one percent the area of the original, with less than one percent the population. But from the air it looked good, the lights and bustle credible. For special events, the streets could be packed with a million people—everyone on the continent who could be spared from essential work. And the place wasn't really a fraud; the Tourists knew this was a reconstruction. The point was, it was an *authentic* reconstruction, as could only be created by a people one step from the original source—that was the official line. And in fact, the people of Middle America had made enormous sacrifices over almost twenty years to have this ready in time for the Caravan.

The car rental was down a fifteen-story spiral, just above the train terminal. *That* was for real, though the next arrival was a half hour away. Hamid got out, smelling the cool mustiness of the stone cavern, hearing only the echoes of his own steps. Millions of tonnes of ceramic and stone stood between them and the sky. Even an Outsider couldn't see through that . . . he hoped. One sleepy-eyed attendant watched him fill out the forms. Hamid stared at the display, sweating even in the cool; would the guy in back notice? He almost laughed at the thought. His first sally into crime was the least of his worries. If Ravna&Tines were plugged into the credit net, then in a sense they really *could* see down here—and the bogus number Larry had supplied was all that kept him invisible.

They left in a Millennium Commander, the sort of car a Tourist might use to bum around in olden times. Hamid drove north through the underground, then east, and when finally they saw open sky again, they were driving south. Ahead was the warehouse district . . . and hanging above it, the slug's barge, its spheres and cupolas green against the brightening sky. So huge. It looked near, but Hamid knew it was a good five thousand meters up.

A helicopter might be able to drop someone on its topside, or maybe land on one of the verandas—though it would be a tight fit under the overhang. But Hamid couldn't fly a chopper, and wasn't even sure how to rent one at this time of day. No, he and the Blab were going to try something a lot more straightforward, something he had done every couple of weeks since the Tourists arrived.

They were getting near the incoming lot, where Feds and Tourists held payments-to-date in escrow. Up ahead there would be cameras spotted on the roofs. He tinted all but the driver-side window, and pushed down on the Blab's shoulders with his free hand. "Play hide for a few minutes."

"Okay."

Three hundred meters more and they were at the outer gate. He saw the usual three cops out front, and a fourth in an armored box to the side. If Ortega was feeling the heat, it could all end right here.

They looked *real* nervous, but they spent most of their time scanning the sky. They knew something was up, but they thought it was out of their hands. They took a quick glance at the Millennium Commander and waved him through. The inner fence was almost as easy, though here he had to enter his Guide ID. . . . If Ravna&Tines were watching the nets, Hamid and the Blab were running on borrowed time now.

He pulled into the empty parking lot at the main warehouse, choosing a slot with just the right position relative to the guard box. "Keep quiet a little while, Blab," he said. He hopped out and walked across the gravel yard. Maybe he should move faster, as if panicked? But no, the guard had already seen him. *Okay, play it cool.* He waved, kept walking. The glow of morning was already dimming the security lamps that covered the lot. No stars shared the sky with the clouds and the barges.

It was kind of a joke that merchandise from the Beyond was socked away here. The warehouse was big, maybe two hundred meters on a side, but an old place, sheet plastic and aging wood timbers.

The armored door buzzed even before Hamid touched it. He pushed his way through. "Hi, Phil."

Luck! The other guards must be on rounds. Phil Lucas was a friendly sort, but not too bright, and not very familiar with the Blab. Lucas sat in the middle of the guard cubby, and the armored partition that separated him from the visitor trap was raised. To the left was a second door that opened into the warehouse itself. "Hi, Ham." The guard looked back at him nervously. "Awful early to see you."

"Yeah. Got a little problem. There's a Tourist out in the Commander." He waved through the armored window. "He's drunk out of his mind. I need to get him Upstairs and quietly."

Phil licked his lips. "Christ. Everything happens at once. Look, I'm sorry, Ham. We've got orders from the top at Federal Security: nothing comes down, nothing goes up. There's some kind of a ruckus going on amongst the Outsiders. If they start shooting, we want it to be at each other, not us."

"That's the point. We think this fellow is part of the problem. If we can get him back, things should cool off. You should have a note on him. It's Antris ban Reempt."

"Oh. *Him.*" Ban Reempt was the most obnoxious Tourist of all. If he'd been an ordinary Middle American, he would have racked up a century of jail time in the last six months. Fortunately, he'd never killed anyone, so his antics were just barely ignorable. Lucas pecked at his dataset. "No, we don't have anything."

"Nuts. Everything stays jammed unless we can get this guy Upstairs." Hamid paused judiciously, as if giving the matter serious thought. "Look, I'm going back to the car, see if I can call somebody to confirm this."

Lucas was dubious. "Okay, but it's gotta be from the top, Ham."

"Right."

The door buzzed open, and Hamid was jogging back across the parking lot. Things really seemed on track. Thank God he'd always been friendly with the cops running security here. The security people regarded most of the Guides as college-trained snots—

and with some reason. But Hamid had had coffee with these guys more than once. He knew the system . . . he even knew the incoming phone number for security confirmations.

Halfway across the lot, Hamid suddenly realized that he didn't have the shakes anymore. The scheme, the ad-libbing: it almost seemed normal—a skill he'd never guessed he had. Maybe that's what desperation does to a fellow. . . . Somehow this was almost fun.

He pulled open the car door. "Back! Not yet." He pushed the eager Blab onto the passenger seat. "Big game, Blab." He rummaged through his satchel, retrieved the two comm sets. One was an ordinary head and throat model; the other had been modified for the Blab. He fastened the mike under the collar of his windbreaker. The earphone shouldn't be needed, but it was small; he put it on, turned the volume down. Then he strapped the other commset around the Blab's neck, turned off *its* mike, and clipped the receiver to her ear. "The game, Blab: Imitation. Imitation." He patted the commset on her shoulder. The Blab was fairly bouncing around the Commander's cab. "For sure. Sure, sure! Who, who?"

"Joe Ortega. Try it: 'We must all pull together . . .' "

The words came back from the Blab as fast as he spoke them, but changed into the voice of the Middle American President. He rolled down the driver-side window; this worked best if there was eye contact. Besides, he might need her out of the car. "Okay. Stay here. I'll go get us the sucker." She rattled his instructions back in pompous tones.

One last thing: He punched a number into the car phone, and set its timer and no video option. Then he was out of the car, jogging back to the guard box. This sort of trick had worked often enough at school.

Pray that it would work now. Pray that she wouldn't ad lib.

He turned off the throat mike as Lucas buzzed him back into the visitor trap. "I got to the top. Someone— maybe even the Chief of Federal Security—will call back on the Red Line."

Phil's eyebrows went up. "That would do it." Hamid's prestige had just taken a giant step up.

Hamid made a show of impatient pacing about the visitor trap. He stopped at the outer door with his back to the guard. Now he really *was* impatient. Then the phone rang, and he heard Phil pick it up.

"Escrow One, Agent Lucas speaking, sir!"

From where he was standing, Hamid could see the Blab. She was in the driver's seat, looking curiously at the dash phone. Hamid turned on the throat mike and murmured, "Lucas, this is Joseph Stanley Ortega."

Almost simultaneously, "Lucas, this is Joseph Stanley Ortega," came from the phone behind him. The words were weighted with all the importance Hamid could wish, and something else: a furtiveness not in the public speeches. That was probably because of Hamid's original delivery, but it didn't sound too bad.

In any case, Phil Lucas was impressed. "Sir!"

"Agent Lucas, we have a problem." Hamid concentrated on his words, and tried to ignore the Ortega echo. For him, that was the hardest part of the trick, especially when he had to speak more than a brief sentence. "There could be nuclear fire, unless the Tourists cool off. I'm with the National Command Authorities in deep shelter: it's that serious." Maybe that would explain why there was no video.

Phil's voice quavered. "Yes, sir." *He* wasn't in deep shelter.

"Have you verified—" *clicket* "—my ID?" The click was in Hamid's earphone; he didn't hear it on the guard's set. A loose connection in the headpiece?

"Yes, sir. I mean . . . just one moment." Sounds of hurried keyboard tapping. There should be no problem with a voiceprint match, and Hamid needed things nailed tight to bring this off. "Yes sir, you're fine. I mean—"

"Good. Now listen carefully: the Guide, Thompson, has a Tourist with him. We need that Outsider returned, *quickly and quietly*. Get the lift ready, and keep everybody clear of these two. If Thompson fails, millions may die. Give him whatever he asks for." Out in the car, the Blab was having a high old time. Her front talons were hooked awkwardly over the steering wheel. She twisted it back and forth, "driving" and "talking" at the same time: the apotheosis of life—to be taken for a person by real people!

"Yes, sir!"

"Very well. Let's—" *clicket-click* "—get moving on this." And on that last click, the Ortega voice was gone. *God damned cheapjack commset!*

Lucas was silent a moment, respectfully waiting for his President to continue. Then, "Yes, sir. What must we do?"

Out in the Millennium Commander, the Blab was the picture of consternation. She turned toward him, eyes wide. *What do I say now?* Hamid repeated the line, as loud as he dared. No Ortega. *She can't hear anything I'm saying!* He shut off his mike.

"Sir? Are you still there?"

"Line must be dead," Hamid said casually, and gave the Blab a little wave to come running.

"Phone light says I still have a connection, Ham. . . . Mr. President, can you hear me? You were saying what we must do. Mr. President?"

The Blab didn't recognize his wave. Too small. He

tried again. She tapped a talon against her muzzle. *Blab! Don't ad lib!* "Well, uh," came Ortega's voice, "don't rush me. I'm thinking. I'm thinking! . . . We must all pull together or else millions may die. Don't you think? I mean, it makes sense—" which it did not, and less so by the second. Lucas was making "uh-huh" sounds, trying to fit reason on the blabber. His tone was steadily more puzzled, even suspicious.

No help for it. Hamid slammed his fist against the transp armor, and waved wildly to the Blab. *Come here!* Ortega's voice died in mid-syllable. He turned to see Lucas staring at him, surprise and uneasiness on his face. "Something's going on here, and I don't like it—" Somewhere in his mind, Phil had figured out he was being taken, yet the rest of him was carried forward by the inertia of the everyday. He leaned over the counter, to get Hamid's line of view on the lot.

The original plan was completely screwed, yet strangely he felt no panic, no doubt; there were still options: Hamid smiled—and jumped across the counter, driving the smaller man into the corner of wall and counter. Phil's hand reached wildly for the tab that would bring the partition down. Hamid just pushed him harder against the wall . . . and grabbed the guard's pistol from its holster. He jammed the barrel into the other's middle. "Quiet down, Phil."

"*Son of a bitch!*" But the other stopped struggling. Hamid heard the Blab slam into the outer door.

"Okay. Kick the outside release." The door buzzed. A moment later, the Blab was in the visitor trap, bouncing around his legs.

"Heh heh heh! That was good. That was really good!" The crackle was Lazy Larry's but the voice was still Ortega's.

"Now buzz the inner door." The other gave his

head a tight shake. Hamid punched Lucas's gut with the point of the pistol. *"Now!"* For an instant, Phil seemed frozen. Then he kneed the control tab, and the inner door buzzed. Hamid pushed it ajar with his foot, then heaved Lucas away from the counter. The other bounced to his feet, his eyes staring at the muzzle of the pistol, his face very pale. *Dead men don't raise alarums.* The thought was clear on his face.

Hamid hesitated, almost as shocked by his success as Lucas was. "Don't worry, Phil." He shifted his aim and fired a burst over Lucas's shoulder . . . into the warehouse security processor. Fire and debris flashed back into the room—and now alarms sounded everywhere.

He pushed through the door, the Blab close behind. The armor clicked shut behind them; odds were, it would stay locked now that the security processor was down. Nobody in sight, but he heard shouting. Hamid ran down the aisle of upgoing goods. They kept the agrav lift at the back of the building, under the main ceiling hatch. Things were definitely not going to plan, but if the lift was there, he could still—

"There he is!"

Hamid dived down an aisle, jigged this way and that between pallets . . . and then began walking very quietly. He was in the downcoming section now, surrounded by the goods that had been delivered thus far by the Caravan. These were the items that would lift Middle America beyond Old Earth's twenty-first century. Towering ten meters above his head were stacks of room-temperature fusion electrics. With them—and the means to produce more—Middle America could trash its methanol economy and fixed fusion plants. Two aisles over were the raw agrav units. These looked more like piles of fabric than anything high tech. Yet the warehouse lifter was built around one, and with them Middle America would soon make aircars as easily as automobiles.

Hamid knew there were cameras in the ceiling above the lights. Hopefully they were as dead as the security processor. Footsteps one aisle over. Hamid eased into the dark between two pallets. Quiet, quiet. The Blab didn't feel like being quiet. She raced down the aisle ahead of him, raking the spaces between the pallets with a painfully loud imitation of his pistol. They'd see her in a second. He ran the other direction a few meters, and fired a burst into the air.

"Jesus! How many did asshole Lucas let in?" Someone very close replied, "That's still low-power stuff." Much quieter: "We'll show these guys some firepower." Hamid suddenly guessed there were only two of them. And with the guard box jammed, they might be trapped in here till the alarm brought guards from outside.

He backed away from the voices, continued toward the rear of the warehouse.

"Boo!" The Blab was on the pallets above him, talking to someone on the ground. Explosive shells smashed into the fusion electrics around her. The sounds bounced back and forth through the warehouse. Whatever it was, it was a cannon compared to his pistol. No doubt it was totally unauthorized for indoors, but that did Hamid little good. He raced forward, heedless of the destruction. "Get down!" he screamed at the pallets. A bundle of shadow and light materialized in front of him and streaked down the aisle.

A second roar of cannon fire, tearing through the space he had just been. But something else was happening now. Blue light shone from somewhere in the racks of fusion electrics, sending brightness and crisp shadows across the walls ahead. It felt as if someone had opened a furnace door behind him. He looked back. The blue was spreading, an arc-welder light that promised burns yet unfelt. He looked quickly away, afterimages dancing on his eyes, afterimages of the pallet shelves *sagging* in the heat.

The autosprinklers kicked on, an instant rainstorm. But this was a fire that water would not quench—and might even fuel. The water exploded into steam, knocking Hamid to his knees. He bounced up sprinting, falling, sprinting again. The agrav lift should be around the next row of pallets. In the back of his mind, something was analyzing the disaster. That explosive cannon fire had started things, a runaway melt in the fusion electrics. They were supposedly safer than meth engines—but they could melt down. This sort of destruction in a Middle American nuclear plant would have meant rad poisoning over a continent. But the Tourists claimed their machines melted clean—shedding low-energy photons and an enormous flood of particles that normal matter scarcely responded to. Hamid felt an urge to hysterical laughter; Slow Zone astronomers light years away might notice this someday, a wiggle on their neutrino scopes, one more datum for their flawed cosmologies.

There was lightning in the rainstorm now, flashes between the pallets and across the aisle—into the raw agrav units. The clothlike material jerked and rippled, individual units floating upwards. Magic carpets released by a genie.

Then giant hands clapped him, sound that was pain, and the rain was gone, replaced by a hot wet wind that swept around and up. Morning light shown through the steamy mist. The explosion had blasted open the roof. A rainbow arced across the ruins. Hamid was crawling now. Sticky wet ran down his

face, dripped redly on the floor. The pallets bearing
the fusion electrics had collapsed. Fifteen meters
away, molten plastic slurried atop flowing metal.

He could see the agrav lift now, what was left of it.
The lift sagged like an old candle in the flow of
molten metal. So. No way up. He pulled himself
back from the glare and leaned against the stacked
agravs. They slid and vibrated behind him. The cloth
was soft, yet it blocked the heat, and some of the
noise. The pinkish blue of a dawn sky shown through
the last scraps of mist. The Lothlrimarre barge hung
there, four spherical pressure vessels embedded in
intricate ramps and crenellations.

Jeeze. Most of the warehouse roof was just . . .
gone. A huge tear showed through the far wall.
There! The two guards. They were facing away from
him, one half leaning on the other. Chasing him was
very far from their minds at the moment. They were
picking their way through the jumble, trying to get
out of the warehouse. Unfortunately, a rivulet of
silver metal crossed their path. One false step and
they'd be ankle deep in stuff. But they were lucky,
and in fifteen seconds passed from sight around the
outside of the building.

No doubt he could get out that way, too. . . . But
that wasn't why he was here. Hamid struggled to his
feet, and began shouting for the Blab. The hissing,
popping sounds were loud, but not like before. If she
were conscious, she'd hear him. He wiped blood
from his lips and limped along the row of agrav piles.
Don't die, Blab. Don't die.

There was motion everywhere. The piles of agravs
had come alive. The top ones simply lifted off, tumbled upwards, rolling and unrolling. The lower layers
strained and jerked. Normal matter might not notice
the flood of never-never particles from the melt-

down; the agravs were clearly not normal. Auras flickered around the ones trapped at the bottom. But this was not the eye-sizzling burn of the fusion electrics. This was a soft thing, an awakening rather than an explosion. Hamid's eyes were caught on the rising. Hundreds of them just floating off, gray and russet banners in the morning light. He leaned back. Straight up, the farthest ones were tiny specks against the blue. *Maybe—*

Something banged into his legs, almost dumping him back on the floor. "Wow. So loud." The Blab had found *him*! Hamid knelt and grabbed her around the neck. She looked fine! A whole lot better than he did, anyway. Like most smaller animals, she could take a lot of bouncing around. He ran his hands down her shoulders. There were some nicks, a spattering of blood. And she looked subdued, not quite the hellion of before. "Loud. Loud," she kept saying.

"I know, Blab. But that's the worst." He looked back into the sky. At the rising agravs . . . at the Lothlrimarre barge. *It would be crazy to try . . .* but he heard sirens outside.

He patted the Blab, then stood and clambered up the nearest pile of agravs. The material, hundreds of separate units piled like blankets, gave beneath his boots like so much foam rubber. He slid back a ways after each step. He grabbed at the edges of the units above him, and pulled himself near the top. He wanted to test one that was free to rise. Hamid grabbed the top layer, already rippling in an unsensed wind. He pulled out his pocket knife and slashed at the material. It parted smoothly, with the resistence of heavy felt. He ripped off a strip of the material, stuffed it in his pocket, then grabbed again at the top layer. The unit fluttered in his hands, a four-meter square straining for the sky. It slowly tipped him backwards. His feet left the pile. It was rising as fast as the unloaded ones!

"Wait for me! Wait!" The Blab jumped desperately at his boots. Two meters up, three meters. Hamid gulped, and let go. He crashed to the concrete, lay stunned for a moment, imagining what would have happened if he'd dithered an instant longer. . . . Still. He took the scrap of agrav from his pocket, stared at it as it tugged on his fingers. There was a pattern in the reddish-gray fabric, intricate and recursive. The Tourists said it was in a different class from the fusion electrics. The electrics involved advanced technology, but were constructable within the Slow Zone. Agrav, on the other hand . . . the effect could be explained in theory, but its practical use depended on instant-by-instant restabilization at atomic levels. The Tourists claimed there were billions of protein-sized processors in the fabric. This was an import—not just from the Beyond—but from Transhuman Space. Till now, Hamid had been a skeptic. Flying was such a prosaic thing. But . . . these things had no simple logic. They were more like living creatures, or complex control systems. They seemed a lot like the "smart matter" Larry claimed was common in Transhuman technology.

Hamid cut the strip into two different-sized pieces. The cut edges were smooth, quite unlike cuts in cloth or leather. He let the fragments go. . . . They drifted slowly upwards, like leaves on a breeze. But after a few seconds, the large one took the lead, falling higher and higher above the smaller. *I could come down just by trimming the fabric!* And he remembered how the carpet had drifted sideways, in the direction of his grasp.

The sirens were louder. He looked at the pile of agravs. Funny. A week ago he had been worried about flying commercial air to Westland. "You want games, Blab? This is the biggest yet."

He climbed back up the pile. The top layer was just beginning to twitch. They had maybe thirty seconds, if it was like the others. He pulled the fabric around him, tying it under his arms. "Blab! Get your ass up here!"

She came, but not quite with the usual glee. Things had been rough this morning—or maybe she was just brighter than he was. He grabbed her, and tied the other end of the agrav under her shoulders. As the agrav twitched toward flight, the cloth seemed to shrink. He could still cut the fabric, but the knots were tight. He grabbed the Blab under her hind quarters and drew her up to his chest—just like Pop used to do when the Blab was a pup. Only now, she was big. Her forelegs stuck long over his shoulders.

The fabric came taut around his armpits. Now he was standing. Now—his feet left the pile. He looked *down* at the melted pallets, the silver metal rivers that dug deep through the warehouse floor. The Blab was making the sounds of a small boy crying.

They were through the roof. Hamid shuddered as the morning chill turned his soaked clothing icy. The sun was at the horizon, its brilliance no help against the cold. Shadows grew long and crisp from the buildings. The guts of the warehouse lay open below them; from here it looked dark, but lightning still flickered. More reddish-gray squares floated up from the ruins. In the gravel lot fronting the warehouse, there were fire trucks and armored vehicles. Men ran back and forth from the guard box. A squad was moving around the side of the building. Two guys by the armored cars pointed at him, and others just stopped to stare. A boy and his not-dog, swinging beneath a wrong-way parachute. He'd seen enough

Feds 'n' Crooks to know they could shoot him down easily, any number of ways. One of the figures climbed into the armored car. If they were half as trigger-happy as the guards inside the warehouse . . .

Half a minute passed. The scene below could fit between his feet now. The Blab wasn't crying anymore, and he guessed the chill was no problem for her. The Blab's neck and head extended over his shoulder. He could feel her looking back and forth. "Wow," she said softly. "Wow."

Rockabye baby. They swung back and forth beneath the agrav. Back and forth. The swings were getting wider each time! In a sickening whirl, the sky and ground traded places. He was buried head first in agrav fabric. He struggled out of the mess. They weren't hanging below the agrav now, they were *lying* on top of it. This was crazy. How could it be stable with them on top? In a second it would dump them back under. He held tight to the Blab . . . but no more swinging. It was as if the hanging-down position had been the unstable one. More evidence that the agrav was smart matter, its processors using underlying nature to produce seemingly unnatural results.

The damn thing really was a flying carpet! Of course, with all the knots, the four-meter square of fabric was twisted and crumpled. It looked more like the Blab's nest of blankets back home than the flying carpets of fantasy.

The warehouse district was out of sight beneath the carpet. In the spaces around and above them, dozens of agravs paced him—some just a few meters away, some bare specks in the sky. Westward, they were coming even with the tops of the Marquette towers: brown and ivory walls, vast mirrors of windows reflecting back the landscape of morning. Southward, Ann Arbor was a tiny crisscross of streets, almost lost in the bristle of leafless trees. The quad was clearly visible, the interior walks, the tiny speck of red that was Morale Hall. He'd had roughly this view every time they flew back from the farm, but now . . . there was nothing around him. It was just Hamid and the Blab . . . and the air stretching away forever beneath them. Hamid gulped, and didn't look down for a while.

They were still rising. The breeze came straight down upon them—and it seemed to be getting stronger. Hamid shivered uncontrollably, teeth chattering. How high up were they? Three thousand meters? Four? He was going numb, and when he moved he could hear ice crackling in his jacket. He felt dizzy and nauseated—five thousand meters was about the highest you'd want to go without oxygen on Middle America. He *thought* he could stop the rise; if not, they were headed for space, along with the rest of the agravs.

But he had to do more than slow the rise, or descend. He looked up at the Lothlrimarre's barge. It was much nearer—and two hundred meters to the east. If he couldn't move this thing sideways, he'd need the slug's active cooperation.

It was something he had thought about—for maybe all of five seconds—back in the warehouse. If the agrav had been an ordinary lighter-than-air craft, there'd be no hope. Without props or jets, a balloon goes where the wind says; the only control comes from finding the *altitude* where the wind and you want the same thing. But when he grabbed that first carpet, it really had slid horizontally toward the side he was holding. . . .

He crept toward the edge. The agrav yielded beneath his knees, but didn't tilt more than a small boat would. Next to him, the Blab looked over the

edge, straight down. Her head jerked this way and
that as she scanned the landscape. "Wow," she kept
saying. Could she really understand what she was
seeing?

The wind shifted a little. It came a bit from the
side now, not straight from above. He really did
have control! Hamid smiled around chattering teeth.

The carpet rose faster and faster. The downward
wind was an arctic blast. They must be going up at
fifteen or twenty klicks per hour. The Lothlrimarre
barge loomed huge above them . . . now almost
beside them.

God, they were *above* it now! Hamid pulled out
his knife, picked desperately at the blade opener
with numbed fingers. It came open abruptly—and
almost popped out of his shaking hand. He trimmed
small pieces from the edge of the carpet. The wind
from heaven stayed just as strong. Bigger pieces! He
tore wildly at the cloth. One large strip, two. And
the wind eased . . . stopped. Hamid bent over the
edge of the carpet, and stuffed his vertigo back down
his throat. *Perfect.* They were directly over the barge,
and closing.

The nearest of the four pressure spheres was so
close it blocked his view of the others. Hamid could
see the human habitat, the conference area. They
would touch down on a broad flat area next to the
sphere. The aiming couldn't have been better. Hamid
guessed the slug must be maneuvering too, moving
the barge precisely under his visitor.

There was a flash of heat, and an invisible fist
slammed into the carpet. Hamid and the Blab
tumbled—now beneath the agrav, now above. He
had a glimpse of the barge. A jet of yellow-white
spewed from the sphere, ammonia and hydrogen at
one thousand atmospheres. The top pressure sphere
had been breached. The spear of superpressured gas

was surrounded by pale flame where the hydrogen and atmospheric oxygen burned.

The barge fell out of view, leaving thunder and burning mists. Hamid held onto the Blab and as much of the carpet as he could wrap around them. The tumbling stopped; they were upside down in the heavy swaddling. Hamid looked out:

"Overhead" was the brown and gray of farmland in late autumn. Marquette was to his left. He bent around, peeked into the sky. There! The barge was several klicks away. The top pressure vessel was spreading fire and mist, but the lower ones looked okay. Pale violet flickered from between the spheres. Moments later, thunder echoed across the sky. The slug was fighting back!

He twisted in the jumble of cloth, trying to see the high sky. To the north . . . a single blue-glowing trail lanced southwards . . . split into five separate, jigging paths that cooled through orange to red. It was beautiful . . . but somehow like a jagged claw sketched against the sky. The claw tips dimmed to nothing, but whatever caused them still raced forward. The attackers' answering fire slagged the north-facing detail of the barge. It crumpled like trash plastic in a fire. The bottom pressure vessels still looked okay, but if the visitor's deck got zapped like that, Larry would be a dead man.

Multiple sonic booms rocked the carpet. Things swept past, too small and fast to clearly see. The barge's guns still flickered violet, but the craft was rising now—faster than he had ever seen it move.

After a moment, the carpet drifted through one more tumble, and they sat heads up. The morning had been transformed. Strange clouds were banked around and above him, some burning, some glowing, all netted with the brownish of nitrogen oxides. The stench of ammonia burned his eyes and mouth.

The Blab was making noises through her mouth, true coughing and choking sounds.

The Tourists were long gone. The Lothlrimarre was a dot at the top of the sky. All the other agravs had passed by. He and the Blab were alone in the burning clouds. *Probably not for long.* Hamid began sawing at the agrav fabric—tearing off a slice, testing for an upwelling breeze, then tearing off another. They drifted through the cloud deck into a light drizzle, a strange rain that burned the skin as it wet them. He slid the carpet sideways into the sunlight, and they could breathe again. Things looked almost normal, except where the clouds cast a great bloody shadow across the farmland.

Where best to land? Hamid looked over the edge of the carpet . . . and saw the enemy waiting. It was a cylinder, tapered, with a pair of small fins at one end. It drifted through the carpet's shadow, and he realized the enemy craft was *close*. It couldn't be more than ten meters long, less than two meters across at the widest. It hung silent, pacing the carpet's slow descent. Hamid looked up, and saw the others—four more dark shapes. They circled in, like killer fish nosing at a possible lunch. One slid right over them, so slow and near he could have run his palm down its length. There were no ports, no breaks in the dull finish. But the fins—red glowed dim from within them, and Hamid felt a wave of heat as they passed.

The silent parade went on for a minute, each killer getting its look. The Blab's head followed the craft around and around. Her eyes were wide, and she was making the terrified whistling noises of the night before. The air was still, but for the faint updraft of the carpet's descent. Or was it? . . . The sound grew, a hissing sound like Tines had made during his phone call. Only now it came from all the killers, and there were overtones lurking at the edge of sensibility, tones that never could have come from an ordinary telephone.

"Blab." He reached to stroke her neck. She slashed at his hand, her needle-teeth slicing deep. Hamid gasped in pain, and rolled back from her. The Blab's pelt was puffed out as far as he had ever seen it. She looked twice normal size, a very large carnivore with death glittering in her eyes. Her long neck snapped this way and that, trying to track all the killers at once. Fore and rear talons dragged long rips through the carpet. She climbed onto the thickest folds of the carpet, and *shrieked* at the killers . . . and collapsed.

For a moment, Hamid couldn't move. His hand, the scream: razors across his hand, icepicks jammed in his ears. He struggled to his knees and crawled to the Blabber. "Blab?" No answer, no motion. He touched her flank: limp as something fresh dead.

In twenty years, Hamid Thompson had never had close friends, but he had never been alone, either. Until now. He looked up from the Blabber's body, at the circling shapes.

Alone at four thousand meters. He didn't have much choice when one of the killer fish came directly at him, when something wide and dark opened from its belly. The darkness swept around them, swallowing all.

Hamid had never been in space before. Under other circumstances, he would have reveled in the experience. The glimpse he'd had of Middle America from low orbit was like a beautiful dream. But now, all he could see through the floor of his cage was a bluish dot, nearly lost in the sun's glare. He pushed hard against the clear softness, and rolled onto his back. It was harder than a one-handed pushup to do that. He guessed the mothership was doing four or five gees . . . and had been for hours.

When they had pulled him off the attack craft, Hamid had been semiconscious. He had no idea what acceleration that shark boat reached, but it was more than he could take. He remembered that glimpse of Middle America, blue and serene. Then . . . they'd taken the Blab—or her body—away. *Who?* There had been a human, the Ravna woman. She had done something to his hand; it wasn't bleeding anymore. And . . . and there had been the Blabber, up and walking around. No, the pelt pattern had been all wrong. *That must have been Tines.* There had been the hissing voice, and some kind of argument with Ravna.

Hamid stared up at the sunlight on the ceiling and walls. His own shadow lay spread-eagled on the ceiling. In the first hazy hours, he had thought it was another prisoner. The walls were gray, seamless, but with scrape marks and stains, as though heavy equipment was used here. He thought there was a door in the ceiling, but he couldn't remember for sure. There was no sign of one now. The room was an empty cubicle, featureless, its floor showing clear to the stars: surely not an ordinary brig. There were no toilet facilities—and at five gees they wouldn't have helped. The air was thick with the stench of himself. . . . Hamid guessed the room was an airlock. The transparent floor might be nothing more than a figment of some field generator's imagination. A flick of a switch and Hamid would be swept away forever.

The Blabber gone, Pop gone, maybe Larry and the slug gone. . . . Hamid raised his good hand a few centimeters and clenched his fist. Lying here was the first time he'd ever thought about killing anyone. He thought about it a lot now. . . . It kept the fear tied down.

"Mr. Thompson." Ravna's voice. Hamid suppressed a twitch of surprise: after hours of rage, to hear the enemy. "Mr. Thompson, we are going to free fall in fifteen seconds. Do not be alarmed."

So, airline courtesy of a sudden.

The force that had squished him flat these hours, that had made it an exercise even to breathe, slowly lessened. From beyond the walls and ceiling he heard small popping noises. For a panicky instant, it seemed as though the floor had disappeared and he was falling through. He twisted. His hand hit the barrier . . . and he floated slowly across the room, toward the wall that had been the ceiling. A door had opened. He drifted through, into a hall that would have looked normal except for the intricate pattern of grooves and ledges that covered the walls.

"Thirty meters down the hall is a latrine," came Ravna's voice. "There are clean clothes that should fit you. When you are done . . . when you are done, we will talk."

Damn right. Hamid squared his shoulders and pulled himself down the hall.

She didn't look like a killer. There was anger—tension?—on her face, the face of someone who has been awake a long time and has fought hard—and doesn't expect to win.

Hamid drifted slowly into the—conference room? bridge?—trying to size everything up at once. It was a large room with a low ceiling. Moving across it was easy in zero gee, slow bounces from floor to ceiling and back. The wall curved around, transparent along most of its circumference. There were stars and night dark beyond.

Ravna had been standing in a splash of light. Now she moved back a meter, into the general dimness. Somehow she slipped her foot into the floor, anchoring herself. She waved him to the other side of a table. They stood in the half crouch of zero gee, less than two meters apart. Even so, she looked taller than he had guessed from the phone call. Her mass might be close to his. The rest of her was as he remembered, though she looked very tired. Her gaze flickered across him, and away. "Hello, Mr. Thompson. The floor will hold your foot, if you tap it gently."

Hamid didn't take the advice; he held onto the table edge and jammed his feet against the floor. He would have something to brace against if the time came to move quickly. "Where is my Blabber?" His voice came out hoarse, more desperate than demanding.

"Your pet is dead."

There was a tiny hesitation before the last word. She was as bad a liar as ever. Hamid pushed back the rage: if the Blab was alive, there was something still possible beyond revenge. "Oh." He kept his face blank.

"However, we intend to return you safely to home." She gestured at the star fields around them. "The six-gee boost was to avoid unnecessary fighting with the Lothlrimarre being. We will coast outwards some further, perhaps even go into ram drive. But Mr. Tines will take you back to Middle America in one of our attack boats. There will be no problem to land you without attracting notice . . . perhaps on the western continent, somewhere out of the way." Her tone was distant. He noticed that she never looked directly at him for more than an instant. Now she was staring just to one side of his face. He remembered the phone call, how she seemed to ignore his video. Up close, she was just as attractive as before— more. Just once he would like to see her smile. *And somewhere there was unease that he could be so attracted by a murderous stranger.*

If only, "If only I could understand *why*. Why did you kill the Blab? Why did you kill my father?"

Ravna's eyes narrowed. "That cheating piece of filth? He is too tricky to kill. He was gone when we visited his farm. I'm not sure I have killed anyone on this operation. The Lothlrimarre is still functioning, I know that." She sighed. "We were all very lucky. You have no idea what Tines has been like these last days. . . . He called you last night."

Hamid nodded numbly.

"Well, he was mellow then. He tried to kill me when I took over the ship. Another day like this and he would have been dead—and most likely your planet would have been so, too."

Hamid remembered the Lothlrimarre's theory about the tines's need. And now that the creature had the Blab . . . "So now Tines is satisfied?"

Ravna nodded vaguely, missing the quaver in his voice. "He's harmless now and very confused, poor guy. Assimilation is hard. It will be a few weeks . . . but he'll stabilize, probably turn out better than he ever was."

Whatever that means.

She pushed back from the table, stopped herself with a hand on the low ceiling. Apparently their meeting was over. "Don't worry. He should be well enough to take you home quite soon. Now I will show you your—"

"Don't rush him, Rav. Why should he want to go back to Middle America?" The voice was a pleasant tenor, human-sounding but a little slurred.

Ravna bounced off the ceiling. "I thought you were going to stay out of this! Of course the boy is going back to Middle America. That's his home; that's where he fits."

"I wonder." The unseen speaker laughed. He sounded cheerfully—*joyfully*—drunk. "Your name is shit down there, Hamid, did you know that?"

"Huh?"

"Yup. You slagged the Caravan's entire shipment of fusion electrics. 'Course you had a little help from the Federal Police, but that fact is being ignored. Much worse, you destroyed most of the agrav units. *Whee*. Up, up and away. And there's no way those can be replaced short of a trip back to the Outsi—"

"Shut up!" Ravna's anger rode over the good cheer. "The agrav units were a cheap trick. Nothing that subtle can work in the Zone for long. Five years from now they would all have faded."

"Sure, sure. I know that, and you know that. But both Middle America and the Tourists figure you've trashed this Caravan, Hamid. You'd be a fool to go back."

Ravna shouted something in a language Hamid had never heard.

"English, Rav, English. I want him to understand what is happening."

"*He is going back!*" Ravna's voice was furious, almost desperate. "We *agreed!*"

"I know, Rav." A little of the rampant joy left the voice. It sounded truly sympathetic. "And I'm sorry. But I was different then, and I understand things better now. . . . Hey, I'll be down in a minute, okay?"

She closed her eyes. It's hard to slump in free fall, but Ravna came close, her shoulders and arms relaxing, her body drifting slowly up from the floor. "Oh, Lord," she said softly.

Out in the hall, someone was whistling a tune that had been popular in Marquette six months ago. A shadow floated down the walls, followed by . . . *the*

Blab? Hamid lurched off the table, flailed wildly for a handhold. He steadied himself, got a closer look.

No. Not the Blab. It was of the same race certainly, but this one had an entirely different pattern of black and white. The great patch of black around one eye and white around the other would have been laughable . . . if you didn't know what you were looking at: at last to see Mr. Tines.

Man and alien regarded each other for a long moment. It was a little smaller than the Blab. It wore a checkered orange scarf about its neck. Its paws looked no more flexible than his Blab's . . . but he didn't doubt the intelligence that looked back from its eyes. The tines drifted to the ceiling, and anchored itself with a deft swipe of paw and talons. There were faint sounds in the air now, squeaks and twitters almost beyond hearing. If he listened close enough, Hamid guessed he would hear the hissing, too.

The tines looked at him, and laughed pleasantly— the tenor voice of a minute before. "Don't rush me! I'm not all here yet."

Hamid looked at the doorway. There were two more there, one with a jeweled collar—the leader? They glided through the air and tied down next to the first. Hamid saw more shadows floating down the hall.

"How many?" he asked.

"I'm six now." He thought it was a different tines that answered, but the voice was the same.

The three floated in the doorway. One wore no scarf or jewelry . . . and looked very familiar.

"Blab!" Hamid pushed off the table. He went into a spin that missed the door by several meters. The Blabber—it must be her—twisted around and fled the room.

"Stay away!" For an instant the tines's voice

changed, held the same edge as the night before.
Hamid stood on the wall next to the doorway and
looked down the hall. The Blab was there, sitting on
the closed door at the far end. Hamid's orientation
flipped . . . the hall could just as well be a deep,
bright-lit well, with the Blab trapped at the bottom
of it.

"Blab?" He said softly, aware of the tines behind
him.

She looked up at him. "I can't play the old games
anymore, Hamid," she said in her softest femvoice.
He stared for a moment, uncomprehending. Over
the years, the Blab said plenty of things that—by
accident or in the listeners' imagination—might seem
humanly intelligent. Here, for the first time, he knew
that he was hearing sense. . . . And he guessed what
Ravna meant when she said the Blab was dead.

Hamid backed away from the edge of the pit. He
looked at the other tines, remembered that their
speech came as easily from one as the other. "You're
like a hive of roaches, aren't you?"

"A little," the tenor voice came from somewhere
among them.

"But telepathic," Hamid said.

The one who had been his friend answered, but in
the tenor voice: "Yes, between myselves. But it's no
sixth sense. You've known about it all your life. I like
to talk a lot. Blabber." The squeaking and the hissing: just the edge of all they were saying to each
other across their two-hundred-kilohertz bandwidth.
"I'm sorry I flinched. Myselves are still confused. I
don't know quite who I am."

The Blab pushed off and drifted back into the
bridge. She grabbed a piece of ceiling as she came
even with Hamid. She extended her head toward
him, tentatively, as though he were a stranger. *I feel
the same way about you,* thought Hamid. But he

reached out to brush her neck with his fingers. She twitched back, glided across the room to nestle among the other tines.

Hamid stared at them staring back. He had a sudden image: a pack of long-necked rats beadily analyzing their prey. "So. Who is the real Mr. Tines? The monster who'd smash a world, or the nice guy I'm hearing now?"

Ravna answered, her voice tired, distant. "The monster tines is gone . . . or going. Don't you see? The pack was unbalanced. It was dying."

"There were five in my pack, Hamid. Not a bad number: some of the brightest packs are that small. But I was down from seven—two of myselves had been killed. The ones remaining were mismatched, and only one of them was female." Tines paused. "I know humans can go for years without contact with the opposite sex, and suffer only mild discomfort—"

Tell me about it.

"—but tines are very different. If a pack's sex ratio gets too lopsided, especially if there is a mismatch of skills, then the mind disintegrates. . . . Things can get very nasty in the process." Hamid noticed that all the time it talked, the two tines next to the one with the orange scarf had been nibbling at the scarf's knots. They moved quickly, perfectly coordinated, untying and retying the knots. *Tines doesn't need hands.* Or put another way, he already had six. Hamid was seeing the equivalent of a human playing nervously with his tie.

"Ravna lied when she said the Blab is dead. I forgive her: she wants you off our ship, with no more questions, no more hassle. But the Blabber isn't dead. She was *rescued* . . . from being an animal the rest of her life. And her rescue saved the pack. I feel so . . . happy. Better even than when I was seven. I can understand things that have been puzzles for years. Your Blab is far more language-oriented than any of my other selves. I could never talk like this without her."

Ravna had drifted toward the pack. Now she had her feet planted on the floor beneath them. Her head brushed the shoulder of one, was even with the eyes of another. "Imagine the Blabber as like the verbal hemisphere of a human brain," she said to Hamid.

"Not quite," Tines said. "A human hemisphere can almost carry on by itself. The Blab by itself could never be a person."

Hamid remembered how the Blab's greatest desire had often seemed just to *be* a real person. And listening to this creature, he heard echoes of the Blab. It would be easy to accept what they were saying. . . . Yet if you turned the words just a little, you had enslavement and rape—the slug's theory with frosting.

Hamid turned away from all the eyes and looked across the star clouds. *How much should I believe? How much should I seem to believe?* "One of the Tourists wanted to sell us a gadget, an 'ftl radio.' Did you know that we used it to ask about the tines? Do you know what we found?" He told them about the horrors Larry had found around the galactic rim.

Ravna exchanged a glance with the tines by her head. For a moment the only sound was the twittering and hissing. Then Tines spoke. "Imagine the most ghastly villains of Earth's history. Whatever they are, whatever holocausts they set, I assure you much worse has happened elsewhere. . . . Now imagine that this regime was so vast, so effectively *evil* that no honest historians survived. What stories do you suppose would be spread about the races they exterminated?"

"Okay. So—"

"Tines are not monsters. On average, we are no more bloodthirsty than you humans. But we are descended from packs of wolf-like creatures. We are deadly warriors. Given reasonable equipment and numbers, we can outfight most anything in the Slow Zone." Hamid remembered the shark pack of attack boats. With one animal in each, and radio communication . . . no team of human pilots could match their coordination. We once were a great power in our part of the Slow Zone. We had enemies, even when there was no war. Would you trust creatures who live indefinitely, but whose personalities may drift from friendly to indifferent— even to inimical—as their components die and are replaced?"

"And you're such a peach of a guy because you've got the Blab?"

"*Yes!* Though you liked . . . I know you would have liked me when I was seven. But the Blab has a lovely outlook; she makes it fun to be alive."

Hamid looked at Ravna and the pack who surrounded her. So the tines had been great fighters. That he believed. So they were now virtually extinct, having run into something even deadlier. That he could believe, too. Beyond that . . . he'd be a fool to believe anything. He could imagine Tines as a friend, he wanted Ravna as one. But all the talk, all the seeming argument—it could just as well be manipulation. One thing was sure: if he returned to Middle America, he would never know the truth. He might live the rest of his life safe and cozy, but he wouldn't have the Blab, and he would never know what had really happened to her.

He gave Ravna a lopsided smile. "Back to square one then. I want passage to the Beyond with you."

"Out of the question. I—I made that clear from the beginning."

Hamid pushed nearer, stopped a meter in front of her. "Why won't you look at me?" he said softly. "Why do you hate me so much?"

For a full second, her eyes looked straight into his. "I *don't* hate you!" Her face clouded, as if she were about to weep. "It's just that you're such a God-*damned* disappointment!" She pushed back abruptly, knocking the tines out of her way.

He followed her slowly back to the conference table. She "stood" there, talking to herself in some unknown language. "She's swearing to her ancestors," murmured a tines that drifted close by Hamid's head. "Her kind is big on that sort of thing."

Hamid anchored himself across from her. He looked at her face. Young, no older than twenty it looked. But Outsiders had some control over aging. Besides, Ravna had spent at least the last ten years in relativistic flight. "You hired my—you hired Hussein Thompson to adopt me, didn't you?"

She nodded.

"Why?"

She looked back at him for a moment, this time not flinching away. Finally she sighed. "Okay, I will try but . . . there are many things you from the Slow Zone do not understand. Middle America is close to the Beyond, but you see out through a tiny hole. You can have even less concept of what lies beyond the Beyond, in the Transhuman reaches." She was beginning to sound like Lazy Larry.

"I'm willing to start with the version for five-year-olds."

"Okay." The faintest of smiles crossed her face. It was everything he'd guessed it would be. He wondered how he could make her do it again. " 'Once upon a time,' " the smile again, a little wider! "there was a very wise and good man, as wise and good as any mere human or human equivalent can ever be: a mathematical genius, a great general, an even greater peacemaker. He lived five hundred years' subjective, and half that time he was fighting a very great evil."

The Tines put in, "Just a part of that evil chewed up my race for breakfast."

Ravna nodded. "Eventually it chewed up our hero, too. He's been dead almost a century objective. The enemy has been very alert to keep him dead. Tines and I may be the last people trying to bring him back. . . . How much do you know about cloning, Mr. Thompson?"

Hamid couldn't answer for a moment; it was too clear where all this was going. "The Tourists claim they can build a viable zygote from almost any body cell. They say it's easy, but that what you get is no more than an identical twin of the original."

"That is about right. In fact, the clone is often *much* less than an identical twin. The uterine environment determines much of an individual's adult characteristics. Consider mathematical ability. There is a genetic component—but part of mathematical genius comes from the fetus getting just the right testosterone overdose. A little too much and you have a *dummy*.

"Tines and I have been running for a long time. Fifty years ago we reached Lothlrimarre—the back end of nowhere if there ever was one. We had a clonable cell from the great man. We did our best with the humaniform medical equipment that was available. The newborn *looked* healthy enough. . . ."

Rustle, hiss.

"But why not just raise the—child—yourself?" Hamid said. "Why hire someone to take him into the Slow Zone?"

Ravna bit her lip and looked away. It was Tines who replied: "Two reasons. The enemy wants you permanently dead. Raising you in the Slow Zone was the best way to keep you out of sight. The other reason is more subtle. We don't have records of your original memories; we can't make a perfect copy. But if we could give you an upbringing that mimicked the original's . . . then we'd have someone with the same outlook."

"Like having the original back, with a bad case of amnesia."

Tines chuckled. "Right. And things went very well at first. It was great good luck to run into Hussein Thompson at Lothlrimarre. He seemed a bright fellow, willing to work for his money. He brought the newborn in suspended animation back to Middle America, and married a woman equally bright, to be your mother.

"We had everything figured, the original's background imitated better than we had ever hoped. I even gave up one of my selves, a newborn, to be with you."

"I guess I know most of the rest," said Hamid. "Everything went fine for the first eight years—" the happy years of loving family—"till it became clear that I wasn't a math genius. Then your hired hand didn't know what to do, and your plan fell apart."

"It didn't have to!" Ravna slapped the table. The motion pulled her body up, almost free of the foot anchors. "The math ability was a big part, but there was still a chance—if Thompson hadn't welshed on us." She glared at Hamid, and then at the pack. "The original's parents died when he was ten years old. Hussein and his woman were supposed to disappear when the clone was ten, in a faked air crash. *That was the agreement!* Instead—" she swallowed. "We talked to him. He wouldn't meet in person. He was full of excuses, the clever bastard. 'I didn't see what good it would do to hurt the boy any more,' he said. 'He's no superman, just a good kid. I wanted him to be happy!' " She choked on her own indignation. "*Happy!* If he knew what we have been through, what the stakes are—"

Hamid's face felt numb, frozen. He wondered what it would be like to throw up in zero gee. "What— what about my mother?" he said in a very small voice.

Ravna gave her head a quick shake. "She tried to persuade Thompson. When that didn't work, she left you. By then it was too late; besides, that sort of abandonment is not the trauma the original experienced. But she did her part of the bargain; we paid her most of what we promised. . . . We came to Middle America expecting to find someone very wonderful, living again. Instead, we found—"

"—a piece of trash?" He couldn't get any anger into the question.

She gave a shaky sigh. ". . . no, I don't really think that. Hussein Thompson probably did raise a good person, and that's more than most can claim. But if you were the one we had hoped, you would be known all over Middle America by now, the greatest inventor, the greatest mover since the colony began. And that would be just the beginning." She seemed to be looking through him . . . remembering?

Tines made a diffident throat-clearing sound. "Not a piece of trash at all. And not just a 'good kid,' either. A part of me lived with Hamid for twenty years; the Blabber's memories are about as clear as a tines fragment's can be. Hamid is not just a failed dream to me, Rav. He's different, but I like to be around him almost as much as . . . the other one. And when the crunch came—well, I saw him fight back. Given his background, even the original couldn't have done better. Hitching a ride on a raw agrav was the sort of daring that—"

"Okay, Tiny, the boy is daring and quick. But there's a difference between suicidal foolishness and calculated risk-taking. This late in life, there's no way he'll become more than a 'good man.'" Sarcasm lilted in the words.

"We could do worse, Rav."

"We *must* do far better, and you know it! See here. It's two years' subjective to get out of the Zone, and our suspension gear is failed. I will *not* accept seeing his face every day for two years. He goes back to Middle America." She kicked off, drifted toward the tines that hung over Hamid.

"I think not," said Tines. "If he doesn't want to go, I won't fly him back."

Anger and—strangely—panic played on Ravna's face. "This isn't how you were talking last week."

"Heh heh heh." Lazy Larry's cackle. "I've changed. Haven't you noticed?"

She grabbed a piece of ceiling and looked down at Hamid, calculating. "Boy: I don't think you understand. We're in a hurry; we won't be stopping any place like Lothlrimarre. There is one last way we might bring the original back to life—perhaps even with his own memories. You'll end up in Transhuman space if you come with us. The chances are that none of us will surv—" She stopped, and a slow smile spread across her face. Not a friendly smile. "Have you not thought what use your body might still be to us? You know nothing of what we plan. We may find ways of using you like a—like a blank data cartridge."

Hamid looked back at her, hoping no doubts showed on his face. "Maybe. But I'll have two years to prepare, won't I?"

They glared at each other for a long moment, the greatest eye contact yet. "So be it," she said at last. She drifted a little closer. "Some advice. We'll be

two years cooped up here. It's a big ship. Stay out of
my way." She drew back and pulled herself across
the ceiling, faster and faster. She arrowed into the
hallway beyond, and out of sight.

Hamid Thompson had his ticket to the Outside.
Some tickets cost more than others. How much would
he pay for his?

Eight hours later, the ship was under ram drive,
outward bound. Hamid sat in the bridge, alone. The
"windows" on one side of the room showed the view
aft. Middle America's sun cast daylight across the
room.

Invisible ahead of them, the interplanetary medium was being scooped in, fuel for the ram. The
acceleration was barely perceptible, perhaps a fiftieth of a gee. The ram drive was for the long haul.
That acceleration would continue indefinitely, eventually rising to almost half a gravity—and bringing
them near light speed.

Middle America was a fleck of blue, trailing a
white dot and a yellow one. It would be many hours
before his world and its moons were lost from sight—
and many days before they were lost to telescopic
view.

Hamid had been here an hour—two?—since shortly
after Tines showed him his quarters.

The inside of his head felt like an abandoned bat-
tlefield. A monster had become his good buddy. The
man he hated turned out to be the father he had
wanted . . . and his mother now seemed an uncaring
manipulator. *And now I can never go back and ask
you truly what you were, truly if you loved me.*

He felt something wet on his face. One good thing
about gravity, even a fiftieth of a gee: it cleared the
tears from your eyes.

He must be very careful these next two years.

There was much to learn, and even more to guess at. What was lie and what was truth? There were things about the story that . . . How could one human being be as important as Ravna and Tines claimed? Next to the Transhumans, no human equivalent could count for much.

It might well be that these two believed the story they told him—*and that could be the most frightening possibility of all*. They talked about the Great Man as though he were some sort of messiah. Hamid had read of similar things in Earth history: twentieth-century Nazis longing for Hitler, the fanatics of the Afghan Jihad scheming to bring back their Imam. The story Larry got from the ansible could be true, and the Great Man might have been accomplice to the murder of a thousand worlds.

Hamid found himself laughing. *Where does that put me?* Could the clone of a monster rise above the original?

"What's funny, Hamid?" Tines had entered the bridge quietly. Now he settled himself on the table and posts around Hamid. The one that had been the Blab sat just a meter away.

"Nothing. Just thinking."

They sat for several minutes in silence, watching the sky. There was a wavering there—like hot air over a stove—the tiniest evidence of the fields that formed the ram around them. He glanced at the tines. Four of them were looking out the windows. The other two looked back at him, their eyes as dark and soft as the Blab's had ever been.

"Please don't think badly of Ravna," Tines said. "She had a real thing going with the almost-you of before. . . . They loved each other very much."

"I guessed."

The two heads turned back to the sky. These next two years he must watch this creature, try to decide. . . . But suspicions aside, the more he saw of Tines, the more he liked him. Hamid could almost imagine that he had not lost the Blab, but gained five of her siblings. And the bigmouth had finally become a real person.

The companionable silence stretched on. After a moment, the one that had been the Blab edged across the table and bumped her head against his shoulder. Hamid hesitated, then stroked her neck. They watched the sun and the fleck of blue a moment more. "You know," said Tines, but in the femvoice that was the Blab's favorite, "I will miss that place. And most of all . . . I will miss the cats and the dogs."

I've got plenty of loose ends to tie up—both before and after the Blabber. In this future, the centuries after our twentieth are very interesting—but discouraging and mystifying to extreme tech optimists such as myself. Computer power increases, but somehow never produces the reasoning entities we expect. In the twenty-first century, the AI gurus of the twentieth are seen as old fogies whose wild predictions never came true. Instead, humankind spreads through the solar system and then to the nearby stars. Some of our descendants never learn the truth. Others, whose slow boats and relativistic rockets take them galactic outward, eventually reach the Beyond. (Still others, on missions toward the galactic center, end in mindless destruction . . . or maybe not: the most tragic situtation of all might be a colony at the edge of the Unthinking Depths, where even the brightest humans are retarded.)

The Beyond is an interesting place, almost like the wild interstellar playgrounds of 1930s sf, except that there are the Transhuman Reaches just a little further *out, beckoning empires to remove themselves from human ken. Traders to those Reaches would be very strange beings . . . when they come back at all.*

In particular, what about Hamid and the Blab? How did the tines race get zapped, and what about the Great Man who Hamid isn't? I think some readers believe that fictional universes are born full grown, that stories simply explore an already existing place in the writer's mind. That's not the case with my stories. I do have ideas—but too many, as often as not. For instance, the tines culture would be very interesting, both in and out of the Slow Zone. Sex, drugs, religion—everything would be wacko for them. An orgy and a choir practice might be the same thing for packs of tines. And as for government . . .

I've got the answers here somewhere. I just have to recognize them. I . . . um . . . hey, don't rush me. I'm thinking. I'm thinking!

Here is an excerpt from the new novel by Timothy Zahn, coming in October 1988 from Baen Books:

TIMOTHY ZAHN

DEADMAN SWITCH

I was playing singleton chess in a corner of the crew lounge when we reached the Cloud.

Without warning, oddly enough, though the effect sphere's edge was supposed to be both stationary and well established. But reach it without warning we did. From the rear of the *Bellwether* came the faint *thunggk* of massive circuit breakers firing as the Mjollnir drive spontaneously kicked out, followed an instant later by a round of curses from the others in the lounge as the ultra-high-frequency electric current in the deck lost its Mjollnir-space identity of a pseudograv generator and crewers and drinks went scattering every which way.

And then, abruptly, there was silence. A dark silence, as suddenly everyone seemed to remember what was abut to happen.

A rook was drifting in front of my eyes, spiraling slowly about its long axis. Carefully, I reached out and plucked it from the air, feeling a sudden chill in my heart. We were at the edge of the Cloud, ten light-years out from Solitaire . . . and in a few minutes, up on the bridge, someone was going to die.

For in honor of their gods they have done everything detestable that God hates; yes, in honor of their gods, they even burn their own sons and daughters as sacrifices—

A tone from the intercom broke into my thoughts. "Sorry about that," Captain Jose Bartholomy said. Behind his carefully cultivated Starlit accent his voice was trying to be as unruffled as usual . . . but I don't think anyone aboard the *Bellwether* was really fooled. "Space-normal, for anyone who hasn't figured it out already. Approximately fifteen minutes to Mjollnir again; stand ready." He paused, and I heard him take a deep breath. "Mr. Benedar, please report to the bridge."

I didn't have to look to know that all eyes in the lounge had turned to me. Carefully, I eased out of my seat, hanging onto the arm until I'd adjusted adequately to the weightlessness and then giving myself a push toward the door. My movement seemed to break the others out of their paralysis—two of the crewers headed to the lockers for handvacs, while the rest suddenly seemed to remember there were glasses and floating snacks that needed to be collected and got to it. In the brisk and uncomfortable flurry of activity, I reached the door and left.

Randon was waiting for me just outside the bridge. "Benedar," he nodded, both voice and face tighter than he probably wanted them to be.

"Why?" I asked quietly, knowing he would understand what I meant.

He did, but chose to ignore the question. "Come in here," he said instead, waving at the door release and grabbing the jamb handle as the panel slid open.

"I'd rather not," I said.

"Come in here," he repeated. His voice made it clear he meant it.

Swallowing hard, I gave myself a slight push and entered the bridge.

Captain Bartholomy and First Officer Gielincki were there, of course: Gielincki because it was technically her shift as bridge officer, Bartholomy because he wasn't the type of man to foist a duty like this off on his subordinates. Standing beside them on the gripcarpet were Aikman and DeMont, the former with a small recorder hanging loosely from his hand, the latter with a medical kit gripped tightly in his. Flanking the helm chair to their right were two of Randon's shields, Daiv and Duge Ifversn, just beginning to move back . . . and in the chair itself sat a man.

The *Bellwether*'s sacrifice.

I couldn't see anything of him but one hand, strapped to the left chair arm, and the back of his head, similarly bound to the headrest. I didn't want to see anything more, either—not of him, not of anything else that was about to happen up here. But Randon was looking back at me. . . .

The days of my life are few enough: turn your eyes away, leave me a little joy, before I go to the place of no return, to the land of darkness and shadow dark as death . . .

Taking a deep breath, I set my feet into the gripcarpet and moved forward.

Daiv Ifversn had been heading toward Aikman as we entered; now, instead, he turned toward us. "The prisoner is secured, sir, as per orders," he told Randon, his face and voice making it clear he didn't care for this duty at all. "Further orders?"

Randon shook his head. "You two may leave."

"Yes, sir." Daiv caught his brother's eye, and the two of them headed for the door.

And all was ready. Taking a step toward the man in the chair, Aikman set his recorder down on one of the panel's grips, positioning it where it could take in the entire room. "Robern Roxbury Trembley," he said, his voice as coldly official as the atmosphere surrounding us, "you have been charged, tried, and convicted of the crimes of murder and high treason, said crimes having been committed on the world of Miland under the jurisdiction of the laws of the Four Worlds of the Patri."

From my position next to Randon and Captain Bartholomy, I could now see the man in profile. His chest was fluttering rapidly with short, shallow breaths, his face drawn and pale with the scent of death heavy on it . . . but through it all came the distinct sense that he was indeed guilty of the crimes for which he was about to die.

It came as little comfort.

"You have therefore," Aikman continued impassively, "been sentenced to death, by a duly authorized judiciary of your peers, under the laws of the Four Worlds of the Patri and their colonies. Said execution is to be carried out by lethal injection aboard this ship, the *Bellwether*, registered from the Patri world of Portslava, under the direction of Dr. Kurt DeMont, authorized by the governor of Solitaire.

"Robern Roxbury Trembley, do you have any last words?"

Trembley started to shake his head, discovered the headband prevented that. "No," he whispered, voice cracking slightly with the strain.

Aikman half turned, nodded at DeMont. Lips pressed tightly together, the doctor stepped forward, moving around the back of the helm chair to Trembley's right arm. Opening his medical kit, he withdrew a small hypo, already prepared. Trembley closed his eyes, face taut with fear and the approach of death . . . and DeMont touched the hypo nozzle to his arm.

Trembley jerked, inhaling sharply. "Connye," he whispered, lower jaw trembling as he exhaled a long, ragged breath.

His eyes never opened again . . . and a minute later he was dead.

DeMont gazed at the readouts in his kit for another minute before he confirmed it officially. "Execution carried out as ordered," he said, his voice both tired and grim. "Time: fifteen hundred twenty-seven hours, ship's chrono, Anno Patri date 14 Octyab 422." He raised his eyes to Bartholomy. "He's ready, Captain."

Bartholomy nodded, visibly steeled himself, and moved forward. Unstrapping Trembley's arms, he reached gingerly past the body to a black keyboard that had been plugged into the main helm panel. It came alive with indicator lights and prompts at his touch, and he set it down onto the main panel's front grip, positioning it over the main helm controls and directly in front of the chair. "Do I need to do anything else?" he asked Aikman, his voice almost a whisper.

"No," Aikman shook his head. He threw a glance at me, and I could sense the malicious satisfaction there at my presence. The big pious Watcher, forced to watch a man being executed. "No, from here on in it's just sit back and enjoy the ride."

Bartholomy snorted, a flash of dislike flickering out toward Aikman as he moved away from the body.

And as if on cue, the body stirred.

I knew what to expect; but even so, the sight of it was shattering. Trembley was *dead*—everything about him, every cue my Watcher training could detect told me he was dead . . . and to see his arms lift slowly away from the chair sent a horrible chill straight to the center of my being. And yet, at the same time, I couldn't force my eyes to turn away. There was an almost hypnotic fascination to the scene that held my intellect even while it repelled my emotions.

Trembley's arms were moving forward now, reaching out toward the black Deadman Switch panel. For a moment they hesitated, as if unsure of themselves. Then the hands stirred, the fingers curved over, and the arms lowered to the Mjollnir switch. One hand groped for position . . . paused . . . touched it—

And abruptly, gravity returned. We were on Mjollnir drive again, on our way through the Cloud.

With a dead man at the controls.

"Why?" I asked Randon again.

"Because you're the first Watcher to travel to Solitaire," he said. The words were directed to me; but his eyes remained on Trembley. The morbid fascination I'd felt still had Randon in its grip. "Hard to believe, isn't it?" he continued, his voice distant. "Seventy years after the discovery of the Deadman Switch and there still hasn't been a Watcher who's taken the trip in."

I shivered, my skin crawling. The Deadman Switch had hardly been "discovered"—the first ship to get to Solitaire had done so on pure idiot luck . . . if *luck* was the proper word. A university's scientific expedition had been nosing around the edge of the Cloud for days, trying to figure out why a Mjollnir drive couldn't operate within that region of space, when the drive had suddenly and impossibly kicked in, sending them off on the ten-hour trip inward to the Solitaire system. Busy with their readings and instruments, no one on board realized until they reached the system that the man